## About the Author

Jonathan Dransfield was a child when man first stood on the moon. There was an expectation that the next place to visit would be Mars. It never happened, but the awe and wonder of the solar system and the universe has lived with him since.

When the current interest in visiting the red planet resurfaced he felt that crazy schemes like sending people on a one-way trip were not the way to go. As an architect he was used to designing things and solving problems.

The key problem is weight. To date we have dropped only robots onto the surface, as the problem of a manned mission is getting the crew back off the planet. Solving this is the key.

Perhaps it was the fact that Dransfield and his partner have nine kids between them that compelled him to write this book. He also knows that kids at times can be smarter than adults, especially with modern technology.

Dransfield is a visual person and used his drawing talents to develop the plot. *The Other Things* is an illustrated book – and a study on how to go to Mars and get some peace and quiet.

# The Other Things

# The Other Things

## Jonathan Dransfield

**UNBOUND DIGITAL**

This edition first published in 2019

Unbound

6th Floor Mutual House, 70 Conduit Street, London W1S 2GF

www.unbound.com

© Jonathan Dransfield, 2019

This book is a work of fiction and, except in the case of historical fact, any resemblance to actual persons, living or dead, is purely coincidental.

ISBN (eBook): 978-1-91261-887-3

ISBN (Paperback): 978-1-91261-886-6

Cover design by Mecob

Printed and bound in Great Britain by Clays Ltd, Elcograf S.p.A.

*To Kirsty, Kathryn and the kids.*

*With grateful thanks to Denis Ryan for his support over the years.*

Dear Reader,

The book you are holding came about in a rather different way to most others. It was funded directly by readers through a new website: Unbound.

Unbound is the creation of three writers. We started the company because we believed there had to be a better deal for both writers and readers. On the Unbound website, authors share the ideas for the books they want to write directly with readers. If enough of you support the book by pledging for it in advance, we produce a beautifully bound special subscribers' edition and distribute a regular edition and e-book wherever books are sold, in shops and online.

This new way of publishing is actually a very old idea (Samuel Johnson funded his dictionary this way). We're just using the internet to build each writer a network of patrons. Here, at the back of this book, you'll find the names of all the people who made it happen.

Publishing in this way means readers are no longer just passive consumers of the books they buy, and authors are free to write the books they really want. They get a much fairer return too – half the profits their books generate, rather than a tiny percentage of the cover price.

If you're not yet a subscriber, we hope that you'll want to join our publishing revolution and have your name listed in one of our books in the future. To get you started, here is a £5 discount on your first pledge. Just visit unbound.com, make your pledge and type DRANSFIELD19 in the promo code box when you check out.

Thank you for your support,

Dan, Justin and John
Founders, Unbound

## Super Patrons

Julia Adamson
Paul Barritt
Nick Beecroft
K H Bottomley
Rima Boz
Sherry Brennan
Roderick Burgess
Ingrid Chauvet
Janet Chequer
Kristen Cutlip
Philippa Dennison
Adam Dransfield
Graham Dransfield
Owen Dransfield
Patrick Dransfield
Sam Dransfield
Shakar Elahi
Emerald Gregg
Nicola Guirguis
David Holmes
Sarah Huber
J W Hughes Building Contractors Limited
Adam and Elizabeth Knight

Zulu and Thando Maseko
Kathryn McAdam Freud
Kayd McAdam Freud
Kirsty Mcneil
Tim Murrills
Sarah O'Sullivan
Jonathan Reeves
Jim Rice
Chakib Sbiti
Bernadette Sheehan
Ana Silva
Clive Smith
Jervis Smith
Clive Thomas
Giles Underhill
Nick Warde
Dom Welby
Andy Welsh
Ianthe Wicks
Ann Wilkinson
Rupert Wilkinson
Ian Yardley

'We choose to go to the moon. We choose to go to the moon in
this decade and do *the other things*, not because they are easy, but
because they are hard, because that goal will serve to organise and
measure the best of our energies and skills, because that challenge is
one that we are willing to accept, one we are unwilling to postpone,
and one which we intend to win, and the others, too.'

John F. Kennedy
12 September 1962

# Prologue

Pioneer 1990

*The Pale Blue Dot*

*Speeding beyond the outer planets, the Pioneer spacecraft turned its camera to take a last look back. There, caught on a sunbeam, was what Carl Sagan called 'the Pale Blue Dot'. It was our planet.*

*No larger than a pixel. All of us, and everyone who has ever been, was represented on no more than a digital square.*

*In an instant it revealed how irrelevant our troubles are and how fragile we are in the vastness of space.*

*It also begged a question. Are we alone in the void or just one corner of a universe teeming with life?*

# Chapter 1

## Wilson

*Asteroid Wilson*

Ford Harris had never felt like this before in his life.

His mind and body were twisting and turning between panic, elation and the need to run to the toilet or drink something strong enough to put him to sleep until it was all over. It was probably the most incredible night of his life... so far.

However, Ford couldn't show anything but calm self-belief and confidence as he stared at the screens, his team behind him answering phone calls, checking calculations and scribbling indecipherable scrawls on reams of paper. As time moved on, they were edging closer to him, and finally followed him as he moved steadily out and found a space to stand on the observatory balcony, absolutely still. The team mirrored him with their own heads tilting towards the sky. No one made eye contact as they all stood either staring at the sky or scanning it with binoculars, everyone wanting the best view possible of what they believed was about to happen.

Standing below them was a field of astronomers, each with the task to observe a specific patch of sky and record the exact time the asteroid crossed their field of vision, then relate it back to be recorded against the expected trajectory. One by one they signalled their sighting and joined Ford and his group in searching the sky with binoculars. Beforehand, people had seemed to be in a terrible hurry to do things with gadgets, but it was now really happening and they were witnessing it. The entire Near-Earth Object – NEO – observation operation had been temporarily moved to the disused Mount Peach Observatory, secretly prepared over the last few weeks. This was the team's opportunity to check the asteroid's final path as it passed directly overhead in this remote area of North America. It was the last chance to give the warning or reassurance that the world was or wasn't about to end.

**Mount Peach Observatory**
Dexter Michigan, USA
42.4N 83.9 W
Altitude: 1,033ft
Geology: Wooded, glacial moraines and lakes

The president specifically didn't want a *War of the Worlds* scenario with all-out panic, anarchy and looting, so opted instead for secrecy and the inevitable backlash that would be sure to follow once this was over. 'There's no point having mass panic, violence and chaos if you're going to die anyway – may as well just be getting on with life, eating our greens, like the dinosaurs did.' This wasn't one of the president's best speeches, but luckily there had only been an audience of one – Ford Harris, and he had been on the other end of the phone.

Long ago, with meagre government funding, NASA had launched Project Jukebox – looking for hits – and Ford had enlisted a growing band of trusted amateurs with telescopes and computer software – the NEO team. There are millions of asteroids and comets out there, but they were looking for the rogue ones that might be heading towards Earth. Thanks to social media and the internet, Ford's team co-ordinated this vast network of contributors, without whom they couldn't do their job.

It was an email that had set this whole thing off; Jackie Wilson, its author, was with them tonight in this remote forest in Michigan. He had understood the initial need for total secrecy and was an able and enthusiastic member of the team. Being here was a fitting reward for being the first to spot the asteroid and sending the code 'ONE'. He had seen it when observing Mars and tracked it over several nights. When Wilson had realised it was moving suspiciously and was fairly large, he fired off his warning.

Ford had arrived very late into work that day after dropping his grandson, Buzz, off with his mother. He went straight to his computer and checked his mail. 'Dolores, there's a ONE code.' Ford beckoned and she moved quickly towards him. 'It's from Wilson, and he's got a big one!'

*Field of Astronomers*

So now there they stood, straining upwards at the sky – because that was all they could do. The news of the asteroid's existence had been kept secret until they had felt reasonably certain that it would not impact the planet. False news reports warning of an unseasonal hurricane had allowed for evacuations, but many people had refused to move until finally the real news of it just skimming the Earth was revealed. There would be loss of life, destruction and chaos, Ford was sure. Yet, if their calculations were wrong, it could be absolutely catastrophic.

And now, above the south-western horizon, there was a growing primrose dot. There was a gasp from the crowd. The asteroid was moving at an immense speed against the backdrop of stars. One by one, the hunched shapes peering through their telescopes signalled a thumbs-up as it passed through their lens and relayed the exact time through a phone app to Celeste in the dome.

Then, in one accord, they all rocked back as it tracked overhead, changing and growing into an orange beacon – the brightest thing, save the sun and the moon, that any of these seasoned sky watchers had ever seen.

The air was full of expletives and words like 'amazing', 'incredible', 'awesome'. As the crowd on the balcony rushed around to the other side of the dome, Ford was reluctant to break off from this spectacle, but he had duties to perform. He rushed in to check with Celeste, who was huddled by the great telescope mounting, the glow of the computer screen lighting her intense expression. Ford, still within earshot, had rushed to the opposite window.

The intense orange crescent, now hanging like a Cheshire cat's smile, appeared to float to the north-eastern horizon.

Celeste, without looking up, shouted, 'It's bang on track, Ford! I've sent the signal. I've got Reykjavik online.'


Kirsten Gunnarsdottir stood in the cold and windy Harpa – the concert hall overlooking Reykjavik's majestic harbour. She had worked through the night as a special volunteer, organising the storage of thousands of sheets of glass from its crystalline facades. This beautiful building had been built as a gesture of Icelandic self-confidence in the wake of the notorious banking collapse, which had blighted the country since the start of the millennium. Kirsten was one of the trusted few who had been informed early of what was to come today. The cold glow of dawn was starting to light up the snow-covered peaks across the dark and peaceful water. It was time to leave and gain higher ground. They had barely half an hour before asteroid Wilson was about to change their lives forever. '*Flytir!*' she called to her companions, as they wound their way through neatly stacked piles of glass, leaving behind the filigree temple to the arts, and moved up the Skólavörðustígur, towards the Hallgrimskirkja.

> **Reykjavik**
> Faxafloi Bay, Iceland
> 64.1N 21.6 W
> Altitude: 0ft
> Geology: Volcanic, glacial, coastal

At this moment, all she could think of was Elin, her daughter. When they'd heard the news, torn between duty and family, Kirsten had stayed in Reykjavik to help. After much anguish she'd decided that Elin was safe with her grandfather, and in any case, what could Kirsten do to protect her against a million tons of rock and ice? At least she could be useful here.

If a major calamity were to happen anywhere, Iceland was the best place for it. Constantly on the alert for the next major volcanic eruption and with the sparsest of populations, it had many of the contingencies in place and an organised and stoic spirit. As Kirsten reached the top of the shopping street, her back against the lightening sky, she turned and peered to the western darkness. '*Va otrulegt,*' she whispered to herself. It was like a second moon had appeared in the sky, except this was moving, growing and shining with an intensity of light that was both beautiful and frightening.

Asteroid Wilson was now entering the atmosphere and the red morning rays were mixing with the intense light of friction on its perimeter. This was no time to stand and stare. She had to make it to the great church for shelter.

She was met at the doors by her colleague Magnus, who handed her a pair of dark glasses.

'*Einhverjar frettir?*' she demanded, her normal calm broken for a moment. Any news?

The wildly grinning Magnus, who had been working with the American team of observers, had heard the latest update from Peach Mountain and gave the thumbs-up.

Kirsten surveyed the small, brave crowd who were still outside. Sunglasses adorned each head, with some already in place over eyes. The moment had come. She thought she was going to throw up — she hadn't eaten properly for days, no 'last supper' for her. Rigidly still, she held her stomach, her eyes fixed on the sky. There was no time for any further thoughts as the heavens appeared to unfold in a blinding streak of light, no longer white now but coloured. Still in absolute silence, some of the team dropped to their knees, clutching their heads; others ran screaming into the building, but Kirsten never moved. She wanted to feel it, hear it, see it, taste it. If she was going to die on this day, she wanted to know about it and damn well be there for it.

Two great hands grabbed her and pulled her through the church's mighty wooden doors just as they were shut and barred. Any gap in the boarded windows now streamed with the intense light. In the packed nave, dwarfed by the soaring white arches, people linked arms and waited in silence. Then came a deafening, terrifying noise and a shockwave that assaulted all Kirsten's senses. It felt as if her chest, ears, whole body had been hit with a thousand sledgehammers.

To the north, high above the stark volcanic interior of central Iceland, asteroid Wilson was enjoying its brief visit to Earth, powering its way through the stacked layers of atmosphere. The pressure was creating an immense bubble of superheated ionised plasma, which now enveloped it like an iridescent cloak. The air in front, unable to accommodate its velocity, was stacking up as a massive shockwave with a vacuum tunnel in the great trail behind it. The deep boom of the shockwave, mixed with the continuous ear-splitting crack of the atmosphere closing behind the speeding body, had created the loudest sound ever heard by humankind.

Wilson's encounter lasted all of three minutes, travelling through 1,500 miles of our precious atmosphere. For all but the very closest observers, it did so in majestic silence, an awe-inspiring and beautiful sight. However, no one could anticipate the power of what was to come. That shock and noise was spread over the whole length of its track and was only travelling out at approximately 750mph, thus producing a two-hour cacophony of such power that it could be heard rolling around the whole world, not once but twice over the next three days, as it resonated like a great discordant bell.

The shockwave took three hours to reach Ford and his team near the Great Lakes, where it was still the middle of the night. After the asteroid disappeared over the horizon, there had been an anxious wait, and the crowd shivered in the cold night air. Suddenly a slight glow could be seen above the trees, spreading out as a false dawn, starkly lighting the few high-level clouds present, then brightening the sky as if it were day. Many of those watching instinctively reached out to hold hands, not wanting to break their gaze but needing to share this moment of sublimity.

As the light and colours finally started to fade, Ford stood and watched with a profound sense of relief. 'It can't have hit us,' he muttered to himself, pushing past his colleagues.

He re-entered the dome, where Celeste was still collecting data and reports on her various screens. There were emails, texts and tweets coming in from the epicentre, and live coverage from ships in the Greenland Sea and the Atlantic, where Wilson could be seen in all its glory, like a streaking sun flashing through the morning sky, its long trail of vapour tracing its path through the heavens. Small pieces could be seen breaking off, exploding and disintegrating. Luckily Wilson was a dense and rocky body with enough clout to barrel its way towards its next encounter – with the sun itself.

For Kirsten at the epicentre it had been immediate and not just deafening, but positively bowel-loosening. The erstwhile members of the congregation of the Hallgrimskirkja were in a state of deep shock. A fine layer of dust covered them, and one by one they slowly took their hands from their ears, finally sure that the noise was subsiding. It still cracked and resonated, though now from a distance. Their ringing eardrums added an extra high note as the wall of sound diminished. Kirsten wanted to get out and see what had happened. She helped Magnus, a fellow lecturer at the university, open the door. The sight that met them was extraordinary: Reykjavik looked as if it had been peeled open like a thousand empty sardine cans. Multicoloured corrugated sheeting was everywhere. Roofs and wall claddings had been peeled off the buildings by the force of the shockwave. Even the famous acid green house was now naked, its sheets joining in a great square pointillist work laid out over the city.

*Kirsten Gunnarsdottir*

Above, the sky looked as if it had been ripped from horizon to horizon. The meteor trail was so vast that its collapsing vacuum tube had sucked out any moisture in the morning air into a deep, dark, swirling mass. Wilson, moving at 30,000mph, had pushed the air into rolling billows, a series of tight and endless smoke rings moving east, as if still drawn to their creator. The morning sun lit the underside of this vast tube with a yellow hue. The rest was the ethereal clear-blue sky that is particular to the northern climes.

'*Va!*' Wow! was the only word issued, again and again but all unheard due to the Icelanders' temporary deafness, which would soon affect half the population of the rest of the world. Magnus was tugging on Kirsten's sleeve, but she ignored him as she searched the screen of her phone for a signal. What about Elin? Was she safe? Magnus tugged again, mouthing, then pointing down across the harbour.

A very large hunk of rock hurtling through the atmosphere is not something meteorologists have ever witnessed, nor could predict. The immense pressure of the shockwave pushes down on the land and the sea, while its trailing wake sucks it back up, like running a stick through a pond.

A peculiarly high-walled tsunami was now heading for land.

Far away, once the glow had subsided behind the tree-silhouetted horizon, an eerie quiet had settled over the field of telescopes in Michigan. After experiencing the most extraordinary observation any of the astronomers had ever seen, their appetite only whetted, the gathered throng had collectively missed out on the climax. Akin to listening to a football crowd from outside the stadium, they all wished that they had been in among the action.

All they could do now was follow events through their phones, tablets and laptops. There was a hubbub of activity inside the dome, but only room for the core team. One of the trailers outside the perimeter was serving coffee and had erected a large screen, lighting up the faces of those gathered around. This was the Pure Channel's media centre at Peach Mountain. Although unwelcome because of the bad press they had given to the administration over the years, Pure had set up shop and its reporters were interviewing anyone with a woolly hat and bad clothes sense, on the assumption they were an astronomer. Because so many systems had failed through interference and the shockwave, and only patchy reports were coming out of the epicentre, even interviews with these bit players were going out live.

Ford had been either on the phone or checking data for almost three hours. Communication with Iceland was difficult, but he had compared notes with Jess Jensen in Sweden, whose team mirrored the Michigan set-up but were watching the meteor leave the Earth behind. Even in broad daylight it had been visible and spectacular. There was enormous relief because they would have been right in its path, had it taken a slightly different trajectory or broken up.

Finally, drained and needing air, Ford picked up the special boxes he had brought with him. Standing on the balcony of the dome, he could see his team of amateurs, still chatting in groups or packing up their equipment. Most of them recognised Ford and he caught their attention. 'I just want to thank you all for an amazing job! To express my sense of relief that we are all still here, I've brought a little something to keep the cold out...'

Opening the boxes, he laid out three dozen plastic cups and two bottles of single malt. There could not have been a more welcome offering, even for stargazers well used to cold and frosty nights. The diminishing levels of adrenaline had let the cold in and the warm shock of the aromatic liquid was like a comforting blanket.

Ford clanked the empty bottles, drawing the crowd's attention once more. 'From what we can see, Wilson has been and gone mostly intact, but there may still be some surprises. We have had reports of...' He broke off, distracted by a high-pitched whistle that suddenly enveloped the gathering. The dark trees surrounding them appeared to shiver and rustle.

As the whistle grew louder, it was joined by more earthy tones and a deep growl that seemed to shake the soul. Increasing in volume and intensity, the cacophony of sound was suddenly and violently overlaid with a cracking, splintering wave, accompanied by a slam of air that hit them like a wall, and ebbed and flowed like furnace bellows.

# Chapter 2

## Mo and Jane

*Alim and Mo*

As the train clanked through the underbelly of London, Alim Azim felt a curious mixture of excitement and relief. He resisted the temptation to put his feet up on the opposite seat and instead installed his travel bag and coat there, with his suitcase on the floor of the carriage.

He always felt that this route was the back door into the city. Staring through the dirty rain-flecked window, he enjoyed the transition: the Sussex countryside and then the North Downs and the only bit of tunnel on the whole journey. He viewed the landscape as a history book and he was now passing through millennia of deposited chalk, then emerging into the wide river valley of the metropolis itself. Much of his life was spent searching for rocks in bleak, remote and old landscapes. The continuous metamorphosis of a big city fascinated him. As the train snaked through a changing cityscape there was always another new development to spot.

A slight tingling of his skin and nervous smile gave away his three reasons to be excited: first, the news that the world might end this morning; second, that he had an amazing specimen to show Simon; and third, that he was going to pick up his son, Mo, for one of their precious short breaks together.

Some months ago he had booked a breakfast table on the 35th floor of the Shard. Quite by chance, he and Simon would witness 'the big event' from the best vantage point in London. Originally the arrangement was purely for the usual business with Simon, but now it was the perfect setting for testing his mystery specimen.

This was a regular trip for Alim – some business first, then seeing Mo, his nine-year-old son.

His niche was the Precambrian era, a long and spectacularly boring time when bacteria and simple forms comprised life on Earth.

This 'first life' really intrigued him. Having appeared, it did so little for such a long time. Why?

**Precambrian Era**
The 4-billion-year era before recognisable fossils are found. Consisting of 90 per cent of the Earth's history, ending with the Cambrian explosion, 600 million years ago, when all the precursors of modern life developed.

What was going on to produce such a comfortable place for bacteria and stromatolites that they hardly evolved until the Cambrian explosion?

*Bang!* After almost 4 billion years of slumber, that great change produced all the precursors of life we recognise today.

His quest was not easy: he had to travel the world searching for ancient rocks, as aeons of plate tectonics and erosion had turned it into a real-life detective story. Alim was now one of the leading lights in this limited field – and also an emerging authority on what life could be like elsewhere, often consulted by planetary scientists imagining what life might be like on Titan, or Enceladus, or newly discovered exoplanets.

For all this recognition, his family in Bangladesh were not at all happy with his career. 'If you are going to get a doctorate, be a doctor! What's the point in scratching around in old dirt?'

His free tabloid's headline screamed 'The End of the World!', jolting him back to the recent hysteria about 'Asteroid Wilson' until he realised it was referring to Croydon. As the train clanked and jolted, across the carriage he could see a fine view of Tower Bridge, and with that his thoughts went to Mo on the other side of the river in Hermitage Basin.

London felt strange today. It was as if the city was draining its energy back to the suburbs. The government had advised people and businesses to work from home where possible.

> **Croydon**
> London, England
> 51.4N 0.1W
> Altitude: 200ft
> Points of interest:
> None
> Geology: River valley, near chalk downland

There was anxiety in the air. There had been almost too many reassurances about the asteroid. The original news about exceptionally bad weather had cut no ice with a population uncertain, at the best of times, whether the next day would bring rain or shine. When news of the imminent visitation had finally been revealed, it had been met with distrust, which had now given way to excitement, as this was also a chance to see an extraordinary event. With a day off, people were heading to any vantage point that had a clear view northwards.

Unfortunately, as Alim stepped off the train, lugging his heavy suitcase, he could already see spots of rain dotting the glass roof of the platform. As an experienced weather watcher, he prepared himself for a damp squib of a spectacle.

*Titan and Enceladus*

Emerging from the great brick arches of the station undercroft, he passed the anxious queues for the viewing gallery of Europe's highest building. What mugs they were – far cheaper to have breakfast in the Shard's bistro. He turned the corner to see Simon waiting for him by the lifts.

'Simo!' He beamed, offering an outstretched hand.

'Limo!' came the rhyming retort. Thirty years on and they were still two grown-up public school boys.

**Titan**
The largest moon of Saturn has a thick atmosphere and stable lakes of liquid (methane).

\*

**Enceladus**
Sixth largest moon of Jupiter, vents geysers of water into space from a warm liquid ocean under its crust of ice.

Their table was tucked in the floor-to-ceiling glazed corner with the spectacular panorama of London laid out before them. Even better, they had some privacy. This was fortunate, because the bar was packed and a party atmosphere prevailed. The bar staff were calling it the real 'Restaurant at the End of the Universe', and a large screen was following the action. Alim took in the cloudy view. Fat chance of witnessing anything today! At least he could get on with business.

Once settled, they finally looked at each other over the croissants. 'Well, Limo. What have we got in the bag of wonder?' Simon's joy was not in knowledge specifically, but in the deal. He was an instinctive man who possessed the gift of great memory. He started in real estate, then progressed to antiques, until he discovered the lucrative market in antiquities and fossils.

Alim was his main supplier; he supplemented his research grants by picking up other specimens on his travels. No one was interested in his period.

Today he had a mixed bag and one mystery item, which was so perplexing, it was like having a secret that you couldn't quite believe yourself.

Glancing up at the grey sky, Alim was tempted to check out the live stream from Pure News, but all it showed were studio pundits and badly dressed astronomers in the woods of America.

Simon tapped on the bag. 'Open up then, *frendo*.'

Alim had a habit of packing his finds in newspaper, then in his spare clothes to protect them. Out would come the shirts, socks and vests, then the screwed-up *Sydney Post* or the *Greenland Guardian* would tumble aside, before finally the objects themselves emerged one by one.

This was their routine. They would agree a price, and Simon would rewrap the items in the paper and then place them into his own large navy duffle-style bag. Then Alim would show on his tablet the items he couldn't carry, before returning his clothes to the suitcase.

Suddenly there was a roar from the bar. The other diners, having given up on the cloud-obscured view, had gathered around the TV.

The views on screen were extraordinary, cutting from the original beacon over America to the fireball over Iceland. As the images got more impressive, the pictures broke up. Then the screen cut back to the studios and a headline: 'ASTEROID JUST MISSES!'

Simon expelled a long breath. 'Sheee… it, close!' Then it passed him by. 'OK, Alim Azim, old man! What's in the photos?'

Alim had also been utterly distracted by the images on the TV, but in the absence of live feeds from the epicentre, the coverage now had the air of half-time at a Cup Final.

He and Simon returned to business. Flicking thorough images on his tablet, Alim showed a number of larger specimens that were for sale, and Simon expressed interest in two. Alim had held back the one image he was most interested in. He often kept the best till last and as he announced the ultimate image, Simon's anticipation was palpable. The look of disappointment was superimposed by an exasperated smile. 'You're trying to sell me a sea slug?'

*Sea Angel*

Alim encouraged him to look closer and give his opinion. Magnifying the image, Simon viewed it with renewed scrutiny. It was not often Alim could put a fossil past him that he did not recognise.

'Mmm, you've got me there… It looks like a sea angel, but with tiny bones. Cretaceous maybe, but a weird mix-up.' To Simon it was a puzzle. He didn't even recognise the rocks.

**Sea Angels**
Swimming Sea Slug
Clade:
Gymnosomata
Distribution:
Worldwide
Carnivores

Suddenly there was another gasp from the bar. They turned back as the views of a flattened Reykjavik came through. The camera was catching the high waves deluging the harbour. It turned to the face of a pretty woman who had managed to compose herself to shout a few comments to the struggling reporter.

The studio then cut in. They appeared visibly shocked by the sheer scale of the space rock that had missed Earth and how close it had come to complete disaster.

'Bloody English weather! That would have looked amazing!' Simon dramatically waved his hand across the grey skies.

'Final opinion, Simo?' asked Alim, gesturing to the tablet.

'Oh, sorry, my man. Not interested. Can't sell something I can't name.'

Alim pressed him. 'But you do think it's an animal?'

Simon wondered why he was asking such a stupid question. 'Yes, but a very boring one. Where's it from, anyway?'

Alim just gave him a half-smile before giving his cryptic response: 'Further than you could imagine...' He looked at the big screen again and suddenly felt a desperate urge to leave and get to Mo as quickly as possible.

He swiftly concluded the business and, making his excuses, shot towards the lift. Usually he enjoyed the walk to Mo's school, but the sense of unease had got to him, so he headed for the Tube. As he waited impatiently on the platform, he thought he heard the train rumbling around the corner. The air rushed past as he strained to see the oncoming carriages, but the rumbling continued, the blast of air still rushing. He could hear it, feel it, but not see the damned thing!

Alim dealt with past lives, hacking them out of ancient rocks as fossils. He often pondered the lives lived by these humble creatures, always caught at their moment of death.

He suddenly thought of the past lives down here on the Tube. He recalled Henry Moore's sketches of bodies huddling from the Blitz on these very platforms, flinching from the muffled booms from above. 'Of course!' Alim thought. 'The shockwave.'

*The Tube*

By the time Alim exited, the world had changed. He emerged into the aftermath of the 'big bang', a multi-tonal roar that was passing through the world. London was now almost deserted.

His anxiety became a sense of foreboding. He had seen the tidal waves in Reykjavik, and then remembered the recent Boxing Day tsunami. Growing up in Bangladesh, he was all too aware how estuaries and river deltas could amplify tidal surges into powerful killer inundations.

An immense tidal wave caused by a storm killed over 200,000 people in Bangladesh on 13 November 1970.

Could the wave be heading to London? It was time to get Mo. He had moved Mo to live with his brother after falling out with his disapproving in-laws in Bangladesh.

St Katharine Docks was usually an agreeable shortcut to Mo's school. But today, as Alim rushed past the slick white luxury yachts, his suitcase – now missing its ballast – gained a life of its own. It carted from wheel to wheel, like an unruly puppy. He slipped several times on the wet timber decking, steadying himself on the chain railings, before lunging forward across the cobbled paths, which amplified the crazy clattering of his luggage. By the time he reached Mo's school he was soaked from the sweat of his exertions, damp from the drizzle, deafened by the continuing boom around him and driven mad by that 'bloody case'!

Heritage School was modern, its pupils were well mannered, and it smelled of cabbage. Alim explained his mission to pick up Mo to a quizzical receptionist, who even at the best of times was nonplussed at anything out of the ordinary and was now suffering from temporary deafness and general confusion.

**Hermitage Basin**
London, England
51.5N 0.1W
Altitude: 50ft
Geology: River
valley, clay and
fluvial deposits

'Do you have consent to take Mo out of school?'

Alim politely explained the urgency of the situation, only to be told that an ongoing astronomical event did not fit any of the Department for Education's criteria for school absences.

He countered, 'What about "act of God", you know, *force majeure*?'

The receptionist was now very confused. Force Majeure was her favourite indie band. 'I'm afraid we don't recognise God at this school – it's multifaith!' she finally replied with a bureaucratic air.

Alim demanded to see the headteacher. While he waited, a couple of children cheerfully scuttled past on an errand. He met their curious looks with a half-smile, then turned to see the office door reopen and both the receptionist and the headteacher appear.

Gayle Windlass was a no-nonsense teacher with a passion for the arts and history. She knew Alim of old, as she had once collared him to assist at 'a night with the dinosaurs at the Natural History Museum' for Mo's year.

Gayle grasped his hand. 'Mr Azim! How delightful to see you. We've missed your fascinating talks. Did you see the news? The children watched it in the hall. We are lucky not to be fried chicken, to be sure!'

Alim gestured to the office window. 'Drowned ducks more like. Haven't they warned you? The Thames Barrier is only designed for tidal surges, not full-blown tsunamis! I need to take Mo away now!'

As he explained his fears, Gayle Windlass assessed the situation, looking Alim up and down. He was normally a dapper man, but seeing his sweaty shirt, soggy trousers and agitated air, she realised the veteran scientist had to be serious.

'You can't just take Mo. What about the other children? We have to evacuate them as well. How long have we got and where can we go?'

Alim had heard that a tsunami could travel up to 500mph over open ocean. He looked at his watch.

'No more than an hour and anywhere that's a few storeys high or can float!'

One of Gayle's gifts was delegation and the ability to co-opt help. Alim was now very much on board.

Mo was sitting in the main hall with his classmates, all assembled to watch the big event on the widescreen TV. The teaching staff were now calming the children, still stunned from the shockwave.

The screen was showing large waves hitting the north coast of Scotland and warnings to evacuate low-lying areas. Then Gayle Windlass swept in with Alim shuffling behind her, as if on an invisible lead. Taking up the rear were the receptionist and several teachers.

Gayle had decided on a plan of action. She knew they had to move fast, but without panicking the children. Her receptionist hyperventilated, as school protocol was about to be broken on numerous fronts.

Miss Windlass spoke with calm authority. Even Alim kept quiet and still, although his eyes were searching for his boy in the mass of children.

'We are all going on a school trip, to celebrate the joys of our own neighbourhood. It can sometimes take something big to make us appreciate what we have at our own feet.

'Years 1 and 6 will go to the Tower of London, years 2 and 5 will visit Tower Bridge, and years 3 and 4, HMS *Belfast*.'

Alim worried as the children prepared to file out of the hall in pairs. 'This is taking too long!'

Behind them, the TV screened pictures of high tides of increasing ferocity hitting the east coast of Northumberland, and the shallower waters of the North Sea.

He wished he had hightailed it with Mo back to the Shard, but at least these destinations were high enough and would ride out the flood.

The receptionist was in a complete tizz. What would Ofsted say? The children leaving school without parental permission forms?

At last Alim and the remaining staff were able to leave the hall. Mo was proud yet embarrassed to see his father in the role of Pied Piper, leading a crocodile of children through the back streets towards St Katharine Docks.

He had felt the reassurance of his father's hand briefly on his shoulder as Alim passed along the children. 'That's my dad!' he whispered to his friend.

'He looks like a clown!' was the unkind reply.

On they went, Alim following the news on his smartphone to track the course of the wave. The lines of children passed through the cobbled streets. Unaware of the danger, the kids chattered happily; this was one exciting day! A morning in the hall watching TV, followed by a trip!

Alim was really worried now. He wiped his brow with a handkerchief, anxious about the time that they had left and the height they had to reach to get to safety.

At last they reached Tower Bridge. As the 60 or so children started to ascend the stone steps, a siren went off in the distance and the air was suddenly full of the wailing of police cars.

It felt like an age before the last children reached the higher ground of the bridge itself.

The teaching staff were arguing about admission prices at the exhibition's entrance. Rushing forward, he almost screamed at the person behind the desk, 'Can't you hear those damned sirens? This is an emergency! Just get the kids upstairs.'

As he got to the back of the column, he was able to talk to Mo. 'Don't worry, my boy, we'll soon be out of danger.'

Mo looked confused. Danger? This was supposed to be a trip. There was something strange going on: all around them flocks of seagulls and pigeons were wheeling around, as if sensing the force of nature that was about to arrive.

By now most of the children were in the foyer and climbing the internal stairs. Suddenly a distant rumble grew, and as Alim strained to look east up the river, he saw a high line of water bearing down and realised to his horror that it looked taller than the bridge roadway. The queue of children was still moving too slowly. He was frozen with fear and indecision.

Staring at the foaming wall of water, he decided they would be safer out in the open. Quickly gathering the last dozen children, he yelled frantically, 'Into the centre and hold hands!'

The children ran. Seeing the oncoming wave, they needed no urging to flee. As they reached the centre of the bridge, Alim ordered them to grasp the railings and brace themselves. The wave, which bounced off each row of warehouses, was now one great roller, green at the bottom and foaming at the top.

Mo could see objects in the depth of the wave – branches, plastic chairs, traffic cones and a swirl of all the rubbish discarded along the Thames margins. The little height they had gained by reaching the centre of the bridge was of no use. Alim picked up Mo and held him tight as two other children clung onto his trouser legs. Selfishly he regretted helping the school. Looking into Mo's eyes, he wished they had sped off together to safety an hour ago. Mo's look of trust was heartbreaking. 'At least we're together,' Alim thought, as the wave bore down on them.

*Tower Bridge*

They crouched and averted their eyes from the inevitable. In the darkness of their terror and as the spray and mayhem hit them, they suddenly felt lifted. It was as if a mysterious force were buoying them up, above the boiling waters. Their fingers gripped harder as their feet started slipping. The roadway appeared to be moving beneath their feet. Sirens were ringing in their ears and a recorded voice warned pedestrians to stay behind the barriers.

Daring to open his eyes, Alim could see from the angled roadway that the bridge was opening! The little gap in the middle of the bridge had now become a chasm – the wonders of Victorian technology had come to their rescue. The great bascules were lifting as if to salute the oncoming tsunami. The children clung for their lives to the mesh on the cast-iron balustrades, as the maelstrom rushed beneath, drenching them with foaming spray.

The wave passed them in seconds and then there they were, hanging onto the sloping roadway like a string of drowned rats. Each of the children's faces turned to Alim with unexpected grins. Alim, who had started the day inconvenienced by a mild shower, was now soaked to the skin. He wiped the water from his eyes as he turned and watched the crest of the wave flow upstream and lift HMS *Belfast* off its moorings, pitching its stern up. As it dropped, he heard the crowd of whooping children on its upper deck. For them, the thrills and scares of previous trips to Thorpe Park now paled into insignificance.

Ed Goodheart, bridge master, waved at the sodden survivors through his window. Gone were the times when the bridge would open up to 130 times per day. However, today he had his one opportunity to open it on demand. Seeing the plight of the stranded children, he had taken the only action he could and pulled the levers, setting the great bascules into action. Alim looked up to heaven and thanked his god.


Far beyond the spot where Alim fixed his gaze was another world.

Fifty million miles away on Mars lies the dry bed of a far more ancient river than the Thames and there, with its wheels firmly planted in those dry gravels, the rover worked a marvel of 21st-century engineering.

The sparse clouds above it were wispy and white, set against the orange glow of a tenuous atmosphere. Around it were the shapes of rounded hills and shallow valleys. Within this landscape of shifting sands and static boulders were outcrops of stratified rocks and sedimentary beds. A dull twilight lit the iron-red and mineral-green hues of this alien terrain, and all was silent.

Not even the rover, working steadily at a task it was not designed for, could be heard, because the air was too thin and there was no one and nothing to hear it. Nothing moved here apart from the odd dust devil and the rover itself, gamely trying to split apart layers of shale with its arm. It was like making a cake wearing boxing gloves. Two taps of a geologist's hammer would have made short work of it, but no one had expected the rover's discovery and it was now following improvised orders from its programmers on Earth. These masters were desperately trying to reset the rover's software to allow it to act more autonomously, because the 20-minute delay in communication made direct operation impossible, and *Oddity* Rover, for all its sophisticated equipment, couldn't work 'outside of the box'.

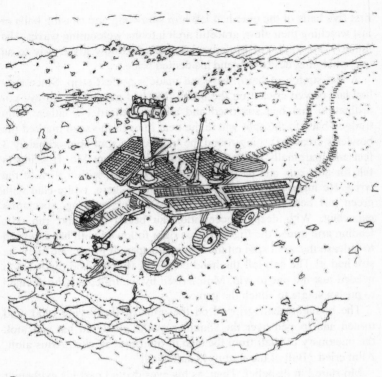

*Rover*

Despite its perky animalistic demeanour (spidery legs, twin camera eyes and robot arms), the rover was no closer to an animal than a vacuum cleaner that had sucked up a laptop. It could compute, but it couldn't think; it could capture images, but it couldn't see. It could measure the temperature, but it couldn't feel the cold and it was oblivious to its own successes and failures. Back on Earth, Patrick Marshall and Dolores Tallon were slowly going crazy with the frustration of it all.

'The problem is, Dr Tallon, it's just not designed to do this!'

'Patrick, this is incredibly important. There must be a way.'

But, for all his skills at programming, not even Patrick could instil a positive mental attitude in a machine!

Two days later Alim's feet were wet again, only this time it was voluntary – fetching a cricket ball from the cold English Channel. The first five balls of the over had left him sprawling and chasing balls or just watching their slow, graceful arch into the welcoming waves. His fatherly admiration of Mo's batting skills had now given way to an overwhelming desire to mend his dented pride.

A flat stretch of hard, wet sand made a perfect strip. Since they had last played cricket on the beach, Mo had gained a hand-eye co-ordination that had surprised and almost pleased his father. Alim trudged back to the spot where the neat lines in the sand marked the bowler's crease. Turning round, he viewed the spot approximately 3 feet and marginally to the leg side of the expectant Mo. His fingers felt for the seam and he carefully tossed the ball with a flick of the wrist. He imagined himself as a young man again, white-clad with green turf between his feet, imaginary fielders waiting, spectators expectant. With deep concentration he began his short run. His leading arm traced the flight and his right followed with hand twisted to unleash the wrist spin on the ball at the apex of its arc. He knew he still had it! The ball left the hand perfectly, flighted and dipped. Mo needed just the one to win. Mesmerised by the trajectory, he decided to push a single to clinch the game.

The bouncing ball gripped on the crust of the drying sand, and turned and looped over the shoulder of the proffered bat and took the imaginary off-bail from the slab of mudstone wicket. Arms aloft, Alim cried, 'Ball of the century! Game tied!'

Mo stared in disbelief. Then, as his eyes drifted past his exuberant father to the far crease, he broke out in the widest of smiles. 'No ball, game won!'

'What! How can you tell that?' exclaimed Alim.

Pointing his bat at a fresh impression of the last run-up, where the heel was obviously outside the crease, Mo explained, 'Footprints in the sand, Daddy!'

They had not come to the red cliffs and sweeping beaches of the Jurassic Coast to play cricket. Whenever he could, Alim took Mo with him on his fossil expeditions. The wash of the tidal wave that had nearly drowned them in London had exposed more fresh rock than usual, and today there were rich pickings. Fossil-hunting helped them bond and Alim proudly observed that Mo had a natural gift for it. He studied and soaked in every word and image he could on the subject. Mo had three languages – Bengali, English and Latin. Two he could speak fluently, and one he used to name ancient animals.

Alim had his fossil-hunter's tool kit with him today. With his bag on his shoulder and the cricket bat over Mo's, looking like the Walrus and the Carpenter, they marched down the sandy beach, its drifts of pebbles leading towards a long line of dark cliffs.

*Jurassic Coast*

Alim's thoughts returned to the events of the past two days. A carpet of foam intermittently lapped over his toes and the rolling pebbles dashed to the beat of the incoming crests. It washed away the angst and adrenaline he had been carrying from the drama on the bridge. He knew now that events were far beyond his control, and some greater purpose had to be behind their extraordinary reprieve.

Mo, able to feel his father's mind wandering off by the relaxation of his hand, slipped his grip and, grabbing the bag from his father, set across the littoral margin, kicking mermaid's breath and knotted seaweed. The triumph of the cricket game was already in the past and now his head was brimming with the joy of the beach and the treasure hidden in the rocks ahead. Nothing could compel his attention more than a new sea-cliff scar and the jumbled pile of dislocated strata blocking his path.

Skidding to a halt in mock-dramatic pose, Mo dropped to his knees and allowed the bag to slip off his shoulder and roll out open in front of him. The beach had gone, the waves had gone – all he could think about now were the nuggets trapped in the rocks. The soft-layered, not-quite-hardened grey, green, brown, dirty stone was familiar and he set about picking out the most promising samples. The frantic little boy was transformed into a methodical, meticulous fossil-hunting machine.

**Grains of Sand and Stars**
It has been estimated that there are ten times as many stars in the universe as grains of sands in all the beaches and deserts on Earth.

He set aside half a dozen likely pieces. From past experience he knew one in six might reveal a prize. Looking for a slightly widened seam, he tapped each rock – just so. On the fourth one, the seam opened to reveal two mirrored plates housing a positive and negative impression of a small pyritised ammonite. He liked these – the iron mineral deposits could be polished to look like gold; it really was like a nugget. Although the next sample was disappointing, he still felt a keen sense of anticipation as he had kept the largest, most promising rock till last. This was bigger than the rest and his intuition told him it would be a good one.

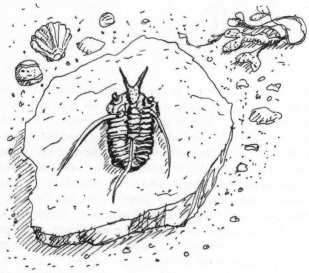

*Horned Trilobite*

By this time his father had caught up and was now watching him, savouring the joy of youth and sense of freedom to be found where the sea meets the land. It took Mo four taps to find the divide. As the rock split open, he cried, 'Horned trilobite!' and the little animal, locked in the rocks for 450 million years, saw the light of day again – if its little stalk-like eyes had been able to see.

With a massive grin Mo studied the segmented body and spiny head. Above the cackle of the passing seagulls he heard his father. 'Class, genus, period?'

'Trilobite, *Cyphaspis*, Devonian,' responded Mo.

'Very good,' replied Alim, as he distractedly surveyed the jumble of fresh rocks, recently freed from the cliff face. Mo watched his father mentally gauging the ages of the strata laid out before them.

**The Devonian**
A geologic period and system of the Paleozoic Era spanning from the end of the Silurian Period, about 420 million years ago, to the beginning of the Carboniferous Period, about 359 million years ago. It is named after Devon, England, where rocks from this period were first studied.

The older rocks were nearer the cliff and the younger ones towards the sea. Mo's two finds had immediately calibrated them in Alim's mind. Leaping forward 200 million years, his father indicated to him where to search next. Major storms, or in this case tidal waves, always brought their rewards to the palaeontologist.

Putting the samples in his bag for later study, Mo moved to pastures new.

Waiting for new instructions, he heard his father muttering a small ditty to himself:

*'She sells sea-shells on the sea-shore.*
*The shells she sells are sea-shells, I'm sure.*
*For if she sells sea-shells on the sea-shore,*
*Then I'm sure she sells sea-shore shells.'*

Mo looked quizzical.

'Oh, it's a tongue twister from my old school days. We did it in geology,' Alim explained. 'It's about Mary Anning, one of my heroes. She walked these shores 200 years ago, just like we're doing, and found the most amazing creatures. Shame about her poor dog, though!'

'What happened?' asked Mo.

'A landslip, like this one. It nearly got her as well! But guess what she found?'

Mo paused to think. 'A dead dog?'

'Yes, but no. Do you remember the plesiosaur and the ichthyosaur from the Natural History Museum?'

Mo looked startled. 'What? Them? Wow! Let's get digging!' With that, Mo threw himself into the task. Alim directed him, while he busied himself carefully cleaning up the beautifully preserved horned trilobite.

They didn't find anything on the scale or significance of Mary's triumphs, but by the end of the afternoon they had amassed a respectable number of interesting specimens. So many, in fact, that Alim had to carry the bag on their happy walk back to the hotel. He was very proud of Mo, not only for his skills in finding the right rocks, but also because he remembered all the creatures' names and their periods.

Unspoken, but drifting in the evening air between them, was a joint thought: 'How can we spend more time together?'

**Gale Crater**
Aeolis Quadrangle
Mars
5.4S 137.8E
Diameter: 154km
Age: 3.5 billion years old
Geology: Impact crater and ancient river bed

On the riverbed in the Gale Crater, the rover was still struggling to split any rocks. It was clumsily trying to find more evidence to confirm that those extraordinary impressions were true fossils and prove, in the rose-coloured half-light of another world, that it had made a discovery of greater significance than even Mary Anning's finds.

# Chapter 3

## Jane, Ford and the President

*The Farm*

During the long night of the near miss, Jane had been glued to the television since the early hours. This was so out of character that Jane had to force herself to watch. She had no option; it was the big event that had dominated her and Ford's lives for months, and this was the only way she could be close to him when it all came to a climax. As the drama of the night unfolded, her relief was palpable that Ford had been right – about the asteroid, at least!

Her shock grew about consequential events unfolding around the globe. She flinched when the endless rolls of thunder broke over the farm and echoed around their verdant valley. That had not been part of Ford's brief! Dawn was finally approaching. As Jane switched off the TV, her weary mind was at ease that they had been spared this threat from outer space, and happy that normal life would return.

There was no point in going to bed and she decided to assuage her annoyance with Ford by indulging in breakfast. Jane wandered into her gingham-fringed kitchen and took the ripest banana from the bowl, slowly shaving off slices onto her muesli. The coffee percolator gurgled and steamed as the early morning light worked its way through the Georgian panes. An entomologist, she now had research to catch up on.

*Jane*

Before starting work, she toyed with the idea of getting the house in order and addressing the chaos that had accumulated over the past tense weeks. Order, order, order! With order you can think, even feel in control again. At least she didn't need to make the bed. Reclined on the sofa during her all-night vigil, Jane had slipped in and out of slumber, to the point where the whole event had gained a dreamlike quality.

Back in the bedroom, as her second cup of coffee blew away any remnants of fatigue, she changed her mind. Ants today, not earwigs! There was always more action with the ants, and if her 'platoon' were still active they were easy to follow. Her 'platoon' were a group of thirty workers she had marked with nail varnish. Red, pink, blue, gold and white; six in each squad like the Brownies. She laughed at her own chipped red nails as she put on her old blue working smock.

Jane walked out into a glorious morning. The few morning clouds were flecked with gold and the old farmyard buildings glowed around her. There was a faint scuffle from the stables and in the distance she could hear the sheep. Through the yard and 100 yards up the track was the main ant's nest.

Sometimes she could entice Ford to help, or Buzz, his grandson, who would always volunteer enthusiastically. Her attempt at marking the ants was only a partial success. For creatures so sensitive to pheromones, the overpowering chemicals of the wet varnish at first drove them mad. Luckily the less than exact art of applying the varnish gave sufficient variation in shape to identify most of her participants. At least a dozen were easily confused; however, 15 ants were easy to identify and she'd named them all: Barry, John, Roddy, Llewelyn, Dylan, Dudley, Owen, Thomas, Richard, Burton, Tom, Jones, Huw, Davies and Catatonia. Her names were scientifically incorrect, as worker ants are female – and not Welsh.

Jane's core view of life was that all living beings had to have something in common, because they had come from a long-distant common ancestor. Each had found a place to survive and thrive, and was part of a 3-billion-year success story of survival and diversity. She knew that she shared a great deal of understanding with her dog and horses, and believed this would not suddenly vanish when you worked your way down the animal orders. The question was, what was left when you got to an ant? Obviously, you couldn't share a joke with an earwig, but in observing their behaviour, you could attempt to define their awareness and intelligence. Her thesis was that by studying the different ways individuals addressed a problem or each other, you could pick apart a conscious level of decision-making. The earwigs and ants were very good subjects, as earwigs lived more solitary lives and ants exhibited the collective awareness of the hive.

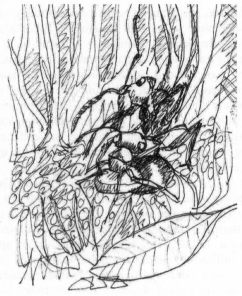

*Dudley*

Dudley appeared. This was good, as Dudley was often an early bird. She marked it down. Out through the leaf mould she scurried, with Jane tracking her movements. At first she followed the pre-set trail, antennae waving to pick up the scent. Jane would generally track an ant as far as she could, taking notes. She was convinced that the ant would change its behaviour if it was aware of being observed, and the closer she got, the more the behaviour might be affected, so observation was always a balancing act. She lost Dudley.

She had lost Dudley because the ant had exhibited the very behaviour she was looking for. The ant had gone off the trail, as some random synapse had triggered. Dudley seldom exhibited any individual behaviour. She was one of the nest. Her value in life was wholly about supporting the hive and her actions were mostly imprinted in her tiny brain as she developed in the cocoon. Ants had been in existence for hundreds of millions of years, and the same set of instructions had consistently served the colonies well.

The ant was now in the undergrowth. Dudley had lived with a heightened reaction to threat due to Jane's interventions. Shadows meant predators. In the undergrowth the ant could function with more ease. It was a predator itself. Hunting was a time when the ant could flip from automation to individual perception, like a pilot turning off the autopilot. Ants can see very well at close quarters, and around these grass roots there was always an effective place to ambush. This undergrowth with its dappled light, moisture and fallen leaf shelters was brimming with life: mites, spiders and grubs. Jane had followed Dudley for 20 yards before losing her, distracted by the persistence of the rumble in the air. In the open an ant would skittle for a few inches and stop, skittle again, more or less in a straight line. Here Dudley was always on the move, rustling each clump of roots to and fro, keeping close to the stalks in the hope of catching something as she came out of the blind side.

After the third attempt Dudley had just backed off. Antennae waving, picking up something, she felt a vibration on her leg bristles. Limbs thrusting, she set off again, catching a flash of movement between the grass stems. Immediately, opening her jaws, she hauled herself past the roots and darted her head and body at a small black ant. To humans, all this happens in a flash, but to an ant, real time is slowed. As Dudley lunged, the smaller ant saw the massive brown jaws flashing, and attempted to raise its abdomen in defence. Instantly Dudley thrust her left-centre leg, swinging its body to twist around the prey. Grasped by its central thorax and held aloft, the smaller ant could only squirt acid ineffectually towards the air.

*Bam!* Job done, ant dead. Dudley's automatic reactions took over. She tracked back to the nest, the black ant frozen in the grip of her jaws. Twenty yards for an ant is, size for size, the equivalent of 5 miles for humans. However, an ant makes very light work of it, running straight and without stopping for 10 minutes – the equivalent of 30mph – to reach home. Time and distance are all relative in our different worlds.

Jane was delighted to see Dudley return successfully, but regretted missing the action. She sat back from her notepad. Even 100 yards away from the farm, she felt lost in the landscape. From the track she could look down on the shingle and corrugated roofs, the bleached wood and rusting iron cladding, towards the green fields and plains beyond the road. Over her shoulder the woods started halfway up the hill. She was in one of the special places on their estate where she could just sit and reflect. She adjusted her hat against the midday sun and felt the first pangs of hunger for lunch.

'May as well break now and have a longer session later,' she thought.

The few clouds of the early morning had all but vanished and the shade of the kitchen was welcome. She turned on the radio. 'Oh the water, oh the shining big sea water...' sang a youthful Truck Longfellow as she rummaged in the fridge. Ignoring the jelly rolls, she picked out some cheese and tomatoes.

The phone rang, and Ford's face showed on the screen. 'Hi, baby, are you OK?' His voice was gravelly with tiredness.

'I'm fine, but how was it with you? I saw some of the crew on Pure News!' Jane replied.

'Jane, it was awesome! Wow, it was close! Just seeing it come over, and the speed of it!' Ford paused and swallowed. 'Guess what? I'm going to be home early. They've laid on a chopper. They said they want me home for a phone call. Can you pick me up from Talladega? About five?'

The rest of the afternoon went quickly. After a light lunch Jane retired to her study. She wrote up her notes and worked on the next episode of 'A Bug's Life'. Jane split her work time between pure research and journalism. Before she met Ford, the painstaking nature of research had driven her to distraction. He had given her this insight: science is not like doing a jigsaw, where each of the pieces is put in place until you have a comprehensive image or theory. Ford marvelled at the ancient philosophers who, by using logic, had worked out many of the discoveries known today. Atoms, the movement of the planets and even quantum theory had all been conjectured long before there were the means to prove them.

Ford's conviction was that if there was no life in the universe, it would be pretty pointless. By accident or design, our very existence gives it significance. We bear witness and understand, and by following our natural logic, like Einstein on the tram, we could make fairly good guesses about the nature of things. Ford likened it to a potter who understood the clay in her hands and could shape it into a jug or bowl. The scientist could form a theory through an understanding of their subject and their reasoning skills, and then test it, like the potter, with experiment to see if it too would hold water.

This perspective had freed Jane to follow her intuition. Her theories about the consciousness of ants had come as a revelation. It seemed logical to her that ants were normally driven by the ancestral, pheromone-induced, collective behaviour patterns of the colony, but the individual worker had to have some level of self-awareness and decision-making capability in areas such as hunting. Her personification of the insects in her articles helped her imagine this and then she could direct her research along a more natural path for her.

Tonight she would cook her favourite dish – Ynys Môns eggs. A recipe from a book called *English Food*, the irony of which still amused her. *Ynys Môn* – Welsh for Anglesey, the last stronghold of the Druids against the onslaught of the Romans, the English and Sunday drinking.

Jane took the Land Rover and parked up on one of the cracked concrete parking lots of their local airport. As the chug of the engine died, she heard a helicopter in the distance. It approached the hard standing and nimbly landed. As the rotors slowed, a figure jumped out. Head slightly bowed, he hoisted a bag over his shoulder and made for the terminus. The chopper revved and lifted off, turning on its axis into the open blue sky. Jane skipped off to greet her partner. A draught of cool air hit her as she entered the building. A dismal place, it had the sort of twentieth-century aluminium-framed ugliness that was a sad replacement for the charm and embodiment of pioneering spirit of the original wooden aerodrome.

Ford shambled through the barriers and his fatigue immediately lifted as he saw Jane. Her younger spirit rekindled his heart as he stooped slightly in their embrace. His bag swung off his shoulder and gently bumped her in the back, adding bruising impetus to the firmly planted kiss.

> **Talladega**
> Lincoln, Alabama, USA
> 33.3N 86.1W
> Altitude: 529ft
> Geology: Forested uplands and flood plains

The sun cast long shadows on the way home. The dog, Macks, barked as Ford and Jane entered the farmyard and rushed to its master as he climbed out of the vehicle. The pair had been comparing notes on the night's event on their journey home. Jane left it until they were safe in their own environment to ask, why the helicopter and why the phone call? Ford's response was guarded. They'd told him the White House was going to call, but now he was doubting it. Surely the president was far too busy visiting and encouraging the flooded communities of the eastern seaboard to break off and call Ford?

Jane poured them both a Menorcan-strength G&T and took a satisfying gulp before attending to dinner. As they settled down to eat, the phone rang. It sounded muffled to Ford, whose ears were still recovering from the boom, but nevertheless the unmistakable voice of Luther Garvey boomed through.

'Ford, I wanted to say that without your diligence we would not have been prepared for all this. It could have been like *The Day of the Triffids*, but at least all the emergency services were on standby.' Luther's voice lowered to a growl. 'I'd like to thank you in person. Can you keep your diary open to meet me in Washington in two weeks' time?'

Jane had been enduring Ford's heightened anxiety of the last few weeks, aware of what was happening but excluded. She had held on to the prospect of normality that would follow this event. The request, even by the president, to 'keep diaries open' released her pent-up rage.

'Well, stuff him! Interrupting our dinner! We are due some peace and quiet. I've had more of this disaster crap than I can take! If that bloody thing had hit us there'd be no sodding diaries or bloody meetings. Who does he think he is dragging you off when you deserve a holiday?'

She looked Ford in the eyes for a good five seconds. Then, with her crooked smile, she decided to let it go and announced, 'Dinner!'


'Oh, good grief, I'm turning into my pa!' Ford patted himself all over as he stumbled out of his bedroom. His hair stood on end as he continually rubbed it to think. 'Where's my watch?' He pulled it out of his dressing-gown pocket. 'What the hell...?'

Jane was smirking as she followed him out of the bedroom, carrying papers, her glasses on her head.

'Deep breath, Fordy,' she said with a yawn. He ignored her, still rummaging and bumping his way around the living room. 'You really should do yoga, you know.' Jane was gently mocking him now.

Ford pictured his father in the lotus position and giggled half hysterically.

'What's so funny?' Jane laughed too.

'Nothing really. Where's the charger? The thingy charger, where is it? Oh God, that's all I need.' Ford wasn't thinking.

'Try Buzz's room.'

Finally, with all his essential belongings together for the day ahead, Ford sat down. He put everything on the table in lines. They sat silently at the sun-bleached table as Jane poured coffee and Ford rubbed his hair.

'Oh God, honey… How can I be getting nervous about the flight when it's me who flies the damn plane?'

Jane held his hand gently. 'I wish you wouldn't fly. You're going to be distracted.' She then let go. 'Look, he's only going to say thank you. You don't have to do anything. Breathe, relax, be yourself – it'll be fine.'

'Tie!' Ford jumped up, hands on head. 'I need a tie!'

'Oh, come on, Ford. You've talked to him enough, you've met him…'

'Once! I've met him once, and not in the White House. Today it's the Oval Office!'

Ford checked everything on the table again, making sure.

'I'd better go.' They embraced and Jane stroked his face.

'You're going to be great. I am so proud of you – you brilliant man!'

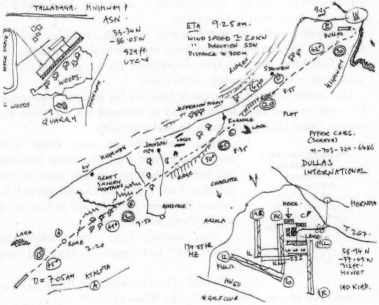

*Flight Route*

Ford decided to take his car, not the camper van, to the airport. He couldn't afford to break down. Ford kept his beloved North American T28 Trojan plane at a nearby airfield, but he barely noticed the journey this morning. There was a clear blue sky, perfect for flying, with the wind sock showing just a faint breeze. It was only when he placed his belongings and kit on the passenger seat that he started to look forward to his flight.

Flying was one of Ford's great passions – the sky to him was freedom. He had his best ideas there in the blueness, without people. Ford had 600 miles to cover, following the forests north-east to Washington. He wagged the rudder and set the trim, throttled up and into the sky.

Although Ford loved the speed of his beloved aircraft, far below he had always wanted to walk the route of the Appalachian Trail. He imagined himself and Buzz making the hike together, although he knew Buzz was hard to involve in anything that didn't involve a screen and some nifty finger work. Ford occasionally let Buzz have a go in the plane, operating the lever and the joystick. It broke the boredom of the long flight from New Mexico. Buzz was a natural, with amazing hand–eye coordination – something Ford liked to believe had been inherited from him.

Eventually, with his radio turned up high, Ford neared his destination. Descending into any large airport was always fraught, but today Ford had been given special clearance. He was going to see the 'main man' and everyone seemed to know.

The runway seemed ridiculously large for his compact two-seater. The scale was so hard to judge and he bumped his way onto the runway. Darn! He had so wanted to land gracefully.

**Washington Dulles International Airport**
Virginia, USA
38.6N 77.0W
Altitude: 313ft
Geology: Mesozoic basin on the border of the North American and African Plates

Ford made for an area filled with expensive private jets. The main terminal had been opened by Kennedy himself, but this time Ford didn't get to pass through it. Instead he went through the offices of a small private jet company.

'Nice landing, Ford. Forget where the airport was?' Jack laughed as he signed Ford out.

Ahead of him a diminutive figure held up a card: *Ford Harris*. 'Hiya, you for the White House?'

Ford smiled. 'You got me!'

'It's stupid, but we have to hold these things. Name's Soraya, and now I'll take your bags, fella. Hey, you're going to see the president! You tell him from me he's a good man, one of us.'

She took his bags despite his protestations, and carefully placed them in the trunk. 'Can't afford to break anything.'

*Ford's Plane*

Soraya, his driver, was all of 5 feet tall and totally dwarfed by the big black sedan. Chewing gum and leaning to the side, she viewed Ford through the mirror. 'You look familiar – on the news, the asteroid thing! I couldn't hear for days. They said it was your fault!'

'Sorry, I didn't catch that?' Ford joked.

'They said you should have warned us.'

Ford shuffled uneasily. Pure Corporation's news outlets, always ready to attack the president and his men, had singled Ford out as the boffin who got it wrong.

Bowling along the I267, Soraya caught his eye in the mirror. 'Hey, you been to space? You're from NASA, right?'

'Not everyone from NASA goes into space.'

'I'd love to go to space!' responded Soraya. 'A space chauffeur, now that's cool! Wanna go to Mars, mister? That's $10 billion plus tip!'

Soraya didn't usually chat too much, but Ford intrigued her. He was nice, she liked his kind eyes, and he was famous.

'So, you discovered the space rock?'

'No, but we tracked the asteroid—'

'You got a big telescope?' Soraya cut in.

'We've got gear for tracking, telescopes, radar, all sorts. Usually supporting our missions. It's not that difficult.'

*Soraya's Car*

'Why the big secret? I bet you knew ages ago.'

'Before it got past Mars.' Ford was going into more detail than he should. 'At first, we were very worried, as it was heading right at us. It was right on target.'

'Could you have shot it down?'

'It was just too big. It'd have been more dangerous if we'd shattered it.'

Coming off the I267, Soraya was quiet as she concentrated on the traffic, then blasted her horn. 'Loser!' she mouthed at a motorist. 'OK, how did you do it? How'd you make it miss?'

Ford remembered the feeling of dread as they did their first calculations. 'Well, as the meteor passed by Mars, its gravity pulled the asteroid, just enough to miss us. We must have recalculated it a thousand times.'

'Were you certain?'

'Yes, at least 95 per cent.'

'Doesn't sound that good,' Soraya retorted.

'Well, we were by the time it got here. We'd narrowed it down to a 2-mile corridor, just over Iceland. We had to keep quiet at first, because everyone would have panicked.'

Soraya flashed a big smile. 'Especially if you lived in Iceland, eating a whale!'

'Well, originally it was going to hit Zanzibar, ruining their breakfast.'

'Poor Uncle Farrokh!' Soraya thought of her family home.

Finally, as they pulled off East Street onto 15th, Soraya turned to Ford. 'Tradesman's entrance, I'm told. Don't worry, I've got clearance. I'm to wait for you. Just ask for Ray, OK?'

**Washington DC**
District of Columbia,
USA
38.5N 77.0W
Altitude: 350ft
Geology: Coastal
river basin and
meteor impact site

# Chapter 4

## The Meeting

*Meeting with Luther*

The US president, Luther Garvey, stood framed in one of the Oval Office's elegant curved bay windows, with his back to two seated figures: Stephen Dyer and Rory Ullman, both from the SAD, a division of the CIA operating drone strikes on 'terrorists and drug barons'. They had just reported another strike 'success' to him. Luther took a long, deep breath.

'OK… any collateral damage?' Luther turned slowly and focused on Stephen Dyer's lapel badge, then his thin lips.

'Yes, sir, but only his family.'

'How old were the kids?' asked Luther, staring directly at him.

Stephen shuffled his notes. 'Eight years, ten years and around twelve years, we think, sir.'

Luther closed his eyes. 'I don't like this. I don't like it at all. That's nearly two hundred since this damn thing started.'

Stephen waved his papers. 'This guy was high up on the list, Mr President, sir... a really big cheese in Shapkada. It's a risk we take... sir.'

Luther Garvey turned away. 'Well, I'm weary of it. Ten years, and where are we?'

Rory Ullman seldom said much. 'We do keep getting the bad guys... sir.'

Luther looked at him silently. 'Maybe *we* are making them the bad guys. Maybe we're doing this because it feels clean, detached. We're just risking machines, not our kids. Anything else to report?'

Stephen and Rory answered in unison, 'No, sir.'

Luther sat down and picked up a silver-framed image of his granddaughter and addressed the two men formally. 'Well, maybe it's time to rethink our priorities.'

Stephen shifted uncomfortably in his seat.

'We need to be talking to people, not killing them and their innocent children. Look, we need dialogue. It shouldn't be a world of *us* and *them*. This near catastrophe has shown us that, hasn't it? There are bigger things for us to tackle. How can we come together and stop using all this money and technology for destruction? We can surely use it to inspire lives, not end them.'

Luther stood up again. 'I'm decided to put this campaign on hold.'

Stephen too shot up. 'What, after all this effort? Always on time, on budget and we got results! How can we exert power, sir, if we don't use it? Nobody changed anything by being "nice".'

Luther gave a short cough. 'Well, maybe Gandhi, Jesus, Martin Luther King...'

Stephen flashed him a look. 'Yes, and look what happened to them!'

'We're all dead in the end, Stephen, it's what we do with our lives that counts.'

He waved his arm towards the door. 'Don't worry, we'll think of something to put your capable minds to. I'm not letting you go... yet!' He hit a buzzer on the desk.

Stephen Dyer looked angry and confused and wasn't following

Rory across the room. He had put so much into this. Yes, there had been collateral damage, but surely the target getting hit was what it was all about? He loved his job – his heart was racing now. The analytical side, the weighing-up of risk and cost, the run in the park at lunchtime while his orders were carried out and the missiles hit. It was modern, clean, perfect. He scowled at Luther as he left the room.

Belle, Luther's PA, entered as he took a deep breath.

'Five minutes, please, Belle.'

'Yes, sir, I'll hold him back until you buzz me, OK? He'll come in through the far door.'

Luther leaned back for a few moments. He could lose himself gazing at the presidential seal on the ceiling, and in difficult times he had. Luther settled his mind before hitting the buzzer. This was the most important meeting he'd probably ever have.

A portion of wall opened slowly. Ushered in through one of the servants' doors, Ford blinked, then, spotting the president riffling through a drawer, he hovered.

Luther Garvey got up and swiftly approached. He took Ford's right hand in both of his. 'Thank you!' he said, smiling. 'Can you hear me now?'

Ford cupped his hand to his ear. 'Loud and clear, sir!'

Into his hand Luther had slipped an object. Ford stared down at the charred, heavy pebble. The president stepped back a pace. 'Call me Luther. Yes! That's a bit of the asteroid.' Looking at the main door, he added, 'They suggested a medal for your enterprise, your organisation, your calculations... but I think this is more appropriate. In any case, I have another reward.'

The president continued, 'We should have a drink, but I hear you're flying. I half-expected you to arrive in one of your famous campers. Coffee, then?'

Luther gestured to the stiff gold sofas and they both sat, facing each other. 'Sir...' began Ford.

The president corrected him, 'Luther!'

'Erm, erm... Luther, thank you, but it wasn't just me, it was the team and we didn't change anything, we just tracked it.'

'You got it right and you kept a lid on it when needed. Believe you me, I am not one for secrecy, but I've been here long enough to know some things need to be classified. Folks were not going to react like "the young lady in the green hat", and imagine the chaos on the stock exchanges if we weren't sure it would miss us!'

'There's been enough physical damage without all that. I suppose it just gave us time to plan for it,' mused Ford.

They talked about the effects of the asteroid: how the blast broke every window in Iceland, the tsunamis, the noise that – like Krakatoa – echoed round the world like a bell, how they had been able to plan and agree with other governments the best time to release information, how Ford's team had been central to this, their increasing certainty that all would be OK after all. It had helped Luther's leadership worldwide. For once, politics had had to take a back seat and everyone co-operated. The last three months had brought a change in Luther. They had given a new focus to his presidency. It had also given him time to reflect, and he had decided to do something big.

They paused and sipped coffee.

'We're from the same generation. When I was a child, it was tough, but the future held a vision. We really thought we would be living Kennedy's dream: the moon, new frontiers and progress. Though I never dreamed I'd be in the White House.' In his famous deeper voice he added, 'It's time to rekindle our faith in the future.'

'For the eyes of the world now look into space, to the moon and to the planets beyond... We choose to go to the moon. We choose to go to the moon in this decade and do the other things, not because they are easy, but because they are hard.'
John F. Kennedy – Gary Rice Stadium 12 September 1962

Ford understood. 'Well, yes, sir... Luther. Even as a little kid it felt like a brave new world. It became my life. But in reality, it's just been more *The Simpsons* than *The Jetsons*.'

'Well, Ford, I have three years left in this office to do something significant. I remember sitting with my dad as we landed on the moon. We felt there were no bounds out there, only here on the Earth. Do you remember Kennedy's speech about going to the moon? Well, it feels like a job unfinished. When he said to do "the other things", I thought *we* would be going to the planets. We must not forget our dreams!'

Luther reached for an envelope and handed it to Ford. 'What do they look like?'

Ford opened it and studied the photos it contained.

'They are classified,' Luther told him. 'They have been taken by one of the Mars rovers.'

Ford scratched his head. 'Wow, they look like fossils! They're amazing! If only we could bring them back and study them.'

Luther patted him on the arm. 'Well, that's why you're here. I'm sick of dealing with naysayers. I need someone with an open mind to help me. I want to do something big, that will change our perceptions!' Luther was staring at Kennedy's portrait. 'We *do* these things because it is hard. I want us to be brave again and go to Mars – this time a manned mission.'

Ford looked dumbfounded.

'You must be hungry after your early start?' He called Belle, who laid out sandwiches by the fruit bowl on the table.

'The trouble is that your rovers are slow and inflexible. It's taken us years to find these fossils, which must be all over the place. A manned scientific mission could do it all, and there's something about the human experience that gives it even greater relevance!'

Ford's brain switched to overdrive. Luther then asked, 'What can you tell me about the challenge ahead?'

Off the top of his head, Ford reeled off: 'It's going to be expensive; there are crucial dates; it's a long, long journey; there's a lot of development to do; it's dangerous, so the results have to be worth the risks and we don't know how to get a crew back!'

'Well, you haven't said it's impossible! Politically, we'll have to go before the end of my term. There'll never be enough money and, yes, you have to get the crew back. However, I don't mind how many crazy ideas you come up with – this mission will need them!'

Ford blurted out, 'Crazy ideas for a crazy proposition? Have you any idea of the time and distances involved?'

'Please, tell me,' responded the president.

'OK, Luther. First, how big is this room?'

The president thought for a moment. 'Well, when we had the carpet done it was about 36 feet by 29!'

Ford paced the room, carrying out quick calculations on his phone.

'OK, sir… uh, Luther, to show you the enormity of what you're asking, please sit back at your desk. The White House is now the solar system.'

Carefully picking up some fruit from the bowl, Ford pointed out that the Oval Office walls were elliptical like the orbit of Mars.

He carefully placed a golden plum at the feet of the eagle emblazoned on the carpet.

'That's the sun and as Kepler discovered it's not quite in the centre, because all the planets have elliptical orbits.'

He gave Luther an apple. 'Please could you go and sit at your desk.' He placed a chair opposite but a little closer to the wall.

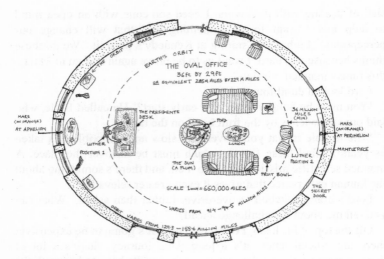

*The Oval Office Plan*

He then put one orange on the mantelpiece and another on the sash window behind Luther's seat.

'The oranges represent Mars when it's closest and furthest from the sun, while your apple is the Earth and you're sitting where it's closest to the sun. The other chair is where it's furthest away from it. Because their orbits are elliptical and the sun isn't at the centre, the distance varies.'

'How far between the oranges, in miles?' asked Luther.

**Orbit of Mars**
At perihelion Mars is 206,655,215km from the Sun and at aphelion it is 249,232,432km distant. That is a variation of just under 42,600,000km. It takes Mars approximately 687 Earth days to complete an orbit.

'About 285 million miles and you are about 95 million from the plum.' Stepping back, Ford felt something give under his foot. 'Oh, shit! I trod on the sun.'

Luther looked at the small portrait of one of his predecessors. 'Don't worry, there've been worse stains on the White House carpets.'

'How far away is the orange behind you?'

Luther squinted at the glare from the window. 'About 7 or 8 feet.'

Ford guided him to the opposite chair and asked Luther the same question about the orange on the mantelpiece.

'About 4 and a half feet, but does it make such a big difference?'

Ford held up a pencil, then handed it to Luther. 'Now, going to the moon is as far as we've ever been, and the width of this pencil represents its relative distance.'

Luther studied the pencil and then the room. 'That's one heck of a lot of pencils! OK. Mars is a very long way away, so we definitely need to go at the right time?'

Ford smiled. 'Fortunately we are closest in about two years. Just when you leave office.'

Luther grimaced and said sternly, 'How long's the whole journey?'

Ford stroked his ear. 'Minimum eight months' journey to get there and four months on the planet and then home, so almost two years in all, and it'll take a great deal of planning,' he mused.

'It'll probably be my final duty to see them off!'

Ford had to put in a reality check. 'Sir, it's hardly any time to get it off the ground! We don't even have a rocket or lander designed to do it. These things take years and years and cost a fortune.'

The president interjected, 'That's why I've chosen *you* to make a plan, a man who comes to the White House in a vintage plane – he must be able to break from conventional thinking. We don't burn you at the stake for it these days.'

This was no comfort to Ford. 'You sometimes have to be brave to tell the truth, and here it is: this is *almost* impossible.'

Luther got up to stand next to the struggling scientist. 'Exactly my point – everyone else I've consulted has said it *is* impossible!' Patting Ford firmly on the back, he said, 'You're my man! Help me get a team together and report back in three months with a possible plan. We'll keep it classified until then.'

Ford was suddenly overwhelmed by Luther's confidence in him. He stood up and promised he would do his best to lead mankind to the red planet.

It was time to leave. Ford walked back the way he'd entered, but he was suddenly lost!

'Where the hell's the door? I'm... sure I came in this way,' he muttered, looking back apologetically at Luther.

The president laughed. 'It's classified, Ford!'

'I'm sorry, sir?'

'Otherwise it wouldn't be a secret door!'

The man tasked with finding the way to Mars finally spotted the handle hidden in the wallpaper.

As it opened, the president called to Ford, 'Just one more thing. I've got someone to help you. He's called Stephen...'

*Ford lost in The Oval Office*

Ford was in a daze. As he left the Oval Office, he saw Soraya was waiting in the car. She got out and opened the door. This was the commission of a lifetime, but ridiculous. Why didn't he explain the difficulties more fully to the president? Of course, he felt flattered and buoyed up by the success of the Wilson operation, but...

Soraya was trying to catch Ford's eye, but he was too absorbed in the clutch of papers on his lap. On leaving he had been given a folder marked 'Confidential'. Laid out plainly was what Luther wanted to achieve.

It was candid, starting with budget (too little), the time frame (impossible), the technology (undeveloped) and the risks of failure (high).

Ford was the only person in NASA that Luther Garvey thought had the right 'left brain' to take it seriously. Ford's use of hundreds of amateur astronomers had not only saved money, but also improved accuracy when tracking Wilson. The president had also been impressed by how Ford had brought the old observatory back into use to track the event.

The president promised the mechanism of state and the personnel needed would be made available, as well as the diplomatic outreach for multinational co-operation.

Luther was cancelling military programmes to free up resources.

The president knew it was the only time he could go for something so risky. It was his second term and he did not need to worry about re-election. If the other party were elected, they wouldn't support it, so it was imperative to get it 'off the ground' now.

The president had been frustrated in achieving many of his original goals. But there was one thing he could do. To be a leader you have to lead. The world was a mess, but if humanity could see a bigger picture, it might proceed with greater consideration and care.

If life was found on Mars, it would put humanity's sea of troubles into true perspective. There was one simple question: 'If not now, when?'

The initial report was to be confidential. Ford was to keep this only between his colleagues and close family. He looked up from his papers and became aware of Soraya's presence. 'Thanks for waiting all that time.'

Soraya took her opportunity. 'How'd it go? What's he like?'

Ford fumbled in his pocket. 'Great! Full of surprises. He gave me this, by way of thanks.' Ford held up the little scorched rock.

Her eyes widened in the mirror. 'So you save the planet and he gives you a pebble!'

Ford's journey home flew past, and it was getting late by the time he lined up his landing on the distant strip. The wind was north-east, so he landed with the warm light of the setting sun lighting up the woods and the shadows of the terminal almost reaching his path. He was eager to get home and tell Jane – in confidence, of course! She shared his life and would share his secrets. What an adventure it promised to be, and he was going to need all her support.

As Ford approached their farm, he saw the light on in 'the den' – Jane was catching up with her regular 'secret lives' paper for the ETA journal. All this Wilson business had been disruptive. Ford's stress and the tension had completely disturbed her equilibrium. At least if the 'end of the world' scenario had happened she would have had a good excuse for missing her deadline. The sound of the car pulling into the yard stopped her. Ford was excited to tell her all the news, but also felt a little guilty. He'd forgotten to even text her! He knew she worried about him flying his 'old crate' but his mind had been buzzing. She'd even made a leek flan with sweet potatoes and tomato salad to welcome him home.

Ford crossed the dark yard. Macks rushed to greet him. Ford's mind was on Jane, though. He couldn't tell the dog about his day.

Jane's beads rattled as she wrapped her arms around him. 'I wish I could have come with you! Come on, I'll open a bottle.'

'Look, the president gave me this!' Ford opened his hand to show her the precious piece of the asteroid.

'A pebble?' Jane uncovered a lot of these when grubbing about for insects. Then, holding it to the light, she appreciated its significance. Under the scorching were green and yellow tinges of glass and streaks of metal. 'Wow! Of course. It's come a very long way. What else did he give you?'

'A job, honey – a hell of a job!'

Over a bottle of Glyndwr 2010, Ford went through his audience with the president. Jane's mood went from excitement to growing apprehension. She was quiet for a while and didn't want to crush him. Finally, she looked at his expectant face. 'It sounds like a wild goose chase, honey! He's giving you two years to do something that could take twenty. And that "trailer" you've been making for years is still without windows!'

All she could see was massive disruption followed by disappointment. She cleared the table and washed up at the old white sink, gazing out of the window as she tried to see it all in perspective. The low crescent moon and the unmistakable bright red dot of Mars were in close conjunction. That was one of the lovely things about living here – the stars. She had grown up with them in Wales, and it felt like home.

She held her thumb up against the glass and made two dots in the condensation: one for the moon and a small one for Mars. There was no more than 2 inches between them, so maybe it wasn't so very far after all. Life was never going to be quiet with Ford and she just loved his enthusiasm, even if she felt compelled to crush it at times.

Ford was now standing by her, drying cloth ready in hand.

'OK, cariad, just go for it!' said Jane. 'There's one thing, though. Promise me, please?'

Ford would have agreed to anything to have her support.

Jane looked out of the window again and drew a small square lower down in the condensation.

'Just finish that bloody trailer!'

# Chapter 5

## The Team Begins

Ford had worked late into the night to the rhythm of the grandfather clock to prepare the briefs and Jane had taken the opportunity for an early night. In the early hours, the farmyard cock's crow broke the night as Ford finally got on to the budget 'brief'. The dark sky was losing its depth and a faint glow was in the east. Aware he would need some sleep before travelling to headquarters, he kept this report brief.

He wrote: 'A billion dollars short of any sensible budget. You are going to have to do a lot of politics, make alliances and make sure the teams don't waste a penny on peripherals. This boat will not be lost from a lack of luxuries, but for the want of a nail.'

Bed at last, tiptoeing across the creaking boards, he very cautiously joined Jane's sleeping form.

*Jane Sleeping*

The meeting room that would become the headquarters of the mission dated back to the Apollo days and was anything but high tech. Tired walls, brown chipped veneer table and mauve chairs – the kind that are mistakenly bought to 'brighten the place up'. Opening a dark panelled door revealed a large whiteboard, which also served as a projection screen. On the west wall was a long strip window with a view over the wooded suburbs, with the bright haze of the ocean shimmering above the city beyond. Opposite hung a series of old photographs of crews of historic missions. Underfoot was a carpet, coffee-stained and threadbare.

In order to instil a sense of urgency, the chairs were stacked. His team were now standing and checking each other out around the Formica table – a mix of familiar faces and new kids, as if on the first day of big school.

Ford felt nervous. He was not unfamiliar with leadership, but this was new territory, as the pace would be daunting.

After his meeting with Luther Garvey, Ford had split his time between planning and putting together the team. With only ten weeks to complete their initial work, the task would be split between four groups with specific areas to investigate. If they didn't get it right, there would be no project. Ford felt like a new national football team manager. To be successful he'd need to bring together their individual skills and inspire them to work as one unit. He was fairly sure of his own players, as they had all worked together for years and were hot off the trail of tracking Wilson. Some of the new faces came with formidable reputations. But the politics and the PR were two completely new disciplines, and he feared these 'wild cards' Stephen and Yasmin might need high maintenance. He quaked at the sight of the health-and-safety manager, the infamous Edward Stalk, already checking out the room for hidden risks.

The room smelled of a mix of coffee and the lilies Sharon had arranged when she'd helped Ford set up the meeting. Sharon took a broad brief in her role as mission planner and understood *esprit de corps*. She had also persuaded him to expand the meeting into a social event later on.

Ford had prepared a short speech. Looking up over his glasses, he was surprised to hear an authoritative voice start up to his left. 'I am Stephen Dyer...' There was a dramatic pause. 'My duty over the last few years has been identifying problems and eradicating them. I'm hard-nosed and don't do bullshit! My thankless role in this mission will be to put your proposals through the mill – a devil's advocate.' Then, with a slow, thin smile, he nodded at Ford.

Stephen appeared pleased with the first move on his mental chessboard.

Ford bristled inwardly before trying to make light of it. 'Anyone else like to set out their stall…?'

He was perplexed. It was not the brief he had been promised by the White House. He changed his tack. Instead of a prolonged group gathering, he cut his speech and announced he was going to meet each group individually, ending with Stephen. His truncated speech summed up the mission: 'Four issues to solve: time, equipment, crew and budget, and two outcomes: remarkable science and a safe return.'

*Time* – Luther's agenda was totally artificial; the only feasible time to visit Mars was when it was closest to Earth as the distance between them was so great. Their elliptical orbits passed each other every twenty-one months. In three years' time the distance between the two would be the shortest. It was sheer luck that Luther's political timeframe worked perfectly with the science.

In any event, it was a long time to be in space. As distances go: if the moon is one small step, say a yard, Mars is 200 more – a real giant leap.

When you got there you would want to stay long enough to make it all worthwhile. In any case, you would have to time your return so that the Earth was still at its closest. Almost two years in space!

Team One's task: timescales, provisions, supplies, and fuel needed to make it there and back. Fortunately they could build on established knowledge, as many rockets had been sent to Mars, but the biggest lander was the size of an empty SUV. This trip would need the equivalent of the SUV, its passengers, a large caravan, a petrol station and a small supermarket, and with a return ticket!

*Equipment* – Team Two: the hardware needed to make this incredible journey.

Politicians do not weigh up all the factors in setting their goals.

Winston Churchill did not have a plan for winning the Second World War. 'KBO!' he would exclaim – something would turn up.

To be successful in life, it helps to be an optimist.

The fact that the USA had no rocket big enough for the task had not crossed Luther's mind. Where there's a will there's a way, was his mother's maxim. It's not rocket science to know you will need a rocket, but for this mission, at least two would be necessary.

If the Earth were an apple and the moon a grape, Mars would be a lime.

*Sizes of Earth, Moon and Mars*

A mighty Saturn V rocket leaving Earth was a spectacular sight, but for all its size it had only had to deliver the tiny command module to the surface. Due to the moon's small gravity (one-tenth of Earth), Eagle needed only two small rockets, one to land and the other to blast the capsule back at 2,000mph to join the command module, which then thrust them home.

Mars' gravity is four times the moon's, so getting back off the surface needs a more powerful affair, which makes landing far more taxing. There's little atmosphere to break the descent and no soft seas to splash down in, so lots of fuel will be also be needed. The long journey means another large rocket is required. The whole thing soon becomes an exponential nightmare and the weight of everything is crucial.

Three men can be stuffed in a tin can and be OK for a few days to the moon, but for months of travel, a home is a necessity.

Space isn't empty, it's full of hostile radiation. We would appreciate our world and the moon all the more if we understood the protection they give us, cutting out the malicious forces thrown at us by the sun and every other local cosmic cataclysm. This home must also be a shield.

Ford was well aware that there would be strict limits to the payload, because it affected the size of the rockets, the amount of fuel and the project's viability.

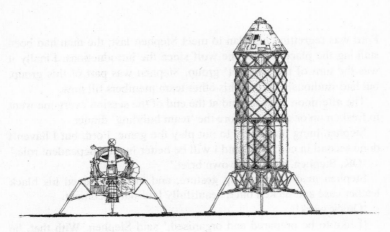

*Lunar and Mars Landers*

No matter how many times Ford worked it out, the astronauts' weight could be no more than 200kg. Solving this was Team Two's biggest task.

*Crew* – Team Three was the HR department. In this case 'Human Resources' was a reasonably accurate description, as people could do things that machines couldn't. The longest-surviving rover had covered just over 20 miles.

In Ford's opinion this assignment would count for nothing if it did not deliver scientific results. The payload really bothered him, as 200kg equalled only two or three crew. Where would they find these new 'Renaissance' people? It would be fine if the likes of Melvyn Bragg had a pilot's licence or Lewis Hamilton had a PhD in geology, and even then, who would clean the toilets? They definitely needed at least six crew to cover all the disciplines required.

**Lunar Module – 1968**
Weight on Moon: 1.5 tons
Escape Velocity: 1.47 miles per second

*

**Mars Expedition – Present**
Weight on Mars: 12 tons
Escape Velocity: 3 miles per second

The HR team would have to find them and plan for their needs, training and safety. The qualities of the people would make or break the mission.

Who but an idiot would want to do it? Those with these superlative qualities had to be intelligent enough to see the risks and run a mile. There would be a lot of time sorting the sheep from the goats.

Ford was regretting his plan to meet Stephen last; the man had been stalking the place like a lone wolf since the introductions. Finally it was the turn of the 'Budget' group. Stephen was part of this group, but had studiously ignored his other team members till now.

The afternoon wore on and at the end of the session everyone went to freshen up or change before the 'team building' dinner.

Stephen hung on. 'Sorry to not play the game, Ford, but I haven't done second in command and I will be better in an independent role.'

'OK, Stephen, write your own brief.'

Stephen made a palms-up gesture, and instead opened his black leather case and picked out a beautifully laid-out document.

'Quick work!'

'I like to be prepared and organised,' said Stephen. With that, he turned and left.

Stephen absented himself from the dinner in a curt email. Ford's keynote address was now to be made this evening.

Sharon had arranged quite an event.

LA-born and bred, she kept her mother's membership of the Flint Hills Country Club. With her charm and influence, she had secured the prestigious Sky Room, which she felt would make an auspicious start.

**Los Angeles**
California, USA
34.0N 118.1W
Altitude: 233ft
Geology: Plate
boundary

Situated on a ridge were a collection of buildings looking lost in time. In the 1930s this had been countryside, but now it was surrounded by a mishmash of 1950s and 1960s mansions. If it hadn't been for the golf course, there would have been no open space left – just a sea of leafy suburbia. Pulling into the car park, Ford had noticed a couple of characters hanging round the entrance. They approached him on his way to the door. At first he tried to whisk past them, like a businessman side-stepping a beggar.

All smiles, they were not to be brushed off. 'Mr Harris, are you here to celebrate your success in tracking the meteorite?'

Ford felt suspicious. 'What's it to do with you?'

'Oh, we're not staking you out. We're from the *Pasadena Globe* and we regularly check out the celebs here.'

'Well, I'm no "celeb".'

'Oh, you are now, Mr Harris, "the man who deafened the planet".'

'I'm sorry, I didn't catch that, and I'm a little late,' Ford retorted as he dodged them and broke free towards the door.

'Just a word for our readers, please?'

Softening, he turned and shouted back at the young reporters. 'I didn't invent Wilson – it was "an act of God"! You should be grateful that we're all still here.'

Professor Philip Brook was nervous. In all his years he had never got over the terror of facing an audience. He was sheltering in the marbled bathroom before the meal. Ensconced in a cubicle, he read through his short speech and rechecked his slides. Finally he emerged, stopping briefly at the art deco mirror. He straightened his tie and tucked in his shirt. Philip was not part of the mission, but was there to deliver something so compelling that no one would doubt why they were there, nor the need for a manned mission to Mars.

*Menu*

Under Sharon's cool direction, the wood-panelled Sky Room had been transformed and a single long table set out with thirteen chairs. She had hung up four huge images of Mars on the walls, each showing one quarter view of the planet. An orange tablecloth and green china gave it a slight 1970s feel. She had positioned the specially printed menus and place names. The teams filed in from the bar, to a background soundtrack of 'Rocket Man'. The smell of earthy pepperiness pervaded the space as the diners took their places. The double doors flung open and the waiting staff stormed in, wielding bottles of wine and water.

On their tail, with his shambling gait, was Professor Brook.

'Hello, Ford. Where do you want me?' he bellowed, waving heartily as Ford gestured to the seat next to him. Standing next to Ford, the 'Prof' tinkled his wine glass and all eyes turned to him.

The nerves vanished as he started his discourse. 'Look at the screen, please. These images are from Gale Crater and they're classified. Because, quite frankly, we couldn't quite believe them.

'First up, sedimentary rocks with iron in them. Like those formed in a warm sea on Earth, where the iron is laid down by microbes.

*Fossil 1*

'Of course, this is very interesting, but there's oodles of iron on Mars, so it's maybe from a different origin. Then this grabbed our attention. I will zoom in. Any guesses?' He looked at Rocky Bari, the chief engineer.

'A carburettor pipe?'

Slightly taken aback, the Prof replied, 'Well, that *would* be amazing!'

'It's a shell, a big shell?' offered Dolores Tallon, the chief scientist.

'Exactly! It appears to be a shell or least a piece of one.' Then the Prof looked over his glasses. 'However, you can be fooled by the light and pure chance, like the "Face of Mars".

*The Face of Mars*

'But then we saw this…'

A silence fell on the room as the next slide came up. On the screen was a photograph of stones, cracked and stacked.

The central stone had two impressions; one had a distinct outline of a small figure with wings, and the second a part of a matching wing, with the rest lost where the rock had been cracked open.

There was a collective gasp in the room.

'It's a goddamn angel, like on a Rolls Royce!'

**The Face of Mars**
Cydonia
Mars
40.8N 9.5W
Length: 2km
Age: 3.5 billion years old
Geology: Cydonian mesa

'Yes, the "Angel of Mars", I call it. The question is…' Philip took a long slug of white wine, then focused again on the screen. 'The question is, what is it? This image has been shared with many palaeontologists, zoologists and geologists. We haven't told them its provenance. Their overwhelming response was that this was once a living creature, and extraordinarily complex.'

To quieten the resultant hubbub Philip clinked his glass again to propose a toast. 'Here's to the *Oddity* Rover, who in ten years has travelled twenty-five miles and found this! Here's to you, because your task will be to take this discovery and find out what happened to its descendants. Here's to those who will go there, and here's to life on Mars!'

*Fossil 2*

'Before Philip leaves us, I'd like to reinforce one point,' said Ford. 'The *Oddity* Rover has no capacity to analyse things much further than the photos we have. A manned mission can travel distances and do science way, way beyond the capacity of any robot or rover, and this discovery is a game changer. Our mission is now an imperative.'

Ford took the stage.

As Philip left the room, Dolores and Rocky looked sideways at each other with 'Do you believe it?' expressions. Dolores, with her fine-boned features and sad brown eyes, nudged Rocky and whispered, 'What do you think?'

Rocky's face was one that only a mother could love – a human cliff, hence 'Rocky'. His mother had called him Ricardo. He had hands that could lift a truck, but a brain that could make it fly.

Dolores nudged him again and winked. 'I've a buddy in imaging and they've been really pumped up about something... If Philip Brook thinks it's kosher, it's no hoax.'

She didn't envy Rocky's brief. She could work out a scientific programme and the mechanics, but he had to provide the hardware, which was nonexistent, and without that nothing was going to happen.

Opposite them, Floyd and Elton, 'the accountants', had an even more difficult task. 'Who made up that budget? Stanley Kubrick? It might be OK if we were filming it!'

'I think that's been done already!' said Elton with a smile.

He then leaned forward, drawing Floyd into the conspiracy. 'We have to cut the research. It's expensive, especially with that lot,' he said, gesturing at the scientists.

Elton added, 'We need partnership! Use someone else's budget and ideas. Europe's a partner already, and what about China? They're throwing money at space... Or India.'

Further down the table sat Sharon. She was a planner supreme. The Mars-themed dinner was her idea – the menus and even the music were all her inspirations. She was obsessed with food and the belief that it was the glue that held a home together. But tonight she wasn't hungry. So she picked at her rocket salad and checked her lists. Sharon had planned missions to land probes on asteroids, while her husband had trouble with the shopping list. She fired a couple of texts off home to set her mind at rest before engaging with her neighbours.

Imran was her fellow mission planner. 'I suspect this will be the last time we'll relax together.'

Sharon's eyebrows lifted. 'Relax? I'm too excited to be relaxed, aren't you?'

Imran explained that he couldn't get excited about an impossible mission.

Sharon realised she would need to be the driver in this partnership. 'They got to the moon in six years, and we've come a long way since then!'

Imran was aware there were times when remarkable things could happen. His father had seen technology go from biplanes to jets in the decade of the Second World War, so why not?

> Moon landing conspiracy theories claim that some or all elements of the Apollo programme and the associated moon landings were hoaxes staged by NASA.

'OK, it's just... where do we start?'

Sharon was certain of this answer. 'Coming home, of course. Let's start with that?'

'I suppose. We've been to Mars, landed there, but never tried to bring anything back yet! OK, that's the tough bit.' There was a brief pause while the waiters removed the plates.

Sharon was distracted by Patrick Marshall, who was going to have to work out these practicalities. He had been listening intently. 'As Ford said, it's all about payload. The less we take, the less we need.' Patrick was not just an extraordinary designer and engineer, but could skin a rabbit and light a fire without matches. He fished an ice cube from his water. 'There's a lot of this on Mars, so we have a supply of hydrogen and oxygen – rocket fuel.'

Imran raised and examined his own glass of water, turning it slowly and considering the technicalities in his mind. 'But this is a long way from being rocket fuel.'

Patrick leaned over and chinked it with his own glass of deep-red Vieux Chateau Champs de Mars. 'This wine's close, though!'

Sharon had chosen the hefty Bordeaux for its name, and now raised her glass and joined the impromptu toast. 'OK then, that's the first task: turning water into rocket fuel!'

*Wine and Water*

Edward Stalk was a naturally worried man. As safety and mission assurance manager, this was a distinct advantage. The effects of small cumulative events or avoidable risks were nearly always the cause of catastrophes in this field and most could have been foreseen.

The breathing of pure oxygen in the early space programme, coupled with a minor electrical fault, caused a fire in the capsule during a launch rehearsal. Then the door mechanism took five minutes to open, meaning the astronauts Grissom, White and Chaffee, despite having expressed their fears, were doomed, not by an accident, but by lack of thought and worrying through the details.

Astronauts, from an elite corps of test pilots, had resisted being 'spam in a can' and had not wished to place their trust in fully automated missions, nor in ground controllers. They insisted on being able to pilot their spacecraft, proving to be life-savers in both the Mercury and Apollo programmes. In any mission to Mars, with its twenty-minute gap in communications, self-sufficiency would be essential.

Space flight is inherently dangerous, so why add to it by not eliminating all 'avoidable' risks? was Edward's mantra. His concerns about the consumption of alcohol during what he categorised as a work meeting caused him such anxiety that he had nearly refused to attend. It was only after he had conducted an impromptu health-and-safety audit on the evening's soirée that he could relax and participate.

"IT ISN'T THAT WE DON'T TRUST YOU, JOE, BUT THIS TIME WE'VE DECIDED TO GO OVER YOUR HEAD" APOLLO 1 CREW.

*Apollo 1 Crew*

He was baffled by Sharon's lack of appreciation when he handed her his unofficial report, just before the start of proceedings. But then Edward had never understood his fellow human beings.

He had been single since the last millennium. Tonight he had Henrietta Crumb as a captive audience and there was something about the dark-rimmed glasses and the tweed skirt that reminded him of his mother.

This was the mask Henrietta wore to be taken seriously in the male-orientated culture of NASA.

Normally Edward was very quiet, but tonight his inhibitions had left him and he went into overdrive, showing off his dreary expertise to the poor woman.

Henrietta was looking a little desperate.

'Oh, Ed, you can't hog Hen all night, you know!' interjected Yasmin. Turning round to Henrietta, she winked. 'He's so much the enthusiast, he puts us all to shame!'

Yasmin understood people. She was not an engineer or astrophysicist, and she was not concerned with budgets, timescales or rockets; her whole focus was about who was going to go to Mars. Her first question was, how do you pick their crew?

Henrietta, as 'Payload Investigator', would be team leader for the crew and their equipment. She was an old hand from the shuttle programme. There was never any shortage of would-be astronauts and it always started with a process of elimination.

'Well, Yasmin, we have four main physical obstacles to tackle before we can even look at their skills and abilities. The Russians have done a lot of research on this, and the length of the mission means that the lack of gravity, high doses of radiation, and boredom can wreak conflict and havoc.

'We actually need a bunch of energetic couch potatoes!' Henrietta continued with her analysis. 'The lack of gravity could mean that the astronauts are too weak to do much on arrival, and they lose bone mass if they don't exercise in certain ways. You lose the ability to grow your bones after your teens!'

Yasmin was trying to take all this in when she was interrupted by the arrival of her main course, Olympus Mons eggs. 'What about the radiation?'

Henrietta finished her mouthful of red pepper with its hot, spicy filling before answering. She explained that in deep space and even on Mars, the environment was awash with radiation. The radiation and the bone loss were an even greater worry than rocket failure, because you couldn't eliminate all the risks.

'Here's the thing: after adolescence your body steadily loses the ability to repair itself, and the latent damage of radiation can stay with you for life. We may have to choose an older crew who, put simply, have less time to develop cancer.'

Yasmin smiled. 'I could contact my dad's champion pub quiz team. They fit all those criteria!'

Henrietta brushed her hair from her eyes. 'Sorry, Yasmin, no room for the beer!'

Cutting the music with the last strains of 'Life on Mars' dying on the speakers, Ford then took the microphone. He got straight to the point.

'The question of life! Is it unique, or as common as stardust? You've all been asking, can those fossils be true? If they are, it doesn't make us less special, just the universe more so. We could have discovered something that will change humanity's vision of itself. In the night sky, instead of seeing stars, we will see worlds teaming with life, even civilisations.'

He took a sip of water and continued. 'Now, if this *is* a fossil – is that reason enough to risk lives to examine the history of a dead planet? Maybe, maybe not. When life on Earth took off, there was no stopping it. Even in the deepest mines and oceans, in the high stratosphere, living in rocks, scalding waters and frozen wastes, life is there. If we go we must seek out the secret places, where there is still heat and water, where it may have clung on, or even blossomed. No rover will do that in our lifetimes. If we are successful, we may find something on that cold, remote red planet that will change our world.'

A silence descended on the room as they took this in before Ford spoke again. 'Just one more thing. We all have commitments, families, friends, ongoing projects. The next few months, and hopefully years, are going to be very busy, so put your houses in order, explain to your loved ones that this is important. Ask for their forbearance and support. For the sake of my own relationship, this weekend I'm going to finish my trailer!'

# Chapter 6

## Koma Heim

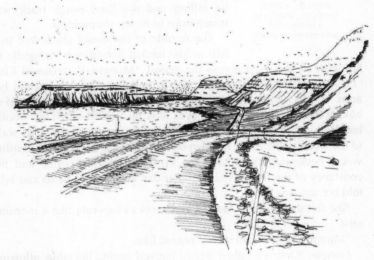

*Icelandic Road*

It was a long and dramatic drive from Reykjavik to Akureyri. Winding through the narrow plains and ancient lava fields that skirt the limbs of stratified hills and mountains, Kirsten's view through the salt-speckled windscreen was a monochrome of charcoal blacks and icy whites, broken only by the ethereal blues and golds breaking through the grey clouds.

In the summer Kirsten would have jumped at the chance to cut across the barren wilderness of central Iceland to see the long volcanic fissure that had opened up at Bárðarbunga; even now she would have moved heaven and earth to witness it.

> **Akureyri**
> North Iceland
> 65.4N 18.1W
> Altitude: 0ft
> Geology: Coastal
> town on fjord

However, she had been insanely busy helping with the recovery in the capital, and now had to get back to see Elin.

Out here, little seemed to have changed except for the repairs to the lonely farms, and the stark mountains seemed darker and more brooding than ever. The weather had been patchy and to her relief, as she drove through the deep northern fjords, the sun broke out, illuminating the white peaks with a warm gold.

**Bárðarbunga**
South Iceland
64.4N 17.3W
Altitude: 1,800ft
Geology: Subglacial
volcano and
subterranean system

She needed this encouragement on the last leg of the journey. Although the short winter days were finally lengthening, night would be falling and the final rough track was treacherous in its icy slipperiness.

The rumble of the diesel shuddered to a halt as she hauled herself out. A bundle of knitwear hurled itself across the gravel. 'Mummia!' screamed Elin. '*Pu ert heima!*' The little girl was in midair as Kirsten opened her arms. A wide smile returned to Kirsten's face as she saw the wisp of blonde hair and the deep-blue eyes look up from beneath the woolly hat. Bag in one hand and child in the other, she made the short walk to the weather-bleached wooden door. She heard her father's familiar voice, beckoning them to come in. The smell of coffee and the constancy of the lives lived day after day in the same fields and hills told her she was home.

She felt the stress of the last two weeks evaporate like a morning mist.

'Mummy, on TV you were!' purred Elin.

Gunnar, Kirsten's father, busied himself setting the table, allowing mother and daughter some precious time together. Elin was used to her mother's absences, but the drama of the event had made her return all the more special. She settled down on Kirsten's lap on the old wooden chair. 'An adventure. Can we do? Please, Mummia! My holiday it is.' Elin caught Kirsten's eye. 'Volcano hunting?'

Apart from the simple household rhythms of bedtime and stories, cooking and eating, and a hundred and one mundane tasks that leave a child happy and secure, the best thing Elin liked was to accompany her mother on her trips. Any deficit in parenting was made up by the intensity of these excursions. Even a summer trip in Iceland would entail 4×4 vehicles, fording rivers, hiking and camping. They were special times and she had the added interest of helping her mother's research.

They would interrogate the landscape. Elin would find rocks, take measurements or be a sounding board for Kirsten's thoughts.

Since the drama of Eyjafjallajökull, they had been dreaming about the next adventure.

Elin mirrored her mother's enthusiasm for any eruption, like a son might naturally follow his father's football team. She was very bright for her age and had the ability to absorb facts like blotting paper.

Iceland is an anomaly. A cross between land and a raised seabed, it is part of the Mid-Atlantic Ridge where the tectonic plates of America and Europe away move from each other, creating new land from the molten interior. One half of the island heads west and the other east, on average 25mm per year.

**Eyjafjallajökull**
South Iceland
63.4N 19.4W
Altitude: 5,417ft
Geology: Subglacial volcano

The Earth's population has the illusion of living on a solid planet. But here Icelanders are all too aware that we all exist on a thin crust of rock floating on a sea of magma. The latest eruption had created a long crevice a mile long, where spouts of lava were bursting into the skies and across the grey wilderness.

'Why not, *litla elskan*? It will be such fun, but I also want to rest and spend time with Grandad and Grandma.'

On cue, the sound of a second motor could be heard and Gunnar called them back to the kitchen to receive Kirsten's mother and sit down to eat. Kirsten's mother, Oddny, arrived in a flurry. They sat around the large wooden table and swapped tales while savouring Gunnar's hearty *kjötsúpa*. Elin sat transfixed, listening to their news. While Kirsten had been helping to mop up downtown Reykjavik, Oddny had been putting back the stained glass into the Akureyrarkirkja, removed as a precaution against the asteroid. Stifling her mirth, she explained how the MHB (Museum of Practical Jokes) had sent a mock delegation of Coventry Cathedral officials to reclaim the central panel.

'They offered me a post, you know,' recalled Kirsten.

'Well, I'm glad you didn't accept it,' replied Oddny with a laugh.

Every year the famous Museum of Practical Jokes invited the vain and the pompous to be their new director. If you accepted it, your name went with the others on the broom-cupboard door in the gift shop.

Unlike her mother, Elin was desperate to visit the world-famous museum. 'When can we go?' she implored. Kirsten did not approve of the MHB. It didn't show Iceland as a serious place for the arts.

Gunnar asked if it was true the museum was closed due to flooding, like the opera house.

'Of course not, Daddy, they are on the hill. If they say they are open, they are closed and if they say they are closed, they are open. It's a joke!'

Gunnar took another mouthful of stew. 'Not a very good one!'

'Well, to go I want, anyway,' reminded Elin.

Kirsten watched Elin continue with her meal, starting with the least favourite bits as if following some obsessive food routine. Her concentration was only broken when Kirsten told her parents about their prospective trip to the volcano.

Later in the evening Elin was snuggled in bed and Kirsten retold her the fable of the evil Katla and the volcano. Little Elin then closed her eyes and lay as still as she possibly could. The less she moved, the more she could imagine. Her mind could leave the darkened room and fly like Katla, or be invisible like an elf, or just walk in the wilderness, hand in hand with her mother.

'That child's obsessed. Volcano, volcano, volcano! It's lucky she lives in Iceland!' Gunnar had a very dry sense of humour.

Much of Kirsten's determination came from her father. He had tracked down Elin's father in Germany and persuaded him to support the child financially; not that he ever told her how he had done it. He interrogated Kirsten about her proposed trip. He might have wanted to join them, but the farm was getting busy.

'Stay away from the glacier!' he warned her.

The main calderas were covered by 850 metres of ice, and enormous bodies of meltwater could burst out. These could be far more dangerous than a normal volcano, and there were dramatic scars on the landscape to testify to the power of a subglacial eruption.

The danger didn't seem to worry Oddny. 'Just make sure Elin takes her watercolours,' was her only concern. It was nice to have a mother who didn't worry about anything.

So, four days later, setting off on the expedition was Elin's idea of heaven. They drove through snowscapes, forded frozen rivers and sheltered in emergency huts. They also had hours and hours to talk.

It was exacting driving, and although Elin started with her childish news, the longer they drove, the wider the topics became. Kirsten, losing all worries apart from keeping on the road, relaxed and revealed so much more of her life and thoughts than she ever would if they baked cakes together.

Then in the gloomy distance they could see a flash of red and the rising smoke. As melting snowfields gave way to blackened shingle, they finally pulled up onto a barren ridge.

Elin's heart was fit to burst. Laid out before her was a world split apart – its molten core spewing out with unimaginable force and beauty.

It was then she knew that understanding her planet would be her life, her quest, her future.

*Kirsten and Elin by Eruption*

# Chapter 7

## The Quest to Find Solutions

The teams got busy immediately, each working out their own agenda. Rocky and Dolores had decided to split their efforts. Rocky would do the rockets, as he had to get the project off the ground, and Dolores was to work on the landers, living quarters and scientific payloads.

Being a rocket engineer, Rocky knew exactly what he needed. His problem was NASA didn't have any suitable rockets at this time.

Dolores, the scientist, had to break new ground. She was to provide safe and adequate living quarters for the journey and on Mars itself. Most importantly, she had to deliver the precious cargo to the planet and get it back. The earlier landers had used disposable heat shields, parachutes, protective balloons or 'sky cranes' to slow the craft from 13,000mph to zero in a matter of minutes. For this mission, the sheer weight would make all this redundant. They needed some radical thinking and designs to succeed. For Dolores it would start with pure science and a drawing board. Rocky would start with a calling card and a Yellow Pages.

There was a strange alliance between Rocky and Yasmin from HR and PR. Their lack of heavy-duty rockets meant they would have to beg, borrow or steal one and a great deal of negotiations might be needed with other nations' space agencies. Yasmin's charm was a perfect counter for the bluff Rocky.

> **International Space Station (ISS)**
> Orbit height: 408km
> Speed of orbit:
> 7.66km/s
> Length: 72.8m
> (239ft)
> Width: 108.5m
> (356ft)

In all the years since the Apollo programme, nobody had built anything to match the Saturn V. And since the retirement of the shuttle, NASA had been more or less dependent on Russian technology. In fact, only the Russian and the European space agencies had the large rockets that could take the mission into space, and even then the mission would need to be laboriously assembled in orbit, like the components of the International Space Station.

There were other possibilities. Maybe the burgeoning space industries of India or China could fill the gap? Or even the private sector? The Pure Corporation, who had already been launching their own satellites, had great ambitions for space tourism and even aspirations to get to Mars – a one-way ticket concept that took out all the difficult bits and condemned the participants to never being able to return to Earth.

Yasmin and Rocky were deep in their deliberations when Ford joined them. Yasmin had sat Rocky down in front of her beloved whiteboard, where she delivered conceptual buzz words in the hope that that they would yield some profound answers.

She had written 'What do we need?' in bold letters on the board.

'A rocket – a BFR,' answered Rocky.

'How's it going?' enquired Ford.

'Apparently we need something called a BFR,' chimed in Yasmin.

Ford smirked. 'How many Big F***ing Rockets are out there?'

Rocky took up the marker pen and wrote a list of large rockets past and present, where they were made and how many rockets they might need to put the mission together in orbit.

| 1 or 2no | Saturn V | (USA – out of production) |
|---|---|---|
| 2no | Space Launch System | (USA – in development) |
| 2no | Pure Proton | (USA – in development) |
| 4no | Ariane | (Europe – French) |
| 6no | Angara | (Russia) |
| 8no | Long March | (China) |
| 9no | GSLV D5s | (India) |

Yasmin immediately saw the prospect for foreign travel, and in her vision of the Ariane it was not a rocket but the Eiffel Tower.

'Brilliant!' Yasmin clapped. 'Our first port of call must be Paris, then Moscow, then Beijing.'

Ford chipped in. 'We will definitely need the European Space Agency's help! But skip Moscow. We have a trade embargo with Russia, so any approach would have to be very high level.'

'Hey, we also need to talk to my good buddy Milton.' Rocky's friend Milton was the original 'rocket man', an obsessive genius who knew everything there was to know about every rocket ever produced.

He was now curator of rockets at the Samsonian Institute. He'd have some ideas, for sure.

Ford got a call to 'discuss' things with Stephen. According to the president, he was there to help, Ford told himself again and again.

Stephen had invited Ford 'for tea' at an address just up the hill from the Pasadena headquarters.

In the late afternoon Ford made his way there, the dust trailing behind him as he turned around a bend and there, perched on a small outcrop, was a small but beautiful house. The steps to the main entrance bridged a bubbling stream via granite stepping stones. From the terrace above, Stephen waved and gestured Ford to join him.

The aloof man of that first day had disappeared. Stephen was all smiles. Dressed in a black tracksuit, he wafted around the glamorous shack, explaining how he had rented it for the quarter.

They settled on the terrace. The view between the two Scots Pines was magnificent, framing the wooded suburbs and the hazy city beyond. This was a house for enjoying sunsets.

'I rented it for the run. It's three miles, a perfect commute. I couldn't survive at the dreadful "Gulag".' This was where Ford stayed with the rest of the team who had to fly in for their meetings. He brought out the résumé that Stephen had given him.

Stephen looked away to the downtown horizon. The city of Los Angeles was spread before them. 'There are 4 million Americans out there and another 312 million we can't see. My job was to protect them against the bad guys. A talk abandoned because the president wants to get the glory of a "grand project" and wash his hands of his guilty feelings... That city only functions because there are people who pick up the rubbish, unblock the sewers and police the streets. It can't all be opera houses and gleaming spires. Give me one good reason why we should waste our resources looking at rocks on a dead planet when there's a war going on and our very values are under attack?'

Ford ran his fingers through his hair as he considered this. 'Nothing positive comes out of war. We have to learn to live with each other – we are all mere humans after all.'

Stephen looked scornful, but Ford ignored him and took a deep breath. 'In my view, we have a unique status on this earth. We are able to understand it. We give it more relevance by witnessing it. Each piece of knowledge we gain opens up new possibilities and it endorses our own existence here. It's what gives us meaning and makes us worth defending. You have been fighting people who want to turn the clock back to an age of ignorance. We should combat that by striving for knowledge.'

There was a long silence. The trees rustled, and the brook babbled. Finally, Stephen broke the silence. 'Bullshit!'

Ford smiled. 'That's just cool, Stephen. We don't have to fight about it. We need a sceptic – you can set deadlines and judge our efforts. There's a big world out there that will be testing us too. In any case, you're a military man. If you've signed up for it, you just need to get on with the job and be professional.'


Henrietta, Patrick and Dolores sat sipping coffee. They were comparing weights. Patrick was about 90kg; Dolores's trim figure weighed in at 50kg. Henrietta announced, dunking a biscuit, she was 'about the same'.

'Ford reckoned 180kg for all the crew. How does that work out?'

'Well... two of me or... Maybe three of you ladies allowing for the biscuits.'

'Women?' corrected Henrietta.

Dolores wrote down 'stores and supplies', and listed space suits, clothes, bedding, scientific equipment, vehicles, food, water and personal items. With an estimate of the weights required, it soon multiplied into several tons.

On a separate piece of paper, in her neat handwriting, Dolores put the heading 'skills', underlined, with three bullet points:

- *Technical*
- *Welfare*
- *Science*

Under 'Technical' she wrote *pilot*.

'Do we need them nowadays? We land the rovers automatically,' questioned Henrietta.

'Do we crash them automatically as well?' replied Dolores bluntly.

The need for a pilot was demonstrated in the stark light of a lunar morning half a century ago. It was Neil Armstrong, not the on-board computer, who landed the lunar module on the Sea of Tranquillity. A quarter of a million miles from home, he steered it to a safe landing ground with Buzz Aldrin by his side, calling out essential data. The computer had overloaded and the designated spot was a field of boulders.

In the small, cramped confinement of the Eagle, shrouded in the deep pin-lit blackness of space, the two of them had stared down intently at the stark, bright, alien landscape of the surface below.

Still in view of the orbiting command module, Armstrong pirouetted Eagle for a final visual inspection.

When he felt the braking and the sudden weight of his body returning as the engine fired to start the descent, Armstrong's heart was in his mouth. Leaning forward, the surface loomed through the triangular window. It was forbidding and frightening and – like being over the ocean – all sense of scale was lost.

The larger craters simply gave way to smaller ones.

Ignoring the frantic bleeping of the computers and the pessimistic fuel gauges, an unfazed Armstrong deftly worked the thrusters to avoid the menacing boulders before landing Eagle perfectly in a spray of dust.

*Eagle Landing*

Mars would be far more difficult, which is why the pilot was first on the list, plus a co-pilot – like Aldrin – in case of illness.

Pilots are at the top of a pyramid of support, with engineers and mechanics making things work. In space this applies not only to the hardware, but also the software and systems that run the show. The further away from Earth, the more difficult it would become; engineering and computer skills would be essential.

If going to the moon was like the ferry across the Mersey, this mission was like a round-the-world cruise – except in a container.

**Skills required**
**Technical** – pilot –
co-pilot – engineer –
computer
programmer
**Welfare** – medic –
dietitian – sanititian
**Science** –
palaeontologist –
geologist – biologist
**General** – explorer –
leader

Most of the time would be spent just keeping alive. Who would prepare the food? Who would deal with the toilet, cleaning, recycling? Who was going to fix cuts, deal with illness and maintain the life-support systems? They needed a welfare team on this heroic mission.

And this was before they did any science and discovery.

'To strive, to seek, to find, and not to yield.'

To seek? Evidence of life, be it alive or dead. It would be triumph enough to prove that those 'fossils' were real and abundant. But what if life had survived?

Earth would suddenly have a family. And if life could exist in a place like Mars, think of all the water worlds that could exist in and beyond our solar system. It needed someone who knew about fossils, someone who knew about the terrain and someone who knew about life – a palaeontologist, a geologist and a biologist. Like Shackleton's mission a century before, they would need a leader and explorer.

When they finished their list, with far more roles than the possible size of the crew, it was clear they'd need to find some remarkably talented people.

Ford had returned with Stephen to NASA's jet propulsion laboratory – JPL – and was doing the rounds.

As he made his way to the budget group, the afternoon sunshine raised his spirits. Brushing his hair back, Ford smiled to himself.

The president had chosen him because he was trusted to 'think different'. OK! The budget would be tight. It cost $2.5 billion for the last rover and he had allowed for three times that budget. 'It must be possible,' he thought.

On entering their room, he found the glum faces of Elton, Floyd and Stephen looking at the estimates he had originally prepared. It was like joining a coven of the undead. Elton and Floyd greeted him with gloomy protests.

Stephen was sitting opposite them with arms crossed behind his head. He had obviously made his presence felt already and was uncharacteristically buoyant. 'I'm sorry, Ford, but I've told these two to sharpen their goddamn pencils or we'll get someone else on the job. The less money we pour into this thing, the better.'

**The Jet Propulsion Laboratory**
La Canada
Flintridge,
California, USA
34.1N 118.1W
Altitude: 1,188ft
Geology: Forest
mountain range and
canyon and seismic
area

A sense of gratitude flooded over Ford. 'Thank you, Stephen!'

Then addressing the affronted faces of Elton and Floyd, he said, 'It's quite simple: the budget is the budget. We'll have to cut our suit to match the cloth until we find someone else to join in.'

'But... But...' responded Floyd.

'No buts,' stepped in Stephen. 'We'll tell the teams that's all they have got for now and if we need more, we'll have to take on other partners.'

The week went by in a blur. By Friday afternoon they had all covered a great deal of ground. Ford felt both elated and exhausted by the time the cab picked him up to take him to the airstrip. Most of all he was looking forward to getting home and seeing Jane.

# Chapter 8

## Buzz and the Trailer

*Ford Mending the Camper*

Although Ford could have simply jumped into his plane once it was fuelled, he still had to wait for a slot to take off.

He sat in the club room for private pilots. His phone rang; it was Buzz.

'Hi, Granf, wanna play "AirAce"?' Buzz had never been one for words.

'Sure, Buzz. How's your mom?'

'She's OK. You ready?'

Ford put on his earphones and stared at the glowing screen of his phone. Suddenly in this micro world he was on a digital runway, with Buzz's plane on his wing. 'AirAce' was one of Buzz's favourite games, and one where Ford, being a real pilot, had a natural advantage. At first Ford would let Buzz win, but as the boy got better, it got competitive. As their planes crossed the start lines, Ford took the lead.

Engrossed in the game, Ford unconsciously traced the sweeps and dives of his plane with his upper body as it careered around. It caught the attention of the couple opposite. The upwards sweeps got them smiling, when a sudden 'Yes, yes, yes!' as Ford edged Buzz on the line set them off in stifled giggles. He realised he had an audience.

Removing the earphones with one tug and avoiding eye contact, he was relieved to hear the tannoy calling his name. As he got up he heard them say with a snigger, '*Dr Harris.*'


Buzz sat in his room with the games controller and a big screen. Buzz would play for hours, perfecting his techniques against 'AirAces' all around the world. His youthful reactions were quicker than Ford's, but not yet a match for his grandfather's real experience.

Aldrin, or 'Buzz', lived with his mother in Baton Rouge. His father, Armstrong, Ford's only son, was bumming around some far corner of the world and lost to all those who still loved him. Down the chaotic corridor, Buzz could hear his mother in the kitchen, clanking pots and plates as she prepared supper. Buzz was furious as he surveyed the ham sandwich on the desk; clearly he wasn't invited.

**Baton Rouge**
Louisiana, USA
30.3N 91.8W
Altitude: 56ft
Geology: Prairie
surfaces and alluvial
deposits; first bluff of
Mississippi river

It was Mom's date night with 'The Boyf'. He'd liked The Boyf (Anthony) at first. He was funny, if a bit of a bum. However, he was now getting far too exclusive in his visits. Buzz loved his mom, but she drove him mad with her wild flights of delusion and disorder. Certainty was Buzz's craving in life. Tonight he was certain of one thing: they would play music until late, make strange noises, then The Boyf would slip away before dawn. Buzz had had enough disruption in his nine short years. It wasn't until he was four that his mother had contacted Ford and Jane to ask for help. During the brief relationship with Ford's son Armstrong, she had asked him about his unusual name and he had just said, 'My dad works for NASA!'

With that snippet Buzz's mother had tracked Ford down and the first email changed everything. Buzz learned two things: life could be different, and there *was* another world out there. That other world was Ford and Jane's ranch. He called them 'Granf' and 'Granj'.

Buzz lay on his bed and listened to the noises of the city. Above the drone of the traffic, he heard a plane taking off. Living close to the airport, he was constantly aware of its ebb and flow. It was a regular commuter plane, a 737 most likely. He listened to the next arrivals, then, picking up his trusty binoculars, he eased open the window to the sultry evening, climbed out and skipped to the nearest bush. He skirted the clutter in their yard and made it to the fence without being noticed. The wilderness beyond was his adventure park. At this time of the year the trees were bare enough for him to get a view of the airport. He chose his favourite tree by the chapel and climbed.

The top of the tree was his space station, his cockpit and escape. His mom had caught him there once and threatened blue murder if he didn't come down. The Boyf foolishly tried to get him.

That time The Boyf actually pursued him up the tree. He was within an inch of grabbing Buzz's ankle when – *crack!* – gravity did the rest. Down he slipped, grasping at branch after branch, before crashing to earth in a heap. The Boyf hollered with pain. The commotion brought the members of the congregation spilling out and gathering around.

Unfortunately Bud, his workmate, was in the crowd. While Buzz's mom ran to get her phone, the friend pushed to the front. 'Don't worry, Ant, she's gone to call the medics. They'll soon sort you out.' Buzz overheard the hushed reply: 'More likely my wife will. I said I'm on the night shift!'

> **Gravity**
> The gravity on earth is $9.8 m/s^2$
> On Mars: $3.7 m/s^2$
> On the moon: $1.6 m/s^2$

Buzz knew then he was not just a bum, but a cheating bum!

Below the child in the swaying tree was boring old Fairchild Street with single-storey shacks and modern bungalows like his own. They had previously lived in one of those shacks until Ford came to the rescue. Buzz's mom said they were royalty because they didn't live in a trailer and she didn't do the garden or household chores.

Swaying in the bare canopy, he could look out over the city and the airport where Granf would arrive and whisk him off in the 'old crate'. Dusk had settled as he watched the green and red lights of another small aircraft during take-off. He turned and gazed over the city lights and the abrupt outline of the banks of the mighty Mississippi. The same green and red lights tracked the waters, defining the boats as they worked their way along the river.

When he and Mom had moved from the shack, Buzz finally got his own room. Granf had given him two brass bedside lights. Red for port and green for starboard, they had transformed the mattress into an imaginary craft of air, water or even space.

He suddenly heard his mom's voice. 'Buzz, what the hell are you doing up there?'

'Flip!' he thought. He had left it too long. He then heard The Boyf's imperative tones: 'Get down here, you little dirtbag!'

His mother turned on Anthony. 'Shhh… remember the last time?'

'Phony! Cheat!' shouted Buzz.

His mom shrieked, 'Come down! You're supposed to be at home!'

'So is he!' Buzz screamed.

The Boyf shuffled in his sneakers, uneasy with the drift of the conversation.

'Perhaps he could join us for supper, after all?' he suggested lamely.

Buzz could not resist and 'dirtbag' slid down as gracefully as a falling leaf, desperate to be included again.

*Ford Finishing the Trailer*

Ford had got up early, determined to set to on 'The Trailer'. This was no ordinary trailer. It was fashioned from the mangled remains of two crashed campers found at the local scrapyard. He had promised Jane he would finish the hulk, which had cluttered up the yard for months, and soon he had the wheels on and the pop-top fixed and working. With a little trouble he fixed the newly painted doors and there it was – not just a trailer, but a mini-caravan.

Jane came out into the yard. 'If it was that easy, why didn't you finish it last year, then?'

He just smiled and said, 'If it wasn't for "the last minute", nothing would ever happen!'

Jane sceptically cleared her throat. 'By the way, Maria called. She wants us to take Buzz a week early,' said Jane. 'She sounded pretty dodgy.'

'We can't. We're going to Italy.'

'Let's take him. He'll be good company for me while you're in the hall. *Bella Italia*, he'll love it!'

Ford looked very worried. 'Do you think Maria was going bonkers again?'

Jane gave a solemn nod.

That evening Ford cooked for Jane. One of her gifts to Ford was showing him the simple joy of preparing food – natural ingredients and following your instincts.

Jane had brought much more than wholesome food to their lives; she had brought life after death.

They had met in a hotel restaurant, where she was brimming with the success of her first book being accepted. Ford was feeling crushed. He had never felt so alone. It had been five years since his wife Rebecca died. Her death, the devastation it had wreaked on Armstrong, and Ford's stalled career had left him feeling like he was rolling down an endless hill. He didn't know it, but that evening he was going to reach the valley.

It was a boutique hotel, all dark colours and overelaborate table settings. Ford sat at his small table and fumbled with the overgenerous tablecloth as he tucked in his napkin.

Jane was also sitting alone, but in a much happier state of mind, enjoying the luxury of people-watching. After checking out the gregarious family opposite, then the tetchy couple to her right, she spotted Ford. There was a hint of a wounded animal about him as he struggled with his thoughts and napkin. His vulnerability held her gaze. Ford had taken little joy in the steak on a slate and jam jar salad, and decided to retire.

As he stood up and left, he felt a tug on his belt, followed by a tinkling and crashing as slate, glasses, flower vase and red wine bottle were all yanked to the floor by the tablecloth tucked into his trousers.

He just stood there, looking ridiculous. He turned his face to the dark ceiling as if imploring a greater being to give him a break.

Jane could not help herself – she was on the move. She whisked Ford away by the arm. 'Don't worry about that lot and come with me.' She sat him down in a quiet corner of the bar and, using a napkin, sponged his chinos as best she could. She looked up and, stifling her mirth, said, 'Look at you. What a bloody state!'

That was it, their introduction – at last, a silver lining to the dark clouds.


That night at Ford's the crockery stayed on the table and, with the food eaten, they settled down by the fire in the living room, sipping a sweet digestif.

'Is it going to be all right, cariad?' She hoped for Ford's sake it would work out. After all, he had fixed 'the trailer'.

Ford took a deep breath. 'There are issues I can't see how to resolve, but that's what's interesting. I hate the politics – what with Stephen and the press – it feels too... I don't know... negative.'

Jane was positive. 'Well, it *would* be political. It's being sponsored by a politician! Remember, he's the same one who's taken you on because you are different. What's *your* motivation in this?' They stared at the flames as he thought.

'To do something profound,' Ford finally replied in a reflective tone of voice. 'I feel like a mason who has spent his life just building houses, and I want to build something beautiful, something significant.'

'Like a cathedral?' Jane filled in.

He slowly nodded his head. 'Yes, that's it. It has to be extraordinary.'

Jane sipped her drink before answering, 'Well, it would be if you found life! Tell me about the Angel.'

He turned the question around. 'No, you're the biologist. Could it be a trick of the light, a chance illusion?'

He summoned up an image on his iPad. Jane started to review it with analytical scrutiny.

'Well, it's got a face for a start. The body *is* symmetrical and has a detailed structure, which would be a challenge for a random rock shape. The dead giveaway is the broken wing to the top left. That's no accident. And if it is life, it's quite advanced.

'Just remember, there's nothing scientific about this – it's just my observation. However, I would say this: it hasn't just curled up and died. That other wing shows it was not alone. I'd like to think there was a shoal or a flight of them and... Maybe they've just been caught up in a catastrophe. Poor little darlings!'

'Anything else?' asked Ford encouragingly.

Jane lay back on the cushions and put her right arm over his shoulder. 'If it really was an animal, it would have an ecosystem.

There would be many other plants and animals to be found. That shell-like thing on the other slide is just as important. Looking at it, I guess it lived in water. The wings certainly are for moving in a fluid.'

*Fossil 2*

'Thanks, that's fascinating.'

'I'm not finished!' Jane held up her left index finger. 'I don't think it's worth going to Mars to find more of these. I'm convinced already.

'What's really worth doing is finding its great-great-great- etc. grandchildren. They must have been wonderfully adaptive, progressing so far in such a short time compared with Earth. I only see a fraction of my ants' lives, because they're underground most of the time. If I were to go to Mars, I'd look for a nice, deep, warm hole. Have you ever been down a coal mine? It gets very warm very quickly!'

On the generous mantelpiece there stood three globes: one of the Earth, one of the moon and one of Mars. They were a gift set she had given Ford for their first Christmas. She walked over to the fireplace. Picking up the Martian globe, she gave it a whirl. She counted dozens of ancient volcanoes on its

**Pavonis Mons**
Tharsis, Mars
1.48N 247.0E
234 miles wide, 8.7 miles high
Geology: Shield volcano

pockmarked surface and explained to Ford that although they might be inactive, they would be the best places to look for those warm spaces. 'Just make sure your geologist knows their volcanoes!'

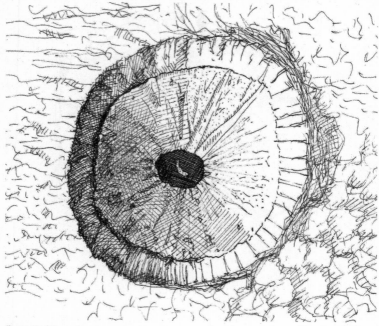

*Pavonis Mons*

# Chapter 9

## Jane Steps In

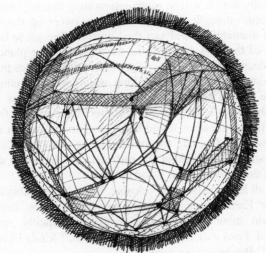

"MARS AS THE ABODE OF LIFE": 1905
by PERCIVAL LOWELL.

*Old Illustration of Mars*

Ford shuddered as he thought of his crazy week ahead. Off to the JPL, then hooking up with Rocky and Yasmin. They were calling in to see Milton 'the rocket man' at the Samsonian.

He was freaking out over the Italian conference. 'I know we've booked the tickets, but hell, I'm just not prepared for it. I'll let everyone down.'

Jane put her foot down. She wanted this trip to Italy badly and especially now Buzz was coming too.

'Look, you can't put all your eggs in the one basket. This is a big deal as well. It's packed full of people who you'll need if this thing is to get off the ground.'

He explained it wasn't the timescale; he just had no time to do the paper. It was the 10th international conference on planetary exploration and he was to speak on potential ecosystems on other planets and moons.

'OK then, cariad, I'll write your paper!' said Jane. 'I'm a biologist, after all.' She'd had a revelation, looking at the globe of Mars. It was a real place, and not that different from their own planet.

Ford considered it. He knew Jane's scientific abilities, and a different take on it could be very interesting.

'OK, why not? It will be more entertaining than my drivel!'

'Brilliant!' thought Jane. She shot up, swept up the Earth globe from the mantelpiece and vanished outside. The globe had contours not only of the land, but also the ocean beds – the planet laid bare, with its deep-sea mountains, ridges and tectonic plates made visible. With the smell of pear drops wafting around her, she returned, hiding the globe behind her. With a flourish she placed a new 'red planet' on the table, with Ford's car-body primer still gleaming freshly on its surface. It was uncanny. It had been transformed into an alien world, which she placed beside the smaller globe of Mars. The difference was extraordinary! Without the distraction of land and sea the very nature of the planets' skins stood out.

Mars, all hard-shelled and volcanic, looked immutable and ancient, while the Earth was a patchwork of zipped plates, deep trenches, plains and mountain ridges, a surface constantly renewed and weathered. Ford was less impressed. 'Mmm, I kinda liked my globe as it was!' But he got the point.

That afternoon, after Ford had left, Jane hunted out her old PhD thesis. The thick, bound pages represented years of research. She remembered the long hours of writing and the field trips to wet and humid deep caves for her research.

Jane thought of her innocence and youthful enthusiasm at that time. Her subject was an extraordinary ant species, white and blind because it had lived entirely underground for over 100 million years. The question she had put was not how it had survived, but for how much longer it could carry on. Her conclusion: the ants had lived through at least one major extinction event without batting an antenna, so there was no reason why they shouldn't be there in another 100 million years. If she could publish a PhD on such an extreme animal, there was no reason why she couldn't tackle this subject now.

She studied the small globe of Mars as if mentally peeling it like an orange. Needing a tea break a little later, she was livid to discover the trailer was still sitting in the yard. It was now late afternoon and the roosting birds circled overhead.

The finished article was a weird yet beautiful thing. Her curiosity took hold and she tentatively went outside and opened the doors, which revealed a beautifully crafted interior. There was a range of birch plywood cupboards, with a bright table that folded down between the seats. This table covered an alcove holding within it a hob next to a small ceramic sink. On either side were shelves, containing wicker hampers for cutlery, crockery and provisions. The double-banked seats were covered in the same William Morris patterned fabric from Jane's childhood home. The whole effect, with the oaken boat-like joinery, proper ship's brass fittings and the deep colours of the Strawberry Thief fabric, was simply gorgeous. On the seat among the cushions was an envelope with Jane's name. She carefully peeled it open to reveal a card. On the front was a simple heart and, turning it over, she read, '*For us, my sweet. XXXX*'.

She had thought the trailer was a 'man den' for Ford. Now she knew it was for them both and she was touched by the little thoughtful details that surrounded her. Through the rear window she could clearly see the red disc of the setting sun dropping through the blues, oranges and greys of the sky. She went back and returned with the two globes, setting them up on the back shelf. She pictured the history of the solar system in her mind.

The two planets had started out in the same swirling void of stellar debris, forming, sweeping and fermenting as they grew and grew. With less material to gather, Mars never reached the size of Earth or Venus, but had settled down to a stable state earlier. The Earth had had a catastrophic youth. As Jane had seen whenever Ford was packing a bag, a small element of chaos could lead to interesting results. Two planets formed near the Earth's orbit and, like squabbling siblings, were too close to share the space happily.

What a sight it would have been, the two still-glowing planets edging ever closer year by year, until one eventful evening a white-hot burst of energy lit up the solar system as they collided and combined into a dazzling mass. This catastrophic event set back the formation of planet Earth by aeons. The lighter shell of the smaller planet was spun into orbit around the central heaving mass, creating the moon, and the heavier elements and iron cores combined to fuse with the Earth's. This chain of events was incredibly fortunate because, like a gyroscope, the moon's gravity stabilised the Earth's axis, giving its inhabitants regular seasons. The momentum of the collision gave enough impetus to keep the planet spinning once every twenty-four hours, unlike Venus or Mercury, whose days have slowed to a sun-baked standstill. The gift of a massive spinning iron core provided the magnetic field that protects the Earth from solar radiation. In all, it created an ideal environment for life to grow and develop into the special sentient beings humans are today.

Jane looked at the two globes again. Start with the simple things. 'The bloody obvious!' Mars has impact craters, but nothing like the intensely pockmarked surfaces of the moon or Mercury. The Earth has no obvious ones. The mountains and ocean trenches on Earth show an active surface in the process of continual renewal, wiping clean the slate of its early history. Mars has scars and stress lines on its surface, so there must have been some movement of its crust. The biggest difference is the number of volcanoes on Mars. These appear to have erased many of the early scars it would have suffered. The volcanoes on Mars are massive, because without the moving tectonic plates, they could just grow in the same place. Both planets have icy poles and a tilted axis, giving them both seasons and days that are around twenty-four hours long.

How could this cold planet have harboured life in those early days? Life would have needed liquid water, so it had to have been warmer and have had a thicker atmosphere. It may have been a little closer to the sun and still warm as it cooled down from a molten ball. The active volcanoes then would have been pumping out the thick atmosphere needed to maintain the rivers and seas whose remnants have been discovered by the rovers and orbiters.

The cool of the evening raised a few goose bumps as Jane mentally pictured this early Martian landscape and gave herself a ringside seat, perched on an outcrop on the planet's surface just before it started to freeze for good. She focused her thoughts further. 'How could such complex animals have developed then, when it took another billion years for life to develop to a similar stage on Earth?'

Well, she was sure that it had started earlier on Mars due to the Earth–moon collision. Then, like her ants in their underground lair, the Earth was too stable to promote rapid change at first. Mars could have been far more dynamic, forcing evolutionary forces forward at a far greater rate.

Screwing her eyes shut, she pictured a Martian seashore. The land was stark – red, blue and black like today, and the lapping water had the milky blue and green tones of a glacial river. Among the rocks on the narrow beaches were crisp white boulders of ice. The sky was blue with orange-tinged clouds. Across the still waters a line of snow-topped hills spread out and, towering beyond them, an ageing volcano was shrouded in its own vapours, wheezing a caustic mix of gases and ash high into the atmosphere.

*Ancient Mars Landscape*

Straining her 'biological brain', Jane wondered where the life was. She thought about her holidays on the Pembrokeshire coast: the roar of the waves, the sting of the wind on her face and the call of the gulls; rock pools, limpets, mounds of seaweed – there would be none of that. Perhaps on the thin line between land and sea something primitive might have grown, a bacterial sludge maybe. Among the shallows there could have been circular mats of stromatolites looking like the bald heads of submerged giants. The milky sea, she imagined, would have been saturated with the vast amounts of carbon dioxide expelled from the volcanoes. Nowadays the poles of Mars still have a dry ice crust (formed from frozen carbon dioxide) topping the water ice below. Every spring extraordinary geysers of sublimating water burst through in a series of spectacular fountains before refreezing in a hail of snow. Those early seas would have fizzed like mineral water. No wonder that first fossil slide showed a shell-like structure.

She could imagine that scenario but, even straining her vivid imagination, she couldn't picture the 'Angel' fossils to be part of this scene. Jane then noticed, closer to home, that – like Mars – the trailer was getting colder. Reluctantly she retreated to the house. As she lit the fire, inspiration dawned on her. These creatures wouldn't have been hanging around the shore line with its noxious airs and radiation; they'd have had far more time to develop in the warm water in the flooded chambers of all those volcanoes. The networks of caves she had visited in her early research were vast. Maybe the lakes of Mars hadn't all vanished with most of the atmosphere, but some had remained underground. The methane plumes that emanate from the ground today could be organic in origin. NASA had found massive reserves of ice just beneath Mars' surface layers. Like Uncle Chedwyn's mine, could increasing subterranean temperatures melt it and let the water flow?

'Now, that's where we need to look,' she whispered to herself with a growing excitement.

Her imagination aflame, Jane was hooked and with the aid of Ford's notes, she refined her ideas and wrote his paper.

# Chapter 10

## Paris

Yasmin had never felt more alive than today. The early-morning chill just added to the shivering frisson of excitement as she grasped Rocky's arm on the Pont des Arts. 'Isn't this romantic?' she pleaded with the stocky engineer as they surveyed the thousands of lovers' padlocks on the railings. This lightning tour of Beijing and Paris had captured her mind. She now understood why someone could be compelled to roam, to drink in the unfamiliar. The clinging heat and insane hubbub of Beijing had been replaced by the mature sophistication of Paris. Even with the clouded skies, the city felt vibrant with colour, and a harmonious integrity from the centuries of thought that defines a culture was evident wherever they went.

Everything was the same yet different from the States – from the city buildings to the manhole covers. Yasmin had also spoken French! She had carefully introduced both herself and Rocky at their meeting at ESA and rounded off the discussions with her best Gallic repertoire, waving her arms about manically. She had studiously ignored the uncomprehending faces, flattering herself that two-thirds of language was about pure communication.

> **Paris**
> Île-de-France, France
> 48.5N 2.2E
> Altitude: 115ft
> Geology:
> Sedimentary basin
> and Seine river
> valley

As another *bateau mouche* passed beneath their feet with its customary following of gulls, she noticed Rocky's eyes were fixed on the Eiffel Tower rising high above the slate-grey skyline.

He pointed to it and shared his thoughts. 'Look, Yasmin, it's 130 years old and almost as tall as three Saturn Vs. It was the tallest structure in Europe for over a century. If they could build something like that when they had only slide rules and steam engines, why is it so darned difficult to produce a rocket today?'

They both knew that in many ways their trip had been a great success. Both their hosts had been enthusiastic, particularly at the China National Space Administration, where their Shenzhou programmes had been producing astronauts for years. It was clear that there would be money on the table, and technical support if required for a very significant and prestigious project.

But to their dismay there were no secret large rockets in the pipeline, and even the regular ones were fully committed. There would be plenty of capacity on the landers, facilities and other kit, but not big rockets.

Yasmin was undeterred by these minor details; her eyes had been opened. 'I get it now, Rocky,' she whispered.

Rocky stooped to catch her words. 'Get what?'

'Why we have go to Mars, of course. It's like coming here – it's so different. I thought everywhere was the same these days, like a little America, but if Beijing and Paris are so wonderful, just think how amazing another planet would be!'

They had two hours to kill before they had to leave for the airport. Yasmin tore off in the direction of the shops.

Rocky might have headed for a fast-food joint but, charged by Yasmin's words, he decided to go to the Louvre. He didn't want to rush around and needed to think. Finding himself in a vast hall of red marble, he sat down wearily and contemplated a pair of statues – Mars, in an impressive hat and not much else, and his lover Venus, with her gentle arm around his back, and hand touching his chest. Mars' muscular body and imperial air reminded him of himself in his prime, but at least he had been wearing a pair of jeans.

'Something will turn up' had been Yasmin's final words before heading off to retail heaven.

'Nothing's going to just turn up – no rockets, no mission!' thought Rocky.

'Who the hell was this Mars anyway? God of War. Everyone knows that.' He was fascinated to read that he was also the god of agriculture, lover of Venus and father of Romulus and Remus, and that his mother Juno had been impregnated by a flower. Life must have been so very different then.

Mars certainly looked quite impressive, resolute even. Maybe Rocky shouldn't give up straightaway. Suddenly he remembered his own responsibilities. 'Gift shop,' he whispered to himself. He couldn't return home empty-handed. There was also a child in Rocky who just loved gift shops, even when filled with art books.

Yasmin and Rocky travelled business class back to Houston where they met Ford who had also flown in for the meeting. They felt relatively refreshed as the cab pulled along the causeway and across the choppy waters of Galveston Bay. Heading north they could now see the looming form of the museum complex flashing by through the street clutter of the dual carriageway. Rocky's disappointment in the unfinished quest was tempered by the prospect of seeing his old friend.

'Milton! What have you done to this place? It was a dump.' Milton was very proud of the improvements he had made to the Samsonian, and even prouder of its collection of aerospace artefacts.

Milton looked at the trio: Yasmin looking like Coco Channel on steroids, Rocky like a bear out of hibernation, and Ford an extra from *Catch-22*.

In a small office, surrounded by photographs of rockets, space shuttles and moon landings, Rocky laid out their problems. He held nothing back.

'Well, you couldn't have chosen a worse time to go,' replied Milton. 'If the China and ESA can't help and the Russians ain't playing ball, you'll have to wait at least ten years before we've got any proper rockets ready.'

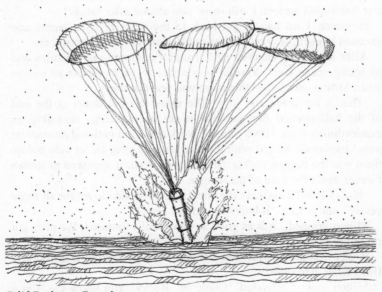

*Solid Rocket on Parachute*

As Rocky had feared, there was no hope. Milton got up to offer another coffee. Then they suddenly noticed a look of inspiration light up his face and he hastily grabbed a catalogue from the shelf.

'We keep our stock in the desert now, as it stops them rotting.' He deftly skimmed through the pages and opened the catalogue to show a photograph of a pencil-like rocket left over from the shuttle programme. 'I've got seven of these if it helps. They are powerful and reusable and I only need one for display. They won't get you all the way there, but... they'll help. You can have them if you promise to bring me back a piece of Mars.'

Rocky and Ford desperately searched the catalogue. 'Hey, these are really cool!' Ford was instantly attracted to a series of 1960s trucks modified for transporting rocket components.

Milton laughed. 'They're from the Apollo. If you can get them to start, you can have them too. But you can't drive them to Mars!'

He prowled the office. Having had another brainwave, he opened a drawer and brought out a large roll of blueprints.

'You could take this to Boeing and ask them to make you another one.' With great reverence he opened out an original set of blueprints of a Saturn V rocket on the desk. 'We've been poring over them on our restoration project. I will show you around after lunch!'

However, Ford had to get back to the other mission teams and excused himself, leaving Rocky and Yasmin to the museum tour.

After inspecting random rocket motors, burned-out capsules and ill-fitting space suits, Yasmin was about to feign illness to escape when Milton announced that there was one last thing.

'This is my pride and joy!' The massive steel doors at the end of the hall opened like curtains in an opera house, revealing an extraordinary sight. 'Five years of work and it's a national monument now,' explained Milton with a proud smile. Lying on its side before them was the biggest rocket they had ever seen. It appeared to stretch forever down the void of the hangar.

'Jesus Christ! That's not the one they left outside to rot for all those years?' said Rocky. 'It looks as good as new!'

Milton grinned. 'It is as good as new, totally restored. We even got rid of the mice.'

Rocky wandered over and banged the side. 'What did you do? Body filler, paint job?'

Milton looked offended. 'Come on, Rocky! You know me. I'm a perfectionist – everything to the last detail, even the wiring. As new! It's put this museum back on the map!'

*Jasmin and Rocky at the Museum*

Rocky stood impassively for what seemed like an age, surveying the massive form. Yasmin gently tugged his tie to get his attention. 'Hello, are you still with us?'

Rocky, his trance broken, turned to Milton. 'It looks just like the real thing. Congratulations!'

'It *is* the real thing,' said Milton. 'It's Apollo 18.'

A shot of adrenaline charged through Rocky and a light bulb sparked. 'I don't suppose…' Hesitating, he thought better of it. 'No, forget it!'

Changing the subject, he asked for Milton to excuse him. 'I couldn't find anything in Paris for the kids. Where's the gift shop?'

This was not Yasmin's kind of shopping and she was itching with impatience when a smiling Rocky finally emerged. She had been waiting in their cab for twenty minutes. 'Just how many children have you got?' she exclaimed at the sight of him struggling with four massive boxes.

Rocky threw her a mischievous look and replied with a twinkle in his eye, 'Not for the kids, they're for the project.'


Ford was distracted as he crossed the car park to HQ. He had slept badly after the museum meeting, his mind churning with the latest problems. He had the taste of failure in his mouth and didn't like it. He kicked a small stone to release some frustration. The stone hit a large black Chrysler, parked near the entrance. Stopping briefly to examine it, he froze as he felt a hand gripping his shoulder.

Then the military training kicked in and he instinctively grasped the hand firmly with his left and, turning slightly, with his right hand caught a handful of shirt, flipping his assailant's off-balance body onto the tarmac. The black-suited figure was no slouch and Ford was too slow to drop onto the semi-prone body. In a flash Ford was countered. His own wrist was turned around his back and his face pushed against a car.

Straining his neck to look over his shoulder, he saw a badge with an electrocuted goose and the words 'Department of Homeland Security' embossed around it. 'Steady now, sir. I only wanted your ID.'

'We have a machine for doing that! Who brought you in?' Ford fumbled for his card.

'We work with Mr Dyer,' he explained as he released his grip and let Ford go.

Ruffled and indignant, Ford made it to his office to find Stephen waiting for him. 'What the hell's going on, Stephen?'

At first Stephen appeared nonplussed, then put on an air of nonchalance. 'Oh, the security? That's just routine in my service.'

Ford was furious. 'Not our kind of routine and you're working for us now!' He crashed his bag down on the desk for emphasis.

'It was in my line of work and the risks don't vanish when you leave. The president promised me cover as part of the deal and none of us can be too careful.'

Mopping a little blood from his lip, Ford tried to suppress his anger. 'You'll be telling me you pack a gun next!'

Stephen touched his jacket pocket. 'I do, actually. Don't you?'

Ford couldn't believe his ears. 'Who do you think I am – Indiana Jones? I insist you leave it in your drawer.' He excused himself to calm down in the bathroom.

On returning he took stock and addressed Stephen. 'OK, so you bring your baggage with you. What else should I know?'

Stephen was candid and explained the sensitivities of his previous work and why he needed protection. Consequently the identities of the team, especially Stephen's, should be strictly on a need-to-know basis, even when the mission went public.

In his words the 'bad guys' he had been dealing with would stop at nothing to attack the state or the president, and the game had now changed for all high-profile projects.

Ford was stressed. 'Well, it's not how we run this organisation.'

'I'm sorry, Ford, I insist. Call it part of my brief... Remember, you've felt pretty spooked by the press and they just hold a pencil. These guys want us to go to hell, not Mars.'

Ford stared at his desk for a moment, then looked up at Stephen. 'OK, it's a new world and we could do without the glare of publicity.' Then, with a forced smile, 'Just don't let your spook use his neutraliser on me!'

Stephen returned the smile with a little more warmth and enquired about the search for the rockets.

Ford shook his head. 'Not good.' He explained they had only a roll of old blueprints and the offer of half a dozen secondhand boosters from the Samsonian to show for it.

Stephen looked quizzical. 'Why's Rocky looking so upbeat then? I saw him arrive this morning with a load of boxes...'

Ford shrugged. 'Maybe he enjoyed Paris? I can't think of anything else. There's no way we can design and build our own rocket in time.'


When Ford entered the meeting room the familiar scent of coffee hung in the air, and a gaggle of his colleagues surrounded Yasmin as she regaled them with her impressions of Beijing and Paris. She was wearing a new scarf and shoes to prove it. She had also brought something back for everybody.

To the sceptical accountants, Floyd and Elton, she announced the offers of funding from the European and Chinese space agencies.

Yasmin relayed to the mission planners and scientists that both agencies had made promises of engineering and hardware and offered the use of the ESA launch facilities in tropical French Guyana, which she selflessly volunteered to check out herself.

Edward was thrilled with the weighty tomes on European procurement rules, health-and-safety directives, and non-discriminatory selection criteria, which would have to be adopted if they were to go ahead in partnership.

The huddle was broken by a barely perceptible cough. They turned to look at the figure of Mr Dyer, clad in a black tracksuit. 'Don't get too excited, my friends. You can't get the project off the ground without a rocket. Where is it? In fact, where's Rocky?'

Yasmin knew exactly where he was. 'In his office. He didn't want to be disturbed for a few hours.'

'Sounds like he's in hiding,' said Stephen with a laugh.

Ford broke the gloom. 'No one said it would be easy. Remember, we are doing this *because* it is difficult. Get on with your work and I will see each team during the morning. Leave Rocky to think it through.'

Rocky had barricaded himself in his office. He was utterly rational and straight down the line, but also a tenacious problem solver. No way was he going to let this one get away.

The statue of Mars had aroused the scrapper in him. The glimmer of a chance offered by the solid rocket boosters was now firing his ambition and he was following his instincts.

With his gift shop goodies he could get straight on it and cut out months of painful computer modelling. The sweet odour of glue permeated the room as he worked away. As well as the plastic components within the boxes he'd raided the kitchen to augment his collection.

He worked with little concern for the finer points of the craft, discarding unwanted components and improvising with others. Three unfinished space shuttles had been tossed aside.

Rockets consist mostly of concentric tubes, linked by short cones. Festoons of clingfilm, paper towers and silver foil littered the desk as he adapted their cardboard cores. After hours of frenetic cutting and gluing, there in the middle of the devastated room stood two model rockets. The first one was squat, just over a foot tall, with six solid rocket boosters set around a central lattice; a short tube with the familiar conical shape of a re-entry vehicle sat on top. Towering beside it, at over 2 feet high, was an instantly recognisable form.

While Rocky worked away, Stephen was with the accountants, working out the cost benefits of the multinational involvement. He grabbed Ford by the arm as he passed by the office. 'You'll need to get even more partners on board if they haven't found a rocket. I can bring in the Pure Corporation. They worked on the drones with us.'

Ford knew that Pure already used drones to spy on celebrities and had ambitious commercial space ambitions. However, he disliked these large corporations and how they could devastate social enterprises and feared that all the higher motivations would be left behind in the wake of shareholders' profits. Ford suggested that they should leave their powder dry and see what Rocky came up with.

Stephen gave him a disparaging look. 'Don't hold your breath!'

But rather than the figure of desperation he feared to see, by the time Ford tapped on the office door, Rocky was animated. Perhaps it was all that glue, but he was convinced he had the problem solved. 'Ford!' he exclaimed, blocking the doorway. 'I've cracked it! Get the meeting room ready!'

On a continent far, far away, two young brothers had already been toiling on their own project. It is never easy being an orphan and times had been particularly hard for these boys for most of their lives.

*Zulu and Bheki in Workshop*

The only consolation was that they were not alone. Sadly there were plenty of orphans in Zimbabwe and, as orphanages go, at least their home had a community spirit and kind-hearted people running it.

They slumped exhausted on the dirt floor in opposite corners of the rusting iron-clad workshop.

Zulu was proud of their contraption – almost as proud as he was of his little brother, who never ceased to amaze and annoy him in equal measure.

Bheki was examining his knees when an oily rag came flying and attached itself to his face. 'Go check the weather, little frog!' his big brother signed demonstrably at him.

He reluctantly dragged himself into the evening air. The first three stars of the night blinked in the glowing sky. The air was cooling and a taste of red dust lingered on. He sensed a breeze kicking up. 'Hey, Zulu! The wind is coming.'

With Zulu's hand on his shoulder they watched how the vanes fluttered and slowly moved. The hand gripped Bheki as the rotor swung into the gathering breeze. The vanes were moving freely and the lights of the workshop flickered and grew steadier as the current flowed. 'The little frog's a genius!' shouted Zulu as he whirled Bheki round the yard.

Zulu had done much of the hard graft, especially sorting through the heaps of scrap from which they had made their turbine, but this had been Bheki's idea and design. Hours of patient study at the Rhodes Library had paid off. Across the yard they heard the patter of Mr Herman's sandals. '*Fantastisch, jongens!* That's just amazing! Is it running those lights?' He pointed towards the shed.

'Yes, Mr Herman, that's the power of the wind!'

Mr Herman did a little jig. 'We must get the children to see this!'

Later that evening Zulu realised one drawback of their wonderful invention. 'Ach! It's real noisy!'

Of course he knew this would mean nothing to his brother. Bheki hadn't even heard the sound of Wilson as it rolled over Africa, but he had felt it deep in his chest. While everyone else strained their ears, he had taken an even deeper breath to discern it.

Despite the noise, Zulu slept like a log, their efforts rewarding him with a leaden sleep. The next morning Bheki struggled to rouse him.

Zulu slowly dragged his discordant clothes to him and dressed while still beneath the blanket. Sensing Mr Herman was about to enter the room, he sprang from his bunk, fully clothed and ready for action.

A meagre breakfast was all they had to sustain them for the coming day. Bheki had been excused from class to help his brother.

The testing and connecting had to be done with care. Their salvaged batteries sat in serried ranks, waiting to be charged. If they weren't set up correctly, precious power would be wasted. Finally it was complete, and the two boys stood back in the hope that the electrons were flowing. Then Zulu hastily signed, 'Time for class! I'm going up the hill.'

In the rising morning heat the hot crystalline surface was difficult to walk on, even for his hardened feet. This was his land and the delicately curved igneous batholith, with its great skull shapes of rock, defined their surroundings. Granite landscapes are found throughout the world, but there was something particular about the balancing stones, the bulbous outcrops and fluorescent lichens that set the Matopos Hills apart. The red earth, blue sky and green thorn bush created a rich frame around the canvas of these dark-grey natural sculptures.

On top of these rocks was laid out the extent of his world. He'd been allowed no further than Bulawayo. He was almost grown up and the sands of time were running out on his stay at the orphanage. He often came up here at night to escape his small world. The clear air and velvet darkness gave Zulu an unmatched view into the cosmos. He'd take Bheki here and they'd dream about the lands beyond the horizon and the wonders of the zodiac above. Bheki would spot the satellites and, as they passed, both of them would marvel at the evidence of a modern world far beyond their simple lives.

It was Zulu's small obsession, this realm beyond. The less he experienced it, the more he wanted it, but the more it scared him.

He would latch on to visitors and, rather than begging for dollars, he scrounged emails. Bheki was his clerk, firing off

**Bulawayo**
Zimbabwe
20.1S 28.3E
Altitude: 4,455ft
Geology: Highveld plain

missives at the library. They had written to tourists, priests and government officials, and kept the best replies in a precious file. Pride of place was a letter from his own president, who'd replied that their email had been received and would be responded to in due course; it even had an official logo.

At first the boys relied on visitors they could pester, but, amazingly, as word of their contraptions had leaked out, the world started to ask about *them*. The wind turbine was not the first thing they had made.

Their first project was the playground with seesaws and roundabouts from axles and old tractor wheels. Then came a mobile phone-charging station and a small income for the boys. As well as the engineering, their homespun farming techniques were a testament to Bheki's inventiveness. Their inverted plastic bottles, like a field of topless hourglasses, not only collected rain and dew for the young shoots, but also acted as mini greenhouses. The boys glowed with pride when they wandered through their towering corn.

Normally Zulu would have left at 16, but with Bheki still young, he'd been allowed to remain.

Their next project was to harness a turbine to granite stones and grind the corn. To them, milling corn by wind power was a novel and amazing invention.

Zulu saw the sun was getting close to its zenith and decided he had to move. The small stones scattered as he landed on the ground. Watching out for the thorns, he worked his way down and back along the dusty path to the school. He still attended the lessons that would help him in the future. He was very excited because this was their exchange session with their twinned school in Baton Rouge, USA.

*Zulu and Bheki on Hill*

Mr Herman initially worried that it would upset the children to be exposed to the wealth and complexities of Western life; he was wrong. They loved it, and this applied to both sides of the equation. The African children sent letters and drawings, whose nondigital format had to be carefully explained to the Americans. In return they emailed short films.

Zulu settled in next to Bheki. The performances by the American children often had the kids in stitches, especially when a nerdy kid called Buzz attempted a stumbling rap called 'Ma and The Boyf'. For once, their own world seemed sane and normal, and they were fleetingly glad that they didn't have parents.


The door was locked and a small crowd was waiting impatiently outside room 501. The difference between waiting for a train and being late for one is all you need to understand Einstein's theory of relativity.

Rocky was nervous and as he frantically shuffled chairs around, he had a terrible vision of deckchairs and a floating life belt. Was this a crazy idea? Could they ever pull it off? Wiping the beads of sweat off his brow, he plumbed the depth of a lifetime's experience, reflecting that he'd never started an enterprise with all the answers.

With a broad apologetic grin, he opened the door and invited his colleagues in to a miniature 'theatre in the round'. In the centre were two objects shrouded in thin black cloth.

His audience were sitting spread out like the numbers on a clock.

He wasn't a great speaker and paced the room like an expectant father. He spoke in bullet points, counterposing the enormity of the task with possible outcomes.

'Can anyone supply the large rockets needed? No.

'Do we have the time to develop them? No.

'Can we construct the mission in orbit like the ISS? No, it would take years.

'Should we go home now? Not yet.'

Rocky then turned to Ford. 'I came back from Paris with no answers, to find Milton had them after all. This most demanding of missions is led by a man who drives a fifty-year-old van. Well! At least he won't think I'm crazy.'

He took a sip of water. Then he pulled the cloth off the first mystery object.

On an occasional table, about a foot high, was a strange-looking rocket. It consisted of six rockets set around a lattice, made of glue-filled drinking straws, which cradled a lander made from an energy drink. He'd carefully glued on three legs from a model lunar module and attached six gas canisters from a soda syphon around the can's girth with rubber bands. It all culminated in a hand-made cone and a pencil.

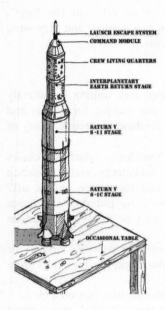
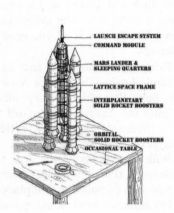

*Model Rockets*

The rockets had been cannibalised from the space shuttle kits bought at the Samsonian and were a perfect representation of the six solid rocket boosters offered by Milton. He worked round the model, tapping each of the lower three rockets. 'These blast us into orbit and fall back to Earth to be returned to good old Milt.' The rubber bands twanged as he slid them off, leaving the upper three still strapped around the cylinder.

'This is the mainframe, the Mars lander, sleeping quarters, command module and escape tower.' He then tapped the remaining three rockets. 'These bad boys then kick us out of orbit to Mars itself.'

Stephen gave a little cough and the attention moved on from Rocky. Holding his hand half aloft, he waited for a second to increase the impact. 'So you've sent an energy drink to Mars! Where's the rest of it?'

The engineer with newly acquired French lifted the second cloth. '*Voilà!*'

The room around him was deathly quiet as they took it in. Then, slightly apologetically, Rocky said, 'I found this in the Samsonian.'

He had revealed the second rocket. It was a perfect model of a

Saturn V, also from the gift shop, but with the top section substituted with two tall peppercorn containers. At the apex were another Apollo command module and an escape rocket. A piece of black cardboard connected the spice containers to the lower rocket.

A whisper from the back disturbed him. 'Where's the salt?'

Standing back, he could see it looked absurd, but he knew it all made sense.

Before he could regain the audience, Elton and Floyd interrupted. The accountants weren't renowned for their gaiety; sarcasm was their forte.

'Are we going to Arrakis?' piped up Floyd. The reference to the spice planet was lost on most of the room, except Edward.

Rocky had lost his flow and a nervous laugh reflected around the walls. He was now on a countdown to an explosion of red-faced rage.

> **Arrakis (aka Dune)**
> Fictional planet
> Star system: Canopus
> Geology: Planetary
> Desert – Spice
> deposits

Ford stood up and stretched out his arms, like a hovering falcon. 'Listen, this is serious. Rocky's been halfway round the planet and returned with a proposition. I asked him to think outside the box.'

Yasmin was feeling Rocky's distress.

Stephen sensed the stage was set to pick things apart. 'Toy box, I say! You're offering us six secondhand boosters and a vehicle that's been out of production for nearly 50 years. You can't be serious! This is a joke!'

It was too much for the old chief engineer. He carefully placed the black cloths back over the models and, gesturing in the direction of his doubters, fired off an expletive, turned on his heel and stormed out.

'Nut screws up and bolts!' said Floyd with a snigger.

The echo from the slamming door had hardly dissipated when everyone except Yasmin was sent back to their tasks.

'Stephen, my office at five!' Ford barked out. 'Yasmin, please find Rocky and bring him to me.'

As the afternoon sun cast its warm light on his desk, Ford picked up his worn book of *Dr Beaton's Guide to Project Management* and turned to 'Personnel and Team Conflict'.

There was a knock on the door and in came Yasmin and Rocky, who slammed an envelope down on the desktop. 'Lateral thinking, my ass. Put me on a desert island and I'll build you a raft – a speed boat with a workshop – but I won't have a bunch of lardy bums laughing at me while I do it.' It was obviously a resignation letter, and Ford closed the book on the chapter 'Empathy'.

'What do *they* know? They know nothing. I've seen caravan parks with more imagination! Personally, I'm fascinated! Come on, for God's sake, man, show us your plan again.' He gently ushered him back towards the presentation room.

Rocky shrugged it off. 'I don't see the point. It's a crazy idea! Stuff 'em, I'm off.'

'Listen, man! I'll tell you if it's crazy.' Ford was desperate. 'Look, weird can be wonderful.'

He'd managed to guide Rocky to the shrouded shapes. Ford made them a coffee.

'Come on, we're on your side.'

Removing the covers again, Rocky went through the whole launch and docking sequence, demonstrating with the models how the Saturn V with the maintenance crew, main quarters, supplies and return rocket would take off and get into low Earth orbit. Then the second 'booster' rocket containing the actual Mars crew, the lander and solid rocket burners would join the first in orbit and dock.

He detached each stage, as would happen during the rocket's flight. On board would be the technical crew who would help prepare the mission. He took off the command module capsule and put it in his breast pocket, then inserted the rest into the tubular space frame of the second rocket. They nested together perfectly.

Space-walking from the capsule, the maintenance crew would make all the attachments and connections to prepare the ensemble for the outbound journey. They would then return to Earth in their re-entry capsule, leaving the intrepid Martian astronauts to prepare for their journey.

Rocky ran through it again in case they'd missed something. At the head of the Mars rocket were the command module and the other re-entry capsule for their return to Earth. Behind it were the lander and sleeping quarters. Next came the living quarters and stores, and then the return rocket and three boosters. Holding it all together was a lattice of rings.

He walked to the window and pointed the contraption towards the wooded hilltops that surrounded the valley to the east. A full moon was rising above the rim of the ridge. Pretending to propel it at the glowing orb, Rocky explained.

'If we shoot this to the moon, it will slingshot and speed towards Mars double quick.' He stripped off the last of the pencil-like forms.

'We jettison these boosters and I reckon we'll get them there in eight months.'

He held up his index finger. 'Big issue, though – even with a diddly-squat payload we can't take enough fuel to get back off the surface.'

Ford, having had his hopes raised, felt them dashed on the rocks. 'Listen, fella, this ain't no one-way mission.'

Rocky gave a wicked smile. 'Yep! Of course we need to refuel and – guess what? – we can do it on the surface.'

Yasmin's delicate eyebrows turned quizzical. 'What if it doesn't work? You're stuck!'

Suddenly Rocky's face transformed with a knowing smile. '*Exactamundo!* We send a probe down there first! There's ice just under the surface. With the right bit of kit we can make hydrogen and oxygen. The crew can sit in orbit until they know it's working.'

'What if the refuelling fails? How do we get them back?'

'Ah! Remember Apollo 13? They used the rockets and fuel from their lander to get them home, and likewise we can use the fuel for landing on Mars to bring them back to Earth if we can't make it down.'

Ford needed to think. He sat down and examined his hands as if counting sheep. Yasmin sensed him working through the stages.

He wrinkled his brow when he saw a flaw. 'You'll need a damned stable orbit, for one, and how long will we be stuck there?'

'Give us a break, man! I'm working the problem!'

Ford sat up and peered over his reading glasses at the now silent engineer. 'That's not crazy, that's a plan! It's cool!' Then, with a slight shake of the head, he added, 'There's one thing missing. Where the hell do you get your Saturn V?'

'Don't you listen? I told you. Milton! The Samsonian!'

Ford looked puzzled. Rocky enlightened him: 'I don't mean the model.'

Yasmin cut in; after all, she'd been there with Rocky and Milton and Ford had gone home before their tour. 'No, he's got a very big rocket. Never seen a bigger one!'

Ford looked deep into Yasmin's wide eyes. 'What? Where's it hiding?'

'Nowhere. It's on display! You missed it, because you went home early.'

Ford thought about the last time he had visited the Samsonian as a proper tourist, with Armstrong, his son. 'You can't mean that old heap that's been rotting outside for all those years?'

Now it was Rocky's turn to clap his hands. 'Like your camper van?'

'Nothing wrong with my camper van. I've restored it!' declared Ford with hurt pride.

'So has Milton!'

'OK, so it's been given a lick of paint, but it's still just an exhibit.'

'You obviously don't know Milton. He's an obsessive. When he restores something, he doesn't do half measures – it's back to the original flight condition! Yasmin was there. That's when I bought the models.'

Yasmin joined in. 'We nearly missed our plane. I thought you were getting those for your kids.' With a frown she continued, 'Didn't Milt say it was a national monument? That means it's kinda protected!'

Rocky wasn't to be put off. 'Maybe, but if the president has declared it a national monument, he can "un-declare" it. This is his project, after all.'

Ford scratched his nose. 'Milton won't let you take it! There's no way he'll agree.'

Rocky fumbled with a piece of paper from his top pocket. 'Don't need to. I've got his holiday dates! Anyway, he'll understand – he's a rocket man. Look. This beauty was made to go to the moon, not stay in Houston. With a few parachutes, we can recover most of it anyway – really enhance its value. The first Martian rocket!'

Ford was impressed. 'So I can throw your letter in the bin?'

As Ford returned to his office, he felt tired. That prospect of losing Rocky had been unnerving. Without his ace engineer, there was no project.

'Good grief,' he thought, 'I have to deal with Stephen again.' His heart sank. He had to give him another dressing-down, but he hardly had the energy.

Entering the office, Stephen was already sitting in Ford's chair and reading a newspaper with a supercilious smirk.

Stephen gave the paper a shake and laid it on the desk. He greeted Ford. 'In the news again?'

Slightly confused, Ford read the open pages. 'What? This is ridiculous. I never said that! And that's a flaming lie!'

Stephen just couldn't help himself. 'At least you're not blaming it on me!'

On the gossip pages of the *Pasadena Globe* was an archive photo of Ford with the headline 'Blame it on God!' As was typical of the Pure Corporation's papers style, the roving reporters who by chance had encountered Ford at the country club finally realised they had the makings of a scurrilous piece of journalism.

It claimed Ford and his previous team were living it up at NASA's expense, to celebrate their role in the Wilson operation. Rather than applauding their discovery, the paper was on a witch hunt.

It was grinding out a point that the world should have been warned about all the effects of the 'Big Bang' and been informed earlier. For them, the 'witch' was Luther Garvey, and Ford was one of his 'familiars' and therefore fair game. Ford's throwaway line about an 'act of God' had been taken literally.

Ford was just taking all this in when he was interrupted by the ringing of his phone. He let it go to voicemail.

He scoured the paper, then listened to the message. 'You will burn in hell!' was the short recording.

Stephen had just caught the gist of it. Gesturing to the newspaper, he happily informed Ford, 'It came out yesterday, and word's got round. They were at the gate today. You know, "Antichrist" or "You will be damned!" placards. The local news stations were there too.'

'What! When did this happen?' Ford was now apoplectic.

'During the meeting, but our "spooks" have dealt with it.'

This didn't reassure Ford. 'What did they do? Baton charge them? Use tear gas?'

Stephen held his palms up. 'Don't worry, our guys are quite subtle. They photo-ID them, download their data and have a word with the ringleaders.'

'Data?' Ford quizzed.

'There's always something. They just give them a glimpse of it – a recent text to a lover, a dirty download, a dodgy bank receipt or a late tax return. It never fails.' Stephen circled the desk. 'I'm sorry about this morning, but now there's even more reason for security and you'll find that these guys have their uses. By the way, I've asked them to look out for you when you leave.'

Ford lowered himself slowly into the seat of his hired car, then eased the pedal and pulled out through the gate. A flash of the lights of not one, but three parked cars burst through the dusk behind him, and he had the distinct feeling that he was being followed. He took a swift right turn, but they followed like links on a chain. Easing his foot off the accelerator, he quickly glanced behind him. The ad hoc caravan was still there, keeping pace and following his twisting route. Putting his foot down again, he felt the car bottom out on one of the crests of the hilly roads.

After the fourth turn and the third hill Ford had enough. He was an ex-fighter pilot, for heaven's sake! He accelerated, leaving them in his dust before he hit the next crest. With wheels lifting off the ground, he stabbed on the brake pedal and pulled hard right on the wheel. The screeching car skidded round in a cloud of rubberised smoke. Easing his foot off, he allowed the momentum of the car to settle it backward into a vacant parking slot by the gates of a hacienda-style mansion. He killed the lights, just as the first vehicle breasted the hill and shot past. Having lost its quarry, the driver slammed on the brakes, only for the next car to roar over the summit. There was a screech of metal, followed by a hiss of released steam as it shunted the first vehicle's rear. The last one glided to a halt parallel to Ford. 'Better slip away back down the hill,' advised the shades-wearing figure. 'We'll sort this out.'

The neighbours emerged to view the argument in the street. From the first vehicle, a rusty-red pick-up with 'You have been judged!' emblazoned on the side, emerged a bear of a bearded man and a slight, long-nosed woman. Both wore matching T-shirts with 'Jesus saves' and 'God invests' printed on their fronts. In the other car were the cub reporters from the local rag. It's one thing taking the name of the Lord in vain, but smashing into your pick-up is unforgivable. The press, rather than observing the news, were now in the thick of it. As the argument boiled over, Walt Slammer of Homeland Security joined the throng. Boy, was he going to enjoy sorting this one out.


Ford had hardly settled into his room at the 'Gulag' when there was a knock on the door. It opened a little and Sharon's immaculate face peered round. 'I hear there was a spot of bother at the gate today. Wanna talk?'

The rooms were big enough to work and entertain in.

'Sure, and you'll only have heard half of it. I was going to have a Scotch. Want to join me?'

Sharon was in her tracksuit. He'd never seen her without make-up or a hair out of place. Pouring a stiff drink in the toothpaste tumblers, he recounted the journey home, his incomprehension as to why he was being targeted, and, triumphantly, how he'd outwitted his pursuers.

'Oh, it's either politics or just bad luck – or maybe Stephen,' said Sharon. 'He's the kind of guy who attracts flies! Let's forget him. There's bigger issues.'

He was slightly uncomfortable about having the younger woman in his room. 'Well, that's one big issue. Apart from the hardware, how do we find the crew?'

Sharon smiled. She was unflappable. 'We've made lots of progress. We now know who we need: two or three ageing super-humans.'

Sharon took a sip of her dram and smiled at Ford. 'As you know, the thing about rocket science is, it's not that difficult, just very complicated and conflicting. We've got some great new astronauts – multitalented, male and female – but they're all in their twenties and thirties and after puberty the body starts to lose its ability to repair itself, so their long-term risks are not good.'

Sharon was referring to the health and radiation risks, which turn a possibility of cancer and bone loss in an older crew into a probability in a younger one, due to the simple fact that they were going to live longer after the mission. 'The "more mature" group, you know, the over-fifties, are rather "old school".'

Ford laughed. 'Yeah, like me!'

'You wouldn't be a bad candidate, actually, but you're the coach, not a player. Anyway, I'm sure there's a solution. We'll just have to widen our net or think laterally. The problem is, the weight is so crucial, everything's at its absolute limits, even when sending two.'

Ford reiterated his mantra. 'Remember, it's all about the science. It's easy to get lost in the mechanics and… we're not doing it for the politicians.'

'I'll drink to that! Another shot, then it's time for bed. It's a long day tomorrow and time is not on our side.'

Pouring Sharon a small one, he tentatively revealed his dilemma about the planetary conference. He'd made the commitment long ago and Jane, who'd made enough sacrifices anyway, was so very keen, but how could it not jeopardise the report?

Sharon stroked his hand. 'No worries, we'll cope. That's why we need a crew of six to go to Mars. We're a team. We can cover for each other.' And then, as an idle after-thought, she added, 'You can't send Stephen, can you?'

# Chapter 11

Italy

*Caradoc*

Jane was in her thirties when she discovered the true Italy.

The Welsh character has been forged by a tenacious people maintaining an independent spirit, despite recurrent waves of invasion. The Romans were first. As a child she'd been hauled up Caer Caradoc, a beautiful mountain and a natural fortress. In that spot, after years of hard resistance under their leader Caradoc, the Welsh had made their last stand.

Hot and sweaty and no lover of educational trips, a twelve-year-old Jane had stood on the ramparts and was surprisingly moved by its underlying intensity – its natural grandeur combined with the knowledge that here the history of her nation had been changed forever.

> **Caer Caradoc**
> Shropshire, England
> 52.5N 2.6W
> Altitude: 1,506ft
> Geology: Extinct volcano

Dreamlike she was transformed into one of the brave, braided defenders, facing down the ordered ranks of the iron-clad Roman fighting machine.

Did the rocks below her feet record the misery of the day? Had the rain washed out every speck of blood? As the fantasy was about to overwhelm her with flashing swords and hails of imaginary arrows, her musings were brought short by Bethan's call. 'Jane! Come on down, we'll miss the coach.'

So it was that she had hence viewed Italy, like perfidious Albion, as a source of invasion and disruption. She was yet to realise that on that day her nation and even her very existence had been cast in the form she now held so dear.

The defeated Caradoc was taken to Rome for execution. Facing his nemesis, the Emperor Claudius, he displayed such integrity that he was pardoned and was able to enjoy the rest of his days as Caractacus, a Roman citizen. Living in the splendour of Rome, he often wondered why this sophisticated state had been so obsessed with stealing the tents and sheep of his simple nation.

For Jane, a weekend break in Rome led to a surprise enchantment with Italy. Instead of the remnants of a terrible imperial power, she found a nation, not unlike her own, with a strong sense of community, an enthusiasm for singing, a passionate love of sport, and better weather.

She also found a philosophy that matched her own temperament. A trip to Herculaneum had introduced her to the work of Philodemus and Epicurus. She'd rejected the chapel of her childhood, which promised joy in the hereafter, but only after sacrifice in real life. The Epicurean philosophy was to attain a happy and tranquil life through self-sufficiency and friendship, which, coupled with the sunshine and good food, made so much more sense.

Later she had discovered Epicurus's genius for scientific conjecture, freeing her own creativity from deterministic thought. There was something that moved her in the ruins of Pompeii, frozen in time by the forces of the restless planet. Confident lives and their deaths, caught unawares in their everyday existence, sharing a common thread of humanity and imparting a sense of frailty about a person's own existence. She had often worried what these people would have thought about gaining an immortality in such a public death. Their body casts displayed their vulnerability among the ancient ruins around them. Would it have given them any consolation that their sacrifice had imparted a unique insight into their lost world?

Jane had not been back to Italy for ages and had been desperate to share it with Ford for years. Then, to her joy, the offer of the paid trip to the conference had come up. Her offer to write the paper was done purely to keep the excursion alive and now she was sitting in front of her computer and beginning to struggle. She felt quite relieved when the dog came in whimpering and yelping, moving between her and the door, a sure sign that he needed attention and a walk.

'Come on, Macks, let's go up to the ridge.' She smiled. 'It's as if he understands me!' she whispered to herself.

Macks was animated and knew that a walk was now a certainty. His canine brain had limited capacity for language other than his own species' limited yelps and barks, but he knew just by the way Jane's body moved that it was going to be a decent walk. The trees were fresh with new growth and the grass was a vivid green. The dog kept pace most of the time, only stopping to mark a fence or a tree. The escarpment was mostly wooded and the walk was like travelling through a long verdant tube. Only on the ridge itself did the vista open over the valley below. Today Jane did not pause or stop and by the time she arrived at the back door, her mind was clear and the dog was happy. Back in the study, she clicked 'Contacts'. One of the first on the list was Alim Azim.

Stuck on a rock shelf, Alim had been chipping away on an unpromising formation just below the famous Burgess Shale in British Columbia. He'd stopped to eat a late packed lunch, unpeeling an egg in the same way he would reveal an ammonite. He was surprised when his phone started vibrating, and it took him a few seconds to place Jane. 'Oh yes, Ford's wife. Of course, we met last year.'

'Can you give me some advice?'

Holding the phone in one hand and the egg in the other, Alim wondered what advice he could give to someone with whom he'd had only the briefest of connections. Jane started to explain her predicament. Alim lodged the phone between his shoulder and his ear. Balancing the egg, he slowly took a slice of ready-buttered bread from the bag. Attentively listening to Jane and attempting to prepare the egg sandwich, he noticed a stray piece of shell. He tried to remove it by rubbing it with his nose. His efforts caused the phone to drop and, clutching at it, he ended up dropping both phone and egg.

Jane, in the middle of asking why evolution might have been faster on Mars, heard a muffled, 'Oh, bloody hell!'

There was a pause and then Alim's voice came back. 'It's a bit like my lunch – catastrophes happen and bring dramatic change. I've lost my bloody egg and am left with just the lettuce and tomato. What kind of sandwich is that? In other words, things can remain very stable until something upsets the status quo. Each time this happens, there's an advance – eggs were one of them! Mars, being so much smaller than Earth, may have accelerated through change much quicker.' Alim paused for thought. 'We are, of course, making the assumption that everything has stopped on Mars. I've seen the 'Angel', but not put a date on it.'

As a biologist, Jane had always been surprised how most of our 'evolutionary action' had happened so late. The human line has been in existence for the briefest snippet, 200,000 years; ants a great deal longer, 140 million years; insects, 400 million years. But 'life' has existed for about 4 billion years. Ten times longer! Thankfully early life hadn't the capacity to get bored.

This period was Alim's forte. He loved bashing around in the lower rocks to find the smallest and most insignificant remains. Other palaeontologists literally looked down on him, as he was always at the bottom of the cliff or the incline, dodging the falling rocks and debris from his colleagues above.

Alim was brimming with excitement. He found the prospect of the Mars fossils fascinating. He'd actually lain awake at night, trying to work it out. He had a lot to share with Jane, as she vigorously took notes. She was charmed by Alim's patient explanation and his obvious attention to detail, and was very impressed that he remembered that Ford had a grandson called Buzz and a dog called Macks.

Although she felt at ease with this strange character, she was surprised when he asked her a personal question.

'Jane, what was the last big change in your life?'

She didn't have to think. 'Meeting Ford.'

'And it changed everything?'

'Absolutely!'

'Well, there you go. That's how things really happen! Random event, big change. There must have been quite a lot of them on Mars.'

As Jane put down the phone, she felt inspired. 'Italia, here we come!'

*Enza and Elisabetta*

Enza was engrossed. This wall had caught her imagination and she was drawing every detail. She was vaguely aware of her mama calling but was too focused to respond. She was meticulously drawing a child's bedroom – at least, what remained of it after 2,000 years. She had watched the carbonised bed and small chair as they were removed to the museum store. Now she was recording the simple, beautiful frescoes on the walls. Painted with the brightest yellow ochre that the Romans possessed, this was definitely a little girl's room. She imagined herself floating around it in a white dress, hair done up, just like the fresco of the girl. Her mama was trying to record the major features of the room and needed Enza to hold the tape. Enza had to finish the flower and little dog motif before bending her attention to the outside world.

'Enza! *Vieni qui!*' finally brought her back to the present. 'Come on, you have to help me, and then Papa needs you to prepare lunch!'

She put down the pad and pencils and tripped down the pile of hard ash that had been her seat for the last hour. As she dutifully held the tape, she studied the layers upon layers of ash still to be cleared from the rest of the house. Pompeii had been a bustling city and so big that much of it still remained under 5 metres of ash, despite more than a century of excavation. Enza had been helping her parents from as early as she could remember.

*Fresco of Lavinia*

**Pompeii**
Campania, Italy
40.4N 14.3E
Altitude: 600ft
Geology: Active
volcano

She spent much of her time in the restaurant kitchen with her father, and only had to slip through the staff gate nearby to find her mama somewhere in the ruins. She had seen many shops and dwellings uncovered, but this one she really loved. It was a family house attached to a restaurant, just like home, and the enchantment of discovering the little girl's bedroom was like having her own Wendy house. Enza was sad when they found a void in the ash that, when filled with resin, revealed an almost perfect tabby cat. As they dug out the rest, she was terrified they'd find the remains of 'Lavinia', named after the lava. The more she studied this room and pictured their life, the more she imagined how her own bedroom might be discovered in millennia to come if it was consumed by the volcano still brooding on the skyline.

She bounded through the crowd of tourists, across the streets, past

126

old shops and graves, down the hill to slip through the gate by the 'House of Mysteries', skidding into the kitchen where her papa was chopping vegetables. 'Gnocchi, Enza!' was his curt order. Enza loved making the simple flour and potato dumplings. It had to be Thursday – *piatto di giorno*. The potatoes were already boiled, so she could start with the pile of flour, her strong little hands massaging the dough into long sausages to be cut up into little gnocchi parcels. 'Hey, Enza, Mama says Jane's coming soon, and she's bringing a boy.'

Lovely *Zia* Jane, who had taken such a shine to Enza. 'She didn't have a boy last time, Papa?'

'Oh, they gained one!'

Jane was Mama's old friend from her time in London. She had come to stay when Enza was very small, but Enza still remembered her.

The clinking of glasses suddenly reminded them of the mountain's presence. Enza had often wondered why they lived on the site of a great catastrophe. Every year they lived here surely had to add to their risk. Had the original inhabitants not realised? They must have felt immune to the malice of the mountain. She too loved this place. It had always been her home.

Her nonno had always said, 'Life's a gamble', even if it was simply making it to the toilet in time.

The restaurant was a simple affair, with a large area for al fresco dining, festooned with vines and, in late summer, abundant bunches of grapes. On the tables were gingham cloths and on the walls were a mixture of black and white photographs of the early excavations and Enza's meticulous drawings. The food they served was simple but delicious. The absence of burgers from the menu was a refreshing change from the other eating places, and the beautifully cooked rustic food was drawing diners to the restaurant as a destination in itself.

'Papa, *finite*!' she called, as the last of the little morsels was completed.

'*Burro e salvia*, Enzachino!' Her papa smiled indulgently as she got to work.

Enza could see the pasta special was already prepared – row upon row of tortellini, ready for the pot. There was a shudder of the glasses again. 'Vulcan is snoring,' her father said to reassure her. Enza inspected the mountain through the steamed-up window. Its perfect conical form had blown apart in the famous eruption. No plumes of smoke. It was just as her father said, the murmurings of a sleeping giant. She asked again the question she had asked one hundred times: 'Will it ever blow again?'

Her father's familiar answer was, 'Every hundred years or so. But probably not like the big time.'

'Why do we live here, Papa?'

Her father suddenly slammed down a large knife on the chopping board and pretended he had cut his finger off, holding up a little piece of sausage. Then, showing her his full set of digits, he just said, 'Everything and everywhere has its hidden dangers.' Waving his knife towards the restaurant door, the vines and the blue sky beyond, he added, 'And where else could we go as wonderful as this?'

Enza didn't reply. She just kept finely chopping the sage and wondered to herself. What amazing places might she find in her life to come?

Her mother breezed in. 'Vincenza, you left your pad and your pencils.' She put them down before going through to organise the service. Both her parents had been precocious children in their own right, and neither really understood just how exceptional their daughter was. Even during term time, Enza would help her father with the evening meal and her mother in the late afternoon. Many children could cook at an early age, but it was Enza's eye for detail in her drawings that really set her apart. Photographs did not follow the same neurophysiological process involving the eye and brain, which made the drawn recording of archaeological remains so important.

It is the careful study that reveals the nuances and shapes that could easily be missed. It was Enza who first spotted that it must have been a little girl's room in the uncovered house.

Enza went through to help her mother, clutching knives, forks and spoons, setting the tables one by one. Looking up from her task, she saw a cat stretching on a wall. Her mind went back to the body of the tabby cat that had been caught as if asleep.

She felt her eyes moisten as she reflected on Lavinia's fate. The cat had set her off, but the intimacy of Lavinia's bedroom and belongings had brought on sadness. Did she escape? Did she grow up? In the busy narrow streets of Naples, were her distant offspring still enjoying the hustle and bustle of family lives not that different from those ancient days?

Napkins! Enza sped round the tables, still feeling the tears well up. Would they find Lavinia curled up like the others, with her parents' bodies in the other room? Then Enza took a deep breath and looked at the mountain again. 'Well, you aren't going to get me, at least not before I've done something worthwhile!' With that, she set her mind to being known for her life, not her death.

Her mother, Elisabetta, broke the trance. 'Did Papa tell you? *Zia* Jane's coming with her boy in two weeks. We'll have to do something special.'

Enza thought for a second. 'I hope he's not like the idiots at school.'

*Dead Cat*

# Chapter 12

## Buzz Gets His Wings

*Plane over Dallas*

Guilt about leaving the mission team to go to the conference had made Ford edgy and nervous. After hours of flying to pick up Buzz, he was now just feeling tired. Above the cloud tops, it felt like time had stopped. There was a bottle-bright gleam to the fields below, and the low shadow of the sun and

**Dallas**
Texas, USA
32.5N 96.5W
Altitude 500ft
Geology: Limestone
escarpment – river
crossing

the skittering ranks of cloud dappled the patchwork of land as it slowly moved beneath the aircraft's wings. To the south-east, the weather was clear and the sun lit up the cotton-wool cumuli, giving each a bright white body and steely silver back. With the wind behind it, the 'old crate' was going at a fair pace. A grid of freeways and fields below soon became a spiderweb of roads and Dallas city centre blocks. Another landmark gone, he thought, happy to follow the highway for a while to his destination.

'I've topped the wind-swept heights with easy grace Where never lark, or ever eagle flew — And, while with silent, lifting mind I've trod The high untrespassed sanctity of space, Put out my hand, and touched the face of God.'
– 'High Flight' by John Gillespie Magee, Jr.

There was a bank of clouds towards starboard and he decided to move a little further north to skirt it. Air is a fluid and when whisking along at 300mph, it can feel like running the rapids. Ford could already feel the bumps of heavier air. He lifted the nose of the 'old crate' and, easing the throttle forward, gained height. Seeing the brooding weather ahead, Ford muttered the airman's poem. It was his companion when alone in the blue or, in this case, approaching the turbulent banks of cloud.

The midway stop at Amarillo felt like a distant memory. The events of the last few weeks had taken his brain and wrung it dry. Ford edged open the canopy to let a stream of air refresh him. It worked for a minute, but the drone of the engine and the strain of the day made it difficult for him to focus. He tried taking deep breaths and singing out loud to refresh his thoughts, repeating again and again the only two verses of 'Amarillo wants me' that he knew. '*Amarillo wants me. No, I won't go back there!*' He suddenly realised they were the wrong lyrics and laughed out loud. He remembered the correct verse: '*Is this the way to Indiana?*'

**Amarillo**
Texas, USA
35.11N 101.5W
Altitude: 500ft
Geology: Playa lakes
– high plains

Flying can be like driving. On a long journey your mind can wander, and Ford's was entering the danger zone, the cumulative tiredness pecking at his consciousness. He needed a stimulant or distractions to re-energise him.

'Wait a minute,' he thought, 'use this time to solve problems!' They'd been working on the landing stage of the project and were stuck on delivering the spacecraft to the surface. They had been through the physics and Sharon had come up with the brilliant idea of sending fuel-generating pods ahead to land conventionally with air bags, like the early rovers. The question was to attain a stable orbit to despatch them with pinpoint accuracy.

The main craft was just too heavy to land in any way they had done before. The genius of the 'sky crane' used to land the 1-ton Curiosity Rover wouldn't cut the mustard for this mission. To decelerate 12 tons from orbit at 5,000mph to zero was a major issue and no one had been able to work it out.

He began to recalculate the sums and as he did, his eyelids started to quiver. He flicked his head, but moments later they started again. There was little to focus on in the growing mass of grey. After each effort his eyes closed tighter and tighter. Slapping his thigh, he attempted to do the calculations of how they could stop something with nothing. Mars' atmosphere was so thin – only a hundredth of Earth's – it didn't have the stopping-power for them to be able to rely on parachutes, and they couldn't carry enough fuel to thrust their way to a standstill. 'What could break the long fall to the planet's surface?' he thought again, as his lids finally drew shut.

**Curiosity Rover**
Landed 6 March 2012
Aeolis Palus – Gale Crater
4.5S 137.4E
Weight: 899kg
Method of landing: Sky crane – lowered from hovering landing vehicle

He slumbered as the plane flew level and then dipped its nose into a shallow dive. The speed accumulated: 275, 325, 350 – the knots grew on the dial – in 30 seconds there'd be no return. At 375mph the aircraft was juddering; at 390mph, the airframe was alive, and Ford was still asleep. The plane hit the cloud bank like a wall; 400mph and five seconds to go.

*Bang!* The jolt rocked through Ford's brain. 'What... what?' Instinctively he pulled back on the stick, the drumming of the wings and scream of the air over the elevators chanting in his ears. Pull, pull! The nose lifted. Feeling groggy, he missed the chance to level off and up went the plane, fighting against gravity, up through the grey massed clouds, engine screaming, forcing the giant metal bird to the heavens, until the point where the momentum equalled the pull of the planet beneath. The aeroplane hung in mid-space, slowly turning against the propeller, and fell on its tail, the pilot now weightless. It pirouetted into a graceful dive. Ford was now fully recovered.

'Oh my God! That's how we do it – fly the damned spacecraft into a stall turn! Use gravity. The escape velocity of Mars is 11,000mph. It's bound to come to a stop at some point.'

Heart beating, with slightly damp underwear, Ford had not only cleared his head for the flight, but also a major obstacle for the mission.

*Trojan in Stall Turn*

Buzz knew that Granf was coming. He started counting the seconds, holding his breath for sixty, then another sixty, then again. He'd worked out how far he was travelling. He'd got the text sent from Amarillo. He knew the times and had worked out the wind speed and direction. By his calculations, Ford was late, and this was why Buzz was holding his breath; it was his way of slowing down the seconds. He hated being incorrect and was fretting that Ford was not on time. Time had been lost because of weather fronts and unplanned aerobatics, otherwise he'd have been spot on. The silence helped him listen for the drone of the Wright 1820 radial engine. Suddenly he picked it up, way in the distance, almost imperceptible but unmistakable. He might have lacked in communication skills, but he made it up with other abilities like mental arithmetic. At his tender age he had worked out sign tables, times tables and square roots of weird numbers, just for entertainment.

'Mom, Granf's coming in!' he called, running from his bedroom. He grabbed her arm and ran out of the house to the car.

'Has he rung, *amorcito*?' Maria asked.

'No, I can hear him!'

She strained her ears. 'Are you sure?'

He was dragging her. 'Come on! Come on! He's due, of course I can!' As they drove to the airport, Buzz was peering intensely through the window. He pointed to a small dot, lost in the steely sky. His mom needed to keep her eyes on the road as she turned up Fairchild Street.

'Stop it!' she said, placing a comforting hand on his wildly jiggling knee. Her car was old enough without further problems caused by Buzz drumming his foot through the floor!

Maria had dreamed of a future with a career, marriage and children. Yet for all her talent and looks, a darkness had crept up in her teens, thwarting all her aspirations except for this child. She could sing like an angel, which only led to shattered dreams and the drugs of the late-night music scene. Tonight she was torn between missing her boy and the desperation to recapture her youth, and the vain hope that Anthony would come good.

She'd had high hopes when she met the wonderfully different young Armstrong in an open-mic bar. Armstrong was stunned by her clear-cut siren voice, and not just the singing. There was a look, a flashing between extremes, that drew him in. Unfortunately they shared an addictive nature that all the talent in the world couldn't tame. They soared the heights of grand folly and delusion, until they crashed down into burned-out animosity. Armstrong moved on, not even considering what he'd left behind.

Buzz's dream was to be part of a real family. The Boyf had no interest in Buzz, just in his mom. He hadn't experienced the balanced attentions of two loving parents and he vainly hoped that an evening with his mom and Granf would be a substitute. His foot stopped drumming as they reached the airport, when his mom blithely announced, 'It's great you can be with Grandpa tonight. Anthony's asked me out.'

Buzz's breathing stuttered and he muttered, 'But, Mom, just family tonight, I thought...'

She flashed him an enigmatic look. 'Sorry, Aldrin, but life's complicated...'

All he could say was, 'It's not complicated, it just sucks.' Then, with venom, 'I hate The Boyf!'

Buzz spent an enjoyable evening with his grandfather. Ford's

steady calm and humour, and their mutual interest in all things that
flew, filled a hole of his psyche. Their takeaway pizza arrived and
Buzz eagerly waited as Ford braved the chaos of the hall to bring it
back to the relative orderliness of the child's room. He watched with
horror as Ford moved one of the beautifully built models to make
room. His grandfather jumped at hearing Jane chastising him. 'Put
that back, cariad!' Buzz had got her down to a T. He had an amazing
gift for mimicry.

It was one of Buzz's saving graces at school. He could make people
laugh and it had rescued the weird, nerdy kid from total ostracism.
Over Coke and beer and the ridiculously large pizza, they played
several rounds of 'AirAce'. To his delight he won the final contest.
Granf's plane had veered off the course to crash into the crowd, as
Buzz took the final flag. He looked round at the slumbering figure of
his grandfather, who'd nodded off mid-game. Buzz got up and eased
Ford's head onto the wing of the sofa, to sleep an uncomfortable night
before the early start to the farm, Jane and then Italy.


'Did you sleep well?' Maria asked over breakfast and Ford struggled
to give an honest answer.

'I don't know. I was asleep at the time! I woke up pretty badly,
though.'

The airport beckoned and Buzz was feeling important. Granf had
printed out the itinerary of the flight especially for him, and called
him 'co-pilot'. Although an indulgence, it didn't stop Buzz studying
it as if they were on a serious mission. He eased into the trainer's seat
and strapped himself in. His placed his bag under his bum so he could
look out and strapped two coffee cups to his feet in the faint hope
that Granf might give him a lesson. When the engine roared to life,
it was as if he'd been injected with pure excitement. They wore old-
fashioned leather caps with goggles, just like in the black and white
films.

Soon they were in the clouds, with Ford informing him at every
turn and change of altitude as if it were a real lesson. Two hours into
the flight Ford announced that all was going so well that they might
as well give Buzz a little practice. With the words 'You have control',
Ford let him fly the aircraft.

'I have control.' And there he was, coffee cups strapped to his feet,
'in control' of 1,400HP of radial engine and airframe.

Ford also needed to refocus his eyes. The same tiredness that had overcome him the previous day had returned. 'Just a few minutes of meditation will clear my head,' thought Ford. The last thing Buzz heard from Granf was, 'Carry on just as you are until I take over.'

Ford drifted into a dream. He was on a long journey, sometimes in space or the offices of NASA. He would open an office door and fall into a black dimensionless void with no space suit. He had to hold his breath and, as time ticked away, he saw through a yellow haze the silver spaceships flying almost within reach, yet too far to grasp. Helpless in the emptiness, he could thrash and kick and wave his arms to no avail. Suddenly he was surrounded by children and Buzz was pulling them to the safety of the ship. Then Ford was back in the office again with Sharon.

Buzz was enjoying the flying. He thought the gentle wheezing over the headphones was Ford's throat mic playing up, but he knew from experience at home that keeping quiet was the best way to keep a good thing going.

Nearing a course correction according to the itinerary, he saw the landscape still matched the course. 'Granf, time to take over!' No answer, more snores. Buzz kicked the rudder and banked to the compass bearing on the paper. 'Granf must be testing me.' On he went, keeping things straight and level until the next turn. Buzz felt worried. It was as if he were in a field of tall corn, lost and alone. This time he shouted as loud as he could, but to no avail. The shouting entered Ford's slumbers, drowned by the scream of rockets in the dream. Buzz could not turn and tap him on the head without losing control.

'Pretend it's "AirAce",' he thought. 'Just keep to the itinerary and Granf will soon be awake.' He could remember all the controls. His remarkable memory for figures ran through his mind like another child's ability to recall the course of a Cup Final. The calming melody of Granf's snoring only gave way to an inner panic when he realised two things: one, they were getting close to their airfield, and two, they were at the end of their range. Meanwhile, Ford was fighting a green Stephen with a pink fire extinguisher.

A plane has to transform itself for landing. Stifling a high-pitched scream, Buzz's bottom lip started to quiver. 'Mom!' he shouted as the roar of the engine stole the scream away. The controls on a trainer aircraft are duplicated, and with tears rolling down his cheeks, the terrified boy heaved with deep sobs, feeling abandoned by everyone he loved. He could see the cockpit controls in misty focus. 'OK, it's really quite simple. First, I need to slow the plane and lose height.'

His right hand eased the throttle back and he started to gently lower the flaps to brake the plane and increase the lift. He could see the familiar airstrip in the far distance and wished fervently that Granf would wake up. Pushing the stick forward, he forced the big bird to lose height. He knew instinctively the rate of descent needed and kept a beady eye on the altimeter as he considered the next adjustment. With his coffee-cupped foot he kicked the rudder and gave a slow bank to bring the 'old crate' into line with the figures on the flight details. Peering back over the cockpit into the outside world, he could see the strip moving into alignment.

The headphone crackled. 'N99ZZ?' demanded the control tower.

Swallowing the last of his sobs, he assumed a persona and replied, 'N99ZZ here!' in his best 'faux Ford' voice.

'Hi, Ford!' came the reply, then a cough and then, more formally, 'N99ZZ, it's nice and quiet here today. Come straight in. The wind's at 10 knots and from 230 degrees.'

The one thing Buzz didn't know how to do was to turn off the radio to stop the control tower listening in. So he banged on the cockpit canopy and bashed his head on the seat to wake his sleeping grandfather, not daring to give the game away. *Bash, bash, bash!*

In Ford's dream, something was trying to get into the spacecraft. Droves of reporters were floating around outside, waving their notebooks.

Buzz's heart raced and his whole body trembled. This wasn't a game – they could both die! 'Come on, remember the last time!' he said to himself. The brake, the air brake! He rummaged for the handle and felt the fuselage judder as it gripped the air. He focused on the narrow strip of grey as the earphones crackled again.

'Wake up, N99ZZ! Don't forget your wheels. Schoolboy error!'

That was not surprising, given the circumstances. No wonder they were going a little fast. He lowered the undercarriage and extended the flaps to regain the trajectory, and saw the treetops beneath the wings and the perimeter fences flashing by. He knew from Ford's commentary on previous flights that you just needed to keep the plane level and allow it to find its own way onto the tarmac. *Bump! Screech!* As he overworked the brakes, a vortex of blue-grey smoke whirled into the distance.

'What, what…? Where…?' came a terrified voice from the rear seat, as Ford finally lost the monsters of the subconscious and awoke, palpitating, into a living nightmare, only to find Buzz had safely brought them home.

Suddenly the control tower crackled again over the headphones. 'Usual bumpy landing, N99ZZ!'

In an enchanted corner of their Icelandic farmstead, the earthy aroma of rising wood smoke evoked the comforting memories of camps with her mother in Elin's mind. The drone of her grandfather's monotone voice soothed the cold air of the morning. Afi turned the sausages on the griddle and moved the bread to avoid the skittish flames. They were huddled in a nook where a warm spring emerged bubbling from a cleft in the dark rock. The steamy vapours moistened the air, rather than warming it. These moments, when the old man and the young child could share their intimacies and questions of life, were special. 'Afi, really Icelandic am I?' questioned Elin as she leaned towards the fire.

'Of course you are.'

Not to be put off, she pursued the questioning. She studied her grandfather as he chomped on a morsel of burned sausage, rescued from the margins of the fire. 'No, I mean from Iceland am I really?'

This time he gave a more complete answer. 'Well, *barnabarn*, your father's German, but your mother's from Iceland. You were born here so, on balance, you're definitely Icelandic!' She still looked confused and frustrated. Gunnar felt quite inadequate. 'Why do you ask?'

The little white face rose to his and replied, 'Absolutely ff-freezing am I!'

'Well, you're off to the warmth of Italy soon. I'm going to take you to Mummia. She's still stuck helping out at the Harpa.'

Gunnar had been fretting about breaking the news that her mother didn't have time to pick her up. He discovered that Elin was already up to date.

'I know, Afi, helping her with her presentation I've been. Mummia is so busy and to help I love. After all, we have such fun during the field trips.'

Gunnar chuckled. 'I thought it was more than school work. What are you doing for her?' He leaned over to grab a bowl of eggs that he'd been scrambling in the trivet.

Elin carefully explained in tortuous detail how she had processed and imported all of Kirsten's photographs into the presentation software. '"The Land of Mars and Iceland" it's called.'

Her grandfather dished out and placed the two camping dishes on their respective laps.

'Ouch, that's hot!' Elin squeaked.

'Too cold, too hot! What's the problem with you, *barnabarn*?'

With a cheeky smile Elin replied, 'I want it like Goldilocks, just right!'

'Where are you getting the images from Mars?'

'Pictures taken by the rovers on Mars I find and I'm matching them to the photos from our trips. Then I tint our images red. It looks just like Mars. Mummia is very pleased with the images, but not the words.'

'Can you paint on the computer? Or is it technical?'

'Technical, Afi, but easy if you're little.' Elin took a huge mouthful of her sandwich into her ever expanding mouth and said, '*Húnffgerðvvekki einsffogvvsvolítið um ffálfa!*' She didn't like the bit about the elves!

'Your mother always loved the *huldufólk*, and she has been friends with this one since your age.' Gunnar gestured towards the steaming opening in the hillside. It was an elves' lair. 'What do have they to do with Mars, though?'

'Well, Afi, you told me that the elves were here long before we were and live hidden underground. God was the God of the whole universe you told me. He is invisible too,' the little girl reasoned. 'So I thought if he made the elves on Earth, why not on Mars?'

Gunnar stroked his moustache and gave his *dótturdóttir* a friendly poke. 'What did Mummia think about your excellent theory?'

'"I think we'll keep to the geography!" she said. She likes the pictures and the layout.'

Elin then completely changed tack. 'Italy, what's it like?'

Gunnar slowly picked up the salt and pepper and held them in front of her eyes.

'If Iceland is salt, Italy is pepper, and like pepper it can be hot, so you should like it!'

# Chapter 13

## The Conference

*Group in Pompeii*

The wrought-iron railings almost burned the little hands as they grasped the handrail. Afi was right – it was hot, especially on this south-facing balcony where Elin was taking in this new country. It wasn't just the heat, it was the light and the earthy hues of the stones that made this place so different. Instead of northern blue light, there was a golden southern glow. It smelled different too. If her homeland was of the sea, Italy was of the land, and all the aromas of the dust, the country's flora and its earthy food. The simple timber-and-tin houses of her hometown now seemed fragile compared with the stone-and-terracotta solidity of these dense and ancient streets. Her mother had been delighted when she discovered that their accommodation was in the centre of Rome, rather than in the modern quarters in Frascati. The Via dei Santi Quattro ran east to west, and as Elin's eyes ran along the busy street from her perch, she gasped at the sight blocking the vista beyond. She recognised it immediately: the looming and curvy mass of the Colosseum. She turned to shout for her mother, but the words

141

died in her throat. A small, slight boy on the balcony next door was staring intently at her. For an instant he appeared startled as her clear blue eyes pierced his. With a nervous shake he broke the moment and darted back into the darkness of his own room.

'Mummia!' Elin shouted. '*Koma, koma!*' Kirsten's low voice came from the room. 'Not now, I need to work on the presentation.' Despite Elin's help, Kirsten had still come ill-prepared and had to submit her paper by the next morning.

**Rome**
Lazio Region, Italy
41.5N 12.3E
Altitude: 69ft
Geology: River valley between seven hills

Buzz was also trying to get attention. 'Granf, Granf! Come here, this is really cool. *Gladiator* is just down the road. I saw it and it's still there!'

'In a minute, kiddo! I need to get sorted,' was Ford's muffled reply.

Jane's cheery tones cut in. 'Poor Granddad's trying to get his head round my, ahem, *his* paper, so we'll leave him be.' Buzz took Jane's hand as she led him back onto the terrace. 'Look, Buzz, it's the Colosseum! I just love it here.' He watched her shake her hair in the breeze, as if washing away the cobwebs of the journey. She waved at the strange-looking girl on the next balcony along. With her bright blonde hair, sculptured face and Icelandic sweater, she looked like a fish out of water.

She waved back. 'Hi! I'm Elin, too I like it here.' Then she turned and vanished back into her own room, leaving Buzz and Jane basking in the sunshine and history.

'Can we go and see it? Please, Jane?' requested Buzz, leaning over the balcony rail.

'Later. I have to help Granf with the work first. You'll have to amuse yourself for a while. Why not explore the hotel and report back, sweetheart?'

Buzz decided to walk down to the ground floor – a building with this many stairs was a bit of a novelty. As he slowly descended, the decoration reminded him of the older parts of his hometown. His determined footsteps echoed behind him down the void, only interrupted by the whir of the descending lift. As he reached the bottom steps, the smiling concierge's eyes were momentarily distracted. Giulio's attention had been drawn to another diminutive figure, emerging as the lift doors glided open. Elin, like Buzz, was unaccustomed to buildings taller than two floors, and a lift was a funfair ride.

She turned to go back up the stairs just as Buzz rushed to reach the lift before the doors closed. *Bang!* They collided and recoiled like two billiard balls.

Buzz and Elin regained their composure but seeing Giulio's concerned face, started to laugh. Then turned to each other and simultaneously declared, 'I saw you on the balcony!'

'Jinx!' they shouted in unison and that was that. Try as Giulio might to engage them in conversation, they both stood, tight-lipped, unspeaking.

'What is this game? A game of silence? What is this "jinx"?'

The two children were now silently daring each other to speak. For an age they stood there staring at each other.

Giulio, totally confused, had started to worry that they'd sustained some kind of injury.

'OK, I may have to call your parents. What are your names?' The silence still prevailed, except now Buzz was pulling faces to break Elin's steely stare. The concierge studied the register and, looking up, declared, 'You must be Aldrin and Elin?'

At that point they both burst out, 'Jinx over!' in gales of laughter.

Buzz had been sent by Jane to explore the hotel and wasn't ready to go back. He wouldn't be able to explore under Giulio's watchful eye. The bright daylight beckoned through the entrance doors, and he plunged into the outside world, swiftly followed by Elin, who'd been given the same brief by her distracted mother.

Turning right out of the hotel, they padded down the hot stone pavement towards the jagged form of the imperial icon. 'My granddad's here for the planet conference. I live with my mom. This is the first time I've left the States.' Buzz wasn't used to talking to girls.

'My mummia is here too for it. With my granddad I live and I've never been to America.'

This puzzled Buzz. 'But you talk American!'

Elin felt quite affronted. 'No, Icelandic I speak, but loads of American programmes we get on TV. Anyway, where's your pa?'

'My mom says he's lost in some weird corner of the world.'

Elin recognised this scenario and replied, 'That's what my mummia says, except Germany she calls it.'

In the next minute Elin saw more cars than she'd ever seen in her life, and some of the worst driving that she would ever see in the rest of it. They were on one side of the hectic circus cutting them off from the Colosseum. It appeared to her that the stream of traffic would never stop, so she started to devise a plan to cross. 'When there's an accident, dash we could into the middle?' she suggested, pointing to a spot.

Buzz replied, 'No need, I've just pressed the button.' And as if by magic, the swirling mass of vehicles screeched to a stop and a little green man signalled it was safe to go. Then there they were, standing outside the Colosseum.

'It's amazing!' said Elin. 'It looks like a football stadium.'

'It *was* a stadium and that's where the name comes from, except this was the biggest,' explained Buzz. 'It was built in 72 BC by the Emperor Vespasian and was used for gladiatorial fights, sea battles, executions, wild animal hunts, plays and poetry readings. Usually there were a lot of killings.'

'Not at the poetry readings?' quizzed Elin.

'Only when they combined those with the wild animals.'

Elin was intrigued, but to her dismay, unlike the famous Museum of Practical Jokes, she saw that children didn't get in free. It was nearly eight euros each! Buzz emptied out his pockets and found just one. Undeterred, Elin announced that she'd heard you could make money on the streets of a big city.

Buzz looked worried. 'They sell drugs in Baton Rouge... or worse!'

*Taktu okkur á staðinn þar sem tveir heimarnir hittast og dansbylgjur líkama okkar berst þar sem saltvatnurinn er freyður Kallar okkur heim.*
Chorus of 'The Song of the Whale'

'No, by singing. You hold out a hat and sing, and give you money people will. Here, take it!' Elin took off her bobble hat for the first time since she'd left Iceland, and began singing in a high, ethereal voice. It cut through the dust and the traffic noise, and very soon a small crowd had gathered, listening intently to the little girl in the sweater and felt skirt and the mournful lament of 'The Song of the Whale'.

Buzz was slightly embarrassed, until coins started dropping into the hat. The numbers had swelled as Elin finished the final chorus, with a surprisingly low but faultless '*Kalla Okkur Heim*'.

'Bravo, bravo!' encouraged the crowd.

Buzz looked in the hat – sixteen euros, enough to get in. But... if they had a little more, they could get ice creams as well. 'Do you know any other songs?' he whispered to Elin.

'"Petrol Rain" by KikiD it is,' came the reply. It was surprising, as it was a strange song for Elin to have in her repertoire, and, even stranger, Buzz knew it! It was a song Jane would sing in the kitchen while peeling onions. She said it stopped her crying. In his head he could hear the snuffling contralto, 'I feel the rainfall of a Titanic moon...'

Jiggling the hat once more, he collected the last donations, then ushered his protegee towards the entrance.

Once inside, Buzz took the opportunity to show off his knowledge of the building. 'These are called "vomitoria". It's where everyone came to be sick when it was really gross.'

'What happened to the poet and the animals?' asked a breathless Elin.

As orange strands of light streamed through the grand arches and openings in the ancient walls, Buzz told Elin about the Greek plays, which, to the rapture of the bored crowds, were interrupted by wild animals emerging from secret ramped trapdoors in the arena. He expanded on the executions, fights and sea battles that had kept the Roman mob entertained and docile.

*Elin in the Colosseum*

'How do you know all this?' she quizzed.
'I just saw it somewhere.'

Elin slapped her forehead with sudden recognition. 'Hey, me too. Buzz, ask my name, will you?' She turned away and made herself some space in the centre of the arena itself. He already knew her name, but humoured her before she replied.

*'Maxima Femina Praelitor my name is, commander of the trolls of the north, of the Köttur Legions, the general, loyal servant to the true founder, Ingólfur Arnarson. Dottir to a einstœð móðir. My vengeance, in this life or the next, I will have.'*

'Wow, that's cool! I love that film,' said Buzz. 'How do you remember that quote?'

Elin smiled. 'We have very long nights in the winter.'

'Maxima is my number one fighter in "Trumper Cards". I make them myself. Here, look.' Out of Buzz's pocket came a mixed collection of homemade cards, each with a photo or drawing and a series of attributes with a score. There were ball players, historical figures, teachers, even relatives, and a number of blanks still to be done. 'I'll fill one out for you when we get back. I'll have to add singing as your attribute.'

'Fighting I'm good at too!' Elin said with a grin.

Buzz tugged on her sleeve. 'Come on, let's get back before we get into trouble!'


The next day, the sliding carriage doors were just closing as two figures made it into the stuffy interior of the Frascati train. Sitting in the carriage were Ford, Jane and Buzz, who immediately recognised Elin, still in her hat and jumper. He gave a nervous smile and turned to look at Ford and Jane.

To her mother's surprise, Elin made a beeline for the empty seat next to the boy sitting further up the carriage.

'Hi, Buzz!'

Kirsten guessed immediately. 'So, you're Buzz! Elin told me all about the Colosseum.'

Ford, distracted from his papers, leaned around to Buzz. 'Colosseum?'

Before he could answer, Kirsten was introducing herself. 'You must be the famous Dr Ford Harris. You know my colleague, Magnus.'

For a moment Ford scrutinised this face he had seen, but never met. 'Dr Kirsten Gunnarsdottir?'

'Yes, I'm speaking before you. I believe we're neighbours.'

*Elin and Kirsten*

Jane recognised Elin. 'Of course, the girl on the balcony! I'm Jane.'

'Ah, Buzz's mum.'

Not quite sure how to describe her relationship with Buzz, she replied, 'I'm Jane Jernigan, Dr Jane Jernigan.'

'Oh, are you presenting today?'

'Not entirely...' Jane answered enigmatically.

'Well, you had a hell of a time. Magnus told me all about it. How is everything up there?' Ford gestured for her to sit by him.

Kirsten wiggled a finger in her ear to assure him that her hearing was back to normal, and that Reykjavik was slowly patching itself up. 'It's a relief to get away. It's been crazy! Are you all prepared?'

Kirsten took the seat next to Ford and engaged him in earnest conversation. Jane left them to it and tried to cajole the Colosseum story out of Buzz, with Elin chipping in with her version of events.

'Boys,' Jane thought. 'Why are they so bad at communication?' Then, catching a view of Ford talking shop with the pretty scientist, added, 'Except when it bloody interests them!'

At first Buzz did not get it. 'You said "amuse yourself", so I did.'

'But I told you to explore the hotel, Buzz.'

'It's not fair! I did! Then I chose to do something different!'

Jane was about to remonstrate. 'But...' She trailed off, reminding herself of the futility of arguing with such a literal-minded child.

Elin had had no such problems and proudly told Jane that 'Mummia sees it as a reflection of an adventurous spirit...'

Jane glanced over at Dr Gunnarsdottir, who was now animatedly expanding to Ford on the sight of Wilson. Her blue eyes were flashing like the sun on clear waters.

The little girl continued '... allowed to kill people at the Colosseum they were, just for being annoying!'

'I can understand that...' replied Jane.

Buzz had removed himself from the conversation. He just stared out of the window at the rows of houses and apartments as they flashed past, and the sections of the antique aqueduct that had once fed Rome. He thought of the endless streams of water flowing in from the far hills, and looked at the lines of washing on every balcony they passed. From togas to Armani in the blink of an eye. How could all this be going on, without him being aware of it? People all over the globe were hanging out their washing, getting on with their lives, and they didn't touch his world in the slightest. He felt very small, but relieved because what he did or didn't do couldn't matter very much.

The conference centre was smart and stylish. People had travelled from all over. *Dov'è la Vita?* – Where is life? – was the name of the conference and it was divided into sections on the solar system (life on the terrestrial planets, moons and comets) and outer space (panspermia, the Drake equation and detecting life on exoplanets).

> **Drake Equation**
> An equation formulated in 1961 by Frank Drake and used to estimate the number of civilisations in the galaxy.

There were introductions, seminars and debates, and an awards dinner. Ford and Kirsten were part of 'The solar system: life on the terrestrial planets', with Ford presenting the prestigious final lecture. He felt frustrated that the news of the 'fossils' was still under wraps and there were rumours of it running around the event.

He was also nervous. Jane's work had introduced concepts that he'd have been reticent to present without the proof that he had but couldn't reveal. He'd encouraged Jane to be instinctive in her research, and she had taken up the baton and run ahead of him.

Kirsten had had no time to work on the format of her own presentation and relied on Elin having prepared the images and script.

As Professor Sigmund Sternenstaub's paper closed with questions of how to explore the hidden seas of Europa, Kirsten was pacing the foyer outside. She felt a tug on her shirt. Elin had come to give her the same advice that she'd often given Elin.

'An examination it's not, Mummia. Enjoy it and do better you will... and don't forget the *huldufólk*!'

Kirsten smiled and tussled her hair.

Kirsten was beckoned to the lectern. She worked her way through the plush seats and up the short gilded stairs to the ornate podium. She arranged her papers and surveyed the seated audience.

'A little time ago, I was asked by NASA to look at some photos of Mars. Very interesting, but why me?

COLD DESERT – ICELAND    COLD DESERT – MARS

*Mars and Iceland*

Then they reeled off a list of Hollywood science-fiction movies... They just said, "These movies were filmed in Iceland. Because it looks like another planet. We tried to talk with someone from Acheron, but they bit our heads off. So we thought, let's ask an Icelander what she thinks of Mars!" So here I am...'

Kirsten presented pairs of photos of Earth and Mars, all prepared by Elin. She didn't say which was which, but pointed out the similarities and differences, focusing on the rock formations and landscape. It was a thought-provoking experience for the audience. It was like being asked to tell whether a particular wine came from Italy or France – you think you know, but then you over-think it and get confused. Kirsten finished by reminding the audience of the recent 'near miss'.

**Acheron (LV-426)**
Mythical moon
orbiting the planet
Calpamos
Named after the river
of woe in Greek
mythology
39 light years from
Earth
Geology: Aluminium
silicates and volcanic

'Remember, we in Reykjavik have been closer to an extraterrestrial body than anyone except the Apollo astronauts. Why spend all that money on space missions when they come to visit you!'

The audience rippled with applause and laughter.

'Oh, there's just one more thing. My daughter Elin, who helped so much with this presentation, would like me to tell you: look out for the *huldufólk* – they are just below the surface.'

Elin ran onto the stage and hugged her mother.

'Ah, bless!' thought Jane. 'I don't think I'll run on and hug Ford.'

*Mount Jefferson*

The audience gave him a rapturous reception as Ford took his place beneath a spectacular panorama of Mount Jefferson on Mars. As he spread his documents on the lectern, he dropped two pages and his fatigue prevented him from calmly reorganising them. He stuttered and struggled through the still unfamiliar script.

There were a few coughs in the hall. Jane felt mortified. The poor man! Had she pushed him too far in her own wilfulness about coming here? He looked so tired, she thought. 'Oh, my God! This is Italy. They might boo him off, like at the opera!'

Ford stopped. There was a dead silence. Peering over his spectacles, he grasped the lectern and scanned the mass of faces. He saw Jane and Buzz, looking uncomfortable. Then, from somewhere, the words 'Take your time, enjoy it' crept into his consciousness. A focus and pace took over and it all began to make sense. He could own these words. The old Ford kicked in.

By the time he had finished, his acknowledgement of Jane's help was drowned out by the clapping.

Once the applause had died down, Dr Michael Hermes rose and asked, 'So, if we are to look under the surface, would we find *huldufólk*?'

A bemused Ford copped out and responded with a smile. '*Huldufólk*? Maybe Dr Gunnarsdottir might answer that question?'

Kirsten stood up and explained. 'The *huldufólk* are elves that live in volcanic vents – warm places. That's where I'd look for real Martians.'

Another question. 'Surely this is all just conjecture, or is there something you're holding back...?'

How Ford would have loved to tell them about the fossils. He had to keep his answer enigmatic.

'We know that life could have developed on Mars and there are tantalising clues like methane in the atmosphere, but until we can go there we might never know.'

'At least she thanked her daughter!' said Jane in a huff, as Ford returned to his seat. He tried to explain how he had thanked her, that it must have been drowned out by the clapping, but it fell on deaf ears. The situation was not helped by the sudden presence of Kirsten, who effusively congratulated Ford on his brilliant paper. She turned to Jane. 'You must be proud of him!'

'I'm proud of both of us! We did it together.'

'A joint paper? But why no credit?'

'Apparently it was drowned out by the applause...'

Kirsten grilled Jane on her input and eventually she gave up the pretence.

'I wrote it and he read it. He's been too busy, and I didn't want to miss the conference and seeing my friends in Pompeii.'

To Jane's immediate dismay, Kirsten told her of her own plans to take Elin to Vesuvius and that Ford had kindly suggested they join them in their tour of Pompeii.

'Surely they would have given him a break, after all the work on Wilson?' Kirsten then made her own disclosure. 'I've been in the same boat. Elin had to put all the slides together for me. I rewrote her script but had to promise to mention her treasured elves.'

As the day passed, the crowd of astrophysicists grew less appealing to Jane. The hot sun on the verdant slopes of Frascati lured her away.

Making her excuses, she offered to take Buzz and Elin for a walk and food. Overlooking the seven hills of Rome was one of the best pizzerias in the world. They devoured the ultra-thin pizzas hot from the wood-fired ovens as they took in the view.

After the business of the conference ended, the copious volumes of local white wine on offer helped fortify Ford. Out of the modern conference hall, he was doing the rounds of the elegant Palladian reception rooms. There were lots of old friends there.

He was surveying the throng when a youthful face popped up, pogoing in front of him to try to gain his attention.

'Hi, Mr Harris?' Jump. 'Great paper!' Jump. 'What about those elves on Mars?' Jump. Ford looked down at what he thought was a very short science student. 'Why not humour the kid?' he thought.

'You mean the *huldufólk*. If they exist here, why not on Mars?' He took another swig of the crisp white wine. 'Half the world believes in supernatural invisible beings, so why not?'

Since he had now focused his full attention on the youthful figure, the jumping had stopped and the dark-brown eyes were full of expectation. Ford was enjoying the fantastical train of thought.

'Why not mermaids, angels, or little green men as well? It'd keep the conspiracy theorists happy!'

As they chatted, Ford asked which college she was at.

'Oh, I've finished my degree in journalism. I work for the *Nuovo Scienziato* now. Can I quote you?' She whisked out a notebook and disappeared into the crowded room, taking notes along the way.


Jane was showing the children some of her favourite places and the pizza she bought them was unlike anything Buzz had tasted. It was all about the thin, freshly baked bread and simple, delicious toppings. It was as if he'd had these things in black and white all his life, and now they were in colour. Jane watched Elin devouring the food and basking in the sunlight. In Elin's home the summer sun could shine all day and night, but never with this warmth. The little girl even thought about taking her hat off, but didn't risk it and just enjoyed being warm to the core.

Jane was enjoying their company. 'Can I show you a secret place?'

They kicked up dust as they wound their way through the narrow streets until they reached a gap in some railings. Crouching, Jane went through and led them into a stony, neglected garden. Her breathing became heavier as they paced up the hill towards an outcrop. Hidden between a ring of cypresses was a small, ancient, circular temple. The two children skipped behind her, then stood as she took in the structure. She seemed to be lost in thought.

'Come on!' They went up a concentric circle of worn steps. There were seven pilasters set in seven short curved walls holding up a corniced dome. The gaps between the walls were all strangely different. They gathered in the middle of the dais and Jane put a finger to her lips. Beyond their silence and the incessant rumble of traffic, they could hear a clear and haunting moan resounding from the walls. As the wind drifted around the surrounding trees and through each opening, the notes changed in a perfect octave.

'Templum Octo Ventis,' declared Jane. 'The Temple of Eight Winds. It's been here for 2,000 years, and guess what? It tells you if it's raining too!'

Buzz was amazed. 'Wow, how's that?'

Looking up, Jane pointed at the oculus. 'There's a hole in the roof!'

Buzz got it. 'That must be the eighth wind. It starts the next scale – listen to it whistling!' All those guitar sessions with Granf had not been lost. 'This is cool! How did you find it?'

For an instant Jane's eyes misted over and she let them into another secret. 'Many years ago, when I was young and foolish, I met an Italian prince. Well, that's what he told me. He was very romantic and he promised to show me something really beautiful if I gave him one kiss.' She smiled to herself. 'I might have been foolish but not stupid, so I said, "Look, show me something beautiful and I'll think about it", so he took me here!'

'Oh, how wonderful! Did you kiss him?' squealed Elin.

'Yuk!' whispered Buzz.

Jane stood in the centre of the dais and told them, 'He took me in his strong arms, right here, and on this spot I looked deep into his dark eyes as he prepared to kiss me.'

'And did he?' implored Elin.

Jane laughed out loud. 'No, sorry, cariad. It started chucking it down!'

'Praise the Lord!' declared Buzz.

'Not then anyway…'

'Have you seen Elin?' Kirsten whispered to Ford, as he earnestly discussed his paper with his old friend Alim Azim.

'Didn't Jane tell you? She took the kids out for a break from all this.'

'So, that's what she meant by "whisk"...'

Kirsten, used to Elin being looked after by others, had no further questions apart from 'Who are you?' to Alim.

Taking her hand, he said, 'Dr Alim Azim. My friends call me "Limo".'

'Well, Doctor, why are you here?'

Alim felt like he was at an airport. 'Business and pleasure!' he joked, clicking his heels together. 'Well, actually, this chap's mates keep asking me to comment on stuff, so I thought I'd bump along.'

'Whisk, chap, mates, bump... I wish they'd speak English!' Kirsten thought to herself. She almost dismissed Alim as a buffoon, but warmed to his charm. 'Actually... they keep asking me about my volcanic landscapes!'

'Oh, I know. I saw your delivery. Iceland's probably the worst place in the world for my research, being so young, but... if you were looking for Ford's Martians, where would you look?'

'Our island is made of volcanoes and glaciers. I remember years ago searching for volcanic tubes. They are tunnels left in the rock as the magma oozes out of the Earth. Up by the glaciers, they get plugged with ice. We spent two days hacking through the ice before we got into the rock tubes beyond. The white ice became bluer and clearer as we worked away, until it was like a pane of glass through which we could see down the cave. In the distance was a great pool of water.'

Kirsten took a sip of wine and carried on. 'When we finally broke through it was like an explosion. There was a whistle of steam. It literally knocked us over, as did the smell! When we got into the cave it had filled with mist, but thick on the walls was a brown stinking mould, which had been growing there for centuries, cut off from the outside world.'

'That's extraordinary! Did you find anything in the pool?' asked Alim.

Kirsten gave a look of faint regret. 'We never got to know. We had to go for respirators and then the weather closed in, and by the time we returned we simply couldn't find it again. Anyway, that's where I'd look on Mars – an old vent blocked with ice, to keep the air at a sufficient pressure and warmth to hold a lake of water, just like mine in Iceland.'

Azim enthusiastically fake-punched Ford's arm, adding, 'Do you think we'll find our angels down there?'

'You know that's classified!' Ford whispered.

Kirsten was intrigued. 'What angels?'

Alim tried to recover. 'Sorry, I meant angles,' he said, and winked at Ford.

Ford hissed. 'It's supposed to be kept under wraps until the president has made his mind up.'

'About what, old man?'

'Another secret…' replied Ford in hushed tones.

'Oh, I love a secret. Have another drink!' Alim dashed off for a refill.

'You are a man of mysteries, Mr Harris!' smiled Kirsten.

As the children slowly burrowed through the throng of chatting scientists, Buzz tried to describe to Elin the arcane rules of his card game 'Trumpers'. 'You put all the skills down in six categories. It can be anyone – your mom, teachers, football players – totally random. You name a skill if you have a big hand, or roll a dice. My Granf beat Albert Einstein – at flying!'

'What are you good at?'

'Maths and flying, like Granf!'

'I'd put geology and imagination as my skills,' she proffered proudly.

Ducking under a swinging elbow, Buzz corrected her. 'Imagination isn't in a category.'

'It would be in mine. OK, fighting?'

Buzz approved. 'Yep, that's cool. Favourite weapons?'

'Rocks!'

'Hi, Granf.' The children had finally made it through the crowd.

'Mummia!' cried Elin and jumped up at Kirsten. 'We went to a temple where Jane kissed a prince.'

'What!' Ford said with a splutter.

'I was adored once, you know.' Jane winked as she arrived.

'You still are, sweetheart!'

She wrinkled her nose at him.

It had been a long and dusty journey back after the conference ended and Buzz was glad to be snuggled into his bed in a compact room off the main suite. Before he knew it he was lost in slumber.

Next door Jane crashed around the bedroom with suppressed rage. Ford had not intended to upset her – actually he'd done nothing wrong, but he should have made more of an effort. 'Men! So inconsiderate, and so happy to plough their own furrow, oblivious to their partners!'

Ford washed himself and brushed his teeth with mixed feelings of relief and post-exhaustion euphoria. In his army days, he'd been drilled to expect the unexpected, so he should have anticipated the pillow that hit him full in the face as he returned, beaming, to the bedroom.

'That's for not giving me any bloody credit for the paper!' said Jane, hurling another. *Thwack!* 'That's for getting drunk without me!'

If Ford had liked the way modern hotels stacked the beds with cushions, he was swiftly going off the idea.

'But, honey...' He ducked an orange satin blur flying across the room.

'That's for asking that bloody woman to join us in Pompeii!'

'Oh, God!' he thought, as the mirage of well-being crumpled and he realised his insensitivity. In a smart move he picked up the remaining cushions from the bed and began his apologies.

Jane stopped to think. With horror, Ford followed her gaze. 'Bed and breakfast next time!' he thought, as he spied the mound of cushions on the luxurious sofa at the end of the L-shaped room. With a satin cushion in each hand, he skilfully parried the next two salvoes. Suddenly the adjoining door to Buzz's room opened and a small pyjama-clad figure entered.

'Pillow fight!' cried Buzz, vanishing, then re-entering the room with his own battery of soft furnishings. All three ended up on the bed – Ford penitent and demanding quarter be given, and Jane and Buzz cackling uncontrollably as they pummelled their prone victim.


After two days Ford, Jane, Buzz, Kirsten and Elin finally made it to the ancient site of Pompeii.

The looming and broken presence of Vesuvius still dominates the landscape. It is part of a ring of fire, where the African plate is forced under the bulk of the European one, where the saturated rock can generate sufficient energy to melt the underlying strata to a pressure-cooker state.

Today it would threaten far more than two Roman towns – the teeming city of Naples with over 3 million lives. However, this is Italy and life goes on regardless, and it is a better place for it.

They passed the gift shop, closed due to 'excessive bureaucracy', and then made their way into the hillside site. Before the pyroclastic flows decapitated the town's buildings, someone could have easily mistaken Pompeii for present-day Sorrento, a reflection of the sophistication of this ancient place. They headed across the rough-paved forum towards a grid of streets. Jane led the way, chatting to Kirsten, with whom she'd now established a congenial rapport. Buzz and Elin followed, swishing 'swords' or acting as shopkeepers, their imaginations gripped by the echoes of the past. Ford tailed behind, distracted by the abundance of detail remaining on the walls and in the courtyards, and even by the carriage ruts worn into the rock from decades of use. He was fascinated by the brothel, with its depictions of services on offer, and the bathhouse, which would have been a health club worth joining.

Jane kept half an eye on the kids in the labyrinth of streets, as she discussed life in the Midwest and Iceland with Kirsten. They stopped at a set of wooden barriers in front of a tall wall, which held back the remaining debris. A call brought two dusty figures out from the excavations with accompanying shrieks. 'Elisabetta! *Bello vederti!*'

'Jane, Jane, *scusami*, my hands are filthy. *Solo cose felici!*' Hiding behind her, and shy at the sight of the children, was Enza. '*Non essere timido*,' said Elisabetta. 'Come meet the children! Remember *Zia* Jane?'

In almost perfect English, Enza stepped out and shook each visitor by the hand, announcing, 'My name is Vincenza. I am a young archaeologist and chef. This is my home. You may call me Enza.'

Then she beckoned the kids to follow her. 'Come see my bedroom!' Enza vanished into the scaffolding beyond and they instinctively followed her. They wove between the half-revealed walls of a dead city. The only signs of life now were lazy cats and twittering birds, which still made Pompeii their home. They arrived at a half-buried doorway and the bedroom of 'Lavinia'.

'I just hope she survived,' said Enza. 'We found her poor cat in the corner. I'm scared of what we'll find in the rest of the house…'

Happily the only traces of Lavinia in the house that day were Enza and her mother.

Enza would never know that when Vesuvius erupted, Lavinia's family had been reluctant to leave their beautiful home and business, and were faced with the dilemma of braving storms of pumice or staying put.

Her father had taken his favourite coin, a spintria. 'Tails we leave, sex we stay,' he thought as the act of flipping it triggered his preference for 'tails'.

*Spintria*

Before the coin hit the floor, he resolved to take the family on the perilous journey through the hot falling ash and leave by the north-eastern gate.

All went well until the cat, terrified by the acrid smells, squirmed out of Lavinia's grip and shot off homeward. She gave chase and vanished from sight. The streets were now so thick with the grey flakes that Lavinia was totally disorientated. The loss of the cat and the bubbling fear forced a well of tears to flow. Lost and alone, she froze in terror, and even her tears solidified with a fine crust of cement that prevented them from rolling down her cheeks. Then the air was rent apart by a sickening series of booms. The very earth shuddered and she felt herself lifted high into the air – to unexpected relief, by the arms of her desperate father.

They were lucky; they fled away from the prevailing winds and ash falls. On and on, through the dark nightmare they ran, dodging the crashing lava bombs until, after an interminable journey, they reached a place of refuge on a small hill in the grey-stained countryside. Many miles away, they could only look back in awe and grief as a 20-mile high column of billions of tons of airborne rock collapsed onto their unfortunate and vulnerable town.

The following day another spewing, superheated mass tore apart the flanks of the fire mountain and finally engulfed their house, their neighbours, and everything they'd ever known from their previous lives – and, worst of all for Lavinia, her cat.

All lay undisturbed for almost two millennia. The toss of a coin and a father's intuition not only saved Lavinia's life, but also Enza's.

Over the centuries and for 82 generations, Lavinia's children and their offspring always bore at least one girl. They would never know it, but Enza and her mother were direct descendants in the female line of the little girl whose bedroom they were so carefully revealing to the modern world.

Buzz and Elin followed Enza's vivid description of the bedroom, comparing it to their own. It seemed so stark, without furnishings, gadgets or even bedding. Suddenly their young guide drew them closer and reached into her canvas drawing bag.

'Look at this,' she smirked, 'I found it under a load of charcoal…' In her hand was a small coin with the Roman numerals VI on it. Before they could wonder what the fuss was about, she turned it over.

'Yeuch!' said Buzz, while Elin just giggled.

'Talk about tails!' she exclaimed, as she made out the tiny embossed rounded bottoms of the two lovers.

'Well, it makes a change from Abraham Lincoln,' offered Buzz.

'Or fish!' added Elin.

The Romans had the concept of *genius* to describe the essential nature of a place, person or even a thing. As a powerful force of nature, Vesuvius had *genius* and so does Pompeii. It must have been a wonderful place to live, and even today the *genius* or magic of the place still hangs on to every nook and cranny.

Each of our visitors felt its presence strongly as they wandered dreamily past the avenue of graves towards Elisabetta's restaurant. Enza took liberties all the way, rushing beyond any barriers into the ruins to show her new friends her favourite haunts. Elisabetta turned a blind eye. She was walking close to Jane, chatting animatedly about the intervening years since they'd last met. Lagging behind the group was Ford, lost in a world of his own. Kirsten waited for him. Her 'Hi' didn't register, and she waved in front of his eyes to brake the trance.

'What's the big secret, then? The one Alim was asking you about?'

Secrets are tyrants willing to be dethroned and as Ford kicked an ancient stone down the dusty road, he decided he could trust her.

He examined Kirsten's face. 'You've security clearance with NASA, haven't you?'

'Sure, grade four,' she replied.

'OK. They've found a fossil on Mars and the president's asked me to plan a manned mission to investigate.'

Kirsten's eyebrows arched. 'What's the problem? That's fantastic!'

'We have to do it within three years!'

'*Fokk!* No wonder you're looking tired!' she said with a laugh, then added, 'Go for it! Why not?!'

Ford crooked his head, as if to the skies above. 'No budget, no rocket, no time, and we can't get the crew back!'

Kirsten picked up the ancient stone Ford had just kicked. 'My country was founded by a desperate people. They had no resources, and guess what? They did it, risking their lives to voyage to a godforsaken place and make it their home! That's my blood. Can I help?'

He looked thankfully at Kirsten Gunnarsdottir, and then to the restaurant. 'That would be so very kind, but first, lunchtime!'

Jane couldn't hide anything from her dear friend Elisabetta, so by the time they all sat down, there was the biggest elephant in the room since Hannibal. When Elisabetta returned from the kitchen with her husband, he was in on it too.

Buzz took no notice. Enza had provided them with crayons and paper, which he was rapidly converting into 'Trumpers' cards.

He guided the girls through their skills. He was more than happy to fill them out on the cards, especially as he was 'No way!' going to eat the whitebait first course. He scored himself high on 'pilot', 'computers' and 'navigation'.

Enza's strengths were 'artist/photographer', 'archaeologist' and 'cook', and Elin's, 'geologist', 'orienteering', 'adventurer' and 'storyteller'.

Enza retreated into the kitchen with her father. They returned with steaming bowls of delicious homemade pasta, while Buzz finished the cards. He loved pasta and this was a real treat. He chatted with the girls, paying no attention to the adults, until he caught the words 'I hear you're planning a trip to Mars?' from the garrulous Giulio.

*Italian Meal*

Ford recalled Benjamin Franklin's words 'Three may keep a secret if two of them are dead' and realised that all the adults now knew.

Intrigued, the children's chatter stopped as they tuned into the conversation.

The long story of the president and the project came out, lubricated by the wine produced from the very vines that surrounded them.

The children grasped the enormity of Ford's story and a thrill erupted among them.

A manned trip to Mars! Then their imaginations were squashed as Ford recounted the brick wall he'd met with. 'Goddammit! The mission needs a crew of six to be done properly and we'd struggle to get even two astronauts back off the planet!' Ford looked around the table. 'As my friend Alim told me, "You're basically stuffed, squire!"'

Giulio laughed. '*Nessun problema, invia piccolo popolo!* Send small people!'

Ford thought 'That's very easy to say,' but replied, 'What do you mean? Dwarfs? Hobbits? You've been watching too many films lately.'

The three children stared intently at each other, then down at their cards, their skills laid out before them. Slowly their eyes met again with a recognition of the answer. The adults jumped with surprise as the 'Trumpers' cards hit the table with a loud smack, and 'the small people' shouted in unison: 'Send us! We can do it!'

*Trumpers Cards*

The adults in the room laughed with indulgent mirth, as Ford thoughtfully studied the cards. The president had selected him to 'think outside of the box'. Ford scrutinised the children, his curious brain churning, and then considered the adults, now distractedly chatting. There was a second pile of cards, which he thumbed through with amusement, for they were the scores for each of the 'growps' – Buzz's term for grown-ups. Enza had drawn a cameo of them above their skills.

Ford placed Enza and Elisabetta's cards together. 'So, just how good is Enza at archaeology?' he asked Elisabetta.

'Oh, *brillante*! She has such an eye! And her drawings are exquisite. We make a *grande* team!' Regarding the empty bowl, he knew she could cook.

He turned to Kirsten. 'And Elin at geology?'

'Like a fish in a fjord. I get twice as much done when she's around. She's like a sponge, and she's as tough as shark skin.'

Ford shuffled to Buzz's card. 'And why've you scored yourself more than me at flying, young man?'

Buzz blushed. 'Not saying.' He looked embarrassed. 'Not in front of everyone.'

Ford leaned forward. 'Whisper it.'

With a deep breath he said, 'I don't fall asleep in the cockpit!'

'Between us, young man.' Ford winked.

At this point Giulio returned with the *carne*. Ford said silently to himself, 'Well, that's food for thought...' And suddenly a subconscious burden lifted from his shoulders. He could now enjoy tucking into the pig's liver with gusto.

# Chapter 14

## Out of Africa

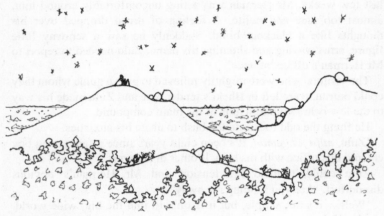

*Zulu and the Stars*

The thorn thicket rustled. Zulu squatted on the vivid lichen-speckled rocks. 'Monkey see, monkey do!' he whispered.

The corpulent couple bent low and urgently asked, 'Do you think it's a lion?'

'Follow me!' Zulu scrambled to a wind-sculpted boulder while they tagged behind, like desperate ducklings. The three heads peered around the crystalline curve of their refuge. Suddenly, from behind the bush, trotted the forms of three zebras: a stallion, mare and foal. Their black coarse manes and pyjama stripes vividly contrasted with the dappled canvas around them. Zulu rose slowly and crept forward towards the family, followed by the tourists. They faced each other for several minutes until the animals sniffed the wind and trotted off.

Kurt looked down at his camera, happy that he had many shots to enjoy back home. Rising, he caught Zulu's full attention. 'What would you have done if it had been a lion?' He was desperate for a frisson of danger.

Zulu gave it some thought. 'Ach! I'd run very fast in the opposite direction.'

'Wow! No way! You can't run faster than a lion?' Kurt responded incredulously.

Zulu gave his broad, gleaming white smile. 'No... just faster than you!'

Zulu's pride in their windmill, still humming happily in the background, had not assuaged the uneasy feeling he'd had over the last few weeks. Mr Herman was acting uncomfortably around him, almost too nice and polite. A feeling of dread dropped over his thoughts like a blackout blind. Suddenly he saw a scrawny little figure, arms waving and shouting his name. Zulu needed to report to Mr Herman's office 'at once'.

The visitors, who were mightily relieved to gain a guide whom they could outrun, were left in Bheki's tender care and Zulu made his way to the low ochre-coloured huts of the main compound.

He flung the odd rock into the bush to abate his anxieties.

'Zulu, *mijn jongeman*. It's been eight years since a sad, young boy entered this office with his baby brother in his arms.'

Zulu couldn't stand the tension and Mr Herman's obvious discomfort. 'Are you sending me away?'

'Well... it's not simple, but it is time to join the big, wide world. You're eighteen now and that's two more years than we're supposed to allow.'

Zulu knew there was no welcoming 'big, wide world' out there – only the prospect of unemployment, tough living or at best life as a servant in some post-colonial household. 'I've more chance of touching the stars than joining the big, wide world! Ach! Who's going to look out for Bheki?'

'Oh... Bheki'll be OK. He's deaf, but he has extraordinary talents, as have you! If you can't touch the stars, we'll find a way for you on this earth.'

Zulu shivered. 'But... I have no family except this. Everyone has family and you are cutting me off! The outside world might offer me work, but who will care for me? Where can I run to when things don't work out?'

A tear started to roll down his dark cheek. He swiftly brushed it off. He was trying to be a man, but the scared little boy still leaked out of his eyes and he knew that Mr Herman was no Daddy. The only man who had that gift was lost when Zulu was very young. Zulu took a deep breath. 'OK, what can I do?'

Mr Herman looked at his notes. He had been in this position so many times before. 'I want to help you study. But we have limited funds – perhaps we can ask those contacts to help? Let's get Bheki on to the emails and make a plan. What about that Welsh woman?'

The grey London skies did not dull the pungent aromas and the smell of baking bread pervading the restaurant. Mo was trying to get his father's attention against the cacophony of raised voices and busy waiters. This was a Formica-table version of heaven for the boy. Salt lassi, fresh bread, hot kebabs and his father's attention.

'How was Ramadan for you, my lad?'

'Boring! What about you, Daddy?'

'Oh, very difficult. I've been at the conference, so fasting was damned impossible. I did miss breakfast twice, to keep my hand in,' he said, helping himself to a morsel of spiced lamb and green minty yoghurt. 'Guess what I've got in my pocket? A reward for your school results!'

Mo loved surprises so drummed his hands on the table vigorously.

Alim waved two tickets in the air. 'The Oval this afternoon. T20 match – it'll be fun.'

Mo even enjoyed the long bus ride to the ground, and they had barely taken their seats before Mo was enthusiastically waving his '6' card as the third ball arced into the roaring crowd.

Alim wafted away the smoke of a clandestine cigarette and sipped his beer, waiting for a lull in the match in order to talk seriously.

'Hydration break? What the heck's that!' complained Alim as the players took 'drinks'. This gave him a golden opportunity to talk. 'I spoke to the school, and they're happy to give you extra holiday, as they're still mopping up after the floods. I'm off to the States to help NASA with their "interpretations". Would you like to come and see some real space rockets and the "Big Country"?'

Heading west at 40,000 feet, Jane was sleeping and Buzz was playing on his tablet. Ford was catching up on the reports sent by Sharon. The science and engineering teams had come up with some radical ideas. He was so excited, he nearly woke up Jane; then the words 'why', 'nerdy' and 'don't you ever' came to mind.

The teams proposed a series of generators, dropped onto the

surface, which would push heated probes deep into the ground. This would melt the subsurface ice and produce steam to generate the electricity needed to split the condensed steam into oxygen and hydrogen. Tiny compressors would pump the gases into cylinders, to provide the fuel to get off the planet.

Ford admired several hand-drawn illustrations showing the 'modules'. Six would be sufficient, and they were light enough to be delivered to the surface in the conventional gas bags used to land the smaller rovers.

A big issue was to land them close enough to the mothership. If they bounced over a wide landing ground, the whole mission time might be taken up with retrieving them or, worse, it might leave the astronauts stranded.

How could they achieve a totally stable orbit to be delivered with absolute precision? In addition, they could only estimate the ground conditions, so if any generators crashed or didn't find water ice, the crew could get stranded. These were questions that needed to be answered and Ford's rested mind was back to a well-honed sharpness.

He stared out of the window, working out a way to achieve a stable orbit. Ford still retained his joy of flight, and always insisted on a window seat. The dark night skies were pierced by the intense moonlight that caught the clouds below, like a never-ending carpet of lamb's wool.

Craning his neck, Ford saw the moon, almost full. He recalled the times it had guided him home on long night flights. Knowing the time, he could use the moon to check his orientation. 'Totally predictable,' he thought. The moon's orbit was known to the very millimetre.

'Of course!' came a flash of brilliance. 'Why not use Phobos, Mars' largest moon? We know its orbit precisely!'

The orbits of the moons are known accurately enough for the Mars rovers to photograph their eclipses of the sun. They are too small to cover its disc and the moons look like potato-shaped blemishes, rather than the Earth's fantastic spectacle. A lunar eclipse of the sun from the Earth is a beautiful and transcendental experience, as the mechanics of the cosmos unfold before the fortunate observer. It is also one of the most extraordinary sights in the whole universe.

The width of the moon appears to be the same as the sun's when seen from Earth. This can allow a view of not only the sun's atmosphere and tiny red solar flares, but also the exquisite ring of diamonds, created as the edges of the sun are seen through the moon's hills and valleys.

*Eclipse*

The process takes at least an hour, with the light diminishing and temperature dropping, and whirling birds preparing to roost.

The sun is so brilliant that only at the final second can the black disc of the moon be seen to cover the sun exactly, like a bullet hole in the fabric of the sky. The world stands still for no more than a few brief minutes, but the experience will last a lifetime.

Suddenly a number of solutions crashed into place in Ford's mind. If the astronauts landed on Phobos first, they would have a completely stable place from which to launch the components of the mission with absolute precision.

The homecoming rocket stages could remain on the tiny moon, waiting securely for the returning crew. They could even stay on the tiny satellite until the fuel generators were working.

'Wow!' he thought. 'That would be an amazing double.' Mars' moons were probably captured asteroids, so they'd be the first astronauts to land not only on another planet, but also on an asteroid.

Even if the landing on Mars had to be aborted, there'd be some wonderful scientific discoveries to be made on Phobos they'd be able to take home. If they pulled the whole thing off, it would be two missions for the price of one!

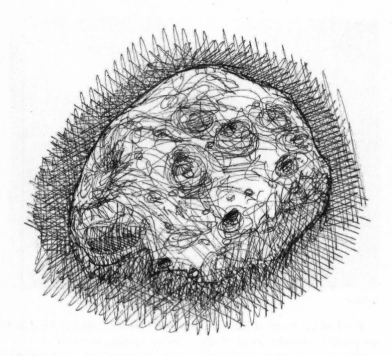

*Phobos*

Ford was very pleased with himself and ordered a large glass of red wine, and a cola for Buzz. 'How's it going, kiddo?' He poked the engrossed child. Buzz was playing a game that only kids seemed to excel at. Ford had tried it himself, but got stuck on level three; Buzz was on level nine.

**Phobos – Son of Mars**
Largest of Mars' moons
Size: irregular, 27 x 22 x 18km
Orbit: approx. 9,375km
Orbital speed: 2.14km/s
Geology: Conglomerate of rocks and ice

He leaned fondly against the still-snoozing Jane, and mused on the problem of the crew's weight, thinking again of their al fresco meal in the shadow of Vesuvius. 'Send us, we can do it!' That's what they'd said.

His mind to wandered down that train of thought and he considered himself at that age.

'Hell, I would have loved to go. We'd expected to see whole families in space in the twenty-first century, watching *Lost in Space* and all.' Then, 'Mmm, families... Clever as they are, these kids ain't alone in their precociousness. They work with their mothers or fathers, or me in Buzz's case. Maybe... they'd be like little avatars.' A potato crisp melted on his tongue, until he washed it down with another sip of heady red wine.

'An expert crew on the ground, controlling their little "mini-me"s in space.' With a guttural spasm he choked on the next sip as he remembered Armstrong. 'I couldn't ever control him in my own yard!'

Stephen's feet pounded down the gravel paths as the glaucous pines gave way to the mellow hues of oaks and chestnuts. His steps beat out his thoughts, his mind churning over his schemes. The more he worked with the project team, the more he wanted to get out of LA.

He had hoped that scientists and engineers would be logical, but this lot were totally unpredictable. All this 'thinking outside the box' and jokes about Schrödinger drove him insane. His only allies seemed to be the accountants; at least they shared his jaded view of the world.

The sooner he could put this stupidity to bed, the sooner he would be back to doing 'real work'. While Ford had been in Italy, Stephen had been playing 'Mr Nice Guy', getting to know his colleagues' work and ideas. Now Ford was back, he was working out how to debunk them. The old trick of inflating the costs was welcomed by his own little cohort and quite defensible, as projects like these usually went wildly over budget.

Stephen had warmed to the scheme of using the Saturn V from the Samsonian, convinced – it being a 'national treasure' – it was a convenient blind alley. He revelled in the fact that even the 'boffins' were scornful about what a skeleton crew could achieve.

As he pushed himself on the final stretch into headquarters, he decided to send in his own report to the president.

Sharon and Imran had put together the tightest mission plan they had ever made. There were still unresolved issues and they were glad to have Ford back with refreshed vigour.

The president's schedule dictated they'd need to have the astronauts trained and equipment ready in eighteen months. As they planned to assemble elements in Earth's orbit, two crews would be required: one for the mission and a second to help with construction.

The two rockets needed to take off almost simultaneously and the mission would blast out of orbit on the great curved arc for eight months to bring them into the welcoming gravitational pull of Mars.

On approach a long rocket 'burn' would brake them into orbit. Then they'd launch their fuel generators onto the planet's surface, leaving them in orbit for two weeks while they confirmed that everything was working; if it wasn't, they'd still have sufficient fuel in the lander to return to Earth.

If everything went well, the lander would attempt a completely new method to reach the surface of Mars. The landing would need to be extraordinarily precise, right in the centre of the fuel cells. The crew would be on the surface for four months. From the base they'd have a radius of 150 miles to explore. On their return they'd blast off to join their mothership waiting high above.

Then a return journey of another eight months before splashing down to a hero's welcome.

That was the best plan they could come up with, and it was far from perfect.

Landing on Phobos came as a gift from heaven. As a keen golfer, Sharon knew the difference between holing from a bunker or the green.

Yet three brooding issues still cast their shadows.

*One – the budget.* Stephen was keeping his team's cards so close to his chest, they had no idea what he'd be reporting.

*Two – health and safety.* They were in the hands of 'mission killer' Edward Stalk to approve their assessments. Safety was paramount and he was totally independent in his judgement.

*Three – justification.* The scientific objectives were crucial and still far from being resolved.

# Chapter 15

## The Presentation

A fly buzzed lazily around the Oval Office. Luther Garvey was exhausted. He'd just entertained the Chinese ambassador before a meeting with the chiefs of staff of the armed forces. Watching its descent towards the fruit bowl, he growled, 'How d'you get past security?'

It seemed an age since Ford's capers around that big carpet, and tomorrow they were to present the conclusions of his 'pet project' in person. He'd asked for the report up front and to his surprise there were three in his in-tray. The main report was a weighty tome with a picture stuck on it and blue text. There was also an unsolicited report from Stephen Dyer, beautifully produced on exquisite paper. The third was an addendum by Ford, called 'The Other Things'. This contained all the other solutions that the team had come up with. These ideas ranged from sound ideas, such as storing the mission's water and waste in an external skin around it to limit the damage from cosmic rays, to criminal – stealing the Saturn V from the Samsonian – and crazy – the 'mini-me' crew.

Luther skimmed the main report. 'Great attempt, but no cigar,' he whispered to himself.

Stephen's finely embossed work looked like a funeral announcement. Skipping over it, he started to read 'The Other Things'.

The concept of a 'wee-wrapped' spaceship tickled Luther. Stealing a rocket from the museum had him in stitches. Then he read with astonishment about the kindergarten crew and heaved with suppressed laughter.

Belle heard the grunting sound over the intercom. In panic she dashed to the cabinet on the wall and burst into the room, wielding the two pads of the emergency defibrillator, to find her patient sobbing hysterically into his 'Stars and Stripes' handkerchief.

She rushed over. 'Are you OK, Mr President?'

Luther dabbed away the tears, and with a grin as broad as the Mississippi said, 'Never been better, Belle.'

Ford and Sharon arrived early for their presentation. They were surprised to find Stephen there and full of himself. 'You do know the president and I go back a long way? He wants to see me first.'

Belle came in and took Stephen into the inner sanctum.

Stephen entered the office and took out a copy of his report.

'Thank you, Stephen, I've already seen that. Please sit,' said Luther. 'I read a lot of reports, but tell me in your own words about these misgivings.'

Stephen explained how the project wasn't credible and the team had been stumbling around, cooking up dumb ideas to cover up the fact that it was ill-conceived, and he wasn't going to put his name to it. Most of all, he was the only one honest enough to say so. Only his team had been realistic in their costing and the project was going to be way over budget.

Luther thumbed through the thick, textured paper of Stephen's report. Then he assured him that it was useful to have a second opinion.

'If this falls flat on its face, I guess you are keen to get back to Washington, Stephen?'

For a moment Stephen's hopes rose. 'Yes, sir!'

Standing up, Luther shook his hand. 'Time to let the other guys make their pitch. They've come a long way.' As Stephen was leaving, the president gave a little cough. 'By the way, I didn't get here by being too realistic. It can get in the way of your dreams. Your budget is good – just what I'd anticipated.'

Sharon was in awe as she entered the room. No secret doors this time. She soon fell to earth. Without pleasantries, or even an offer of coffee, a stern-faced Luther cut to the chase. 'No need for presentations. I've read the reports.'

'Reports?' Sharon was confused.

Luther picked up the main report. 'I asked for a plan to get us to Mars and back, but this doesn't slice the salami.' He then held up the addendum. 'Why the "Other Things" thing? I asked for one report!'

Ford shifted uneasily in his seat. 'I put all our crazy ideas in there. Some were untested and others politically difficult…'

Luther retorted, 'Do you think politics is more difficult than science and engineering?'

'Erm…' Ford answered cogently.

'You're both boffins. Can you tell me what Niels Bohr said about difficult problems?'

Sharon came to the rescue. '"Your theory is crazy, but it's not crazy enough to be true"?'

A smile broke over Luther's face. 'Oh, I like that! My quote was "Every great and deep difficulty bears in itself its own solution. It forces us to change our thinking in order to find it", but that will do fine!'

**Niels Bohr**
1885–1962
Danish physicist and philosopher, received the Nobel Prize in Physics for his foundational contribution to the understanding of atomic structure and quantum theory.

He picked up Stephen's clandestine report. 'There's also a doubter in your ranks with a very convincing case to abandon the whole idea. Can you give me one good reason why not?'

Luther was content to wait as a myriad of thoughts went through Ford and Sharon's minds as they struggled find the compelling answer.

Slowly Sharon took a good look at the famous room, in case it was her last opportunity. She closed her eyes and spoke.

'This office is like a myth, but now I'm here, I can see it's real! I believe by existing we make the universe a more tangible place. Without life, what's the point? If we find life on Mars, it's obviously part of the fabric of everything, not just special to Earth!'

Luther put the two reports together. 'Do you mind if I borrow that in my speech?'

'What speech, sir?' quizzed Ford.

'When I announce the mission!' Luther continued. 'Remember, I'm the politician – that's what I do, and you do the science. The main report didn't contain all the answers. When I read "The Other Things", I laughed like a drain. Then I slept on it and realised there were strokes of genius. That Saturn V was built to go into space, not a museum, and it resolves major deficiencies of the budget and timescales. But what really got me was sending the kids.'

Sharon listened in shock. 'What kids?' she whispered to Ford.

He looked sheepish. 'Oh, just an idea I threw in.'

Luther filled her in. 'An option where precocious children carry out the mission and work with their parents. It solves your weight problem. If I put both documents together, we have a plan. Let's train up three teams, one with two seasoned astronauts – say... "The Right Stuff"? – one with three light adults, maybe... "The Elves", and one with six kids.'

He looked down at the smaller report. 'We'll have to keep this classified, though, so let's just call them "The Other Things". The training will go right to the wire, so there's time to see who performs best... And by the way, as for politics, let's make them an international team, to spread the flak if you blow them up.'

Soraya was idly polishing the windscreen of her waiting black sedan as she saw Ford and Sharon emerge from the shaded back entrance of the White House and approach the car park.

'Hiya, fella! Oh, and you, lady. The airport again?'

'Sure!' replied Ford distractedly.

'Second time around for Mr Rocket Man, must be something brewing. Hey, I saw you in the rags again – here, look.' From under her backside she pulled out a Pure Corporation magazine. Sharon skimmed it and found a picture of Ford, looking the worse for wear, and the headline 'Rocket Man Now Believes in Fairies!'

'I thought you said it was tough in Italy?' Sharon flashed her eyes at him. 'Forget the fairies. Two questions: why'd you keep your "great idea" so secret, and did the president really give us the go-ahead?'

'Yes, sounded like it! Look, I'm sorry about the kids idea, I just wasn't confident in it. Lucky I put it in, though, it might have saved the day.'

Sharon leaned over to get his full attention. 'No, Ford! I'm serious. It nearly lost the day by being left out. Next time you share these things with me, OK? We've got a long way to go now!'

Ford grinned. 'Thirty million miles and back, I suppose.'

'Nah, the airport ain't that far. We'll be there in half an hour,' interjected Soraya, enthusiastically chewing her gum. 'You going to space again, Mr Starman?'

Ford was not too keen to discuss it. 'No, not me personally. Anyway, it's classified.'

'Me too – classified chauffeur. Nah, sorry, licensed! Listen, if you need someone to drive your rocket, I'm your woman!' She swerved to avoid an approaching car. 'If you can drive here, you can drive anywhere!'

Ford took a deep breath. 'You'd have to have been a pilot first!'

He could see Soraya's face light up in the rear-view mirror.

'That's me – first female pilot in New York – boats, not planes, though!'

'They don't count,' replied Ford, relieved.

'Nonsense, boats are far more like spaceships. The clue's in the name!'

A pause, then: 'OK, we'll call you first!'

The flight back gave Ford and Sharon time enough to plan. They poured over the papers Luther had given them. They could see his extraordinary talent. He had taken their findings and turned them around overnight. The main gist was: don't waste a minute; the next administration will kill the deal.

Luther had already laid the diplomatic groundwork to bring in other space agencies straightaway. They also needed to order the hardware, 'steal' the rocket, and choose and train the crews immediately. Luther had included a special presidential order for the Saturn V, and the curator's holiday schedule.

As for the kids – there should only be one American; the rest should come from all over the globe, and particularly one from Africa.

If the mission was going to be about anything, it was about one world and a future for its children's children.

# Chapter 16

## Removed for Restoration

It was the dead of night, an unusual time to visit a museum. But this was no ordinary trip. Rocky and his team had been coaxing ancient diesel engines into life since early evening and as the convoy finally left its desert home, a mist of white smoke fogged the air as it spluttered its way to the city.

The sound of rumbling trucks, amplified by the glistening tarmac, forced Rocky to bark orders over the crackling intercom. All was in place, and since getting the 'go-ahead', he had been working all hours to prepare for tonight's audacious foray.

Their route had to be meticulously planned to allow the massive trailers to navigate their way without getting stuck at junctions or under bridges. Leading the pack was the massive wasp-yellow 32-wheeled crane that would do the lifting. Each trailer or triple trailer had a cradle to take its cargo. In Rocky's breast pocket was the signed consent from the president to remove the exhibit.

The flashing lights of police patrols were at each major junction, smoothing the passage along the route. It would take four hours to accomplish their mission. Rocky felt like a thief in the night, because Milton was on holiday and had not even been consulted. This was the man whose trust Rocky had gained on his recent visits to inspect the object of tonight's escapade, the man who had so enthusiastically helped him to examine the prize exhibit, not suspecting the subplot.

Rocky put such thoughts aside as he dropped down from the cab with the museum keys in his pocket and the codes for the alarms. In a flash they had the gigantic cargo doors open and the crane was slipping into the tight aperture, like a squeeze of yellow oil paint in reverse. The object of their desire was massive. Even the smallest third stage of the rocket, at 60 feet long, appeared daunting enough. The team held their collective breath as the first rocket was lifted, then rolled onto the trailer. Consent or not, they had decided to keep the lights off to minimise attention. In the torchlit gloom, one by one, they lifted each stage off its stand onto the waiting trailers. One false move could have caused irreparable damage to the fragile sections.

Suddenly, as they gingerly moved the last 140-feet-long behemoth onto its train of three equally spaced trailers, the lights split the night.

Mr Marley, the janitor's third assistant, had been rudely roused from his dreams by the hushed commotion. Throwing on whatever clothes he could find, he stood in awe of the sight before him. His flannel underpants and wife's pink dressing gown did not give him an air of authority. Only his hat belied his position to challenge the proceedings. Rocky rushed over, frantically waving his ID tags.

'It's OK, routine maintenance. Surely you were informed?' he blustered.

Marley slowly scrutinised the ID tags and then the letter of consent produced from Rocky's pocket. Shaking his greying head, he just said in a low drawl, 'This ain't right, there's somethin' missing. You can't just take them and leave nothing.'

'Oh, my goodness!' thought Rocky. 'We're not going to have to knock him on the head and throw him in the trunk?'

'They always leave a sign!'

Then Rocky got it. 'Oh! Of course, I've got them in the case.'

To Marley's relief, out came three framed signs reading, 'This exhibit has been temporarily removed for restoration'.

There was a long pause as he took a look at the trailers and the signs. 'OK, sir, I guess that's fine. Make sure you close the doors properly.'

Glad to return to his bed, Marley trudged back. But then he stopped and addressed Rocky again. 'Hey! Wait a minute. Ain't they just been restored?'

Rocky gave a wave. 'This is to restore them to their original purpose.'

Then they were on the road, with the rocket that would have sent Apollo 18 to the moon. Heading straight out of town, the convoy only raised the attention of passing dogs and drunks, whose stories would never be heard or listened to.

Out on the straight highways and leading south, the darkness began to give way to an eastern glow, and small, friendly farmsteads started to appear, with the odd lamp being flicked on as 'early birds' rose to tend their animals. Rumbling on at 40mph, the widest convoy to ever grace these roads passed like a ghost in a forest. Rocky anxiously rode shotgun in the front wagon. Small talk with his driver Gus was perfunctory and avoided any explanation. These were guys who had shifted stuff before and knew not to ask too many questions.

*Rocket Convoy*

As the first rays of the rising sun kissed the tall poplars ringing the base, Rocky's relief was palpable. They'd made it before the build-up of the heavy morning traffic. The rocket stages were deposited in launch order in the vast hangar, to be prepared for their ultimate destiny.

Rocky had a sudden moment of fear and doubt. These machines were made in the same year as Ford's camper van. Considering their vintage, how could they possibly be suitable for a modern mission?

Then he remembered Ford's adage: 'When my camper breaks down, I need a spanner; when my car breaks down, I need a tow truck and a computer.'

Buzz was overjoyed about extending his break at his grandparents' rural heaven. His mum had pleaded for at least an extra two weeks. The Boyf had done a bunk and, at the edge of sanity, she wasn't able to look after her poor son.

He busied himself around the farm with Jane and tended the lambs with the two farmhands, Eric and Ernie. The afternoons were spent looking at the ant nests. Buzz could stay fixed in a position for hours, but even he was getting fidgety sitting on an old log.

'Why'd you find ants so interesting, when Granf plans rocket missions?' he asked innocently. He was fascinated by the colony, but it was like a school project compared with the grown-up stuff of rocket science.

Jane told him how she saw it. 'Buzz, this is big science. It's about intelligence. I'm trying to figure out if these creatures have any identity outside that of the nest. Are they even aware of living?'

Buzz was already sure. 'It's obvious, Granj. Dudley knows what she's doing. I've watched her – she's really smart.'

Jane ruffled his hair; he hated that. 'Well, there's the rub. Classically they seem too small to be able to process the information to make their own decisions and act as we observe. We're either reading too much into it or there's something else happening.'

Buzz was sure of his own observations. 'What else is happening?'

Jane smiled at him. Why couldn't his mum be like this? She was always cross.

'It's complicated,' Jane pronounced.

He sat staring across the valley. 'Everything's complicated,' he returned in frustration.

Jane tried harder. 'OK, the ants' brains appear too small to do a lot, but they do so much more. It's like they have an extra spark! I'm sure they work on a quantum level, which is how the universe works deep down, where it's kind of fuzzy. It allows for all sorts of possibilities. A lot people find it difficult to understand because everything's uncertain.'

Buzz could identify with that. 'It sounds just like home!'

The afternoon light was diminishing and the bright beacon of Venus was clearly visible. Buzz looked around at the sky, the trees, the rocks and the grass. He wore a quizzical expression, as if sniffing the air. 'My mind's not a machine, neither is an ant's. I think all life has the same spark, that quantum thingy. It's just that we have more sparks than they have.'

'At least some of us do,' reflected Jane. 'Hey, we have to get back home for the president's speech!'

There was hardly time for the kettle to boil before the radio crackled with the live broadcast by Luther Garvey.

'I have come here today to Rice University to be on the very spot where my great predecessor made us a promise in the 1960s.

'Let me quote. "For the eyes of the world now look into space, to the moon and to the planets beyond, and we have vowed that we shall not see it governed by a hostile flag of conquest, but by a banner of freedom and peace." He gave this commitment. "We choose to go to the moon. We choose to go to the moon in this decade and do the other things, not because they are easy, but because they are hard, because that goal will serve to organise and measure the best of our energies and skills, because that challenge is one that we are willing to accept, one we are unwilling to postpone, and one which we intend to win, and the others, too."

'Well, we as a nation fulfilled that promise to go to the moon, but nearly fifty years later, what about "the other things"? Sure, we have sent probes and robots to the other planets, but the dream of humanity freeing itself from the bonds of Earth has passed us by.

'Maybe we can forgive ourselves for our lapse. To quote another great man, "The Earth is the only world known so far to harbour life... and the Earth is where we make our stand" – and maybe we've been too busy making our stand.

'However, this year, two events have made us look again into space. One was evident to all, the other I will reveal today. Our space visitor, asteroid Wilson, forced us to regard the heavens with fear and trepidation, and only by God's grace did we not follow the fate of the dinosaurs.

'We should take it as a message not to dwell entirely on the delights or woes of our planet, but to always look for the bigger picture. Those new horizons have been focused by an extraordinary discovery.

'Our rovers on Mars have been working beyond expectations for years. One has recently found what could be a fossil, not of some small microbe, but of a creature so highly developed, it would show that complex life was not unique to this planet. It hints at the prospect of a universe abundant with living beings.

'I asked a young scientist the other day, why should we boldly go and investigate this thing? She said these words: "I believe by existing we make the universe a more tangible place. Without life, what's the point? If we find life on Mars, it's obviously part of the fabric of everything, not just special to Earth."

'We would be foolish to ignore these events and get on with our humdrum lives. I believe it's time to complete the dream and do "the other things".

'I have decided to send a human mission to Mars, not for America but for the world, to investigate this extraordinary discovery. What's more, we shall do it by the end of the decade and not because it's easy; we will do it because it is hard.'

The sputter of the flat-4 1600cc engine suddenly filled the yard.

'Oh my goodness, it's Ford!' exclaimed Jane. She'd lost track of time. Ford was home early and in time to follow the speech on the VW's radio.

Jane and Buzz danced out to greet him.

'Well done, cariad! We've just heard the speech. It's official!'

Ford's natural enthusiasm bubbled over as he told them of the latest developments. 'Guess what! We've got the rocket! Rocky liberated it.'

'Wow!' exclaimed Buzz. 'A real rocket!'

Jane made them all a cup of tea. The farmhouse table creaked under the weight of sandwiches and three sets of elbows. The odd crumb fell onto the gingham tablecloth as Buzz listened intently to his grandfather – the drama at the White House and how they'd nearly lost the mission, but for his idea.

'Does that mean I can go to Mars, Granf?'

Ford ruffled Buzz's hair. He flashed Ford a peeved glance as he hastily rearranged it.

'Well, someone's going to go, but don't hold your breath. Three teams are being evaluated, and there's a world full of people to volunteer. We're working with the Europeans and they're very particular in their selection ethics.'

'Just like FIFA?' chipped in Jane.


Luther was always cautious of the mercurial CEO of the Pure Corporation, Victor Relish. Relish had at one time patronised Garvey, hoping he'd toe the line, but discovered Luther's inconvenient independence of mind. Since then, Victor had encouraged his empire to subtly undermine Luther wherever possible.

Now anyone associated with Luther got the same treatment. Luther Garvey knew not to go toe to toe with Victor, so when they met at the reception after the announcement it was all warm smiles but cold hearts.

'Luther, I'm surprised you haven't come to us to do your big project. NASA is history. Surely it's time for the private sector to run the show?'

'My dear Victor, there are no profit margins in this, it's purely scientific. Besides, your corporation have hardly been sympathetic.'

'A good contract is worth a lot of sympathy,' said Victor with a laugh. Then he added sinisterly, 'We've got better people too. That man's a buffoon.'

This annoyed Luther, as no details had been announced yet. He looked Victor wearily in the eye, considering what to say. 'I've seen you play the buffoon yourself, but you're a shrewd guy.' After a brief pause he continued, 'So what could you offer our mission?'

Victor took a sip of coffee.

'All or nothing, but I don't like to get involved with public projects – all that red tape! Anyway, I've the corporation to consider and we're keeping our options open on the new presidential candidates. I think it may be time for a woman.'

Victor Relish could indeed play the buffoon. He was the epitome of the 'self-made man' and played the innocent commoner when it served him.

He was born to hard-working parents, but his father had died when he was young, after a lawyer in an expensive convertible knocked his father off his pushbike. The injustice of seeing how wealth was used to exonerate the careless driver made Victor determined to fight his way through life. His first break was at the age of seventeen, when he converted his scooter and installed a small pizza oven behind the driver. He could deliver and cook pizzas at the same time. By the age of twenty-four it was a worldwide franchise, Pure Pizzas. He found that with wealth came the respect he craved, and his talent for spotting a gap in the market came again when he worked on the company's first websites. He saw the possibilities of the web for distributing news that was, like his pizzas, hot, spicy and for common tastes.

Now he had a drum to bang: like him, anyone could be successful. He never considered that although anyone might be successful in the competitive market he loved, it was dependent on winners and losers. His media empire, the Pure Corporation, was built on the ethos of supporting the winners and damning the losers. It had been so successful that it was now branching into space by launching its own satellites.

'Yes, I think you should watch Peggy Tyler – she's got far to go.'

'Oh my goodness, her!' thought Luther. Victor was referring to the rising star of the opposition party. 'From my point of view, perhaps the further the better!' said the president, shaking Victor's hand. 'Always good to see you,' he added disingenuously.

# Chapter 17

## Choosing the Astronauts

*Men Wanted*

Victor hadn't anticipated the advent of social media when the phenomenon of Alumni had taken over the planet. What better medium to find the astronauts? There was a cohort of NASA's finest as a core, but now the stage was a multinational mission, there were complications. Ingrid de Gaul had been showing Henrietta and Yasmin how the Europeans did it. In her smooth French accent she explained, 'You know, the methodology always the same. Strict criteria to choose. Non-discrimination, there is equal chance for the women and the men. No, how you say, mention of age, or the disability. Completely fair.'

'OK, how'd ya choose anybody, if ya can't discriminate?' quizzed Henrietta.

'*Ce n'est pas un problème*. Two methods *en* application. In the north of Europe they use it to help them to make the rational judgements. In the south they make selection first and use it to justify their choice.'

'So, as long as all the boxes are ticked, it's all OK, then?'

'*Oui. Important!* Advertising non-exclusive, all the world welcome.'

'Mmm, we usually put the ad in *The Astronaut's Journal* – not the widest of readerships. Hey! How about posting it on Alumni?' Yasmin loved Alumni. 'I saw a post we could base it on the other day.' She searched on her phone.

'*The Times* – 1913. "Men wanted for hazardous journey, small wages, bitter cold, long months of complete darkness, constant danger, safe return doubtful, honour and recognition in case of success. Ernest Shackleton." It just about fits the bill! And they came back!'

They put an edited version on Alumni next to a photo of Mars, changing the word 'men' to 'crew' and ending it with a list of skills. It went viral!


The invitation went to the four corners of the world, including a small orphanage in Zimbabwe.

Zulu saw it when Jane replied to one of his many emails, giving him a link to the page. 'Try this' was her comment. Bheki brought him the message. 'Can we both go?'

Zulu studied the missive. 'Who's going to pick us? We're not Americans, we're too young and don't have any experience.'

'Jeez, Zulu, it doesn't say that. We got the skills on the list. Look, "engineers and botanists". We design and make machines and we look after plants! We're hands-on guys!'

'But we're kids, we're not educated, we're from Africa and you're deaf!'

'Sorry, I didn't hear that!'

Zulu made many hand gestures in Bheki's face, some of them rude. 'Ha, ha!'

'Ach! We're good, man. We're *politically correct*!'


Through the rain-streaked panes, Kirsten saw that the long Icelandic summer days were ebbing into depressing winter nights. 'Another two months and it'll be dark.' She braced herself and considered the merits of crisp snow and the glimmer of the northern lights. No, she wasn't looking forward to it at all. An email popped up on her screen, and she had a premonition that it might be interesting. 'Uh, NASA...' She clicked it. As she read it she realised that her trip to Italy hadn't been in vain. *Vow!* Winter in LA, and a role in the biggest show on the planet. Ford had nominated her to plan the geological goals of the mission and the expedition training, and they'd pay for Elin to go too. Among the attachments were two application forms for the crew.

Elin was kneeling in front of a little green shelf where she'd arranged the rocks she'd collected with her mother. She'd left a gap for a fragment of meteor. The country had been showered by them and she knew she'd find one soon. Her favourites were beautiful black obsidian samples. As she rearranged the rocks, she sang a little song:

*'Burn, set, be my rock of fire, a pebble for my heart's desire,*
*Lay me down on a river bed, a sandy stone for my head.'*

Opposite was her adventure kit: boots, backpack, waterproofs and Katla, her toy witch. The rain was clattering on the tin roof, so she didn't hear her mother enter. Two busy-fingered hands tickled her in the ribs, and up went half of the contents of the shelf as she reacted. 'Mummia, *ekki*!' she shrieked.

Her mother looked elated as she told her, 'We're going to Los Angeles. I've been offered a job and we can both go!'

She knew all about LA from the TV. 'Can we live in Bel Air?' She did a little jig, bouncing on the bed and rapping to an unheard beat.

*'Now, all about how this is a story*
*flipped-turned upside down my life got*
*And a minute I'd like you to take,*
*right there just sit,*
*how I became the princessa of a town called Falleg Loft I'll tell you.*
*In north Iceland town born and raised...'*

Her mother hugged her and told her about the offer. Elin listened intently, then interrupted. 'Look after Afi and Amma who's going to?' she asked, with a furrowed brow.

'Don't they look after you?'

'Oh no,' said Elin. 'Round the house I help, jokes I tell and talk to Afi when Amma's away. Besides nothing will they will have to do. Only left with the animals they will be.'

She sensed her mother stifling a laugh. 'Don't worry, they'll be OK. You can look after me instead. Also, they sent an astronaut application form!'

Recalling Pompeii, Elin couldn't restrain her excitement. 'For me?'
Kirsten laughed. 'Well, they sent two... Now that would be the
biggest adventure for us, a trip to Mars!'

'The first princess of Mars, can I be! You can be queen. Bring
Katla, can I? The red elves she wants to meet.'


A warm breeze wafted through the vines as the family sat down to eat
after the long lunchtime shift. Enza served the tortellini she had made
with the lightest of pasta, wrapped round a pungent mushroom and
garlic filling. The creamy balance of the cheese and asparagus sauce
lifted their hearts and stomachs. Her father, distracted on his phone,
jolted to attention as the dish was served. 'I was just looking at this
Alumni post. It's Ford's mission! Volunteers needed!'

Elisabetta calmed him down. '*Allora, amore*, they'll only want
proper astronauts.'

'Italians have always been the best explorers: Marco Polo,
Columbus!'

There was a small moment for grace before they ate. Not another
word was said until her father gesticulated, waving his arms across
the table. 'If they're going for two years they'll need to eat properly.
They need a chef!' Elisabetta took the phone. 'Look at the skills. We
tick some of the boxes!'

Enza beamed. 'We are the perfect family, then!'

Her mother looked at Enza. 'Let's work on the Temple of Mars
tomorrow, and beg his blessing.'


The Grand Canyon walls stretched high above the river as it wended
its way through the cake-like strata. Russet and buff ochres, blue and
grey skies, and a fringe of green lining the red water made a palette
of this epic landscape. Alim scrutinised the sedimentary beds like the
leaves of a mile-high encyclopedia. Counting the 40 major layers, he
saw a snapshot of half the history of the Earth: from the rocks at their
feet, laid down 2 billion years ago, when only single-celled organisms
thrived, to a point high above them where the landscape met the sky,
and a world full of exotic flora and fauna. Alim's hand traced the
layers to a spot about halfway up. 'Can you see all these layers? In all
that time, life only went from a sludge to bacteria, and then where the
colour changes, it got interesting.

'Three things changed everything: oxygen, sex and teeth!'

He pointed to another change. 'You get the development of complex organisms, like sponges and fungi and corals, until – *whoosh!* – the extraordinary last fifth, an explosion of evolution of all the life we have today.'

> **The Grand Canyon**
> Colorado, USA
> 36.1N 112.4W
> Altitude: 2,600ft
> 277 miles long
> Geology: River valley canyon

Alim was going to show Mo the American West and this couldn't be a more awe-inspiring place. He'd come here as a young man and been blown away by seeing a dynamic planet laying down its story, millennium upon millennium.

'Is there a canyon like this on Mars, Baba?'

'The Valles Marineris would dwarf this one – it's five times longer and four times as deep. What a story that would tell!' He shook his bag of tools. 'It's why we're here. I want to find a layer where we'll find something like that fossil from Mars, and then we'll work out how it could have happened so early.'

He parked his dusty bottom on a rock that contained the forgotten remnants of thousands of tiny life forms and carefully lit a cigarette, while lamenting his lack of fitness. 'I'd love to go and see it myself, but you have to be "A1 fit"!'

Mo sat down, leaning on his father's knees. He scrutinised the valley. 'I'm fit! I'd be your eyes. You've taught me everything.'

> **The Valles Marineris**
> Mars
> 13.9s 59.2W
> Altitude: 23,000ft deep
> 2,500 miles long
> Geology: Largest canyon in the solar system

Alim replied with a snort, 'You're too young, my boy, and besides, it's too dangerous!'

Mo was having none of it. 'I've seen the advert. It didn't mention age, and it can't be more dangerous than going to school. If you hadn't turned up, I would have drowned with my class!'

His father considered his point. 'A stroke of luck, of course, and we're also lucky to be on top of all this evolution, but unfortunately – like my fossils one day – we'll be gone.'

Alim reflected further on the matter. 'You're right! We should make the most of it, my boy! Let's send off the damned applications!'

He didn't take it seriously. Does anyone ever expect to win the lottery? What Mo knew was that you can't win without a ticket.

They were almost out of the canyon when they stopped again. The river now looked like a tiny red ribbon. 'Everything below us is simple life, where nothing had even ventured onto the land, and above us is diversity.' Alim pointed to a line in the cliff just over their shoulders. 'That's where I want us to look, where we'd find our little fella if it lived on this planet.'

They reached a narrow band of limestone that stretched like buried snow towards Las Vegas.

Alim took out the tools but, before he could even start, Mo was chipping away. 'There's loads of them!' He started to work carefully. 'We've seen these before: they're nautiloids.'

Alim was pleased. The fossils were the right mix of shells and soft bodies, and proper animals, like a squid with a cone-shaped shell. He explained to Mo that if his role with NASA was to interpret the fossils found by the rover, he could only start with something similar on Earth. 'What we have to work out is how it happened so quickly on Mars.'

His son looked quizzically. 'Or why so long on Earth?' Mo suggested.

'What do you think?' questioned his father.

'It's just chance, innit? It's like if I toss a coin loads and loads of times, at some point I'll get a string of heads. If I do it a thousand times, like, I'll maybe get ten in a row at some point. I'd be amazed if it happens straight off, but there's no reason why not. If I did the lottery, why not one, two, three, four, five, six and bonus ball seven! Because it's no different from any other set of numbers. It's better, 'cause it reminds me it's all just chance. Maybe Mars got lucky.' For an instant he thought of the cold, barren planet today and added, 'Then unlucky!'

Alim smiled a benevolent smile. 'Well, school may be dangerous, but at least they're teaching you maths!'

Behind them a buzzard wheeled its way across the sky, was picked up by a thermal and escaped into the wide blue yonder.


Henrietta and Yasmin were really enjoying presenting their report to Ford and Stephen. Henrietta started. 'We've had over a million hits on the advert, and half of them have filled in the questionnaire.'

Yasmin took over with her typical enthusiasm. 'Hey, there's all sorts of people, not just astronauts. All ages, all sexes and from the four corners of the globe.'

'There'd hardly be a million astronauts out there, and globes don't have corners!' Stephen said bluntly. 'It's too many – you'll never sort out the time wasters. Even I filled out the questionnaire out of interest, but there's no way I'd go.'

Yasmin clapped her hands. 'Oh, Stephen, we'd love to send you!'

'Yeah, and I'd like to send my ex!'

Henrietta explained that ESA had written them a program to use for elimination. ESA had embedded strict criteria within the questions, with each stage designed to reduce the pool of applicants by half. Then, opening a laptop, Henrietta started to run the program. There were 491,520 'applicants'. As the program rolled, the numbers diminished until, after the 12th stage, they were left with 240. 'Much more manageable!'

Ford was intrigued. 'Well, I filled it out, just to test it. Am I still there?'

Yasmin shuffled a bit. 'Er, well, no. Neither is Stephen. You're both needed here, so automatic veto! But we're not just relying on social media. We have our cadre of astronauts, and several scientists we're interested in. We are going to whittle it down to a squad of 12 and see how they perform.'

Stephen picked up the laptop and started to scan the list of 'weeded' applicants. 'Your algorithms are ridiculous. It's a load of old men, women and kids!'

Henrietta carefully took the computer from Stephen. 'There's no problem with the program. I'm afraid it's going to be more like *Lost in Space* than *Star Trek*. We can't take anyone between the ages of 15 and 40, because of the health risks. The astronauts will have to be light, with at least two core skills, and be an international mix.'

Stephen waved a hand dismissively. 'You can get rid of the kids for a start. Who's going to sanction sending kids into space?'

At this point Ford intervened. 'Actually, the president! He's given us the OK for their evaluation.'

Henrietta had been altogether sceptical at first, but four issues had convinced her. Firstly, there were children out there who had the skills; secondly, children appeared to be less susceptible to the health issues than adults; thirdly, and most importantly, they were light, so a full crew could be sent.

Stephen was finding this irritating. 'You said four issues?'

'Ah, yes,' said Henrietta, 'the fourth – we don't have to make the decision, it's down to the president.'

Among the many names on the shortlist were candidates from Iceland, Italy, Zimbabwe, London and Baton Rouge.

# Chapter 18

## Testing Times

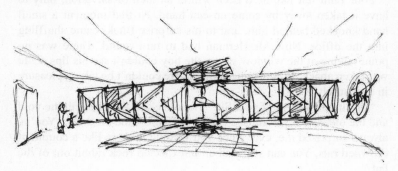

*G Machine*

The acrid smell of dust filled Zulu's nostrils as he frantically swept the yard. He had been doing every job he could, hoping that, by showing his usefulness, it might persuade Mr Herman to give him a reprieve. He was a proud young man and was not prepared to beg for it.

It felt like living on a knife edge. So when one of the youngsters shouted for him, he nearly jumped out of his skin. 'Mr Herman wants to see you.'

'OK, this is it!' His mind ran over whether there was anything he could have done to change the outcome. On the way he dragged his feet. The red dust kicked up as he crossed the courtyard. The surrounding granite outcrops looked like sombre giants. He took a deep breath on the threshold of the office and thought, 'I need to keep myself together.' He pinched himself to break away from the anxiety.

*Knock, knock!* The door was ajar and it gave way a little each time he rapped.

'Come in, my boy,' called Mr Herman. Zulu peeked round and his erstwhile father figure could not even face him. Mr Herman was standing, looking out of the grime-streaked panes. The poster on the wall of a far-eyed prophet quoted some comforting words. Zulu was glad he didn't have to face his mentor; it would have been worse for both of them.

'Do I have to go away, then?' Zulu broke the silence, taking in the details of the office, with the realisation that it would soon become just a memory.

'Yes,' replied Mr Herman. 'I was about to offer you a few more months, especially seeing you working so hard, but not now.'

Poor Zulu felt like he'd been within an inch of salvation, only to have it taken away by some unseen hand. At that moment a small hand knocked behind him, and to his surprise Bheki came shuffling into the office. Now Mr Herman had to turn round. There was no point talking at the window where the boy couldn't see his lips. Zulu was taken aback. Why was he smiling? He couldn't be taking pleasure in this, surely?

'Do sit down, both of you. Sit!' The old clock ticked to fill the void and the older man scrutinised the fresh faces of the brothers. 'You've always surprised me, ever since you washed up here like a couple of drowned rats. You can still pull an unexpected rock rabbit out of the hat.'

The two boys were wondering what on earth he could be talking about.

'Zulu, I know your greatest fear was leaving Bheki. Well, I've some sad news. I'm losing both of you!'

The boys looked at each other. 'What have we done? Why are you sending us both away?'

'I'm not doing the sending. I've told you to be careful with your wishes, as they sometimes come true. You're off to the USA!'


The votive offerings of olive oil and salt at the Temple of Mars had worked their magic. Enza had laid them on the small altar in the ruins. An email had just invited Enza and her mother for evaluation in the States. Giulio was putting a brave face on it. He'd been rejected. Someone had to run the restaurant and with the season ending he'd cope. Anyway, they'd soon be back.


Ford saw Buzz's name on the long list of applicants. Buzz had not mentioned it, in case Ford would have said no. Henrietta assured him that it had gone through according to due process.

Mo and his father were also called, much to Alim's alarm.

It was a bright morning with a slight scent of autumn in the air, as the light streamed through the vertical windows of the hangar door.

An apprehensive crowd had gathered in the vastness of the testing facilities. Whether novices or old stagers, there was no one here who didn't feel a frisson of anticipation.

To the left were the clean-cut men and women from the astronauts' pool, then a badly dressed group of scientists. In the centre was a smart Chinese contingent, and to the right a host of 'can't quite believe I'm here' Alumni applicants.

Yasmin took the stage, and with a large electronic blackboard, she explained the formula for the next week. The first hurdle was designed to weed out those unable to withstand the rigours of space flight and isolation. They could call themselves only by their allocated number, and could leave at any time, sworn to secrecy, with the promise of a cash reward when the mission started. 'What goes on in the hangar stays in the hangar!'

Across the crowded room, Buzz was excited to see his friends Elin and Enza standing with their mothers. They rushed through to meet him.

'Buzz, we all made it!' they screamed.

Buzz looked at the other 237 people there.

'There's a whole heap of people here,' he whispered to Enza.

She was wide-eyed with excitement. 'What they going to do with us?'

'Granf told me it's all physical at first. They throw us about a lot!'

Elin was intrigued. 'Wow, other kids there are, and oldies. One, his cigarette he had to put out!'

There was a maelstrom of activity where they had to change into their designated white, blue or red overalls.

Coming back into the hall, they were taken in mixed groups of six to a field of forty airstream trailers.

The flat dirt parking lot resembled a scene from Mars, as the stainless-steel streamlined shapes gleamed in the sun against the red desert earth.

Elin walked with her mother, her spirit of adventure melting as she eyed their fellow applicants. Each trailer or 'pod' had a black tent outside where the applicants were blindfolded before being called for the tests.

The pod interiors were white plastic with blackout windows. There was a cramped WC and padded benches where they'd live, eat and sleep for the next seven days. By each door was a large red button that they could press at any time if they wanted to go home.

By the end of the first morning at least 10 people had opted to push the red button.

In the pod the seats were arranged to face each other. Elin and her mother sat impassively in their blue overalls, and before they could introduce themselves, even by their numbers, the intercom crackled. 'Candidate numbers 68 and 69, please make your way to the airlock.'

Everyone hurriedly checked their badges and two slight middle-aged women got up and hurried out without speaking. Nobody dared talk, until a grey-haired man proffered a hand.

'I'm not a man, but a number. Seven!' Laughing, he pointed to his red overalls. 'I'm from the astronaut corps!'

Kirsten laughed herself. 'We're 123 and 124 – scientists.'

He took a long look at Elin. 'They must start them young in…?'

'Iceland,' answered the girl proudly.

He moved to one of the vacant seats. 'Don't worry, we won't see many coming back. I've done this before!'

'Good, there's room for my elf,' Elin said, beaming. They chatted with Number 7, and he was regaling them with tales of the space station.

Numbers 68 and 69 never returned. Number 7 was called and returned looking green-faced.

The monotony wore on until finally Kirsten and Elin were called. Blindfolded, they left the trailer for the great hangar.

Elin brimmed with excitement as she removed the blindfold. They were in a large circular room with a lattice-like structure in the middle. This looked better than anything at Disneyland. 'Mummia, it's fantastic, and no height restrictions!'

The technician explained the procedure and Elin and Kirsten were strapped in at opposite ends of the vast armature. 'Just hit the button when it gets too much. Don't worry, everyone does it. It goes to 20G!'

The lights grew dim as they started spinning, and they were pressed back in their seats like they would be in a sports car.

Pleasant at first, it built up speed, and Kirsten felt uncomfortable, head pressed onto the chair. The room was tumbling past faster and faster.

A grey haze clouded her vision as she fought against hitting the stop button. Kirsten gritted her teeth as her lips stretched. 'I can't let Elin down!'

'Wheeeeee!' Elin was shouting, almost immune to the forces thrown upon her. '*Hraðar, hraðar!*' she hollered. Faster, faster! The bright swirling spotlights merely added to the fun for her.

Just before Kirsten passed out, eyes bulging, saliva dribbling around her cheeks, she hit the button. They helped her to the chairs by the door, where many took their chance to escape, especially after hearing the request that they swap ends for the second run. '*Yndislegt*, Mummia!' Elin came skipping over. 'Another go we have. Did you enjoy it?'

> **Centrifuge**
> Astronauts and pilots endure forces above anything encountered in everyday life. Standing = 1G; taking off in a rocket = 3G: effectively three times as heavy – equivalent to the most extreme funfair rides. An untrained individual will black out between 4G and 6G. The centrifuge trains individuals to withstand these forces.

Kirsten hadn't felt so ill since a *Jannith* with her college friends.

Mo was mortified when the technicians came to get them. His old man was already skulking in the 'airlock' having a crafty cigarette. Alim swiftly extinguished it with his heel. He dived back inside, waving his hands through the air. Mo couldn't believe his irresponsibility. 'Dad, you're *so* embarrassing!'

They were taken to Room 2. In the middle sat a contraption looking like a cross between an electric chair and a pneumatic drill. On the arm rests were a series of coloured buttons, and on the panel opposite a console of coloured lights. The chair had heavy straps, resembling blood pressure cuffs.

Mo was first. Every part of him was strapped down.

Mo's only movement was in his hands, which could just reach all the buttons. He had to recall the colours and press the buttons to match the lights.

The run started and Mo's deft fingers hit the correct buttons almost instantly.

Then the chair beneath him started to move, first like a bumpy road, then intensifying until he felt like a biscuit tin in a rockfall. As the shaking built up, so did the flashing, and his fingers fought to co-ordinate with his darting eyes.

His quick reactions and young stomach matched the challenge and he only missed a couple of hits.

Watching his son in this instrument of torture filled Alim with great trepidation and a need for the gents. How was he going to get through this hell? He recalled another hell he'd endured. Caught in the teeth of an Antarctic blizzard while chipping out metamorphic rocks, he'd kept up his spirits by singing.

**Juddering Machine** Tests and trains pilots, especially helicopter pilots, to operate in conditions of extreme vibration. The vibrations of a rocket travelling into orbit, or during re-entry, are extreme.

As the machine wound up and became a gizzard-stretching judder, Mo couldn't believe his ears when his father's voice rose above the clatter.

'*The morning breaks my heart...*' – lights flashed and Alim's fingers hit the buttons – '*... you're shaking me apart...*' – red, blue, red, green – '*...Winter snowfall, winter snowfall is no blanket for my bed...*' It was the only song to which Alim knew all the words, and the louder he sang, the less he thought of his wobbling belly, juddering teeth and loosening bowels. '*... summer sun is long dead...*'

The machine finished its inquisition and, exhausted and desperate to escape, Alim stumbled back to discover to his surprise that he'd almost matched Mo's score.

For the two orphans, it was already like being on Mars compared with home.

'I'm not going in there!' Zulu signed to Bheki, staring into the ice-blue waters. Nestled in an echo-filled hall, a tank designed for practising space walks spread out before them.

'You'll make a great hippo,' Bheki signed.

'We can't swim!' Zulu mouthed.

'You don't need to swim on Mars!'

The attendants interrupted, 'Please get into the spacesuits.'

The boys were lowered to join the awaiting frogmen and were shown the tasks ahead. They were left suspended in the blue void, in eerie silence except for the wheeze of the oxygen.

As the bubbles subsided, they peered out into a world of minimalist abstraction. Being non-swimmers was an advantage for them. Breaststroke didn't work in the cosmos. They had two handheld thrusters and a small squirt of the triggers set them off in the generally desired direction. There were a number of semi-floating platforms tethered to the depths. They felt their suits tauten as they descended, the intercoms giving them instructions.

Bheki at first felt frozen and confused, but his brother's signals calmed him.

They were children of the granite of their homeland and had seldom been freed from its earthly bounds; now the heavy weight of their lives was lifted from their shoulders for the first time.

Bheki felt the exhilaration of this freedom and his heart raced as he followed Zulu. Many had already failed there, either dropping components, shooting past the modules or unable to communicate visually. These two boys were completely used to working in harmony and silence.

The **Weightless Tank** has been continuously used to train astronauts to carry out repairs and operations during space walks. There is no resistance in space, so the trainees have to learn to work in an environment where every action taken has an opposite reaction, and none of the normal earthly resistance can be relied upon.

Compared with making things from a scrapyard, it was easy to fix the parts in the locations on the large tubular structure. But this void was unnerving. The timeless, dimensionless abstraction tempted the mind to wander and the imagination to fill the emptiness.

Zulu was always aware of danger behind a thicket or an outcrop of rocks. But here he felt the threat in every direction he wasn't looking. On land it was only behind him, here also above and below.

His anxiety was rising when he peered into the deep and saw shadowy monsters coming towards them. He was engulfed in a rush of bubbles as a smooth black form grasped his shoulder. Convinced that the creature's teeth would rip open his suit, he fought off the unfortunate frogman who'd come to guide him back.

When the boys walked to their pod, the sun was hanging red in the sky. As they trod the churned earth, they saw that the numbers of trailers had been reduced by half.

On entering, they saw three new faces staring at them. They took their seats with downcast eyes and sat dumbly, swinging their legs. Of their original group, only the feisty American woman remained and she alone shared a smile with them. The silence was deafening and Zulu was relieved when she eventually nudged him. 'Hey! How'd it go? I've not done this since my days on the barge!' Her accent was strange.

'Kugona!'

She recognised his accent though. 'Hey, you from Africa – brother? Pa's from Zanzibar!'

'We're from Zimbabwe. This is my brother, he's called "Number

2"!' Zulu smirked and gave Bheki a shove. The boy's face stretched with a smile that would disarm a dik-dik. 'We went swimming!'

It was a strange night for everyone: airline-style meals, squeezing into the bathrooms and sleeping uncomfortably. It was a mini-test of the claustrophobia they'd endure if selected. There was a trickle of escapees throughout the night, diminishing the numbers still further.

The dawn's golden hue cast itself on the silver camp, unseen by the inmates in their shuttered pods. Only Alim witnessed the break of day as he stole into his smoking chamber.

To heighten the sense of uncertainty, they were kept waiting until the afternoon. Those who have endured years in captivity, from Cervantes to Mandela, have all learned that patience is essential to survive a long confinement.

Enza shared her iPod with her mother. By lunchtime she'd been driven to the edge of reason by Giustino Biebero and was desperate to be called to their next test.

The relief was short-lived for Elisabetta. This equipment looked like an ancient celestial orb. There was a series of pivoted rings, with a seat in the centre. They allowed the body to spin on three axes. Enza stood in glee. 'Mama, you go first – *fantastico*!'

Elisabetta had survived the centrifuge, but this was three dimensions.

Enza was shocked. She was used to seeing her mother take everything in her stride. 'I'll show her how to do it!'

She rushed forward to the waiting bench. As the machine started to move, her body slowly revolved forward. She kept her eyes open as the lights streamed in, trailing blazing streaks, as the machine accelerated and weaved continuously. The stretch and twist exhilarated her. For her young body, unblemished by alcohol, tobacco or any other substances, it was a brush with the thrill of intoxication as she felt the rush of blood to her head and toes.

The complete feeling of abandonment brought a sense of well-being she had never experienced before.

By the time Enza had finished, Elisabetta was sitting with her head between her hands. 'I can't do it, *piccola*!' She started sobbing. 'I've let you down.'

Enza desperately tried to reassure her. 'But it's fun, Mama!'

Elisabetta howled. 'I can't do it! We'll have to go home!' Two of the assistants started guiding her to the door. She broke away and turned back. 'What about Enza?'

'Oh, she did very well!'


The tap of someone walking determinedly resounded along the empty corridors of the JPL, followed by the crash of opening double doors and an angry knock. Then the raging rocket man burst in.

'Oh, hi, Milton! How's it going?' was the shame-faced chief engineer's weak response.

'It's gone, goddammit, that's how it's flaming going! You're behind this, you dishonest, despicable, deceiving creep! All this "Oh, Milton, we're so interested in your rocket" and all that bilious bull! To think I offered you sons-of-bitches part of my collection and wasted my precious time helping your pathetic pursuits!'

Ford raised a hand.

'No! You dare stop me!' screamed Milton. 'You come over in the dead of night and steal the pride of America, the heart of the museum, my joy and the focus of all my energies for as long as I can goddamn think.'

Pointing his index finger at Rocky, he spat, 'And *you, you* have the disgraceful, despicable disrespect to take it when I'm on a well-earned holiday, without a word, consultation or even a nod to the most basic conservation principles, and leave behind a goddamn note! A flaming note! *Removed for restoration!*'

There was no stopping the man.

'I have never experienced such bare-faced, lowdown, turpitudinous cheek.' Milton took a deep breath. 'Removed for restoration... removed for restoration... restoration for freakin' what?'

Ford had only one word of defence: 'Flight!'

The red face turned to Ford. 'Flight! Whaddya mean, flight?'

Ford looked down at his feet. 'It's like this, Milton. When we saw what an obsessive... no... immaculate job you had made of the restoration, we realised you had solved our problem. There was a ready-made rocket waiting to take our mission to space, and we just felt that after all the dedication you had put in... you kinda might have objected...'

'What, you gonna fly that thing?'

'Yep.'

'You mean you're going to *fly* my baby?'

'Yes, Milt.'

'You're going to set her free?'

'Sure.'

'Like Elsa?'

Rocky interjected. 'More like *Free Willy*.'

Milton stared indignantly. 'I don't watch films like that!' Turning to Ford, he asked, 'You actually mean you're going to fly her?'

'Yes, Milton, she's going to take us to Mars!'

The anger flooded again over Milton's face. 'You cretins, stupid baboons, untrusting rats! Why didn't you just *ask*? The years I've slaved over that beauty, the unappreciated sweat, for what? For a load of dumb, gum-chewing kids to gawp and take selfies with. "Generation Stupid" casting their banal, thoughtless lives onto a self-indulgent post on Alumni, where the peak of achievement is 100 likes.

'Fly that magnificent bird – why didn't you say?'

'We didn't think you'd agree.'

'Hell, yes! That's what she was made for, not to slumber in a museum.'

There was a pause for reflection.

'Besides, if we can retrieve any of the stages she'll really have historic value. Not just the rocket that never made it to the moon.'

Milton joined the team.


In the editorial conference of Pure Media's *Daily Planet*, another heated debate was under way. Victor was laying it on the line.

'It's not for me to dictate editorial policy, but what's the point of owning a newspaper if it doesn't support the corporation? We have interests in space and I don't like big government, and especially not this mission.'

'But, sir, *editorial freedom is a horse that pulls a cartload of responsibilities*. I have it framed on the wall!'

This was how Victor wanted it. 'Yes, responsibilities to me!'


By day three, the testing and isolation had taken their toll and a large proportion of the Alumni cadre had voted with their feet.

The prospect of being locked up for two years in a celestial caravan had hit home. Yasmin addressed the diminished crowd gathered in the hangar. 'Till now, everyone has gone home of their own volition. Well done for sticking it out so far. Now it's time to put a few parameters in place to sort the cats from the dogs.

'First we're going to take some blood samples.'

Three would-be astronauts fainted and were helped out.

Enza was confused and isolated. She nervously looked around the great edifice and caught the eye of a slight black-haired girl.

Chao-xing was trying to stay focused, but couldn't ignore the sad-eyed girl. She gave Enza a discreet smile. When they were asked to line up in designated groups, Enza sneaked in behind Chao-xing.

Living in a tourist spot like Pompeii, she had no problems introducing herself to strangers. 'Hi,' she said tentatively, 'is that your mama?'

'Oh, my mom. Yes, she a pilot. Why you on your own?'

'Mama couldn't stand being thrown around. She spends her time in the ground, not above it!'

'Why you still here, then?'

'We'd never actually gone together and they didn't tell me to leave or perhaps I just didn't press the button.' Then she remembered the 'Trumpers'. 'And... I've got skills and I'm little... and I loved the rides.'

'Oh, me too. They ask for good parent–child teamwork. Mom is biologist as well as pilot. She study effects of flight. She teach me everything. We all "only child" in China, so we have strong bond!'

Enza thought of her skills again. 'Me too. I'm artistic and can cook, and I help my mama with her work.'

Chao-xing grinned. 'Oh I cook too. I love noodles!'

'*Amo* pasta!' replied Enza, thrilled to find common ground. Marco Polo would have been delighted.

The girls were each called through. They were measured and weighed; then their reactions, eyesight and hearing were tested. Bone mass, BMI, blood tests and finally a whole-body MRI scan finished the intense examination. It took all day and was exhausting.

Bheki and Zulu waited in line. It had been one big adventure and even the pods were luxurious compared with the orphanage.

However, this medical examination brought back the intense memories of the terrible day they had arrived at the orphanage, when they were prodded and poked as if they were cattle. They'd only encountered stethoscopes and an ageing X-ray machine before. To see the workings of your body being reconstructed before your eyes was as magical as the diagnosis given by the spiritual doctor in the village.

It only reinforced Zulu's respect for her. He thought of the times she'd helped with the problems with the livestock or crops. He aired his thoughts.

> **Amadlozi**
> African mythological figures of the Zulu people. They are the ancestors of the Zulu, and can be summoned for assistance.

'This is how the *amadlozi* do it, brother. Their energy flows through you to find out the illness. SRI scan – spiritual resonance imaging!'

He beat an imaginary drum frantically and shook his head to the shamanic beat, before descending into hysterical laughter. 'They need machines to do it instead!'

Elin and her mother had survived the ordeal intact. Unlike most adults, Kirsten had relished the physical testing, and the hours in the pods were no worse than the winter darkness on the edge of the Arctic.

Until then Elin had been proud of her mother's performance, then blew it at the medicals. They were supposed to present in their underwear.

'*Ekki, Móðir,*' Elin screamed. Kirsten had totally stripped off. 'A swimming pool this isn't! So embarrassing are you!'

Buzz had never been to the doctor's on his own. Even his mother would fuss over him when he was ill. During his medical evaluation he was sullen and listless until he saw the big MRI machine.

'Wow, that's cool!' His scan was delayed until the assistants had completely described the theory and its workings. 'You're gonna model me in the computer? Shame it can't run around and fight!'

Mo was surprised he heard his father announce that he only smoked and drank socially.

'Well, I don't do it antisocially,' said his father with a grin.

When all the remaining candidates had returned to collapse wearily in their pods, the evaluation team got to work.

Yasmin, Henrietta and Sharon drank coffee and ate cookies as they reviewed the process. Of the original 240 applicants, there were 119 left.

Waiting for a quorum, they chatted, swapping stories about the events so far – the guy who kept stealing out for a cigarette; the pluckiness of the little girl left without her mother.

Then Yasmin told them about the two African boys. 'When they had the hearing test, the brother tried to cover for the little one. He stood on a chair, looking over the screen, and mimed the answers.'

'Well, there's two we can cross off for a start,' said Henrietta, voicing her presumption.

'No, the kid was so good at lip-reading, all the staff were fooled until the big one fell off the chair!'

The computer weeded out those who were too heavy or unhealthy and had struggled with the physical tests.

Alim survived by the skin of his roll-up.

The computer had chosen most of the astronaut corps and Chinese cadre and, surprisingly, most of the children.

Then there were those on the borderline – mostly scientists and Alumni candidates to be weeded out further. 'We are going to have to get this lot down to the final 50,' said Sharon.

Edward Stalk objected. 'You can't get rid of all the specialists. It's not their fault they are unfit and untrained. You need to balance the odds. And you need to choose 48, not 50.'

He went on to explain his theory of numbers. Twelves are more useful than tens – they are more easily divided, like selling cakes. Twelves were the original digital (finger) counting system. Shepherds would count their sheep by touching the segments of each finger with the tip of their thumb with one hand, then each dozen with the other, rather than counting to 10 using each finger. He excitedly demonstrated how they could count to 144 with only 10 fingers, then looked round for the astonished faces.

Henrietta was rummaging in her handbag.

Sharon was writing an email on her phone.

Yasmin broke away from her daydream of shopping in Paris and brightly smiled. 'Whatever... Time to get on. We'll be here till midnight if we don't watch it.'

Sharon refocused on the task. She might have missed all the number theory, but the salient point of the filters had hit home. 'OK, we'll put in another factor then – they have to have more than one skill!'

They re-ran the program and there was movement between the groups. 'See, the one who took her clothes off is now in the top group!'

'She deserves an extra two marks for that alone!' said Edward, beaming, then wilted under the focus of three pairs of laser eyes. 'Sorry, bad joke!'

After about an hour they had boiled the numbers down to 48.


Enza was disappointed not to go back to the same pod as her new friend. She worried about her mama. She sang softly to her iPod to take her mind off her loneliness.

> '*I'm lost in the big country, and there's no highway to you,*
> *I'm lost in the big country, and there's no highway to you,*
> *Just wander down the lonely streets, hoping to come through,*
> *I'm lost in the big country.*'

'Hey, that's Giustino! He's cool!'

Enza looked to the side and there was a slight woman about the same age as her mother. Enza studied the dark eyes and smooth, tanned face. She felt sure she'd seen her before. 'You look familiar, are you famous?' she asked sheepishly.

'Yeah, I'm famous for being me!'

Enza smiled. 'So am I, *sono quello che sono*! Like to listen?' She handed over one of the earphones and they both sat swinging their legs in harmony to the music.

Soon the tannoy was calling individuals to the airlock until they were alone, with only the *tsch-tsch-tsch* of the music playing in the background.

'Listen, I love this bit... *My heart breaks like a wave across the sea... My heart breaks like a wave across the sea.*'

The woman gave a crooked smile. Then a faraway look entered her eyes.

'That's where *my* heart is!'

Enza laughed for the first time since her mama had left. 'You're funny!'

The woman offered a high five to the little girl. *Smack!*

'Better funny than sad! Hey, we're the only ones left?'

That night they were alone together in the pod, not knowing their fate. It wasn't until late next morning that they were finally called.

They hadn't disclosed their names, but shared life stories. Enza's was short. She knew it had only just begun, yet it was a lifetime for her.

She adored her companion's tales of Zanzibar and New York, the tug boats and the taxis. This woman had done and seen so much. In return, Enza told stories of other people's lives in the Roman city. Most of all she told her about Lavinia, and what she'd hoped had happened to her.

In the next pod along, another group had been trying to sleep. After a terrible night Alim stirred groggily and shuffled to ease his aching neck. Just being confined in the pods was a test for an individual's endurance. Blood was left splattered on the walls of the Russian space station after a fist fight between cosmonauts. The cramped conditions could amplify personal differences exponentially.

Although the caravans dated back to the 1960s, they'd been fitted to have the sort of airline seats you can never comfortably sleep in. 'Bloody ridiculous!' he commented to himself.

'What do you mean, bloody ridiculous?' a grey-faced astronaut snapped in a mocking faux accent.

'They've got Victorian chairs in my club that you can snooze in all afternoon with absolute comfort.'

The picture of Alim snoozing in a London club was too much. 'Do you snore and fart there too?'

Alim was affronted. 'I beg your pardon, old man, I never snore!'

Mo stifled a snort.

'Listen, Limey, you've kept me awake all night, so just shut it and stop shuffling!'

Alim had been called many things in his life, but never a 'Limey'.

'I take exception to that, old man.' Then he muttered, 'Buffoon.'

The pain of a sharp elbow in his ribs jolted Alim upright. After three nights in these cramped conditions, his neighbour had lost it.

'My goodness, it's just like Thursday prep!' His reaction came straight from his youth. In an action akin to his favourite cricket shot, the hook, he cranked his arms high and, swinging left, administered his own sharp elbow jab to his foe's temple.

'Oh, no!' moaned Mo, head in hands. He couldn't believe it – his dad was taking on an astronaut and the temporarily dazed figure was a real tough, chisel-jawed cookie.

'He's going to kill my dad!' Mo reacted in terror. Quick as a ferret, he bounded over and latched onto the astronaut's right arm that was about to be unleashed on Alim's jaw.

In fear for his son, Alim followed and plonked himself on the struggling astronaut's lap, grasping the man's left hand. They thought they had him pinioned but, with a yelp, a row of teeth had latched onto Alim's back.

He stamped his heel on the astronaut's vulnerable toe; the teeth disengaged with a scream of pain, but spurred the giant on to writhe free.

Chinese astronauts opposite couldn't believe their eyes and sprang to the rescue.

Leonard Wong leaped forward and squeezed the shoulder of the thrashing figure, who quivered and went limp. A long face peered out under the dark fringe.

'Great nimoy!' cheered his companion, applauding the deft martial arts move. Leonard was not only a Chinese astronaut, but a black belt in Vulcitsu.

When they were summoned by their minders, they left the figure unconscious in the pod. 'Having a lie-in, old girl,' Alim said to the technician with a grin.

# Chapter 19

## The Hard Work Starts

Milton surveyed his 'stolen' rocket. 'She's a beauty.' Even though they'd scratched the immaculate black and white paintwork.

'Where should we start?' asked Rocky. Milton was standing by the first stage, dwarfed by the five colossal rocket engines.

'Phew-ey, there's a question. The body's good, but the engines? We patched them up but never tested them.' He thought for a while. 'I spent a long time on that wiring, but I couldn't trust it. Fly by wire, it'll save tons of copper.' They made the long walk to the sharp end where the command module and lander had been.

'What about the payload?'

Milton made a mental calculation. 'She'll take quite a bit...We put Skylab in one of these, so that's your weight limit – 77 tons. Phew! There's a lot to pack in, though. The rest will have to go with the other rocket. Hey! There's a whole heap of designing to be done.'

Rocky slapped him on the back. 'That's the fun bit! Glad to have you on board, Milt.'

'Steady, Rocky. I've not quite forgiven you yet!'

Dolores, Patrick and Imran were sweating over thorny problems. The three Ls: living, landing and leaving.

*Living*. With the crew in space for eight months, on the surface for four and eight months back, keeping them breathing, fed and healthy in the harshest of environments was going to be an extraordinary challenge.

*Landing*. Putting the mission on the surface was difficult, because there was so much more weight than ever before. They had to come up with something radical. For instance, Mars has one hundredth the air pressure of Earth to slow any entering body down, and it's only slightly helped by having half the gravity. In a nutshell it's fifty times more difficult landing on Mars than returning to our own planet.

*Leaving*. All the rovers have been on a one-way trip. This mission had to get back home. Apollo returned from the moon, but on Mars the gravity is five times more, and this time they also had to get the bigger crew home. It would need something more substantial than the lunar module.

'Where to start, compadres?' With that, Dolores started the meeting.

Imran made the first pitch for the landing. 'Dump as much on the surface first, then land the crew. Leave the mothership in orbit for coming home. They can take off in their pants if necessary.'

Ford's idea of landing on Phobos was like the base camp on Everest – a stable platform to fire things onto the planet and a car park for the return rocket. They agreed to divide the landings into three operations.

First, the fuel generators. 'The solution's got to be the underground ice. It's all over the place,' Dolores explained. The ice could be metres down and the probes would have to be drilled into the ground to reach it. The idea they devised was elegant. Plutonium in the probes would get very hot and melt the ice, producing steam. Then the steam would build up until it was released through a valve within the hollow shaft. It would force its way through a turbine to generate electricity. Then by cooling into salty water, an electrolyte, the electricity could split it into oxygen and hydrogen. The gases would be collected by separate balloons, ready for use.

They considered mini-drilling rigs until Dolores worked frantically with her calculator. 'Damn, we need eight of them!' She looked at the photo of the Curiosity Rover on the wall. 'We've not got the room.'

Ford had been dealing with admin and needed a break. He'd hoped to join the team once he'd finished. The staff room was empty, but the aroma of coffee lingered on. He poured himself a cup and casually picked up the darts that were given to the project team, as a joke about staying on target. Ford had first played darts in Jane's Welsh local. He always found a few 'arrows' therapeutic. When the team burst into the room, he was on 80.

'I'll show them,' he thought. *Thud* – another triple. 'One hundred and twenty!' he announced.

Patrick had seen the dart hit the board as if in slow motion. The tip sinking into the red fibre, huddling close enough to the two other darts to make a soft *chink* as it came to rest. Inspired, he ran to hug him. 'You're amazing, Ford. You've cracked it!'

Ford felt flattered, but... 'Actually, 180 *would* be amazing.'

'Let me have a go!' Patrick snatched the darts from him and concentrated on the bullseye. A nice, tight group around the magpie proved his revelation. He cracked the problem and poured his coffee with a sense of great satisfaction.

'We don't need drills, we need penetrators – a set of darts. With the speed they'll hit the ground, they'll smash down to the ice and bingo! Look how deep the darts go into the board!'

Imran was making some tea. 'Won't they just break up?'

Patrick smiled. 'Barnes Wallis devised a spinning earthquake bomb. It'd burrow down deep before exploding. Still intact.'

They briefed Ford on their deliberations and Patrick sketched out a rudimentary design. The main body was just like a dart. The heated tip and thickened shaft formed the turbine chamber and electrolyte bath; the flights held three folded balloons. These would deploy to slow the dart to the optimum speed and fill to store the gas later.

Ford gave Patrick a hearty pat on the back and mimicked Jane's father's distinctive growl. 'Good arrows, boyo!'

'That's what Phobos gives you – a stable oche.'

The crew quarters and food could then be dropped like the early rovers in balloon-filled bags. The design of the Mariner module was the next big question mark. Even without the return fuel and kit, there'd be a 'shed load' to drop on the surface, as Patrick put it.

The last crewed lander NASA designed was the space shuttle, which glided home using the drag of the atmosphere to slow it.

'If we glide it,' Dolores chipped in, 'there's not enough lift in the atmosphere. We'd hit the surface long before it slowed and with no runway, the last stage will have to be rockets, just like the lunar module.'

'I know a big brake,' offered Ford. 'You know the planet's a pain to leave.'

Patrick nodded.

'But it's pulling us in when landing?' Dolores pointed out.

Ford thought of his recent plane ride and how he'd pulled up into a stall turn. 'Perhaps we don't try to land it at first,' he thought. 'Could we get any lift?'

Dolores didn't have to do much maths. 'Sure, we're so fast coming in there's a lot of pressure and lift.'

Following the train of thought, Ford continued, 'What if we don't try to land? We go in and then up, like a stall turn?'

Now Imran did the sums. 'Quite a few times, like skimming a pebble on the sea.'

The vision of the Pembrokeshire coast came to Ford's mind.

Carefree days with Jane, skimming rocks into the foam. They would jump in diminishing hops until they stopped and dropped.

'What about a flying saucer?'

'You've been watching too many movies,' joked Dolores.

Ford left them. There'd be a whole lot of hammering out to do before they got there. He had to make two calls.

Sharon picked up. 'Hi, Ford. We're fine. Hectic, but making progress. Even Mr Health and Safety's been helpful... Yes, Edward! He doesn't do people, but he does do process.' Sharon checked her lists. 'The astronauts are going strong. Hey, the kids are cool, they're lovin' it... No, Ford, I can't tell you about Buzz, they are all still numbers.' She chatted for a while longer then continued, 'It's a big day tomorrow: specialist tests – that'll push them out of their comfort zones!'

The team-room sofas were so old that Neil Armstrong might have graced them. The leather creaked as he called Jane.

'Well, hello, cariad!' Her tuneful voice lifted Ford's heart. 'It's been very quiet. Any news of Buzz?' She shuffled to get more comfortable. 'I suppose no news is good news? I won't fix him dinner. He must be hanging in there!'

She was keen to be helpful on the project. 'I've been looking at the images. The detail, it's amazing! There's a whole world out there!'

Seeing the awesome variety of the landscapes from the thousands of photographs taken from Mars Express, she'd even seen dark streaks of what could be running water. These 'Dark Streaks' are areas of Mars, often on the rims of old craters, where salty water appears to rush out. The intense saltiness allows it to remain liquid for a while, in the thin air and freezing temperatures. 'My Uncle Chedwyn was a coal miner, you know. "Hot and sweaty down there" – I can hear his voice now. If you can get water running on the surface, it's bound to be liquid beneath.'

'How deep was Chedwyn's mine?'

'Oh, 1,000 feet... Yes, too far for this mission, but we don't need it that hot.'

He told her that they'd set up a working party and maybe she could liaise with them. She was full of ideas. 'Yes, but there's too much for a small team. Crowdsource it on Alumni. It'd be a real hit, especially after the advert!'

Back at her desk Jane closed her eyes and opened her mind, imagining the scene from the bottom of an incline on the crater's bottom. She had seen the salt lakes of Tunisia with its crusty white salt, baked over hundreds of years. In her mind's eye, those dazzling white or rose-coloured salts were transformed into a translucent green-blue perchlorate skin with a sprinkling of red dust. A salt ridge had built up at her feet, and the undulating and smooth, pore-marked deposits draped the crater's escarpments like fallen sheets from a line. The crater base extended like a frying pan bottom until it met the encircling wall many miles behind. Towards the summit, the salt crusts gave way in a series of horizontal gashes with perhaps a glint of water. On high an orange and white wispy sky glowed with the Martian summer sun. Around midday, a faint ooze of a dark solution ran, bubbled and fizzed down the fissures and gullies, until collecting into long pools trapped by the sinuous dams formed in previous years. For a few days this would repeat itself, leaving the mark of each year like the rings on a tree.

With a tinge of sadness she recalled how Uncle Chedwyn had shown her the springs breaking out on the banks of the brooding slag heaps near his home and spoke softly of the terrible tragedy of Aberfan. A hillside of slag had engulfed the children of the local school, due to the leaching of the waters within.

Jane would sketch her ideas. It helped her see the task ahead of where to find something extraordinary to explore. She examined the annual methane maps where plumes of the gas emanated from within the planet. It doesn't hang around for long, quickly broken down in the harsh environment. It's either biological or geological in origin, either cause of great interest. She overlaid the ice deposits from the other maps. Then the volcanic areas that had sink holes and vents. Many of the circular depressions on Mars may look like impact craters, but are volcanic in origin and hold the key to accessing the interior.

Then the doorbell rang. There was a man standing clutching a black tool case. He was dressed in blue overalls sporting the name 'LEMON', the telecoms company. He flashed an ID card. 'Come to fix the phone, ma'am.' Without ceremony, he barged inside.

'Excuse me! Where do you think you're going? I've just been on it.'

He stood bag in hand and with a condescending smile. 'It's a silent fault. We traced it from the exchange – it could go at any time!' He turned again to go phone hunting.

'You just stop there, boyo!'

'Boyo, ma'am?'

Jane the biologist knew a rat when she smelled one. 'Show me that card!'

He flashed it at her again.

'I said show it to me, not waft it.'

He held it just long enough for Jane to see it was fake. To take the man off guard she gave him a smile and asked very sweetly, 'May I look in the bag, please?'

He felt he had nothing to hide, as this was only a woman.

'Thank you, so much.' She took the bag and examined it. There was a sad collection of tools, a notepad and some suspicious-looking electronic components. It certainly didn't look like the neat professional array that the broadband guy had brought. Jane closed it with a snap, turned and marched down the hall. There was a flash of coloured light as she opened the stained-glass door and flung it vigorously across the yard.

'Follow that! We got rid of our landline last year. All digital now, you see.'

He looked confused and didn't immediately leave. 'You don't understand the technology, ma'am, must be a crossed line.'

Suddenly Jane was in a fury. 'Yes I bloody do. I'll give you flaming crossed lines.' She held the door wide open, pointing determinedly as he reluctantly skulked out. She couldn't resist but to give him a shove across the threshold and he cartwheeled down the weather-worn veranda steps.

'I've not seen that kind of rejection since Christian Barnard's early patients!' laughed the driver as the dusty 'engineer' climbed into the waiting van. 'Sussed you out, did she?'

'They don't have a goddamn phone line to bug!' 'Mr Lemon' explained as he wearily took off his hat and asked. 'What about you?'

The driver smiled and held up his telephoto. 'I got some great action shots.' He flicked through the stills. 'Mad woman assaults humble telecom man! I can see the headlines.'

'Mr Lemon' gave a sheepish smile. 'At least we won't be going home empty-handed. I didn't know she dropped her freakin' landline last year.'

The driver bashed the steering wheel, screaming with laughter. 'Ha, ha, no wonder she rumbled you.'

'Yeah, she won't next time, though!'


The final forty-eight candidates entered the hall, where a series of squares were marked on the ground like a giant chequers board. This was to organise the candidates according to their aptitude. They needed at least two skills. The 'y' co-ordinates were the prime skills and the 'x' co-ordinates the secondary skills.

Each wandered over the grid to where their skills intersected until they had taken their spaces. They looked like a scene from *The Prisoner*. They were then summonsed to the testing labs.

Buzz was in the Pilot/Computing square which he shared with a fit-looking man dressed in red astronaut's overalls. He felt dwarfed by this latter day Trojan. An avuncular hand reached down to ruffle his hair. 'I wish they wouldn't do that!' he screamed internally.

He fiddled with his Xbox controller, his chosen personal item.

The idea was to have something that mattered to them as a point of discussion. Little use without the games centre, except Buzz could play for hours as prop for his imagination as he piloted spaceships, planes and cars behind closed eyes.

**Skills:** pilot – exploration – medicine – biology – mechanics – construction – communications – navigation – computing – recording geology – palaeontology – welfare and nutrition

There were four of them in the pilots' row and Buzz felt very stupid, as all the others were adults and had thousands of hours' experience. Save for the few occasions with Ford he'd only done it 'virtually'.

They were first called through and the butterflies jumped in his stomach as they filed down echoing corridors then up the skeletal steel stairs to a door with a stencilled sign, 'FLIGHT SIMULATOR', in bold, friendly letters.

The others were called first while Buzz nervously passed the time, fiddling with his Xbox controls. The simulator would bump into action, heaving to the constant whoosh of compressed air. In each session at least two catastrophic events must have happened as the machine lurched violently and died.

Then a dark-haired woman beckoned him to the capsule and explained they were to simulate Neil Armstrong's landing and docking on the first moon landing. To their horror, they discovered that he was too small to look out of the triangular window and reach the controls at the same time. Luckily Buzz could see that although the controls resembled Eagle, they were connected with a simple USB plug. He dropped out of sight and plugged in his Xbox controller.

The assistant smiled apologetically. 'I'm sorry, it will need reprogramming.'

Buzz smiled back. 'No problem, I can.' He could see the screen and keyboard just behind the seats. He fiddled with the settings and his handset to match them up to the levers and thrusters until they were working at his fingertips.

'Something to stand on!' Henrietta scooted out and returned with a box of Coca Cola cans waiting for a nearby vending machine. As they set it up they gave him a tip. 'Just miss the boulder field, and watch the fuel.'

Henrietta had a heart for the boy as he teetered on his makeshift platform, peering through the window, twiddling with his toy controls.

As he emerged from the 'flight', he was met with the sound of clapping. 'You did just great, kid!' Hen and the technicians welcomed him out.

'I hit the ground a bit hard,' he apologised modestly.

'Listen, kid, those guys practised it a thousand times and you did it first time and no one died. So... really cool.'

Sometimes it's best not to say too much; Buzz had done this a thousand times in 'The Eagle has Landed' game.


Bheki and Zulu shared the same square, the mechanic – welfare and nutrition combination. There were another four on the mechanics' line and they were called together. The room had five work benches. On each bench was a collection of junk and a number of non-matching filters and an old space suit.

Sharon addressed the room. 'You have three hours to resolve a life or death problem from fifty years ago. You're going to die unless you work out how to adapt these square $CO_2$ filters to fit the round holes of the fans. What's available on the table is all they had on Apollo 13.'

Zulu wildly signed to Bheki, 'Remember the film club?'

At the end of three hours only the boys' effort was happily chugging away, the square filters adapted with cardboard, plastic bags and duct tape with the hose and pump from the space suit all lashed together. The boys had three advantages.

One: There were two of them.

Two: It was second nature for them.

Three: There were only five films in their library and Herman's favourite was *Apollo 13*. They had seen it 65 times.

Sometimes you just get a lucky break.


Three candidates excelled in welfare and nutrition, and Enza was taken through with two fat ladies. They were subjected to a short interview. Yasmin smiled at her.

'You have two distinct skills: nutrition and recording. Why did you put cooking first?'

To Enza it seemed obvious, but she struggled for the words until she remembered her father.

'My papa always say "The discovery of a new dish is more precious to mankind than the discovery of a new star." Good food makes us happy and healthy.'

'OK, we use many freeze-dried ingredients in space trips, but we hope to grow some crops. What would you want?'

*'La scoperta di un piatto nuovo è più preziosa per il genere umano che la scoperta di una nuova stella.'*
– Jean Anthelme Brillat-Savarin

'I would grow garlic and herbs and tomatoes... I have to have olive oil and parmigiano for certain!'

They then entered a mock up of the space station galley.

'This is not a kitchen, it's an assembly line!' Enza exclaimed. 'I need a chopping board and a knife.'

She cleared a small space.

'Remember you can't make dust or bits to float around in a spaceship,' reminded Yasmin.

'I'm very, erm... tidy.' Enza smiled. Already on the table were her requested ingredients, and stored on the wall units were all the basics. She organised everything on the tiny space available and then took a bag and added some dried potato, flour, eggs, salt, pepper and a little olive oil and water, which she mixed into a paste and when it was firm she took it out.

She then smeared the knife with olive oil, which she also sprinkled over the herbs. She chopped the sage, basil and broad-leaved parsley finely and it all stuck together so she could add it easily to the rest of the olive oil she had put in the bag. She then took the dough and kneaded it, deftly turning it into small nuggets of gnocchi. She stood back for a moment and studied the scene. She filled the original bag with hot water and boiled the gnocchi in the microwave so they didn't stick. Then she added the cup of oil, crushed garlic and herbs to warm through. The parmesan was grated to coat the gnocchi. She cut the tomatoes into a fine salad and mixed the herby liquid with the gnocchi.

Enza's bright eyes gleamed as she served it in the special bowls, shaped to nestle in the hand in zero gravity.

'*Buon Appetito! Gnocchi alla Spazio,*' she announced with a flourish.

They descended on the food. In the frenzied silence there was only one comment. 'Best test yet!'

The examinations took the best part of the day before the candidates gathered once again in the hall. They waited apprehensively as the results were analysed. Henrietta had set up a table between two doors on the opposite side.

An expectant hush fell as she announced they'd made their selection, and when she called out their numbers they were to step forward and go through the door indicated.

No one knew which meant success or failure, except when a seasoned astronaut was called to the right door and Alim was called to the left it seemed pretty obvious. Except to Alim, who jogged to the right.

'Left, number 42,' she called after him.

'But it's to your left, my dear!'

She gave him a withering look as he scuttled back over.

The children saw little more as they were next and also called to the left. They were whisked into a changing room and then outside.

Bursting into the cool of the evening and free from the laboratories, tests and pods, they were glad to be back in their own clothes and letting off steam as they gambolled through a tree-lined campus. They were taken to a comfortable common room, with its plush leather settees and dark-painted walls plastered with jaunty comic posters. At the far end there was a roaring wood fire, where the kids sat down looking lost and subdued, like the failed candidates on a reality show.

Breaking their reflection, the door opened and peeping nervously from behind the architrave was a familiar face: Elisabetta.

'Mama!' Enza screamed and flew across the room to her. 'Have you come to take me home?'

There was a long pause as she accustomed herself to the lighting. 'No, I've come to join you!'

Following her were Alim, Kristin, Zulu and Su-lin.

By the flicker of the fire, Sharon explained that no one was going home. This was the time to see how they worked together.

She turned to Alim and Zulu. 'I'm very sorry, you were really chosen to support your youngsters. Zulu, you're now too big and, Alim, you'd run out of cigarettes before we got to the moon!'

Then to Su-lin and Kristin she said, 'You're still in the running, but if we did pick the kids, you'll be supporting them.'

Buzz looked around. Where was Ford?

'Don't worry, Buzz, he's too busy but we have someone here for you. She's called... Soraya.'

'You and me, Buzzy boy!' Soraya bustled in and ruffled his hair.

Dong Dong sniffed. This country was so different. It wasn't just the faces and language. Even the air and light were different. Only the soil here felt familiar. He fiddled nervously with his phone as he waited.

His first long haul flight had awakened him to the true planet. There was so much water. China felt like an endless land, but when he left its coastline and flew for hour upon hour over the vast stretches of ocean towards California, he understood why this was a blue planet.

He was now in no shadow of doubt that there was a lot of water on Mars. He'd been working on a probe to explore the moon's south pole. They'd discovered that those permanently dark craters still harboured ice frozen since its formation. Now he'd been called by his beloved country to join this heroic mission to Mars.

'Hi, Dong Dong? Is that how you pronounce it?'

'Ah yes, as in long!'

'Anyhow, welcome to NASA. It's great to have you on board.'

'We honoured to be invited.' His eyes searched the room, and alighted on a paperweight of the Eagle on Ford's desk.

Dong Dong drew Ford into his confidence. 'Usually they send a delegation, but they trust me and I get to the point.

'Mr Harris, our involvement has to be tangible. We're a developing country and space is an area of great national pride. We've already sent you our best astronauts and scientists for testing.'

He picked up the paperweight. 'I know you can't guarantee to send one of them. So we want to build the lander.'

Ford looked at his lunar module nestled in Dong Dong's hand. He cleared his throat. 'Very interesting, but we've always made our own landers.'

Dong Dong had a great view of Ford's sleek silver workstation. He traced out the carefully etched words on the aluminium casing. 'This says "Designed in California – made in China". This is not 1968. We already work together making great things.'

'Well, she never crashes, so that's a good sign.' Ford did the maths in his head. 'That's almost a billion dollars we'll save,' he thought to himself. 'OK. That sounds brilliant, but don't forget, we work in feet and inches.'

They had lunch and got to know each other. Ford liked Dong Dong. He had a wonderful combination of confidence and a disarming innocence – for Ford, it was a sign of an open mind. He broached his idea for the crew.

'Dong Dong, we are choosing three potential teams to go – one has very young people, because of the weight restrictions. We will be keeping it under wraps because of the obvious sensitivities.'

Dong Dong seemed delighted they had already sent a Chinese mother and daughter for testing. 'What sensitivities?'

Ford played with his food. 'Exposing such young children to space travel has a risk – physical and political.'

Dong Dong looked through the window at the city sprawling into the distance. 'Risk is about statistics. On average seven children are shot dead every day in your country. It puts it all in a certain perspective.'

Ford nodded. 'I'll take you to meet the team.'

# Chapter 20

## Iceland Adventure and Visit to the MOPJ

*Camper Crossing River*

Before the next stage of testing in Iceland, the candidates waited in limbo while the medical assessments were completed. Most had gone home for the duration, except for Buzz, Bheki and Zulu. Buzz's mother wasn't well, and Zulu and Bheki had nowhere to go.

Jane was like a mother hen. She'd opened her heart and door and insisted they stay at the farm, and soon the days in the pods became a distant memory as they enjoyed the farm's freedom.

Elin and Kirsten had returned to the planet's youngest country. Kirsten's energy seemed boundless, helping to arrange the training. Iceland is a famous testing ground for astronauts, and she'd teamed up with Magnus, an expedition organiser par excellence. Neither were impressed with Ford's special request: a visit to the world-famous Museum of Practical Jokes.

Magnus was a bear of a man. He mopped his brow as he considered the proposition. He had three loves in his life: Iceland in all its geological glory, football and a secret regard for Kirsten.

She went over the brief, hardly able to contain her excitement. 'Plan it like we're on Mars: we need some transport and then a hike.

Find an unknown and hostile environment and test us.' She put her finger to her pursed lips. 'The route and details will be down to you!'

There are no shops on Mars, so they'd need to carry everything with them. Iceland can be challenging at any time of the year – except for the abundance of water and atmosphere, the cold and desolation offer an analogy of Martian conditions. Magnus had worked with NASA for years and was familiar with many of the issues. He'd met Kirsten at the University of Reykjavik where he was researching autonomous vehicles.

There's only one major road encircling the island, so it's hardly surprising that no cars are made in Iceland. Many of the other roads are nothing but cinder tracks. However, there is a car industry, adapting imported vehicles with ridiculously large wheels, high axles and loads of storage, designed for driving through deep rivers, jagged rocks and to the top of glaciers.

Magnus was working on a fleet of rugged multi-purpose vehicles which could be driven to the start of a hike then drive autonomously to rendezvous the end of a trail.

To eke out the grant, Magnus had searched out some old bangers. He'd discovered a weather-stripped old farm on the way to the Douglas Dakota crash site on the south-west coast. In the barn were three 1970s VW camper vans. Their paintwork, sandblasted by the dark sand whipped up from the beaches, and the delicate veneer of rust made them the most sexy grunge-mobiles outside of California. He'd fitted them with his autonomous controls with manual overrides. Magnus brimmed with excitement as he realised that these were the perfect vehicles.

Kirsten was having a great deal of trouble booking tickets for the Museum of Practical Jokes. Every time she put her newly registered username and password in she got rebuffed with a message to call the box office number. On calling the box office number she was referred back to the website. On the website it advised her to follow a link to customer services. She pressed the link and found herself on the Disneyland Paris website. Trying another tack, she called the telephone number again and simply waited. After an inordinate time, she heard the ringing tone.

At last, a human being!

'Cornwall County Council Rates Department,' replied the friendly voice.

She screamed, 'I didn't want you!'

The rejected voice replied, 'Do you want the Museum of Practical Jokes?'

'Yes, yes, please!' Kirsten pleaded.

'Well, you've come to the wrong place, but we get a lot of these calls. If you press four we can help you.'

Kirsten was now almost in tears. 'Please, can't you help in person?'

There was a pause, then, 'I'm not allowed because of data protection.'

Kirsten was completely confused. 'What does pressing four do?'

'Oh, it will refer you back to the museum.'

Kirsten had been at this for over an hour and just flipped. 'OK, if I told you we had kidnapped your children and they are all going to die, would you help me?'

A worried voice came back, 'I hope that's a joke!'

'Give me a straight answer and I'll tell you.'

A wavering voice came over. 'You can't book tickets; you pay on the door, if you can find it. Now, please, what about my kids?'

'Call this number: +354 561 6666.' With that Kirsten hung up.

When the woman dialled, it was the box office of the Museum of Practical Jokes and she was referred back to the website.


Ford was nervous as he waited in his office. He needed some reassurance. He had to speak to Yasmin.

A bead of sweat was trickling down her brow as the call came in. She'd just woven her limbs into another impossible knot. The yoga mat squeaked on the parquet floor.

'Oh sugar!' she cursed as Ford's ringtone interrupted the Tibetan mood music.

She casually flicked away the perspiration and unlocked her legs.

'Hi, Ford! I'm just working out. Is it about the interview?'

'Yep, and... Jane's had a spot of bother. The press are trying to bug our place.'

'Oh my God! What happened?'

Ford told her the story.

'Oh well, they've definitely got you on their radar. They've been snooping after Rocky and Sharon too. Change your passwords, and make them complex!'

Ford laughed. 'What! I can't even remember my simple ones!'

'It won't make a difference then! Anyway, this interview will reset the balance. It's a proper paper. Just be straight and honest, and remember you don't have to tell them anything you don't want to.'

He'd hardly ended the call when there was a knock on the office door.

The reporter, Lesley Scrivener, was a man with voluminous pockets. He wore an ancient tweed jacket and had the whiff of stale tobacco. Out came the notebook, pens, phone, pipe, matches and an ancient dictaphone onto the low table between them.

Ford felt a little nervous and Lesley sensed it. 'Don't you enjoy interviews?'

Ford loosened his tie. 'They call me the man who deafened the world.'

Lesley gave a knowing smile.

'We are always looking for a story. Relax and let's tell them the truth.' Lesley clicked the machine on. 'Why do we need to go to Mars? What's so compelling?'

Ford thought for a moment. 'What's the point in anything? Half the world thinks it's fascinating; the other half can't see the point.

'"We have enough crap on Earth to resolve," I hear them say. But… if we only did the immediate, we'd live very hollow lives.' He took a deep breath. 'We have always looked to the heavens with wonder and – guess what? – we're now able to do something about it.'

Lesley looked quizzical. 'Aren't we just as happy watching television or playing golf?'

'Do you know we spend more on golf than space research? What's the more valuable: finding out about a new planet or ruining a good walk? Anyway, the universe is fascinating any way you look at it. My wife studies ants; I study the cosmos. On the very smallest scale the universe is fuzzy and indeterminate, and only when we observe it does it become real. Why not on a big scale? That faint red dot in the sky is now an amazing new world. Does anything make sense, unless there are eyes to see it and minds to understand? We have only a brief sojourn in a seemingly vast continuum of time, but with each bit of knowledge we add, I believe we give a greater credence to the universe.'

Ford glanced at the photograph of the Andromeda galaxy on the wall.

'Besides, I'd like to add more certainty to Drake's equation. Are we alone or not? Drake estimated there were fifty thousand other civilisations in our galaxy alone, and presumably the same number in that one.' He pointed at the photograph.

The reporter stared at the great spiral of stars. Lesley was sceptical. 'But where are these civilisations? Surely they'd be beaming out some kind of message!'

Jane had views on this.

'My wife says I can't find my hat in the morning, so how's a nerd like me going to find it? For instance, SETI's boffins scan the skies on the wavelength of atomic hydrogen. Who's going to air their music on that?'

Lesley lit his pipe with a studied nonchalance. 'Could we even have a conversation with them when the nearest stars are light years away? Isn't it difficult enough to communicate with Mars?'

'Yeah, there's a minimum twenty-minute gap with Mars.'

Lesley guffawed. 'My parents seem to manage. They can go for weeks without talking.' He continued his probing. 'What difference does it make whether we're alone or not, if we can't communicate?'

'Our perception of ourselves is important. If we're alone, we are very special. If we are one of many civilisations, the universe becomes a more extraordinary place. Finding life on Mars could make us change our views of ourselves, our religions, even our very existence. At the moment we are a lonely world lost in space, uncertain if we are unique or ubiquitous.'

Lesley wafted the smoke around.

'Where are you going to look for this life? That 'so-called' fossil's been dead for a long time.'

Ford studied the wild eyebrows through the haze.

'Life on Mars could be deep in the ground or just under a rock. That's why we need a human crew. They have to be able to turn over a lot of rocks or go down a cavern. You can't do that with a rover.'

Ford made them a coffee as Lesley continued the questions. 'You've never headed a mission. Aren't you a little inexperienced? You've made a few gaffes already... certainly upset the fundamentalists.'

A well of irritation rose in Ford. This was ridiculous. 'I'm a scientist, not a priest, and it's got nothing to do with religion. Science ain't about faith, it's about reality!'

'You don't take the Bible very literally. Do you think it needs rewriting if we found life elsewhere?' Lesley asked.

'Look, all religions have their creation myths; mankind has always been inquisitive about our origins. These were the best explanations of primitive societies. The more we know, the more we can move on.'

He took a deep breath. 'Anyway, it's not about me, but having a great team and solving problems. I'm a problem solver.'

Lesley dunked a biscuit in his coffee. 'Have you worked out how to get them home then?'

'We won't go if we can't get home. We can't put the crew at risk.'

This led to an obvious question. 'Who are the crew? When do we find out? I hear you had an extraordinary response to your advert.'

Ford ran his fingers through his hair. 'It's classified. We won't say until they take off... Two good reasons. The training and selection will go on right to the wire and we need the anonymity, because they'll be hounded to death by you lot.'

Lesley feigned a look of hurt. 'Finally, why on earth would anyone want to go? It's a cold, desolate, frozen, isolated, awful place!'

This had crossed Ford's mind many times. 'If he were alive, I would ask Shackleton!'

Shackleton survived in Antarctica against all odds. When his ship got crushed in the ice, he rowed hundreds of miles to get help. Despite all the dangers and disasters, he got all his crew home safe.

The results flew out, skimming through the airways like swifts in the autumn. *Blink, blink, blink,* bringing the news to the chosen ones for the next round of testing.

It was a time for excitement, a time for reflection, a time for fear.

*Blink,* your travel itinerary from Italy. *Blink,* your itinerary from Beijing, *blink,* your itinerary from Iceland, *blink,* your itinerary from London, Washington, etc., all over the world, and each email had a time and place and destination: Iceland.

The would-be astronauts flew in over the barren perimeter of Keflavik airport. Magnus met each flight and whisked them out to the glass and stone surroundings of the Geyser Information Centre, nestled in one of the geothermal areas of the North Atlantic divide.

This would be the last outpost of civilisation they'd see until the end of the exercise. The interior was inspired by the rugged landscape and had a full view of the geyser fields. Every few minutes a plume of white steam would burst from the hot pools, breaking the grey skyline, before slowly dissipating down the valley. The tourist season had drawn to a close and the snows were starting to take hold on the hills.

The sparse clientele took little notice of the group of women, men and children as they made their way to the lecture theatre.

The doors closed and it slowly dawned on each of them that they'd been whittled down to a final eleven. Magnus bustled around, ordering them into three teams: 'The Right Stuff', 'The Elves' and 'The Other Things'.

The process of elimination had selected three astronauts, two men and one woman; a scientist, and an engineer. These were the adults. Milling around were six others, who for all their talents were just children.

Yasmin explained the quest on her beloved flip chart. They were to set out in the three 'Utility vehicles' in the early morning. First they'd examine their kit and were given a budget to spend at the centre to augment any essentials they thought were missing.

This was the first test.

They had a set of maps and the co-ordinates for their journey. Tonight they'd stay in their vehicles at the nearby campsite.

Magnus's growl drew their attention. 'We are here in Iceland because the dynamics of our planet are all on show. Mars might appear lifeless, but it's certainly active. Now I'm going to show you geysers… and not just the ones outside!'

The house lights dimmed and a projector's beam flashed against the far wall. A strange image came into focus, a white crust-like landscape speckled with dark ink blotches and bursting feathers of black gas breaking through the surface.

'Yes, these are geysers – not water like the ones outside, but subliming carbon dioxide, photographed from a Martian orbit. Can you imagine witnessing that?' After a few more explanatory slides the lights came up and he led the way to the door. 'At least we can do a little sight-seeing here and see our own geysers – a first taste of an alien landscape.'

Mars tilts on an axis like Earth and has seasons and frozen polar regions that expand and retreat from winter to summer. In the relative warmth of spring at its south pole, the winter's harvest of carbon dioxide ice starts to sublimate and its gases run through a network of spidery channels before dramatically bursting through the thin water-ice crust in immense spouts hundreds of feet high. Vast networks of these vents create a speckled tapestry on the landscape.

'If I went to Mars, I'd love to see these!'

They picked their way up the bubbling hot-water gravel paths to a large blue pool edged in a salt-hardened, white and yellow crusting. The weak autumn light broke through with casts of sunshine yellow on the grey-toned background.

*Mars Geysers*

By the *Strokkur* they stood in expectation as the waters heaved and juddered from subterranean turmoil. Bheki couldn't decide what was most exciting – the extraordinary waters or the snow. Suddenly, there was a low gurgle and a perfect bubble of white steam rose through the clear-blue liquid creating a giant monstrous eye before bursting in a gush of brilliant vapour, breaking into the brooding skies. They quivered in amazement as the high column dissipated, carried away on the breeze.

In the campsite slightly up the hill stood the three converted camper vans – a red one, a yellow one and a green one. Each had a small cylindrical trailer carrying water and provisions to last two weeks. Their newly painted exteriors looked as fresh as when they left the production line in the 1970s.

Magnus had been galvanised when he received his brief and

enthusiastically set to transforming the vans into his vision of a space ship interior (also circa 1970), each van gaining a cylindrical lining blocking out the windows, apart from four inset ship's portholes. The red van sported an immaculately finished white fibreglass shell, with moulded storage pockets and two fold-down beds (inspired by *2001: A Space Odyssey*). He lavished so much time on the first that he was running out of time and materials, so the blue van now had a thin aluminium checker-plate skin, with two fold-down tubular-framed beds and the third bed fixed in the pop-top roof (*Red Dwarf* or *Doctor Who*). The green one he couldn't complete and just applied several coats of Danish oil in 4mm marine ply backing. The six beds here was his challenge. He fitted a three-seater rock-n-roll bed and two canvas bunks in the pop top, and one hammock was slung in the driving cabin (*Dark Star*).

*Iceland Geysers*

Between the front two seats was a big steel enclosure. It contained 'his box of tricks', where the van could be controlled remotely or by the on-board computer. The dashboard held a series of glowing buttons and USB ports.

The red van was for 'The Right Stuff', the blue for 'The Elves', and the green for 'The Other Things'.

By accident he'd discovered that the thin stressed ply skin, like a

De Havilland Mosquito, was the most weight/cost/strength-efficient material and would subsequently be used for all future missions.

Each team took possession of their vehicles and examined them in depth. The kids' understandable hesitancy was broken by Bheki who'd been watching out for himself for as long as he knew.

'What you waiting for?' he called while frantically signing his instructions.

'He's a waste-man or what!' Mo whispered to Buzz.

This awakened something in Buzz.

'He's my buddy so butt out! He's signing, you dumbo!'

Mo bristled. 'We're not deaf, though.'

'Hey, it's cool, I've been learning it. We don't want them listening to everything.'

Mo suddenly saw the merits in it. 'OK, teach me a sign.'

Buzz was about to unfurl his middle finger, when Bheki grabbed him and paired him with Chao-xing.

He split them into three pairs; Buzz and Chao-xing checked out the front drivers' cabin, Mo and Enza the rear accommodation and Bheki and Elin the engine and the trailer.

By the time they had finished they'd composed a list of questions and a compendium of their kit and provisions.

Then the arguments started, the big issue... who got which bed.

'I'm sleeping in the back,' shouted Mo.

'You go in front,' instructed Bheki.

'No, I'm there!' cut in Buzz.

Through the shrill voices, Enza put her foot down. She understood the psychology of boys. 'You boys can sleep together on the big bed.'

'No way!' they replied in unison. 'We're having the bunks.'

The boys soon sorted out their precarious perches in the front. The girls got the big comfortable bed.

Buzz and Chao-xing eyed each other suspiciously while struggling with the controls.

'It's just the same as Granf's camper except for the big box.'

'Is this the engine?' she asked as she opened a side hatch, only to find nothing but electronics.

'Don't worry, there's a spare one in the trunk,' consoled Buzz.

Chao-xing joined him vainly trying to turn the enamelled steering wheel. Suddenly the door sprang open and the beaming face of Magnus thrust itself into the cabin.

'Oh no, that's far too last century! Here's your controls!'

To their delight he pulled out an Xbox console and plugged it into the USB port on the dash. The lights immediately flashed and Magnus explained the functions.

'I'll guide you tomorrow until you get the hang of it.' Buzz beamed.

Chao-xing's eyes filled with a red mist. She thought the West was the bastion of human rights and equality. 'Hey, where's mine? Are you sexist, or what!'

Mo and Enza opened up the central cupboards. Enza was enthralled by its neatness. Dwarfed in her restaurant kitchen, this was just her size.

'*Una piccola cucina*,' she giggled, seeing the tiny hob and sink under the worktop. She took out all the utensils and pots and pans and made a mental list of what was missing. She might be artistic, but in the kitchen she was organised.

Mo was rooting in the storage and sorting through the maps, tools and the boots. Then he discovered a walkie-talkie. His dad had given him a shortwave radio, so they could communicate anywhere in the world. The crackle of his signal would bring joy into Alim's loneliest days when stuck in some wilderness. Mo loved radios.

Enza clapped her hands. 'We do this together!' They pulled out six bags. There were warm clothes and waterproofs for all of them. Mo examined the waterproofs with the motto, 'No such thing as bad weather, just bad clothing.'

Bheki and Elin were busy out the back. Bheki made a beeline for the engine. Elin started to unload the kit from the trailer, as a faint shower from the geyser settled on them every few minutes.

Tents, backpacks, sleeping bags and food containers bounced down on the deck. '*Va!* It's just like a real expedition,' she shouted at Bheki's bottom, his head still buried in the trunk. Then she banged on the side panel and he turned his head. '*Va!* It's just like a real expedition,' she said again.

'It is a real expedition,' answered Bheki. Turning back, he pointed. 'This engine is just like Mr Herman's!'

Elin was unimpressed. 'Hey, Bheki, come and help me now. We have to make sure we have everything.'

In half an hour the children got together in the back of the van and made their list and set off in the gloaming light to see what they could find at the centre.

As they neared the road a distinct clop of hooves cut through the air. From up the valley a parade of a dozen Icelandic horses broke across their path. Two riders guided them along the slushy road to the shelter of the lower pastures. The children gazed in wonder at the stocky herd until it diminished into a series of dots in the mist.

By the canteen and gift shop was an outward bound emporium and the children shopped in pairs. Bheki raided the clothes with Chao-xing, buying six pairs of gloves, hats, angora vests and scarves. Elin and Mo bought a ground sheet, torches, gas canisters and a compass. Enza and Buzz stocked up on supplies, including lots of chocolate and a packet of Icelandic salt.

Laden with their booty, Elin and Chao-xing caught the familiar sight of their mothers rooting through the other camper. It felt strange to be so close yet separated.

Mo was envious. He hadn't seen his mother in years and his father's sporadic visits were never enough. Buzz recognised his angst, as he was beginning to gain some empathy.

'What's up?'

Mo put on a brave face. 'I miss my ma.'

Buzz welled up, he'd never even seen his dad and Bheki spotted it. 'What's up, man?'

Buzz shook his head as Mo explained, 'We miss our parents.'

Bheki thought for a moment. 'Never had any. I miss my brother, though.'

There was a roar of laughter outside as the kids ate their first meal. Mo's head snapped round to the porthole. 'Do we need bikes?' he exclaimed as he saw two hulking astronauts careering past them festooned with shopping bags.

Elin peered out and sniggered. 'Not where we're going!'

To the soft, low murmur of the wind the children settled down.

Then Enza sat up. 'Where's the toilet?'

This had been lost on them all except Elin. 'On the side of the trailer!'

'Yuck, I can't go there,' objected the girl.

'No, that's just where the shovel is!' said Elin.

Nobody slept. The thrill of it all kept them awake until the early hours.

When Magnus's bushy beard poked in, they were waking, bleary-eyed. 'Off we go in twenty minutes – got everything?'

Bheki had discovered the tell-tale boom of an empty water tank when returning the shovel. 'Water!' he piped up.

The narrow tarmac road forked some miles from the centre, where they were the last to pull off onto a cinder track, which snaked across the low hills following a string of pylons.

Magnus went through the controls with both Buzz and Xing (as they now called her) for the last time. 'Remember, don't stop in the rivers.'

He waved warmly as he left them to the monochrome landscape.

Four faces peered over the seat backs as Buzz and Xing restarted the engine. Mo had been studying the maps and co-ordinates. He laid the map on the silver housing between the drivers. 'Here's the route, innit!' His finger traced its way along the faint grey line skirting the contours and crossing the rivers. 'We take a right in about half a mile.'

This was a maintenance track for the electricity company. Here the thin Earth's crust provides an endless supply of steam and a spider's web of power lines spread out from the geothermal areas.

The old bus trundled along with the trailer clattering from rut to rut. Bheki just stared out. America had been different, Africa was familiar, but here was crazy. It was cold, the light was blue and without trees. It was as if the land had just been born.

His Earth had an ancient past, where their ancestors' spirits were laid down like strata. In this place no one had lived, the only spirits were of the land itself. He watched the gravel-strewn ground pass him by and surprisingly it excited him.

He had dreamed of escaping his orphanage and this was as different as it could get, except perhaps Mars itself.

Suddenly they lurched to a stop. Bheki sensed they were on an incline and he joined the scrum at the front, staring at the white-and-green-laced river ahead. 'Mo, you're useless, the road's run out,' wavered Buzz. It had been taxing enough driving on the rough track by Xbox control, but a raging river cutting across their path was impossible with no press and leap command.

Bheki was not impressed. 'Ach! Get on with it, man!' Crossing rivers was not unknown to him. Neither were they to Elin.

'Mummia just puts her foot down!'

Buzz was more cautious. He ran the van to the water's edge and stared into the depths, fearing what may lurk in the tumbling foam. 'I think we'll need to wade across and check.'

Xing turned to him. 'Under the rear seat there's a depth gauge.'

Buzz tumbled over to the seat backs and then crashed into the padding as the van lurched forward.

Xing was going for it.

'Just don't stop, that's all!' cheered Bheki, and the van cut through the frothing mass. The waters deepened as unseen rocks deflected the van and the electronics struggled to cope with the jarring obstructions.

'Easy, easy, don't over compensate.' Xing kept a steady thumb on the accelerator button, then as suddenly as they entered, they reared up on the far side to the whoops and clamour of all except a sulking Buzz.

'My turn next!' was all he said as he snatched back the controller.

They emerged into a long, flat valley with a line of mountains along its flanks. The brooding presence of Helka dominated the landscape and as Elin had told them of its imminent eruption, they urged Buzz on and were relieved to leave it diminishing in the rear mirrors, except Enza who wondered what all the fuss was about.

**Helka**
'Gateway to hell'
South Iceland
63.6N 19.4W
Altitude: 4,882ft
Geology:
Stratovolcano

The track was now a pumice ribbon meandering through a boulder-strewn plain, devoid of all vegetation and fringed with great drifts of tephra swept up against the jagged escarpments.

As they headed higher up the valley, it softened into faded greens of tough grasses and lichens among the pristine snow drifts. The sharp peaks gave way to rounded summits dappled with year-long scabs of ice. Mo guided them and to his relief a wide lake appeared to confirm his navigation. 'Nearly there!'

Over the narrow pass they threaded down to the wide, flat campsite at Landmannalaugar, with an icy glacial river sweeping to the left and the chaotic line of frozen lava flows to the right. They joined the two lonely camper vans on the hard standing beside the green-roofed huts.

Their journey had taken the best part of the day and the weather was unwelcoming. Bheki and Elin shivered as they stretched their legs outside the van. 'Are we ever going to be warm again?' stammered Bheki as he surveyed the raw chemical colours of the surrounding peaks.

'Grab a towel everyone!' Elin shouted and she skipped off along a long boardwalk towards a patch of rising vapour.

If they'd been wondering where the others had got to, they were enlightened by the happy chatter of 'The Right Stuff' and 'The Elves' getting acquainted. Their voices drifted over from the steaming hot waters that flowed out of the lava flow's margins.

Xing shivered as she stripped on the wet wooden platform. The cold air pierced into her bones until a line of enveloping warmth spread upwards as she lowered herself down the slippery ladder into the welcoming water. Crouching down, she luxuriated in the comfort of the crystal clear water as she half swam, half crawled towards her mother's arms.

The others waddled behind like little ducks until they reached the point where it was hot enough to just bear.

This oasis is fed by seeping springs from the old lava flow, its core still scalding hot years after it solidified on the edge of the valley.

Mo's mind wandered as he relaxed. In front of him the hills glowed with sulphurous yellows and iron reds, to his back the ragged black basaltic cliff towered ominously. He pinched himself to check he wasn't dreaming and then luxuriated in the sense of being anywhere but home.

In the predawn glow Eugene was brimming with confidence. A natural early riser he was the first to bump into Magnus as he prepared to waken the troops and gather them for a briefing.

There was little time, as they had to set off at dawn. He made them check their walkie-talkies, each with a built-in twenty-minute delay, only to be overridden in dire emergencies.

Their vehicles were left ship-shape for the autonomous drive to the rendezvous at the end of the hike.

The children checked their backpacks, adjusting the weight of the clothes, camping gear, water, food and cooking equipment which bore down on their diminutive frames.

Eugene Claymore and Felix Owen were pleased with themselves. The old stagers, with many months in space between them, revelled in their moniker 'The Right Stuff' and were convinced they had an ace up their sleeve.

'With these bikes we'll do this hike in two days. We're going to leave them in our dust!' Eugene shouted as he checked them over.

'What could possibly go wrong?' Felix replied.

Without hesitation, 'Two years in space with you!' Eugene gave him a large grin.

Felix had another plan. 'We're going on a diet by the way!'

'Huh! And how will that help, pray?' Eugene attempted to balance his backpack on the rear rack of the bicycle.

'The weight limit's 31 stone. If we lost a bit of weight, we could take one of the women with us, the scientist!' He gave a wry smile.

Eugene was still struggling with his balancing act. 'You should have got some panniers. By the way, what's with the snotty kids?'

Felix gave a dismissive shrug. 'No worries about them, man! It's just a bit of PC bullshit.'

They set off in twenty-minute intervals, the half-light barely illuminating the well-worn track among the chaotic basalt boulders.

'The Other Things' followed in the tracks of 'The Elves'. Once through the maze of the lower lava field they climbed up onto the limbs of the hills. Plumes of steam condensed in the morning air as they emerged like troops in a battle.

It took time to become accustomed to the heavy backpacks. Elin helped with the adjustments, making them more tolerable. Today they were at their heaviest, with four days' food weighing them down.

Eventually they stopped on a rock-strewn plateau and the sight they beheld was enthralling. The empty interior of the island spread out behind them, with the milky green river far below as it wound out into the plains beyond. Ahead of them seemed like another planet.

The buff weather-worn gullies were topped with a patchwork of mosses, lichens and mini ice fields. Ahead they could make out the three figures of 'The Elves' and way down the valley the wind just carried the curses of 'The Right Stuff' as they dragged their bikes up the unforgiving path.

Every so often, Elin picked up a rock and examined it before casting it aside or surreptitiously slipping it into Buzz's backpack.

Enza clicked away with her camera. Mo and Xing were up front, map in hand as they marched along the route. Bheki kept watch for wild animals.

Famished from their exertions, they huddled on a ring of rocks for a lunch of 'Everest Brod' and sausage and cheese. Bheki started teaching them signing and named familiar items as they followed his hands.

Up the track there was a stone-scattering rumble and the Eugene and Felix flew past, waving from their mountain bikes.

Buzz watched enviously they peddled into the distance. 'I guess it's what adults do and we're just kids!' he signed, as he tried to pick up his pack.

He thought of his own bike lying useless in the garage and the hollow promise from Boyf to mend it one day.

Mo was not used to hiking. Elin had a spring in her step and he had a leak in his boot. A real challenge for a city boy, he found himself lagging behind the others, apart from Buzz, whose pack seemed to have gained weight.

*Iceland Hike*

As they trudged down an incline they hit a wall of steam, blown over from a spring boiling out of a fissure. Sinews strained as they descended into the fog, following the fleeting figures that skipped across a tepid stream before working their way up the other side.

'That you?' Buzz sniggered to Mo as a wave of sulphurous vapour attacked his nostrils.

As the mists lifted, a whole hillside of ice rose before them, hugging the soft shoulder of the ridge. A small, straight, single line of tracks bisected its surface, overlaid with the sinuous bicycle tracks and scuff marks of large boots. They could see they were rapidly catching up with 'The Right Stuff', who were at a slithering sub-walking pace and desperately trying to keep their bikes upright on the near frictionless surface.

Mo started first, run and slide, run and slide until they were all slithering along like a giant concertina.

Eugene was struggling. He'd slipped three times already and when his back wheel pirouetted slowly around, his heart raced as he felt his balance following it down the deep valley.

Bheki dropped his pack and ran, just in time to grasp the man's jacket. He dug his feet in and when the others arrived they hauled him back onto the track.

The children padded along, stabilising the bikes until they reached firm ground. Eugene didn't seem at all grateful and he just gave a casual nod and set off on his way.

Felix winked. 'Thanks, kids,' he said before peddling furiously after his partner.

As their shadows lengthened they reached a high plateau strewn with shards of beautiful black glass.

'How beautiful!' Xing thought as she handed a piece to Elin.

'Obsidian, a natural glass. It's from the felsic lava flows – it's one of my favourites.'

The exquisite mineral was scattered as far as the eye could see. Impervious to weathering it was as sharp as the day it cooled and shattered.

Each picked up some more samples. Buzz sliced bits of the sausage with his while Bheki held his like a knife, unsure what predators might be lurking around the corner.

The wind was freshening and when the drizzle turned into driving rain they hurried their pace. As visibility diminished, Elin got them to spread out so they wouldn't lose the markers as the landscape became a formless haze.

They followed the bike tracks, until through the gloom they made out two bent figures mending punctures.

The men's hands were like bunches of sausages as they struggled with the patches.

Bheki had fixed more punctures than he cared to remember – bikes, cars and wheelbarrows. He thought of Eugene's earlier lack of gratitude. He refrained from offering his services.

The squall passed and the air cleared by the time they reached the ridge above their first night's camp.

The barren undulating land had given way onto a grey scree slope and standing out like a beacon a bright-orange tent stood with the unmistakable figures of three women huddled around a boiling stove. They half slid, half ran down the incline.


Eugene's anger boiled as they pushed their bikes the last couple of miles. The light had failed and they were in serious danger of missing the camp altogether. The moon was yet to rise and the skies had sunk into an inky blackness save the pinpoints of stars.

'Why the hell didn't you ask for lights? I can't see diddly squat.' Eugene stood tall, staring into the unremitting blackness. 'How we gonna find this goddamn place?'

The black ground, velvet sky and dark hills gave nothing away. They stumbled blindly. 'This is hopeless. Can you see anything?'

The Earth has many qualities that help life to flourish. It's not just the atmosphere or the water but also a strong magnetic field.

A lucky accident. Over 4 billion years ago the young Earth collided with a smaller proto-planet. As they coalesced, the heavier elements stuck together and some of the lighter ones were flung out to form our moon.

The moon is a benevolent sibling. Its gyroscopic influence has prevented our poles flipping. The extra momentum, heat and the combined nickel and iron cores of both planets gave us one massive spinning core whose magnetic field reaches far into space, deflecting the steady flow of deadly charged particles blasted at us by the sun.

During the eleven-year solar cycle, the Earth is swamped by this solar ejecta and it tugs and stretches the field until it snaps back, drawing in a cascade of ions streaming towards the polar regions.

Mars had none of these things and the incessant radiation has stripped away its atmosphere, leaving it almost naked and a frozen place.

Felix was at the point of desperation when he perceived the faintest green light high above.

He grabbed Eugene's sleeve. 'Hey! Is that what I think it is?'

'I'm glad to know you think!'

The green glow was cut by a burst of ephemeral bubbles descending from on high, then a scything curtain of light insinuated itself across the darkness. 'Oh, man, this is beautiful! I've only seen it from space.'

The veteran astronauts stood in wonder. The auroral display guided them home to their haven and, wheeling their bikes, they made it to the crest of the valley and spotted the tents below.

The sky was pulsing with red oxygen ions high above the green curtains, as Felix threw his pack down. 'Well, that's worth a few punctures!'

Su-lin offered them tea and supper, but Eugene politely declined. 'No, we're on a diet!'

The next morning Xing blew the goose feather off her nose and uncurled from their canvas nest. The parties packed up and set off in the order they'd arrived.

Xing and Buzz had the task of collecting flora and fauna.

It had been very thin on the ground and looked even less promising as the early light clipped the hills. They understood why this place had been chosen as an analogue for Mars. There was just rock and ice. No scrap of vegetation, not even mosses graced its undulating surface. Even the sky was a Martian pink and only the meltwater in the gullies gave the game away. On Mars the carbon dioxide and water ices would sublime rather than melt.

Mo called Magnus on the walkie-talkie before setting off. Enza was scornful. 'You never get an answer on that thing?'

Mo turned it upside down, explaining, 'There's a button here, for emergencies. On Mars you can't talk – just message.'

Enza looked puzzled. '*Stupido!* If they can send us to Mars we'll need us a better radio!'

'My dad told me about it, innit. When we look at the stars we stare into history. Even the light from the sun is nine minutes old. It's the same with the radio.'

Enza sniffed.

They walked across the barren mountains and around the rims of ice fields. Picking a way through a small pass they found it blocked by a rushing rivulet of meltwater. To their left it had cut a tunnel through a long drift to form a frozen bridge.

The kids picked their way over and made it to the other side. Then Buzz was excitedly pulling on Xing's arm. 'There's samples up there.' From the charcoal-black earth a series of hot streams bubbled down. The warm water had created an eco-climate of moss and algae tresses. To their amazement some of the algae was existing between boiling water and freezing ice.

'How can that live there?' Buzz wondered out loud as he put his finger into the hot water.

Xing looked around at the forbidding climate. 'Where else would you choose?'


Felix's pride had been dented and he'd determined to make up lost time in the obsidian plain. The ground sped on under their knobbly tyres and they were set on overtaking the others by the end of the day. Eugene stood, map in hand, at the spot where the kids had stopped.

Felix pointed towards the stream. 'Let's just power through it.'

Eugene was doubtful. His eye caught the long bank of ice. The tracks of the children were still fresh and they set off in pursuit. The packed gravel gave excellent traction and they were both flying as they met the ice. Felix, losing his nerve, hopped off near the top and started to push. Eugene's back tyre spun and cut through the hard crust. He peddled frantically, cutting a long scar through the drift. The weight and the damage made by the revolving wheels were too much.

Felix started to haul his bike up to the ridge beyond. As he puffed up, there was a muffled crunch and stifled cry. The wind caught his voice as he called, 'Hey, man, are you OK?'

No answer. He wasn't the sort of man who would take no answer as an answer and he pulled back the fur of his parka. Where the hell was he? 'Eugene!' he cried and made out a muffled 'Help' from deep below. He edged gingerly back across the ice bridge. There were cracks and on its apex was a man-and-bike-sized hole. He dropped down and strained to look into the void. Ten feet down he saw Eugene entangled with his cycle, covered in chunks of snow. Half of him was in the river, the rest stuck fast in the fallen ice. Eugene felt injured pride, but as the freezing water lapped against his back, he started to panic.

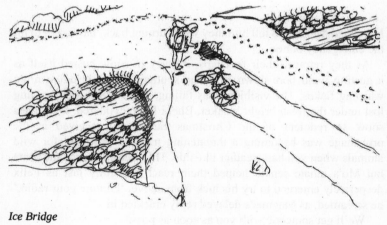

*Ice Bridge*

'Get me out, Felix. I'm screwed down here, it's flaming freezing!'
'Where's the radio, man?'
'In my pack!'
'Damn, it's beneath you in the stream. Mmmm... I'll try to get to you through the tunnel.'
Felix was fearful. He decided to shout for help. At least the kids

would have a radio. He let out two immense cries. 'Heeellllpppp! Heeeellllpppp!' echoed around the impassive hills.

Elin caught the call on the wind. 'Did you hear that?'

They all picked up the second call and, without words, turned on their heels and headed back.


Felix made it to the head of the tunnel where the stream vanished. Peering thirty yards downstream in the translucent light he could just make out the red flash of Eugene's jacket and his pack lying in the water. There was a big problem: the ice tube narrowed to an impossible aperture for his sturdy frame.

Eugene shouted again. 'I'll try to unhook my boot – it's all caught around the chain.' He gave it a good kick. The bike slumped a little and he sunk deeper into the stream. The water was backing up around the pack and the level was rising. If he was worried before, he was panicky now. It was lapping around his head and he was very cold.


Mo called Magnus to tell him they were turning back, but forgot to hit the emergency button.

As they retraced their footsteps, a flurry of snow busied itself as a gusting wind bore down from the southern ridge, bringing more whirling flakes. The visibility was failing. Their tracks were getting lost under the fresh bright blanket. Bheki felt bewildered, the joyous snow so redolent of the Christmas cards they received at the orphanage was becoming a threatening menace. No need for wild animals when you had weather like this. They nearly missed the route but Mo's innate senses helped them reach the gully just as Felix desperately emerged to try his luck from above. 'Gimme your radio,' he screamed, as Magnus's delayed reply crackled in.

'We'll get someone with you as soon as poss.'

The kids weren't going to wait, action was needed. They swarmed over the bridge, Elin and Xing staring into the void and the rest scampering round to the ice tunnel. Bheki brought out one of his special purchases: mountaineering rope.

Eugene had slipped further and he needed to arch his neck to keep his nose clear of the gushing stream. He wanted to reach up to untie his boots but his strength was failing him. Now in his fifties, endless rounds of squat thrusts were a thing of the past. Stuck between the water and the point of exhaustion, an uncontrollable shivering set in. The same thoughts that gripped him on the last launchpad came flooding back.

His numbed mind woke up to an unexpected thump on his chest and the miracle of his boot laces untying themselves. Weightless for an instant he dropped the final few inches before landing with a splash and a flurry of ice. There was another almighty bump as Xing tumbled after him. Her angel face pressed against his.

'I'm so sorry, Mr Eugene.' Before he could make any sense another head burst into his vision. Bheki had squirmed his way through the tunnel. Eugene was unable to climb back up and too big to crawl down the tunnel. Bheki weighed it up, turned and scurried back.

He returned brandishing the toilet spade, hacking away at the ice walls like a demented mole. He hitched rope around Eugene and Xing followed him, squirming their way back to join in a tug of war against time. Felix and the six children took their grip and heaved. Eugene moved until the aperture narrowed and he was stuck fast again. His eyes were filling with watery ice and he was jammed against the translucent roof.

Felix bellowed, 'We have to heave. After me – heave! HEAVE!' The rope tautened again and they dug their heels into the wet gravel to pull on the deadening weight. Eugene, choking, started to thrash around insanely, and the more they pulled the more he seemed to work against them.

'Eugene, get a grip!' Felix screamed as they pulled again, the little line snaking to and fro.

'OMG, what if this doesn't work?'

Felix was really starting to panic now. 'Pull. Pull!' And they pulled again. Closing his eyes, he strained against the rope. Suddenly it felt as if a hidden force had gripped it and it was as if the kids had superhuman strength.

*POP!*

Eugene broke like a cork from a bottle and skidded out into the open air.

They all flew backward into a crumpled heap of bodies and backpacks. Felix fell on Buzz, who fell on Mo, who fell on Elin, who fell on Enza, who fell on Bheki, who fell on Xing, who then fell on Su-lin, who fell on Soraya, who fell on Kirsten.

'The Elves' had arrived!

Magnus had sent out an emergency message to them. Kirsten had dealt with these situations before. 'Put up a tent. We need shelter!'

In the tent they started warming up the torpid man. There was only room for three. Soraya joined Kirsten, gently removing the wet clothing before wrapping him in the sleeping bags. Their busy hands rubbed his body to get the circulation going. With no response, they hastily stripped off to their underwear then snuggled up to share their body heat.

Eugene slowly came to, with the distinct feeling he'd died and gone to heaven.

Mo tugged at Elin's pack. 'Where's the burner?' She undid it with a quizzical look. 'Tea! It's Dad's solution to everything, innit!'

The relief was palpable when the women declared he was 'back in the living land'.

'Hey, Dr Su-lin, Xing, your turn now!' shouted Soraya as she reported his torn tendons.

Eugene looked sheepish when he emerged strapped up and ready to make it off the mountain. They set off into the remains of the daylight. Eugene took stock of the hole in the ice and the trapped bicycle. 'I suppose they'll get it back in the spring.' Then mournfully added, 'Damn! It's on hire!'

They gingerly came off the mountain, straining unused muscles helping Eugene down the scree slopes. Despite their exhaustion, the beauty of the valley still impressed them.

Gone were the bare rocks and ice fields; the vista finishing with the brooding mass of the Eyjafjallajökull ice cap was exquisite. The carpet of green mosses covering the broken volcanic cones was like passing from hell into a verdant and welcoming dale.

They followed the stream as it ploughed downwards towards the speck of a distant hut by the lake beyond. Magnus's team met them on the pass and helped them home, where a blazing fire and hot meal awaited them. They said farewell to Eugene, who was trundled away in a high-wheeled rescue vehicle. Virgil, the reserve, would be joining them in the morning.

The boys scoffed at the girls fastidiously choosing rocks to weigh down their perfectly well pinned out tents. They were hungry and in a hurry to eat. The campsite was a stone's throw from the hut and sheltered by the lakeside hills. They crossed the stream on a string of wobbly stones, then moved up to the glowing lights of the welcoming wooden edifice.

No Michelin-starred restaurant could have served a more welcome meal.

The kids graciously shared out some of their chocolate before retiring back across the gurgling waters.

Soraya held up the kettle to the remaining adults. 'Cawffi?'

Felix gave a conspiratorial smile. 'I've got something better!' He brought out one of their 'essentials'. A crystal clear bottle of Icelandic vodka and two lemons.

'Well, there's no shortage of ice.' Kirsten beamed as she searched for tall glasses.

'Wasted on Virgil.' Felix chinked his glass with Soraya. 'We go back to the shuttle. He don't drink and he don't smoke.'

'He married?' Soraya wondered.

'Nope! Hangs out with his brothers on some tiny island.'

'You married then?'

Felix shrugged his shoulders.

'I was happily married for seventeen years.'

'What happened?'

'She wasn't.'

Soraya touched his hand in sympathy.

'What about you?'

'Oh, I kiss frogs, but found no princes. Maybe one day.'

Felix flirted with a cheesy smile. 'There's room in my tent tonight.'

'Not with you in it, mister.'

Felix changed the subject. 'Why you wanna go, girl?'

'Don't girl me. I'm a mechanic and I've driven, sailed or flown everything except a space rocket.'

'Can you fix rocket engines?'

'They're not "rocket science", man, just an engine. You put fuel in one end and get motion out. The rest is in the manual.'

As the children settled down, the soft breeze was picking up and they dropped into a well-earned sleep with the canvas cracking and rippling above their heads.

In high spirits the adults stumbled across the stepping stones, pulling their hats down against the gathering gusts.

Xing woke up first, torn from her vivid dreams by the press of stretched canvas against her face. The quiet of the early evening was now a banshee wail of an Atlantic storm.

She buried her head, only to find Enza also stirring.

'*Che succede?*' Enza failed to sit up, bounced back by the wind on the tent. There was a commotion.

'We're blowin' away, bruv,' came through the canvas. 'We've lost our pegs and the tent's blown down. It's wild.'

Elin tried the zip. The opening crack revealed the shivering form of Mo. Beyond him were the boys, struggling like flies in a nylon web. Streams of snow were flying parallel to the ground.

In a still, small voice of calm, Elin commanded, 'Come on, get dressed.' They emerged with a flailing of limbs and gathered up the strewn backpacks while the boys freed themselves.

They salvaged as much as they could carry to the hut.

It was 3am when they forced the door shut against the wind's nipping fingers. Then tripped over a snoring figure on the floor.

Felix woke with a grunt. His tent had also collapsed around him.

As daylight lifted the mirk, the women, who'd survived the tempest, joined them for breakfast. A disaster – blown away on day three! On Mars they'd be dead.

As the wind abated they heard the distant sound of air-cooled engines toiling over the rocky roads. Magnus was in his jeep, heading a convoy of the self-driven camper vans.

With him was a square-jawed guy, Virgil.

'Your new buddy!' said Soraya.

**Thingvellir**
National park and canyon
South Iceland
63.2N 21.0W
Area: 92km$^2$
Geology: Crest of Mid-Atlantic Ridge

Felix nodded and gave him a man hug. Magnus regretfully announced the trail closed and that they'd be pulling out to the more sheltered climate of enchanted Thingvellir.

Enza nibbled her nails as she watched the roaring waters surge past, fording yet another swollen river. If she didn't bite them they'd be 4 feet long by her mother's age!

The continental plates of Europe and America also spread at the same rate. Each time you cut your nails it represents how far New York has moved from London in the same period.

The Earth's skin is a dynamic patchwork like the leather segments of a football, but not stitched together. They float on a vast ball of liquid rock whose convective currents drive the plates in a perpetual dance as they spread and disappear under each other, vying for space on a limited globe.

Thingvellir is an exposed section of the Mid-Atlantic Ridge, a jagged crack stretching from the Arctic to the Antarctic. The fissured landscape is the Earth's new skin, emanating from the mantle deep below. As it spreads, the pressure pushes all the way to the west coast of America, where the Pacific Plate grates against its North American counterpart. Periodically it releases this energy in catastrophic earthquakes.

Fractures dominate Thingvellir's landscape as the earth cracks like parched lips under a desert sun. There's a narrow canyon running north from the Thingvillavatn, where in the middle of its jumbled rocky bottom you can walk between the edge of Europe one side and America on the other.

It had been achingly frustrating to leave the trail, but when they arrived and gathered together, they sensed the energy of this extraordinary place and a shelter from the storm.

> **Thingvillavatn**
> Lake
> South Iceland
> 63.1N 21.1W
> Depth: 114m
> Area: 84km$^2$
> Geology: Rift valley lake

They started the next hike by dropping into the narrow canyon. On a wrinkled ledge of basalt, Elin told her friends about the wonders of plate tectonics.

Buzz stood astride the two continents, straining his legs.

He wondered if his little shove, like the wings of a butterfly, might tip some balance to create a rumble in Los Angeles where he knew his Granf was working at the JPL.

# Chapter 21

## Preparation

*Guarding the Farm*

The crockery faintly tinkled as Ford poured the coffee.

'They say it's not long before the Big One! At least there's no earthquakes on Mars!' he joked as he passed Stephen a cup.

'Why's that?' Stephen quizzed.

'Because they'd be Marsquakes!'

Stephen gave a pained smile and showed off his limited knowledge of the planet. 'That's not very funny. Anyway, there's no plate tectonics either?'

Ford had speculated about this. 'Yes, it must be due to the size of the planet. What do you think?'

With Stephen's repertoire of Martian geology almost exhausted he replied, 'I think I'll have two sugars.' Then dredging deep, 'OK, so why does Mars have such massive volcanoes then?'

It seemed obvious to Ford. 'With no tectonic plates the volcanoes stay put and just grow, rather than creating a chain of islands like Hawaii.' He enjoyed talking science, Stephen didn't.

They hadn't talked for some time. Stephen Dyer had been away. Convinced the project would fail, he'd taken all his leave well before its inevitable demise.

**Plate Tectonics**
A scientific theory accepted since the 1960s with the discovery of sea floor spreading. The lithosphere or Earth's crust is made up of seven large plates which move around up to 4 inches per year. There are volcanoes and ocean ridges where they spread and subduction zones where they slide under each other, causing earthquakes and ocean trenches.
The Big One – Expected large earthquake in Los Angeles area.

'I know that this nonsense will soon be consigned to the dustbin of history, but I was wrong on one thing.'

Ford ran his fingers through his hair, amazed at this admission.

'Unmanned drones were one thing, but that Saturn V is something else. Rocky's Hutzpah is on another level.' His thin lips twitched at the corners into a knowing smile. 'If by some miracle it does go ahead I hope that 'The Other Things' are still in contention.'

Ford couldn't believe his ears. 'Well, you've changed your tune.'

Dyer gave a strange laugh. 'Not really, I just hate kids, so you're welcome to blow them up in that second-hand rocket!'

It was the first time Ford had heard Stephen laugh – a sort of high-pitched sneer.

'You've been in the press again, at least your wife has!' Stephen had a newspaper with him showing Ford's front door and a flying tool bag in midair, beneath a headline, 'Mad Scientist's Mad Wife!'

*The wife of crazy scientist Ford Harris, who upset all the world's religions by calling them 'primitive', showed an unfortunate telecom guy how to 'move on'...*

Ford's face flushed as his anger rose. 'It's goddamn ridiculous. We think the press were trying to bug the place. Who'd be interested in us anyway?'

Stephen gave a contemptuous look. 'You're so naive. The real world is made of opposites. In my other work, it's the "Good Guys" or the "Bad Guys". To the press you are either celebrities or nonentities, and they'll build you up just to knock you down.'

Ford shuffled in his seat, frustrated at the sheer iniquity of it all. 'Why pick on me? I've never been famous, I just do my job!'

Stephen crossed his arms. 'Yes, but you work for the man they want to knock down, so you're in the crosshairs.' He tried to think how to explain it better. 'Look, I've been dealing with the "Bad Guys". The drug barons and crooks are one thing, they think they're above the law. The fanatics think they *are* the law, secure in their own self-righteousness.'

He made that strange laugh again. 'You can't argue with a Hellfire missile, though; I'm sure their last thoughts are, "It's so unfair!"... Look at this.'

He took out his phone and pressed an app with CIA on it. He took a picture of Ford and shared the screen. Information was streaming in: his name, relationships, internet usage, even the films he watched.

Then Stephen pushed the status button and 'LOW RISK' came up.

'Well, at least you won't be sending me a missile.' Ford laughed nervously.

Stephen narrowed his eyes and told him straight, 'These are just algorithms. The press have a different set and you're definitely a target.'

'But I'm a scientist, I deal in facts!'

Stephen gave that look again. 'They don't like facts, just opinions.'

Ford got up. He had very little time for Stephen's 'Real World'.

'But you're the president's man, why don't they get at you?'

Stephen looked very self-satisfied. 'I work for the administration, not the president, and I keep my head down and don't say dumb things at conferences... My vacation made me realise that I don't fit in here, policing you lot. I've now decided to concentrate on the project's hardware, in particular the lander. I like rockets and what's more, when it all goes wrong I can blame the Chinese...'

'"I've now decided"! Bloody cheek!' thought Ford, then realised it was really a great idea.

'You'll have to work in China.' To which Stephen nodded.

'Oh joy!' thought Ford.

They left it at that. Stephen was going to be far away and out of mind.

Ford called Jane. 'That man! I'll kick him out too, if he comes here, telling us we're naive.'

There was a crackle on the line. 'How's Buzz?' Jane asked.

'Good. I spoke to Magnus. He's having a real adventure. He's actually getting on with the other kids. Poor Eugene's had an accident, though, he fell through an ice bridge.'

'How's Bheki? He's a sweetie.' Jane had taken to the boy.

Ford laughed. 'Freezing. It's a real shock to his system! He's gonna enjoy the desert more... Look, be careful, honey.'

Jane still seethed with indignation. 'It's not fair, cariad, these guys try to bug the place, tell their lies and now everyone knows where we live!' She took a breath. 'And the dog's been sick, messing up the bloody yard.'

'Oh no, that's all we need! Is he OK?'

Jane sighed, 'Yeah, just getting old – a fate awaiting us all!'

'I'll stay out of the yard when my time comes! Any luck with the landing sites?'

Photos of Mars were now cluttering Jane's desk. 'The Moreux crater looks interesting, or have you seen the Micoud crater? My God, it looks like the entrance to hell! Deep, dark and mysterious.'

'Just like you, honey!'

'The entrance to hell?'

Ford scanned the paper Stephen had left.

**Micoud Crater**
49.5N 11.eE
Acidalia Planitia –
Mars
52 miles wide
Crater with
underground vents

'Listen, honey, I'll contact security.'

He didn't need to. After putting the phone down he had a call.

'Manny Black here, Homeland Security. We're concerned about your press exposure. There's a flutter in the ether about the mission too. We'd like to post a presence on your farm, sir.'

Ford felt sick. 'What do you mean, flutter in the ether?'

Manny cleared his throat. 'I'm sorry, it's a sign of the times. Anything this symbolic will draw attention, and these security breaches don't help. Mr Dyer knows the score. Anyway, no more press releases and no personal details, especially about the candidates.'

Ford was vexed. 'What do I say to my damned wife? Honey, you're a target!' There was a pause on the line.

'No, I'd couch it like – we're all targets and with this security, you're less so.'

Ford was unimpressed. 'She's not stupid, you know.'


The discreet protection arrived in a large black sedan and Darko Flanelli emerged in a black tie, white shirt and charcoal suit.

The dog was out of sorts and in no mood to welcome visitors.

It snapped at Darko's ankles as he retreated back to the car and honked the horn.

The commotion brought Jane striding across the yard and she shielded her protector from the dog as she guided him into the house.

'Scared of dogs, are we? Mack's a softy compared with the old farm in Corwen.'

'Sorry, ma'am, dogs are my Achilles heel, and I think it just nipped it!'

'Take those sunglasses off and I'll put the kettle on.'

She dabbed the spots of blood off his ankle and applied a plaster.

'I hope you've got something more casual – this is a farm, not a night club!'

Twenty minutes later Darko was on duty in one of Ford's lumberjack shirts and a pair of jeans. Jane found him an axe and told him to get busy chopping wood as the lumber pile had a commanding view.

As dusk fell two figures crept onto a low ridge overlooking the farm. Moving stealthily, they dodged between the boulders to gain the best vantage point. Both were dressed in black with matching balaclavas. They'd been here before, but last time in a telecoms van.

A familiar waft of ripe manure drifted over them as they settled behind a lonely shrub.

'What the hell are you doing?' whispered 'Mr Lemon'.

'Getting the camera ready!'

'Phew! I thought it was a gun!'

'Well, I got some good shots last time, unlike your mess up. You clown!'

'Hey, I've done the ground work now.'

'Lemon' explained how he'd laid bait to sedate the dog and already recced the farm to find Jane always kept her study window slightly open. He pulled out a jemmy and demonstrated his technique. 'I'm going to nip in and set the bug in their broadband.'

'Not in those white sneakers – they'll spot you a mile off!'

'Hey, I'll take the risk. There's no way I'll wear black ones, my friend!'

The photographer carefully surveyed the scene with binoculars.

'Oh hell! The old man's back. He's chopping wood. How you going to get in now? AND the dog's still charging around the back yard. It's having a crap. What kind of sedative did you give it?'

'Laxosomething, some of Grandpa's pills. He always takes them after dinner, he says he can't sleep without them.'

'Oh my God! They'll be laxatives to stop him pooping himself in his sleep! My gran's the same!'

The whispering stopped abruptly as a distant rumble grabbed their attention and a convoy of pick-ups billowed dust along the winding farm track. In the half-light the would-be intruders watched as they pulled up, and a score of morbidly obese protesters unloaded placards from the opened backs of the vehicles.

'Hey, this is our night after all!' whooped the photographer as he pulled the trigger on the massive night camera.

'... and my distraction bang on cue!' beamed 'Mr Lemon' as he grabbed his kit.

Jane's feelings of violation in the unwanted security presence had given way to her humane instincts. Darko now looked like a young Ford as he left the house with the axe, and when he asked if he could leave his meagre rations in the fridge, she decided cooking a proper 'tea' would be the right thing to do. She would make a pie. She was dusting the counter with flour when the commotion outside stopped her dead and she clumsily dropped the bag of flour with a soft thump on the red terracotta tiles. As she opened the front door she could see Darko, axe still in hand, running to the gate as a chanting crowd pressed against the fence. Their garish banners shrieked the messages, 'GOD HATES YOU', 'GOD HATES GARVEY' and 'YOUR SIN NOT GOD'S'.

She'd not seen anything like this since her Sunday school in Corwen. She hurried back through the house and into the yard and let the dog through the side gate to give Darko some support. Macks rushed off and, ignoring Darko, headed straight for the crowd before relieving himself in front of their leading figure.

With Jane's attention firmly fixed on the commotion, a dark-clad figure worked his way unseen towards the yard. Jane rushed back to the front veranda as the crowd were shaking the fence and lighting torches.

The burning brands and visceral chanting created a chilling atavistic air as she watched Darko's silhouette holding the crowd at bay like Horatius on the bridge. She dialled 911 and called for help.

At the rear, 'Mr Lemon' didn't even need his jemmy. Jane had left the back door open and she didn't hear his soft footsteps slip through the kitchen to place the bug. He only needed a minute to swap the filter on the internet connection once he'd found the router.

Suddenly Jane remembered Ford's advice and darted back in the house to turn on the floodlights. The intruder sought refuge in her study when he heard Jane run to the hall cupboard. The whole farm lit up in a tungsten glare as she flipped the switches. There was a sudden gasp outside, then a click and total darkness. She'd blown the main fuse.

In the temporary lull outside and the silence darkness brings, she thought she heard a slight scraping of furniture beyond the kitchen. By the light of her phone she crept down the hall and on the floor were a second set of tell-tale floury footprints that headed for the study. She was terrified. They must have broken through and were in the house! She picked up the trail from the kitchen as well as her rolling pin. With a quavering voice she shouted down the hall.

'Who is it? Get out of my house. I've called the police!'

In the white beam she saw that her study door was ajar. She always left it shut. The footprints vanished beyond the threshold and an unpleasant smell was in the air. At the sound of Jane's voice 'Lemon' was frantically packing away his tools. He'd found the router and set the bug and the window was his escape route. Jane heard the rising sash repeatedly hit the security restraints with bruising thuds.

'Get out of my house!' she screamed again, not yet daring to cross the threshold.

The intruder's only escape was blocked. He'd tried to squeeze through the opening left after the mangled restraints had jammed the sash but to his dismay he found it too small and, disaster, his raised white sneakers had picked up a generous helping of dog doo in its designer treads. He couldn't cope with marks or even creases on them.

After an interminable wait Jane dared to enter the room; with all that banging and splitting of wood surely the imposter had made their escape. She surveyed the scene as the narrow beam flitted around, immediately noticing her desk had been shifted and the nasty smell hung in the air. The door to the old closet where she kept her records was also ajar. Creeping forward she put her ear to the opening. Was that breathing she could hear above her own booming heartbeat? Jane yanked the door open, rolling pin raised high. Nothing... apart from the serried ranks of her research papers caught in the beam. She froze as she felt a soft pressure on her ankle and a hairy presence wind between her lower calves. She jerked her leg away, then a soft mew brought recognition. It was her old red tomcat.

'Oh, Jones, it's you!' she whispered with relief, and squatted down to pet the cat. It suddenly hissed at a sound behind her and straining her eyes in the darkness, she discerned a crouching shadow hiding under the desk. The figure seemed to glow and unfurl, and, panicking, she rushed for the door as it too shot in the same direction. An invisible hand shoved her and wheeling round she instinctively swung the rolling pin to defend herself. The startled shriek of pain was followed by a sickening crash as the figure pitched forward against the doorjamb.

Mr Lemon's consciousness slowly returned, with the smell of coffee and fresh herbs hanging in the candle-lit air and the gentle hands of a woman dressing his scalp. Where the hell was he and how long had he been out? His body felt lifeless, immobile. He strained to move but the police handcuffs binding him to the solid pine chair held firm.

'What's the point of all that nonsense, then?' demanded Jane as Lemon stared wildly round the farm kitchen. Outside, he could hear the police sirens and shouting as they ejected the protesters and in the next room the voice of Darko on the phone.

'Yes, sir, there was a whole gang of them and one got into the house... Jane's shook up but OK and the police are here.'

Lemon's groggy eyes rested on a framed print on the wall – 'The Gates of Paradise 1793'.

'That image is what my husband's really about, not dogma and hatred like you lot. He may be a scientist... a rocket man, but he's soulful. It seems to catch his sense of wonder.'

The whistle of the kettle on the hob blew and Jane fetched a bowl of hot water.

She proffered the sweet tea to the lips of the recumbent figure and bathed his head once again.

'Why don't you nutters leave us alone!'

Lemon protested, 'I'm not one of them. I'm a reporter. My press card's in my wallet.'

She carefully took the wallet out of his pocket and there was his photograph on a 'Pure News' press card. With sudden recognition Jane blurted out, 'You've been here before, the telecom man! You advertised my house to every loony in the country and now look what's happened.'

She poured the tea away. 'You're worse than they are! At least they believe in something. You're not a reporter, you're a bloody burglar.'

*Blake, Gates of Paradise*

# Chapter 22

## Training

*Icelandic Trout*

The night drew in and the children, having fallen behind, pitched their tents alone by the edge of the twinkling lake.

They unpacked and made their nests for the night. The storm now a memory, the wind was soft and the temperature mild.

The question 'What's for supper?' hung in the air. This was the first night they'd have to prepare their own food.

'Bread, noodles and sausage!' Elin pronounced as she shuffled through their supplies.

'No pork for me!' protested Mo.

'OK, cheese and tomato pasta?'

'I can't eat cheese!' declared Xing.

Bheki turned his eyes to the starry heaven. 'Hey, what's wrong with you? I'll have both!'

There was a splash in the shallows.

'Ach! That's a fish!'

261

Thingvellir Lake has some of the best freshwater fishing in the world, famous for its giant trout.

'Hey, what are we waiting for? Find a good stick.' Bheki delved into his pack and brought out his special purchase. A fishing line and hooks.

'Did you say fish?'

He picked out feathers from his sleeping bag and bound them to the hook and trace. His friends returned stickless, so he borrowed a carbon-fibre pole from the front of the tent.

'Stay to my left while I cast.'

The children, like all who watch a fisherman, stood by the lapping waters in keen anticipation.

'Useless on Mars!' he laughed as he flicked the rod, before setting the fly on his chosen spot. As he cast, an enormous moon rose above the broad horizon, spangling the dark waters.

Cast after cast he made, well-practised in the seasonal streams of the Matopos Hills.

Then high above the waters, Buzz spotted the unmistakable beacon of the ISS gliding overhead. 'They're sending bits of us up there!'

The children followed his finger.

'Those samples they took; they're testing them in space! Eugene told me.'


In the depths a cold body stirred, disturbed from her torpor by a long hunger and the tempting vibration of ready food. The crafty old trout was cautious of figures by the bank, but the storm had left her disorientated, and the yellow moonlight echoed the long summer evenings when the surface swarmed with an insect harvest.

Her brain was cold and mechanical. Shifting through the information conveyed through scent, vibration and electrical fields, she created a map of the murky world, letting her instincts home in on her prey or avoid danger, long before her fish eyes focused on these objects of desire or menace.

Tonight the dark figures on the bank were outshone by the moonbeams spreading through the water.

Bheki's skill was to lightly drop the line to mimic the evening dance of the mayfly. The old trout cautiously patrolled the spot, weighing up the odds as she scanned the shimmering surface and the tempting bait. It was not a conscious decision, like choosing a tempting cake. Her conflicting urges tipped into feeding mode and with a silvered flick of her tail she struck, breaking the surface and diving with her nemesis in her pouting mouth.

Bheki felt the tug and pulled, embedding the hook deep beneath the clamped lips and held firm as the strong body flexed against the line, lunging for the safety of deeper waters.

A thrill tremored through the row of children as Bheki strained against his foe. There was a flash as the brown-and-blue-speckled form broke the surface and dived. It was enormous, and even in these winter waters, pulses of adrenaline spurred the fish on to fight against its fate.

It was long and hard but the years of battles with African fish had prepared Bheki well. Exhausted and beaten the creature was finally coaxed into the shore.

'Hey, man! Someone bash it!' cried Bheki as he kept the line taut against a late escape.

Buzz looked at Mo; Elin looked at Enza. Frozen, none of the faint hearts moved. With a sudden splash and a squelching thud the spark of life was extinguished. Xing had crashed a rounded rock into the sleek blue scales just above the gills.

That night 'The Other Things' feasted on the fish, sushi-fresh and with beautiful texture and taste. However squeamish Enza had been to kill the fish, she was in her element cooking it. Last season's wild thyme was gathered and chopped with the raw fish into a trout carpaccio and the fillets were fried in thyme and oil and served with noodles.

They slept like contented kittens that night, but as the night became day, Enza woke fretting about the remaining fish.

As she took the remaining fillet off the bones, a voice emanated from the boys' tent.

'Shouldn't we get going?'

'Shut uppa, Buzz!'

'We're totally behind!'

Then Elin piped up. 'It's a test not a competition!'

He didn't get it. 'What's the difference?'

'Mummia always says not the quickest it is, but who's best at the work. A race, no one said it was. If we go to Mars, it will be what we do there, not how quickly back we come.'

She emerged into the cold, misty air and addressed the two tents. 'We are on an expedition, so work we need to do. Samples I'll take of the rocks and look for fossils with Mo. Buzz, about bugs you're supposed to know, so look for them. Xing will help you! Enza, you can record everything. Empty-handed we can't end up. Bheki, smoke the fish and pack up the gear.'

'Who says she's the boss?' moaned Buzz.

'I do,' affirmed the little girl.

They left the adults to race each other and spent a cold, moody morning among the rocky outcrops and frozen bogs. Enza eagerly donned her fingerless gloves to draw the 'finds'. Bheki scoured the waterfront for junk. In a cleft was a weathered fragment of tin roofing. Delighted, he then foraged back among the mosses and dry grass.

Bheki formed the tin sheeting into a funnel to smoke the fish. His sure hands steadied the structure as he carefully hung the side of trout with wire from the top. He coaxed the smouldering vegetation until the peaty smoke billowed merrily out of the cone. He soaked in the warmth as he tended the fire. Then he carefully packed the gear as the pink flesh slowly turned into an aromatic bronze.

They set off just before noon, following the shoreline as the frigid waters lapped at their feet. Packs groaning with rock samples they headed south until the wide, salty sky and cold Atlantic breeze enveloped their diminutive figures. Bheki proudly carried the fish. He sang as he hiked, forgetting about the cold, but still accustoming himself to the world of a thousand shades of blue and grey. He wondered if the red hues of Mars would feel more like his familiar African palette.

His song stopped abruptly with a new visual shock. Before him was the coast. The blues, whites and aquamarines were expected, but the beach!

He'd seen plenty of pictures of the sea, but nothing like this. The sand was jet black and rocks of white ice played games with his vision. It was like a negative world!

He stood mesmerised and the others stopped with him, then broke with an infectious laughter as he ran skipping through the dark sand, kicking the ice which shattered into explosions of dancing white flakes. They all followed, screaming until they reached the waterline and the crashing breakers.

There is nothing beyond the line of surf, except the ocean stretching south to the icecap at the bottom of the globe.

With this vast horizon to their right, they trekked eastwards, crossing the shallow rivers that punctuated the shoreline until they reached the looming slopes of the Eyjafjallajökull glacier as it met the ocean.

*Icelandic Coast*

Exhausted, Buzz tugged Mo's sleeve. 'Are we there yet?'

Mo checked his co-ordinates. 'Nearly there, innit!' Then around a bluff they spotted the shapes of the three faithful camper vans laid up by the grey ribbon of a road. He called Magnus to announce their arrival.

By the time Magnus's response of 'Mission Accomplished' came through, 'The Other Things' had been warmly welcomed by the adults and were soon unpacking bags to pool their remaining rations for a celebration dinner. The introduction of the smoked trout transformed the meagre menu.

Repacking the rocks and mosses, Enza reassured Buzz and Xing. 'Don't worry, I've drawn the fish to go with your samples.'

Felix triumphantly winked at Virgil. 'We won, man!'

Virgil sported an increasingly perplexed look as they all swapped notes.

'What's all this about samples?' he whispered.

Felix spun round and kicked an ice rock. 'Damn! Eugene was taking the samples. Weren't you briefed?'

'I thought it was just a race!'

Felix shouldered his bag. 'Quick, man! Grab some rocks and stuff.'

Tomorrow they'd be heading to the capital to present their reports and for the long-awaited visit to the world-famous Museum of Practical Jokes.

Rumbling through the untidy suburbs of Reykjavik, they headed for the university. The clean Scandinavian lines made the JPL look like a budget hotel. Magnus and Eugene – now on crutches – welcomed them into a wood-lined lecture theatre.

They presented their samples and reports, then retired for a short lunch. The excitement was palpable as they set off to the Museum of Practical Jokes. Even Kirsten allowed herself a frisson of anticipation. By luck it was only a short detour off the main road to their final destination, Keflavik airport, so they had plenty of time to enjoy it.

Since it was founded by Ingolfr Arnason, the people of Iceland have been renowned for their love of practical jokes.

The long winter evenings have, almost out of necessity, been broken up by fun and japes and as the Icelanders say, 'If we didn't have a sense of humour we would all be Danish.'

Pulling off the barren tarmac, they whisked past an enormous sign.

*Safn Practicla Brandara* (the Museum of Practical Jokes)

As Eugene was on crutches, the vans drew up in the disabled bays of a vast parking lot.

Eugene limped out as they spotted an arrowed sign.

*Museum – 500m. Remember to pay for your parking – 2,000ISK.*

The children could hardly contain their excitement.

'Come on, Mummia, it's this way!' screeched Elin, dragging her along.

**Ingolfr Arnason** Norwegian Chieftain Founded Iceland in 874 AD and made its first practical joke. He promised his wife Hallveig Frodesdatter they were moving to America.

Under grey slabs of cloud, they trudged past ranks of empty bays.

There was nothing in the distance except a strange-looking kiosk with a blue '*Botts Hughson Pylsa*' sign and a low pyramid-shaped gift shop.

Bewildered, the party confronted the bald bearded man standing behind the sizzling onions.

'Where's the Museum of Practical Jokes?' demanded Felix.

'The clue's in the name!' beamed the hotdogista. The wind moaned as he tapped the side of his nose. 'It's a well-known fact that museums only make money out the parking, gift shops and food and we are a practical people... They just cut out the middle man. Never built it.'

*Ingolfr Arnason*

'That's ridiculous!' retorted Felix.

'The ridiculous is the cornerstone of all humour!' The man smiled. Felix looked puzzled. 'I thought it was timing!'

'Ah, thanks for reminding me. It's also shut on Thursdays!'

Kirsten burst in. 'How can it be shut on Thursdays if it doesn't exist?'

The man stirred his onions. 'It's shut every day, of course!'

Eugene had just caught up. 'You can't have a goddamn museum without galleries or exhibits, fella!'

The poor man looked hurt. 'That's how we ran our banking system! The hot dogs are good!'

As they left the car park, still picking burned onions out of their teeth, Felix pointed to the back of the large entrance sign.

*Thank you for visiting Safn Practicla Brandara*
*The world's first virtual museum (www.thejokesonyou.is).*
*Please remember to drive on the left!*

# Chapter 23

## The President's Last Year

A blank piece of paper stared back at Luther Garvey. His last 'State of the Union' speech, his last year in office. Where to start? A culmination of his life's work then years of lectureships and ceremony. He shook his head at the thought of his high hopes for social reform. Now there was little he could do to salvage his bold ambitions.

'Damn it,' he muttered, 'I'm going to enjoy myself... and get that rocket off the ground.'

He recalled the conversation the vice president, who'd put his hat in the ring for the party nomination but not his commitment to the project. With a grimace he considered the alternative. Although Peggy Tyler hadn't yet been nominated for the opposition, for a man as experienced as Luther, he considered it a slam dunk. What's more, he feared she'd give his stable mate more than a run for his money. Either way he had to get the project off the ground before either of them took up the reins. He scanned the room for inspiration. The images of both John and Martin stared back reproachfully. 'Get on with it, man!' they seemed to scold.

Belle came in with a flourish and brought coffee and a piece of fruit. Luther picked up the halved pear by the remains of the stem and eyed it suspiciously. 'Why the fruit? There's a bowlful yonder?'

'Because you ignore it, sir, and Wilma had a word with me.' She stood looking at him, hand on the hip. 'Remember you've got a conference call with Mr Harris and his team.' Then, with a glance at the bowl again, she said, 'I think his visit was the only time you've touched it!'

As she left the room she called over her shoulder, 'I'll patch you in when everyone's on board, sir.'

There was an interminable wait as Ford desperately tried to end his previous call.

'Yes, honey, you're quite right, can we talk lat... OK, I know it's important but the president is wai... Yes, I know it was his bl... idea, but I can't say that to him... Yes, sweetheart, I'll try to bring it up... I mean, I will. OK. Yes... Yes... I love you!' Ford put the phone down with a sheepish look to his colleagues who were pretending not to notice.

When the conference finally started Luther was feeling decidedly tetchy. 'I hope your comms will be snappier on the mission!'

Ford flustered apologetically. 'I'm sorry, sir, it's just that Jane, my wife, came through on the line and I thought it was the conference call. She was a bit upset!'

'Upset?' quizzed the president.

'Yes, well, more like a bit furious! It was difficult getting her off.'

Luther looked at the cameo on his desk. 'Well, Wilma's never a bit furious, she only has one setting. I guess it's about security... Well, I don't blame her.' Luther tapped the phone to gain attention.

'Hello, Manny, you there? Let's talk about security. What about Ford's wife?'

'I think Jane would be safer with Ford in LA. The press have made her address known to everybody and the farm's too big to guard discreetly.'

Luther tapped the phone again. 'Stephen, what about you? How come you've slipped off to China?'

'You sent me to the wilderness, I've swapped it for a desert, and my old colleagues encouraged me. It's an opportunity to see their methods from the inside.'

'Need any protection over there?'

From the other side of the globe Luther heard Stephen's strange laugh. 'No worries, sir, Jiuquan is the deadest place on the planet and there's guards everywhere and no press at the gates.'

'OK,' followed the president. 'What about the safety of the candidates?'

Sharon broke through. 'Sharon Frankel here, Mission Programmer. We have them holed up in the Mojave doing their isolation training and we take them in the back way when they go to the JPL.'

The president pressed the point. 'I want an absolute news blackout regarding their identities and no blabbing relatives. Can you all achieve that?'

The president moved onto the project. Stephen was almost enthusiastic when he briefed them on his progress on the lander and the fantastic resources the Chinese had thrown into it. Rocky gave a deadpan delivery on the restoration of the Saturn V and the second rocket being assembled by ESA in Toulouse.

'I'm on the farewell tour this year, so you'll all get a visit. Focus, guys! We've only twelve months or this ain't gonna happen,' said Luther.

Before they signed off, the president addressed Ford. 'By the way, rent a nice house for Jane in LA. We'll cover the costs from the security budget. It will get you out of those awful rooms.'

Sharon couldn't help herself. 'Hey, Aunt Naomi's house is vacant. She's in a home and looking to rent. It's a Fifties villa up in Bel Air. All abstract art and modern furniture. Jane'll love it!'

'Sounds perfect and discreet,' added Luther as he signed off.

The president put pen to paper as he gnawed his fruit. He sketched a road, two vanishing lines and then a fork: one leading to the left, one the right. He jotted down a cloud of words above each direction.

Equal and opposites: science – ignorance; generosity – greed; open mind – closed mind; love – hate; and as he filled the skies above the roads with these laden words he formed his speech around these future choices.

He reflected on how the asteroid made the world take stock, changing minds and policies, and maybe how each of the problems could be used as an impetus to make things better. As the speech took shape he implored his successors to be positive. Most of all he lauded the Mars project as America being able to do the 'Big Things' that make a difference.

It was a start anyway. He picked up the phone. 'Could you get me Victor Relish, Belle?'

He fiddled with the speech, then the line buzzed and it was Victor. 'I'm honoured, a call from the president himself! How can I help?'

Luther took a deep breath. He would need to handle this well; he didn't trust the man. 'I need you to cut us a little slack, Mr Relish. We have enough trouble getting the project off the ground without the press hounding my people. It's now got serious and as it's so precious to me, I'll take steps if I don't get co-operation.'

Victor mulled it over. 'That sounds like a threat, sir. I don't interfere with editorial policy.'

Luther cleared his throat. 'I am the head of state and the buck stops with me. You are the head of your group and it's the same. I don't make threats, just promises. Understood?'

Luther had a long list of the various licence agreements,

government contracts and other business that might unravel if he needed to exert a little more pressure and so did Victor.

'OK, sir, I'll make sure they keep the dogs off, at least while you're here. But... I have my own interests to consider, so we won't be backing it!'

'Thank you, Victor!'

The president's stomach gurgled as Marine One took off. His itinerary was hectic. On this last tour of the Union, he was keen to inspect the restoration of 'Wilson's' damage to the Eastern Seaboard, then his treasured rejuvenation projects in the dysfunctional cities throughout the Midwest.

He was a man of the people and they flocked to see him – except in the high Mojave Desert. As they sped low over the hot landscape the ground pulsed with the pumping of the rotors and, banking around an outcrop, they saw three alien silver cylinders nestled on the desert floor.

'Hey! It actually looks like a moon base!' shouted the president over the engine noise. The red dust swirling, he stepped out onto the baked ground. Henrietta and Sharon met him, heads ducked as they made their introductions and led him across the bouldered surface to the first of the pods. Luther momentarily stopped to take in the desert.

**The Mojave Desert**
California/Nevada/
Utah/Arizona, USA
35.1N 115.3W
Altitude: from 279ft
below sea level to
11,918ft
Geology: Rain
shadow desert

Boundless and bare, the sands stretched far into the distance and he considered what he might leave for posterity.

The three silver pods were splayed out in a tripod shape, limiting the views of their neighbours. From the porthole windows the desert stretched far and wide, and was ever silent except for the howl of the odd coyote and the incessant stutter of the aircon units as they struggled against the baking heat. Apart from the training trips to the JPL, their inhabitants had spent the last three months in 'The Transit Stage' – a process aimed to simulate the mental conditions endured on long interplanetary flight. They wouldn't leave the pods for days and then only for brief forays at night, as if on space walks, tethered and hanging on to the many rails and handles fixed to the smooth aluminium skins and never touching the ground.

The 'Exploration Stage' had, thankfully, just begun with forays into their surroundings. They'd felt ridiculous, dressed in masks and jump suits and always carrying a pack to simulate the cumbersome life support they'd have to wear.

The president was ushered to the first door.

'What?!' Eugene cried as it opened, surprised to see a new face. Eugene was reading on his bed, while Virgil rehydrated lunch and Felix was learning geology online. A locker-room smell wafted past as Eugene stuffed his scattered clothes beneath the mattress. He recognised their visitor.

Luther reeled back outside. 'Has a dog died in there?' Then bravely taking a fresh lungful, he re-entered and sat with the old astronauts, chewing the fat about their past space exploits.

He breathed a sigh of relief as he finally re-emerged into the sunlight.

The party made the transfer to the next pod. It looked mighty familiar. 'Henrietta, where the hell did you get these things?'

She laughed, 'Verner Bros studio! You know the space epic that flopped last year?'

'You mean *The Final Frontier* with Michel Angelo?'

'That's the one! Renamed *The Final Curtain*... They were only too happy to let these go... Obviously, no chance of a sequel...'

Henrietta put her head through the second door. All was in sweet-smelling order. She proudly announced, 'Ladies, we have company!'

'Only women in here!' Kirsten called tetchily over her shoulder as she pounded on the exercise machine. Soraya's head bucked to her music as she worked on the computer and Su-lin was reading.

'Hello there!' Luther stepped over the threshold.

They froze; that voice was unmistakable. One of his many charms was a voice that could melt chocolate. 'Luther Garvey,' they whispered.

This felt calmer, more ordered and certainly more fragrant. 'So, Su-lin, how does all this compare to your own space agency?'

Su-lin thought hard. 'Less disciplined but... more fun!'

'I don't suppose Iceland...?'

Kirsten laughed as she replied, 'Only in that crazy museum!'

He turned to Soraya. 'I've seen you at the White House. How come you're here?'

She looked him straight in the face. 'I'm the best driver you'll meet and cool at mechanics. Besides, DC's getting boring, so what the hell?'

Luther turned back to Su-lin. 'So you're the "Bones" and a pilot?'

'Bones? Ah, you mean medic. I'm a flying doctor.'

'Plane or helicopter?'

'And autogyros,' she replied.

'Wow! Well, you only live once.'

Luther took in the cabin. His Oval Office desk seemed bigger. 'And, Kirsten, as well as your love of practical jokes, you're the scientist?'

'Sir, no one in Iceland actually likes practical jokes – that's the joke! I'm a volcanologist and expedition organiser.'

Luther tried to picture them on the planet and wondered if they'd still be so calm and measured after eight months in space. Their determined natures reassured him. 'Maybe,' he thought.

He walked close to Henrietta after leaving the pod, their two figures casting long shadows on the ground.

'Wouldn't you like to join them, Henrietta?'

'Do you think I'm mad, sir? I haven't finished with this planet yet!' She ushered him forward. 'This is the kids' pod. Let's surprise them!'

As they crossed the 'airlock', there was a monotonous thudding coming from within and raised voices.

'Stop the racket! I'm trying to think!' Enza shouted at Mo as he practised catching a tennis ball against the side of the hull.

'Leave him be!' shouted Buzz, defending his right to a bit of exercise.

'Shut up, you're annoying too!' Elin snapped.

Mo tossed the tennis ball in a slow loop at her head. 'Catch!'

She whacked it back with venom. 'You'll be chasing your balls all over Mars, if you don't watch it!'

The ball ricocheted hard off Bheki's head, as the door swung open. It's a little known fact that every elected president has been good at sports. Even President Roosevelt represented his country in the 1936 Paralympics in Berlin. Luther's figure filled the doorframe, the ball hurling towards his nose. In a flash he deftly intercepted the missile and slipped it into his pocket.

'*Il Presidente!*' Enza stopped dead. 'You tell him, stop it! He's got to listen to you!' she implored.

Henrietta was mortified. 'I'm so sorry, sir, they're usually as good as gold!'

'Ah, just like a real family – no problems here!' laughed the head of state.

Spending time with each of them, the president listened intently.

Bheki was working on designs for a Martian bike.

Xing had been racing Buzz on his flight game.

Enza had been making ravioli with the sage Bheki had been growing.

Elin showed him some earthly rock formations, which looked strangely like the ones she was studying of the Martian surface.

Mo, when not practising his cricket, had been researching exotic life and early soft-bodied fossils, familiarising himself with animals that might resemble the Martian photographs.

Luther studied the pictures with fascination. He took a shine to the boy. He was a 'first' American president in many things and one of them was an appreciation of cricket. His grandpa Constantine had come from Grenada and had shown the young Luther how to catch against a wall, just like Mo.

Nibbling on the pasta, Luther then spoke to the children. They huddled up around him; it looked like Uncle Remus had descended to tell his fables. Rather than cautionary tales he told them the reasons why he'd considered sending them on this dangerous mission.

'I meet many, many people and the younger they are the more enthusiasm they have for new ideas as well as a faith in the future. My jaded generation's just waking up to the damage we've caused. Our salvation lies in the dreams of our youth. If they're inspired by your exploration of another planet, they might believe we can save our own. It will be a very grand thing.' Then he gave some pearls of wisdom. 'Keep up with the training and don't forget your homework!'

The children stepped up and gave him a hug.

'Also, never accept sweets from strangers!' He winked as he slipped them each a bag of savoury snacks.

As he bade them farewell he tossed the ball to Mo, just like his grandfather might have done.

'They're amazing kids. How'd they keep in touch with their parents and schooling?'

Sharon joined them as they emerged. 'We have tutors and they talk to their families all the time, but every day we add slightly greater time delay in the conversations. It's just a few minutes now, but it trains them to deal with the transmission pauses.'

Luther needed to talk to Sharon and asked Henrietta and his bodyguards give them some space.

'I think we're safe enough here.'

He scuffed the ground as he walked, kicking the parched tufts of hardy grass that patiently waited for the rains to come.

'You won't find this on Mars. Have you been to a real sand desert?

I remember walking on the edge of the Sahara. It felt like being on a small boat on an endless ocean. It was scary.'

'It serves its purpose, sir. It's dry, isolated and close enough to do the rest of the training at the JPL. There's also cinder cones and lava tubes within a day's hike. They're just like ones we've seen on Mars.'

Luther wasn't here to talk volcanoes. 'Are we crazy considering those kids?'

They sat on two smooth red boulders while she mulled over the question. The cloudless sky held the thinnest of crescent moons, gorgeously close to the bright jewel of Venus as they set in the gold and blue afterglow. Although the day's heat still hugged the ground, the night air was cooling fast.

Sharon pulled her grey NASA hoodie around her as she replied, 'The men are seasoned astronauts but struggle with the science. The women are doing pretty well all round, and the kids... well, they are actually holding their own. They squabble a bit and need the guidance of their parents, but they are surprisingly resourceful and they're having fun, even in this isolation.'

'So, it's not that crazy?'

She looked up at the sky again. 'Yes, of course it's crazy, but it's not stupid. We shall see... Did you know Venus is bright enough to cast shadows in a dark place like this?'

*Bang! Bang! Bang!*

Her musing was brought short by the sound of what she thought were fire crackers behind them.

Luther had dreaded this sound. He flinched at all unexpected noises. He turned and dived, pushing her to the deck beside him. 'Quick, behind the rocks – that's gunfire!'

As they shuffled back, the president's brain was overloading with dire possibilities and plans of action. They saw three men in the distance firing in the air, and flashes and sparks streaming off some invisible object. There was a high-pitched squeal and an oncoming 'whoosh' as they picked out the target. It seemed as if some gigantic injured spider was spinning towards them. It could be anything, though nothing good.

Luther placed himself protectively across Sharon and shouted 'Brace!' as the object screamed, hitting the ground a mere 10 yards away and clattering along the rock-strewn ground.

The president slowly raised his head as the dust settled, peering at the stricken object, two of its rotors still spinning. It was a broken camera drone, and on the bottom was a small sticker: 'Property of PURE CORP. Reward for return if found.'

'It's a goddamn drone!' he reassured Sharon as he hauled himself to his feet. The sprinting bodyguards arrived hollering, then gingerly approached the stricken article for closer examination.

Manny Black and his companion were eventually allowed into the sumptuous office of the head of the Pure Corporation. 'How can I help you? I trust there's nothing wrong. I'm at your service...' Victor Relish oozed obsequious platitudes to the agent.

'No. I'm here to serve something on you.' Manny placed a subpoena on Victor's endless chrome and leather desk. The embossed document sat accusingly among the alabaster paperweights and staged, silver-edged family photographs.

Numerous sensitive scenarios flashed through his mind as Victor scanned the document. He burst out laughing when he read the indictment of breaking air traffic regulations, pertaining to drones.

'This is ridiculous. Get out of my office! The legal department's on the 12th floor.'

Manny took a deep breath. 'Mr Relish, we have reason to believe that you are responsible for an unmanned aircraft to be flown in such a way to endanger the President of the United States, and as such I shall be sequestrating your personal computers and you will allow my colleague here access to any company files, databases, messages or emails that he may need to help us in our investigations.'

Victor was furious. 'Listen, we send out drones all the time to gather information, there's no law against it!'

Manny smiled. 'This is no poor celeb in a swimming pool. You nearly dropped it on the president.'

'Dropped it? Dropped it? You shot it down!'

'It could have been carrying a bomb, so it was a risk. I'm afraid you chose the wrong target for your cameras this time!' Manny started un-hooking Victor's laptop on the desk.

'You can't do that. We'd had a tip off about a secret training base – how did we know he'd be there?'

'Bad luck...' replied Manny as he placed the laptop in an evidence bag. 'I'll leave you with my friend here and I'm sure you'll be helpful.'

Victor froze for a moment, mentally checking on the secrets encoded on the Pentium chips and flash drive of his Sinclair ZX810.

The door shut firmly behind Manny with a thud.

# Chapter 24

## Beverly Hills

*Ford and Jane Dancing*

'And what did Sharon's auntie do?' quizzed Jane as she strode round the wood-veneered walled living room.

'Costumes! Made a fortune out of costumes. They rebuilt this place in the 1950s when her uncle was teaching at the new university.' Ford was following her.

'And look at the views!' Jane swung her arm imperiously across the immensity of the full-height windows. 'They certainly picked their spot.' She turned quickly into his path. Picking up his arms she whisked him away in a mock waltz. 'What parties they must have had. All those famous actors!'

'I wonder who?' mused Ford.

Jane stopped and thought. 'Elizabeth Taylor, of course! You can be my Richard Burton. Except for the voice!'

Ford looked affronted and in gravely Welsh tones quoted, '*It is spring, moonless night in the small town, starless and Bible-black, the cobble streets silent and the hunched.'*

'Wow! Not bad, cariad! You sound just like Uncle Chedwyn.' Then Jane started the dancing again. 'I can't imagine why Sharon isn't living here instead of staying at the "Gulag"!'

'Sharon couldn't afford it, sugar. Her aunt has been trying to rent it to cover the costs of her care home. Sharon told me she could sell the site for a fortune, but it would break her heart to knock this down.'

**Beverly Hills**
California USA
35.4N 118.2W
Altitude: 258ft
Geology: Tertiary
sedimentary rocks,
oil deposits

'It was really sweet of Sharon to offer it to us.' Suddenly Jane stopped dancing and stared through the expanse of horizontal glass and way out over the valley. 'You spent a lot of time with this Sharon in the "Gulag" all bunking up together. I hope she wasn't too sweet to you then!'

'Honey, that's silly, we are all professionals – scientists, even – and usually far too tired to fraternise,' replied Ford, offended.

Jane pushed him a little further. 'It's just that I know what you men are like: a pretty face, a flash of the eyes and you will forget everything!'

Noticing the direction of the conversation, Ford distractedly surveyed the room. 'Have you seen how the central-heating system is ducted through those vents in the wall? Very 1950s – absolute classic!'

Jane carried on, ignoring the integrated services. 'So, when you all weren't too tired, did you fraternise?'

Ford examined the room further. 'Just an odd glass of wine. Hey, there's even some flush-mounted grills in the floor!'

'Sorry, my love, but I'm doing the grilling. Where would you drink this wine?' Jane delved deeper.

'Just in the bedrooms,' Ford replied nonchalantly.

'What, the bedrooms? Wine in the bedrooms! Yours or hers?'

Ford made to show her the original Bakelite room thermostat but on reflection gave up the idea.

'Everyone's, honey. It depended on who needed to talk about the project. Remember these aren't like a real bedroom. It's more like a university hall of residence.'

Jane had a vision of her own chaotic and debauched student days. 'Well, that's hardly reassuring.'

Ford was feeling distinctly uncomfortable and couldn't understand how the joy of being in this extraordinary house together, at the expense of NASA no less, could suddenly fall apart into a suspicious inquisition. Although he knew how much Jane enjoyed her research and the farm, he had never really comprehended how much his many absences and close relationships with his team gnawed at her with every tick of the old clock in the hall. Finally he turned and faced her full on, snapping, 'Why are you so interested? Come on, honey. Nothing "like that" has ever happened!'

Jane took a deep breath and mentally toyed with the meaning of 'like that' before deciding to let it go.

'I'm a scientist too, you know: behavioural biology. You just happen to be one of my research topics!'

Ford smiled to himself at the thought of it. He felt oddly flattered by her jealousy.

'I'm sorry, honey. It has been so tough on you and I've not been there. It's just been so demanding with the project and all the extra red tape and protocols that the darned Europeans need to do anything!'

This was not quite the right thing to say.

'Wales is still a part of Europe, you know! You've had no bloody red tape and protocols from me when I've been packing up the house, arranging cover for the animals and sorting the dog out!'

'Believe me, Jane, I appreciate it and your support has helped me get on top of things. Only yesterday I saw the first stage fully repaired and – guess what? – the engines had just been tested and had passed with flying colours.'

Ford could've spent all evening telling Jane about the ins and outs of it all, but he sensed now was not the time and they had a new house to explore and enjoy.

The open-plan living room faced east, perched on a sedimentary ridge overlooking the Stone Canyon reservoir, just north of Sunset Boulevard. In summer it provided precious evening shade on the terrace and broad views of the setting sun highlighting the receding ridges to the Santa Monica Hills. The air was clean and fresh as they relaxed in their classic modernist armchairs and watched the lights twinkle around the lake shore as the evening faded into night.

'Are you happy with your role in the project? There's a hell of a lot to do...' Ford asked. He was concerned she wasn't content. Jane still worried that searching for landing sites was beyond her expertise and didn't want to be patronised.

'I watched a spider make a web the other day, something I've done a hundred times. The way the breeze catches the first strand of silk, wafting it through the air until it catches a branch or tree and starts the whole process. For the spider it's instinct; beyond that there's an intelligence in the problem solving. That tiny brain has so much capacity. I find that far more interesting than geological processes or imprints of dead animals. I remember a trip to London as a girl. My dad gave us a choice of the Natural History Museum or the zoo. I chose the zoo. I remember him musing by the tiger cage, quoting: *"When the stars threw down their spears, And water'd heaven with their tears, Did He smile His work to see? Did He who made the lamb make thee?"*

'That's been my question ever since. What makes life tick? What makes me tick? When we go for a walk, I look at the hills and the trees, for sure, but it's the ant holes and the burrows I really relish. That's what I really want to look for on the mission – to find a rabbit hole like Alice and study the wonders within.'

'But that's why they're going down the lava tubes in the desert; you've already identified likely ones on Mars.'

'Well, the ones I found on the satellite photos vent methane... which is promising.'

She then thought for a while. 'Listen, I want to help Buzz with his biology and even Bheki with his horticulture... I'm not saying I won't search for interesting rocks or long-dead animals, but my real passion is to find whatever life's still there.'

For the 'Exploration Phase', the 48,000 square mile desert gave ample opportunity for the kind of journeys the crew would carry out on the planet's surface. With the variation in height from 275 feet below sea level to almost 12,000 feet, it was a perfect fit. In the three months on the surface they would travel a round trip of at least 250 miles, a mere country walk compared with Scott's 1,600-mile expedition to the South Pole, which finished tragically an agonising 11 miles short of safety. Mars was an even more 'awful place' and 250 miles would be a Herculean effort compared with the mere 25 travelled by the *Opportunity* Rover in over a decade of robotic exploration.

Paradoxically, the catastrophic experiment with bicycles in Iceland had not killed the idea, but sparked the engineers' imagination. Weight for weight, bikes are the most efficient form of transport, turning a sluggardly human into a super animal. What was more, cycling would be perfect exercise for weakened bodies after the long spell in zero gravity.

Bheki had been modifying the scrap-heap designs he had already put together back home. He and Zulu had created a tricycle for collecting firewood. It had a place to stow the cargo between the cyclist – Zulu – and the footrests for a passenger on the rear, who could jump off and push when the going got tough – Bheki. With less than half the gravity on Mars and little air impedance, a single person could easily propel the kit and a passenger considerable distances with ease. Bheki and the NASA engineers worked hard to perfect the vehicle. They taught him the basics of computer-aided design and 3D printing, while they learned signing and not to talk to him over the video link while eating a sandwich.

Six 'tandem' tricycles in descending sizes were duly delivered for testing, their sleek titanium frames and contrasting chunky tyres giving them a purposeful appearance. In the Earth's 'normal' gravity the would-be astronauts carried half the weight in the carrier, where their life support packs, shelter, water and food would accompany them on Mars. Happily, the bikes made them look less peculiar in their pseudo space helmets, which from a distance resembled BMX lids.

A sense of excitement rippled through the teams on their first exploration of the desert. They were given instructions and downloaded the data onto their tablets. They'd take separate routes to the cinder cones and perform a variety of tasks on arrival.

They were champing at the bit, except for Kirsten and Mo. Kirsten's head was willing, but her heart was lagging behind. She'd signed up for the mission planning originally, and the prospect of taking two years out of Elin's life at this crucial stage ate away at her psyche like a worm in an apple.

Mo was suffering from cabin fever. Three months cooped up had taken its toll. It wasn't just the inactivity and boredom; it was the almost continuous spat he'd shared with Elin. She was bold and outspoken and it didn't sit well. She had the answer to everything and owned the last word.

Elin had no such issues. She was thrilled at the prospect of an adventure and paired up with Bheki on their trike, communicating by touch and signing in front of his face. This had become their secret language and it made them all feel special.

Buzz and Mo led the way, followed by Xing and Enza, with Elin and Bheki taking the rear. It was to be a long day's travel, following the old dry gullies and coyote tracks around rocky bluffs. The agility of the bikes was surprising. The leader's job was to steer and pedal, and the pillion jumped off and pushed up the steeper slopes.

The sun beat down on them and a steady stream of sweat trickled through their overalls as they picked their way through the stark landscape. The ungainly Joshua trees set an unworldly scene as they sheltered in their welcome shade to collect samples or to take frequent water stops. After a long slog they reached their camping spot where Elin took charge, bossing the moaning boys as their small shovels manically dug a shallow pit in the granular terrain.

Their extraordinary tent was like a spider's web. The radiating tubes inflated with a small pump to form a taut dome. They laid the ground sheet in the shallow depression then pitched the centre pole and piled sand back over the webbing. This would be an essential routine on Mars, as it would shield them against the persistent bombardment of cosmic rays. Here on Earth it provided insulation from the cold desert night, at least.

The boys tumbled inside, throwing their sleeping bags and themselves on the deck. Elin followed like a ferret and shoved them off while barking out chores.

The space filled with steam and earthy aromas as Bheki organised supper, his speciality sadza – a pasty porridge. He broke into his little stash of spices to liven it up along with the tomato pastes from their space larder.

Scouring pads and dish clothes were as alien to Mo as a Kuiper Belt object and he reluctantly learned their use under Elin's watchful eye.

Soon they were all fast asleep, except the restless Mo. To a boy brought up in a pious household, the Museum of Practical Jokes website had been a revelation. One where mischief was encouraged and revenge was sweet. Even in the darkness of the tent he could make out that Xing had kicked off her sleeping bag.

He thought about Elin again and how she'd really annoyed him. He felt bruised by her cold, self-assured disdain. 'Maybe she would appreciate an extra layer or two…' Very, very slowly and carefully he took Xing's bag and eased it first over Elin's head then slowly over her softly breathing form until she was totally enveloped. He retired most satisfied with his work, sensing that Buzz was sniggering softly.

Elin felt wonderful. For once in her life she was warm. Was it still a dream? How lovely, she thought, but no! It was a nightmare and she couldn't move. The taut double bags were like a straitjacket, and the drowsy girl squirmed across the tent like a wounded caterpillar.

Mo sat up, cackling with laughter. 'There's a grub in the tent!' he called. Buzz moved himself closer to Mo, equally amused. That evening Elin had made a neat stack of all the kit. Her blind struggles disturbed the tenuous equilibrium of the pile.

'Look out!' Mo screamed, too late. Collapsing in a steady arc, the kit hit the titanium centre pole. It flexed and kicked under the weight of sand on the roof.

Slowly and alarmingly, flecks of falling silica flicked in the night light as a split widened to the high-pitched ripping sound of taut nylon. A cascade of golden particles streamed through as it gave way on top of the two boys.

Like a very large egg timer, a neat pyramid of grains engulfed the pranksters.

All that could be seen and heard were their writhing limbs and the shrill laughter of the girls. On Mars they would all be dead.

Half a roll of duct tape and a lot more shovelling finally brought repair and order back to their shelter. Mo sought tacit absolution by demonstrably dusting down the girls' sleeping bags and neatly packing them away. He knew Elin was watching him as she stood impassively, hands on hips and he finally forced out an apology.

'Sorry, innit!' he mumbled.

It was a small triumph for Elin and she took the opportunity for one last word. '*Takk*, but more excepting you have to be of *stelpukraftur* – girl power.'

At daybreak Mo's radio crackled into life, giving them their first orders. He hastily handed the handset over to Elin when asked to describe the geology before them. The desert sands of yesterday had given way to a series of cone-shaped hills, whose mixed monotones and red mineral streaks now dominated the horizon. This was familiar territory for the girl: a landscape of cinder cones. It would be another twenty minutes for any response, but the task was self-evident, and they started to follow the weathered gullies to investigate any openings they could find. Within a mile of the camp the terrain got too hard even for the bikes and they proceeded on foot. This at least gave Mo an opportunity to crack open any rocks he thought might contain fossils.

Beyond a small ridge was a hidden hollow and a jagged black square where the rock had broken down to reveal a void below. The radio crackled again. The advice was pretty useless. It told them to go up the track they had just completed. Mo shrugged his shoulders and put his hammer away; the lava tubes would be devoid of interest for his speciality.

The difficulties in communicating in twenty-minute intervals was going to need better protocols than this. 'The Other Things' reported on their intention of investigating the caves. Now they waited for instruction. The boys killed time by throwing rocks down the hole, while Elin and Xing searched the landscape, in case they caught a glimpse of their mothers.

The series of ancient lava tubes near Kelso Depot were exactly the type of feature that could lead the way into warm and interesting places on Mars. The tubes form when slowly flowing lava builds deep channels and crusts over as it spreads out from the main chambers. These get covered by subsequent eruptions to form a network of oval subterranean warrens, revealing themselves as the overlying rocks are weathered down.

Buzz was overjoyed to hear Jane's familiar tones break over the airways. 'Look for olivine within the caves and take samples of any type of slime you can.'

Elin gave a thumbs-up to show the others she knew the silica-based mineral Jane was talking about.

In the cold, dark environment beneath their feet, life still thrived without sunlight or normal nutrition, sustaining itself from iron deposits within the rock.

Modern humans have been on the Earth for at least 200,000 years, yet we are still discovering how it works. Galileo was nearly burned at the stake for telling some simple truths less than 400 years ago. Even plate tectonics were not understood 50 years ago, and the discovery of extreme animals living in previously considered intolerable conditions has allowed us to envision life beyond the safe confines of our everyday world.

Take the water bear or tardigrade: only quarter of an inch long, it can live without water or food for 120 years and withstand pressures six times greater than those found in the deepest oceans. It can also survive temperatures from near absolute zero to well above the boiling point of water and withstand radiation one hundred times more than we can handle.

Within a day's drive of the camp there was a lake whose water is so caustic you could clean your toilet with it and as salty as the water flows discovered on Mars. These extreme examples of life show that life can survive in the strangest place on Earth but until we find life elsewhere, the universe for us hovers between two states: the first, we are alone in the void, making us special and unique, where creation has been gloriously made for just us; the second is that life is ubiquitous and occurs wherever the right ingredients come together. Life may even be a natural phase of matter and energy analogous to the states of gases, liquids or solids.

*Water Bear*

If life were found on Mars and that spark of vitality pervades the universe, it becomes a far more exciting place in which to exist. Like the difference between living in a provincial town like Runcorn, or a dynamic city like New York. No one ever named Runcorn twice.

Our assumptions of life are so adapted to our current environment that we instinctively expect it to need what we need, in particular sunlight and oxygen. It didn't start like that and any planet or space rock with a source of energy and liquid water might be teeming with life.

Those impressions in the rocks of Mars were not the first clues that sophisticated life could have evolved there. Although the seas and thick atmosphere are now long gone, something might survive. This is why the teams were exploring lava tubes on Earth, because they might be a rabbit hole to a Martian wonderland.

The rocks before them were broken by large fissures. As they worked their way to the edge, they found that the debris from the caved-in roof formed stepping stones into the oval interior. As they descended, the bright light streamed around them but did not penetrate too far into the gloom. With a series of satisfying clicks, the helmet lights shot out into the darkness, darting around crazily as they peered into the void. This was a special tunnel, off the usual tourist trail and the preserve of researchers.

There was no sulphurous stench or latent heat as the rocks solidified 8 million years ago. Should they go left or right? Elin's instincts led them up the incline. There was no noise save the echoes of their footsteps.

Enza strode forward. She imagined it to be a grand archaeological journey of discovery. Her mother's heroes ran through her mind. She'd quote Howard Carter, shifting through the dust into the darkened chambers of a young king's tomb: '*sì cose meravigliose*'. Yes, wonderful things.

Bheki felt nervous. He couldn't tell what was behind him as the torch always faced forward. Even in the blackest of African nights, the stars gave some comfort. Hidden creatures were lurking in every shadow.

They travelled up the curving chamber for hundreds of yards until the light of day was a memory. Every so often Elin would stop to examine a patch of rock and beckon Buzz to take samples of some pongy goo. Enza would sit on her pack to sketch the stark shapes caught in the headlights.

'Ach! Can we get back now?' Bheki moaned. The echoing walls gave the others their spatial bearings, but here Bheki felt very lost and scared.

Elin bravely pushed them on. Their pace quickened as the unremitting tunnel dropped downwards until the walls and roof opened into a larger space. Then in the near distance the flash and glimmer of green water lay before them, the light beaming through the depths of a deep pool blocking their path.

Elin worked out the topology and firmly announced, 'Look! The old chamber where from all this lava flowed – it this must have been.' Her beam flashed ahead. 'From somewhere this water must have come...'

Bheki jumped! Staring into the beautiful clear liquid, they saw a strange glow bouncing up off the sandy bottom. Tiptoeing on the rim of the pool, Xing hissed to turn off their torches.

Stomachs in knots, they instinctively held hands as the strange submarine illuminations darted around. These lights were not only getting closer but they could see moving shapes behind the glowing beams.

*Swimming Monsters*

Their grips tightened, and as one they hastily stepped back as these subterranean apparitions glided towards the surface.

The silence was riven as three cyclopses emerged from the rippling waters, light streaming from their foreheads. These forms let out a guttural gasp and a cacophony of shrill, ear-piercing screams split the air.

The children broke ranks, scattering away from the spectres. Desperately blundering into one another or the cave walls, they fumbled blindly to find the switches of their lamps. Elin could have fled all the way back to the entrance, but forced herself to stay with her friends.

Turning, she found the switch and scanned the depths. Her blood froze. To her shock, the beam landed not on Buzz or Mo, but straight in the face of one of the monsters.

The figure seemed wildly animated, the head torch flashing insanely. It advanced and its clammy hands struck out and grasped her tight.

She screwed her eyes shut and screamed, 'Mummia!'

Her mother and 'The Elves' had been on their own trek, not to the lava tubes but to the baking-hot tops of the cinder cones and, seeking shade, had dropped down into a cavernous old chamber at the bottom of the caldera.

To their joy and amazement, they found a welcoming pool, whose limpid, clear, cool waters had been beyond temptation.

*Sirens*

Stripping down to their underwear the dusty and parched women slipped into the refreshing water and in the half-light they made out a curious ethereal glow in the depths. With deep breaths they dived to investigate, swimming beneath a low rock ceiling and up again searching for its origin.

Then the light suddenly vanished. Desperately breaking the surface on the other side, they gasped for breath and with horror saw six screaming trolls standing silhouetted in the black void.

As their torches scanned the darkness, the figures scattered. There was a cacophony of footsteps and squeals, then suddenly, a couple of feet in front of Kirsten, a light flashed on and she saw two unmistakable china-blue eyes.

She grabbed hold of the terrified creature as it let out a bloodcurdling scream.

'Mummia!'

Kirsten stood fast and with soothing words said, 'I'm here, little one!'

# Chapter 25

## Stephen in the Wilderness

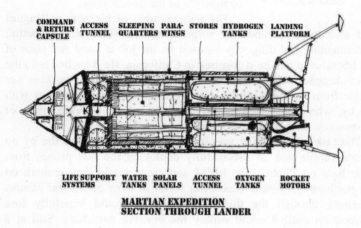

COMMAND & RETURN CAPSULE — ACCESS TUNNEL — SLEEPING QUARTERS — PARA-WINGS — STORES — HYDROGEN TANKS — LANDING PLATFORM

LIFE SUPPORT SYSTEMS — WATER TANKS — SOLAR PANELS — ACCESS TUNNEL — OXYGEN TANKS — ROCKET MOTORS

**MARTIAN EXPEDITION
SECTION THROUGH LANDER**

*Section of Lander*

Stephen Dyer had learned something new.

Tonight there was a celebration, quite an event for this remote outpost. The never-ending grasslands would have been lost in the darkness, if not for the momentary flashes of the spectacular display that boomed, crashed and whizzed before the expectant crowd.

Dong Dong was his host tonight and was at pains to look after the American guest. Sprays of silver and gold bespeckled the black skies, while dancing shadows played on the dark, undulating plains.

Overhead, streaming rockets and globular explosions burst like rows of gigantic alliums.

'A thousand years!' Dong Dong shouted above the booms.

'A thousand years of what?' quizzed Stephen.

'Rockets! We have been making rockets for a thousand years!'

Stephen had considered China to be a technological 'Johnny come lately', but his stay had made him think again. He now understood that, but for the last few hundred years, it was Western civilisation that had lagged behind in many respects. This Eastern enlightenment dawned over 7,000 years ago and spawned a continuum of arts, science and culture reaching to the present day.

**Jiuquan**
Inner Mongolia,
China
40.6N 100.2E
Altitude: 4,865ft
Geology: Rain
shadow desert

The crowd of scientists and technicians cheered at the climax. Then, as the smell of oxidation dissipated on the wind, Dong Dong shepherded Stephen into the hall for the banquet to celebrate the successful completion of the design stage.

The temperament of his new colleagues had also taken Stephen by surprise and he liked it. Respectful, undemanding and diligently focused on the job at hand and none of the liberal crap that he'd despised in California. He'd latched onto the chief designer, often spending hours at her shoulder, working her magic from her workstation. He'd even re-built some bridges with Rocky, who'd join their weekly reviews, albeit by video link, of progress on the MEM – the Mars Excursion Module.

The task of the MEM was fraught with danger. After the by no means simple task of successfully deploying the fuel probes from their base on Phobos, the MEM and crew would then embark on the perilous 3,800-mile descent in series of slow glides and climbs. Crashing through the thin atmosphere it would hopefully lose momentum until it could deploy the massive parachute. Still at a frightening speed the MEM would finally fire its retrorockets and make a controlled landing precisely in the middle of the fuel pods. At least, that was the theory.

If all went well, the crew would frantically set everything up to harvest the fuel to get them back up to Phobos and the mother rocket that would take them home. Only then could they explore the planet.

Dong Dong's passion in life was flight and, having had no opportunity to fly a real aeroplane, he had pioneered the sport of hang-gliding in China. He was also obsessed by the ancient art of zhezhi, or paper folding.

Paper was invented in China in the sixth century, and the beautiful and intricate shapes of boats, hats and umbrellas have been refined over the centuries.

Dong Dong's unique contribution to the mission was to develop a lightweight folding wing system to help the MEM glide through the thin atmosphere. His genius was to transform it to unfurl into an effective parachute. It was a task beyond any computer-aided designer to accomplish, and Dong Dong had spent hours drowning in reams of paper, working out the transformative shapes required for the metamorphosis from neatly stowed panels to wings to parachute.

This had been the turning point: the weight saved would allow for the excess fuel needed to land the massive weight with precision.

Stephen had admired Dong Dong's patient, analytical approach to the task, in the way he enjoyed the precision of chopsticks in picking out the specific morsels of food he decided were worthy of his fastidious palate.

'You must miss your family, Mr Dyer,' Dong Dong enquired attentively as Stephen took in the tables of chatting scientists.

'No, I've just got my mother and we never got on.'

'Well, your work mates?'

Stephen laughed, 'Ha, like a dog misses its fleas!'

The mood around the room changed and glasses were being filled. Dong Dong nudged him.

'This is "*ganbei*", Mr Dyer – our toasts. Only one rule. You must drink up!'

Baijiu is an intensely strong spirit and the first toast was to the heads of the project. They then insisted in toasting their honoured guest, Stephen.

Each time Stephen took a sip, Dong Dong gestured him to knock it all back and tip his glass to the throng, to show its dry bottom.

'You need "*juidan*" – drink courage!'

As toast after toast was made, the room became animated.

For Stephen, the room literally began to spin. The whirling haze was interrupted by Dong Dong. 'Your turn now, Stephen!'

The glasses were filled again and Stephen rose unsteadily to his feet. He proposed '*ganbei*' to Dong Dong, who blushed and declined, saying, 'I am not worthy, Mr Dyer, toast more high person.'

Stephen squinted blearily at the expectant throng, straining to think of someone important. 'To the Emperor!'

A few coughs broke the silence. Dong Dong whispered, 'That was a long time ago – we have a chairman now.'

'Chairman Mao!' Stephen held his glass high. The embarrassing silence grew thicker.

'Not good, Mr Dyer, try something less political?'

'Bruce Goddamn Lee!'

Relieved laughter erupted round the tables.

'Bruce Goddamn Lee!' they shouted, to the chinking of glasses.

News was now spreading around the room that they would soon

have another honoured guest: Luther Garvey, on his state visit to the People's Republic.

Amid the chatter, Stephen toyed with a chicken foot. He knew he must eat something more substantial to absorb the alcohol. He thought he'd be safe with fish. 'Any seafood?' he enquired.

Dong Dong scanned the food-laden wheel and gestured to a dish. 'Well, Stephen, you must try these!'

A row of little eyes stared up at Stephen. Each crab had hairy mittens on its claws. Stephen, now even more woozy with the drink, chased one round the plate with his chopsticks, before skewering it like a lollipop.

They got on with the job. The speed of manufacture was extraordinary. Since committing to the project the Chinese Space Agency had the full weight of the state behind it and the pride of the nation.

It was not lost on Stephen that while his NASA colleagues were struggling to reuse a fifty-year-old piece of hardware, he had a 'state of the art' facility and focused minds to produce an exquisitely engineered vehicle in a fraction of the time it would have taken back home. It was like revisiting the 1960s or the 1940s in the US where the country could command an urgency to do extraordinary things on impossible timescales.

While the teams sweated it out in the desert the MEM took shape in the large air-conditioned hangar. Its shiny titanium and carbon-fibre form now looming large above the teaming blue-overalled technicians. The moon shot of 1968 had a lander that was strangely bug-like compared to the sleek geometric solids of the rockets and orbiters. Although more symmetrical, this one also broke from the tubular pattern of conventional rocketry. It had been based on a hexagonal plan, which allowed a stable three-pointed landing platform and plenty of straight sides to attach the other bits of kit that would be needed on the descent and exploration.

A tubular space frame made up the main body in a diamond lattice, with the thinnest of detachable shells protecting the inner workings. The beauty of this was that only the knuckle joint needed to be designed; the rest was cutting tube to length.

Stephen busied himself distracting the designers with his own flights of fancy and learning as much as he could about Chinese

294

capabilities. He had not had to take his wallet out since he arrived and delighted in the fact that his expense allowances kept rolling in.

They were still a long time off the fitting out of the crew's module, but he fretted about this element in particular. He just couldn't get a straight answer on the numbers to be accommodated. Two, three or six were not numbers he could work around. Eventually the order came through to prepare the crew module for any combination of the twelve potential recruits, and a crate arrived with twelve fibreglass seats, each formed, like a racing driver's, to the precise shapes of their posteriors.

It was a Friday morning. Stephen had been called to the hangar to inspect the fitting of the wings. The delicacy of them astounded him. The thin transparent carbon-fibre fabric was stretched over a web of black interlinking tubes, appearing like a giant mayfly. The technicians were folding them into their closed state, reminiscent of the old films of seafarers stowing the sails in the teeth of a gale. Then he spotted the seats, now unpacked and being carefully stowed in the storage racks to the left. Stephen had been so engrossed with the technicalities of the task at hand that his anger over Ford's 'dumb idea' had abated.

He'd assumed that 'The Other Things' would be weeded out early. Seeing concrete evidence of the idea of sending them into space was still a possibility sent him into a demented fury. He gathered up the straps on their seats, three in each hand, and ignoring their pared down engineering tossed them into the welcoming aluminium bins. He summoned Ford on his video link.

'Ford, what the hell are you doing wasting time and resources on those crackpot schemes? Pick your best team and make the most of it!' Stephen could see he had taken Ford by surprise.

Ford ran his fingers through his hair. He took a deep breath and in reassuring tones told Stephen that the crew evaluation would be going right up to the wire and nothing conclusive had emerged from the training and tests so far.

'Look, whatever the logic you are following, the reality is... you can't send a bunch of kids into space! And... if you don't get it, I'll talk to the president when he's here next month.'

Wilma had done a great deal of travelling in her seven years as first lady. Like many business people discover, it's no holiday, with the forced pleasantries, the staged banquets and the punishing schedules. Their last major trip would be different and she was going to relish it. No hectic negotiations, troubleshooting or high-level treaties to be signed by Luther. They were being feted as an out-going president and his wife, and his itinerary was full of promise.

The first city had always intrigued Wilma as it was twinned with her home town of Atlanta. Compared with that brash skyline, the secret rose of Toulouse was a beautiful sibling. It was their first stop, away from the Parisian seat of pomp and power and a chance to experience a more relaxed French culture. It also happened to be the centre of the European space industry. Wilma's excitement on landing turned to frustrated anger. She couldn't quite believe it when they simply crossed the tarmac into the large hangars where the second rocket with the reusable boosters was being constructed.

**Toulouse**
Occitanie, France
43.4N 1.3E
Altitude: 300ft
Geology: River
valley – alluvial
deposits

She fixed her husband in the eye. 'This evening better be darned good!'

Fortunately, it was.

Harmony returned for the second leg when crowds of adoring citizens swamped the streets of Maputo. They swept past its extraordinarily ornate station as the warm winds of the Indian Ocean beckoned them to the corniche. They stayed at the fabulous Hotel Tello, where Luther's uncle had worked as the head chef in the colonial days, before the winds of change had called him into the bush to join Frelimo in the fierce battle for their independence.

**Maputo**
Capital of
Mozambique
25.6S 32.4E
Altitude: 154ft
Geology: Large
natural bay

The salt cod that evening brought her back to meeting Luther's family for the first time and the exotic fusion of African and Portuguese cuisines that underpinned his upbringing.

This brief African interlude was a mere stepping stone to their final destination of China. They had entertained many delegations from the Oriental power house and were delighted to finally reciprocate. For her husband this was one country whose wealth and ambition could rejuvenate the exploration of the cosmos. Also, to his never-ending gratitude, they'd filled a gaping hole in the budget and he was desperate to see their work at first hand.

There was a distant whinny as a herd of wild brown horses broke cover at the sound of a drone taking off. Stephen and Dong Dong stood, controllers in hand, away from the small crowd, their eyes fixed on the ascending machines. A dark insect-like form was silhouetted against the morning haze, with a strange body suspended swaying beneath.

'Ready!' shouted Stephen as he flicked the switch. The payload dropped like a fruit bat from its tree, the wings picking up lift as Dong Dong edged the controls to guide it into a leisurely glide.

He expertly circled it over their heads in an expanding spiral until, faltering and stalling, he eased the nose upwards, then flicked another switch. The body transformed itself as the three wings opened up like spring buds to unfold into a large blue hexagonal parachute as the thin tethers drew out from the silver tube below. Stephen sidled over to join the president to watch the model landing.

Dong Dong guided the craft as best he could in the persistent breeze to the spot where a large cross had been cut from the luscious grass.

As squirts of compressed air slowed its descent, the craft landed upright with a determined jolt, then appeared to break apart before their eyes.

'Oh dear, those poor astronauts!' cried Wilma, almost forgetting it was just a model.

'No, no, come look closer!' shouted Dong Dong.

The thin dust had settled as they approached to see that the lander had not broken but deployed six symmetrical curved panels to reveal the neat skeletal shape of its hexagonal core sitting on three splayed legs.

These would house all the solar panels, kit and systems they would need for their sojourn on the surface. 'Wait, sir!' shouted Stephen, stopping the small crowd in their tracks.

Dong Dong joined them, controller in hand.

'We're not finished yet.'

A trill emanated from the model as remaining compressed air lifted the central body clear of the outspread clutter and landing gear, simulating the eventual take-off and return to a distant home.

Luther broke into enthusiastic applause. 'You've been having fun, Stephen! And I thought you hated the project!'

For Wilma, this godforsaken windswept plain was no substitute for the Great Wall or the Forbidden City and she tagged along grumpily as they were shepherded into yet another hangar. 'When do we finish with the boys' toys and get to some real culture?' she hissed in Luther's ear.

'Boys' toys?' responded Luther with a knowing smile.

She stopped in her tracks as they entered. 'Oh my goodness, that's beautiful.'

*Lander in Hangar*

Before them was a tall and exquisitely elegant edifice, the sort of spacecraft that elves might fashion. Gleaming gold bells of the rocket motors sat beneath a shining lattice of jet-black carbon-fibre tubes and gilded connectors. Within the delicate cage were nine towering red-and-black cylinders with a matrix of pipes spiralling down towards the motors.

'Gorgeous! My God! It looks like it's designed by Fabergé!'

Dong Dong gestured towards a small fine-featured woman bent over a large silver computer, who, looking up, wiped her hands on her overalls before stretching one out to shake.

'Hi, I'm Ivy Cheung – call me Ives. Everyone else does.'

'You didn't design this, did you?' questioned a surprised Luther.

'Yes, sir, with Rocky!'

'Way to go, Ives!' Wilma beamed. 'Hey, forget the Wall.'

The president was making his thanks and farewells to his hosts as he prepared to leave. He was upbeat and experiencing a welling contentment about the project's progress. Stephen had other thoughts and was trying desperately to put his spanner in the works. He almost tripped up the attentive Chinese host as he attempted to get Luther's attention. It was all to no avail. He'd been ignored, and Stephen saw his chance slipping as the mighty rotors of the Chinese state chopper whirred into action.

Luther stopped abruptly, calculating the length of the flight, his age and viewing the spartan helicopter. He needed an ally. He beckoned to Stephen, who rushed over, hopeful that the president had finally decided to hear his wise council.

In conspiratorial tones Luther mouthed, 'Where's the john?'

It was not the advice Stephen was hoping to give but he stole his chance and guided the president to the restrooms. A serried rank of white porcelain urinals stood like a tropical naval parade. Luther was disconcerted as Stephen not only followed him to the urinal, but stood beside him as if to relieve himself too. The president stared at the cracks in the wall as he tried to pee under close surveillance. 'I'm sorry, Stephen, but you'll have to find your own patch – you're putting me off!'

Stephen moved two along, still desperate to air his complaint. 'Sir! I had to talk... You know those dorks in LA are still contemplating putting a bunch of kids in this thing? They even sent the special seats for them.'

Luther was a captured audience so just said in low, slow tones from the side of his mouth, 'So.'

'It's an insult. You gotta tell them to drop it. There's no way the press or your successor will stomach it. It's a political nightmare and a waste of time and resources.'

Luther gave a little shake and reorganised himself.

'My politics have been about turning nightmares into dreams. Anyway, from what I hear the smart money's on the women. Anything else?'

Stephen was not to be stopped. 'Well, you need a stronger leader than Ford. JPL are an organisational shambles. Look, where the hell's the chief engineer? He should've been here today.'

A whirl of dust pervaded the air as they walked back to the silver bulk of the waiting chopper.

# Chapter 26

## Training Continues

*Lavinia on Rock*

Elisabetta raised her voice above the rattle of pans. 'Time to call Enza.'

She left the kitchen to follow the ancient walk to the top of the old town. It was her favourite spot, where she could get some peace and a decent mobile signal. The swifts were skimming over the bushes as she made her way up. She found the old rounded rock, smoothed by generations of bottoms as their owners surveyed the fabulous vista over the ruins.

Elisabetta settled herself as the setting sun cast a blush over the landscape and the Mediterranean twinkled in a deep red swathe to the hazy line where it met the evening sky. She and Giulio took turns to make the evening call to their daughter.

Enza missed her parents terribly, but she didn't let it spoil her excitement over her grand adventure.

Tonight she bubbled over. They'd been up in the 'Vomit Comet', a zero-gravity aeroplane, and Enza had experienced her first hint of weightlessness. The long days stuck in the desert pods and the 'Mars walks' were over and all the candidates were working hard at their astronautical and specialist skills. Her current task was learning how to sketch while wearing space gloves.

'*Non è giusto,*' she then complained. The kids still had school work to do after training, when the lazy adults could just relax.

'You must be doing very well,' her mother interrupted. 'I shall be joining you next month as your mentor. They're taking you all very seriously.'

Enza was so delighted she even forgot to ask about the fortunes of the restaurant and the minutiae of the daily menu. 'Oh, *giorno felice!*' she trilled.

By the time they ended the call, the sun had set and the evening stars were blinking into action in the darkening sky. Mars and Jupiter shone clearly, bright evening visitors among the western constellations. Elisabetta picked them out. She had become fascinated by the heavens and astronomical news, such as the discovery of six new planets around Kepler 11, a sun-like star 2,000 light years away.

**Kepler 11**, Cygnus
2,000 light years
away
G Type Star – 96 per
cent of the mass of
the Sun
Six planets
8.5 billion years old
The age of this star
means that any
civilisation is either
extraordinarily
advanced, or died out
a long time ago.

It sparked her imagination, and in her mind's eye she pictured some sentient alien sitting on a rock like herself, contemplating their own view of the night sky. The light from our sun would be just another pinprick star in the cosmos and it would have started its journey when Pompeii was in its prime. If this advanced species had extraordinary telescopes, they could be watching that disaster unfolding as if it were today.

Everything in the starry dome is not just separated by space but time. The present does not exist out there. Every twinkling star or smudge of nebula lies somewhere in the past – a star map is really a history book. Tragically, even if a sophisticated civilisation existed around that distant star system it would take their messages or offers of help 2,000 years to arrive and then another two millennia for a response to come back, perhaps saying, 'Sorry, we've got over that, but could you help us with…' It makes the twenty-minute delay with Mars seem like the blink of an eye.

As Elisabetta viewed the skies that sultry night, she felt sad to think no one will ever know what glorious secrets are hidden among the stars stretching out across the heavens. There may be many civilisations out there, but effectively we'll always be alone.

Elisabetta sought out the constellation of Cygnus, trying to discern that particular faint star, whose light started its own epic journey a hundred generations ago. At which time, curiously, Lavinia had been sitting on that very same volcanic rock. Its surface was then fresh and rough, only recently deposited with the thick grey layers of ash that had enveloped Pompeii. Lavinia used to come here to be close to her old friends, home and most of all her beautiful cat, all entombed by the disaster.

It was a quiet place to ponder sad thoughts. Lavinia lived in an age where the stars and planets represented the heroes and deities of her time, and the mysteries of the universe were limited within the bounds of humanity.

She would look across the devastated plain to the long horizon of the pristine sea and dream of the wonders that might lay beyond. She'd heard the stories of monsters, amazing beasts and extraordinary cultures whose sophistication could match even that of her own mighty Roman empire. She lamented that for all the extraordinary achievements of her time – central heating, running water, the roads that could touch the extremities of their known world – they still had no control over the vagaries of nature or the will of the gods. Taking out a small flask of wine, she'd pour a libation on the steaming rock and in the rising heady vapour, would whisper a prayer that her city might rise again and her progeny would flourish and live in a world free from the malice of nature.

On the isolated continents of that far away time, each of the children's ancient ancestors must have asked the same perennial question. Not what lies beyond the depths of space, but what lay beyond their own unyielding forests, mountains or the oceans of their own worlds.

Everything changes, yet nothing is different.


Rocky had always taken time out to indulge the children and when it was proposed to show the candidates how the Saturn V was taking shape in the cavernous Vehicle Assembly Building, he made sure they were given VIP treatment. They knew him as the benevolent friendly bear, who patiently showed them his designs on their trips to the JPL. When they spotted him across the hangar they all ran over, vying for his attention.

As their mobbing abated, the other recruits joined them. The impromptu crowd dwarfed within the edifice. At 160 metres high and a volume of almost 4 million cubic metres, the building is gargantuan enough to form its own weather systems on humid days. Filling the space was the object that it was built for, a partially assembled Saturn V rocket towering above them. It sat solidly on the platform that would inch it to the launch pad.

Rocky felt a small, rough hand grip his. 'Ich! It's like being in giant land, Mr Rocky.'

Bheki's drawl was unmistakable. Rocky looked down and saw two bright eyes gazing up in wonder.

'You've gotta let me go on that thing, Mr Rocky!'

The greying engineer smiled. 'It's not my choice, young man. Anyway, you might miss home!'

'I've never had a real home, Mr Rocky. That's going to be my home!'

They finally moved on, leaving Rocky examining the colossus. The sound of footsteps on the concrete floor heralded the approaching figure of Milton.

'Your phoenix arises!'

Milton modestly wiped his hands.

'It's not mine any more, it's ours!'

Squinting up into the gods he quipped, 'The pointy end's still missing?'

Rocky laughed. 'Don't get technical on me... Yep! It's on the drawing board. 4 tons too heavy, and we need that for the fuel. We keep stripping things out, but if we can't solve it... no mission.'

A New York accent broke into their discussions. 'Don't mind me for earwigging, mister, but it ain't that thirsty.'

They turned to find Soraya adjusting her mission cap.

'Thirsty?'

'You know, desperate. Just find something that's 4 tons and adios! Simple.'

Rocky laughed. 'Yeah! We can get rid of the cosmic ray shielding or the water, but you might not appreciate it after day three.'

She looked hurt. 'Just tryin' to be helpful, mister, but "Madame Kirsten Resourceful" can really pack a tent and she don't take nothin' that ain't got two uses. What's with the shielding stuff anyhow?'

Rocky humoured her. 'Well, it's a special composite made of layers of plastic, lead and carbon fibre which envelops the crew's quarters and keeps them safe from space radiation.'

'Thanks, man, very thoughtful! And I suppose we might just need the water!'

Rocky's metaphorical bath overflowed – a eureka moment. He whispered, 'Shit!' then, 'Soraya – you're a genius! The water, oh, the water! We can use the freakin' water! It absorbs cosmic rays.'

He got out a notebook and made a sketch of the crew quarters and a calculation of the volume of the double skin now filled with water instead of the shielding – 4 cubic metres, thus 4 tons.

'We keep the water around the crew for protection and get rid of the water tanks. Brilliant'.

'Hey, don't spoil us, mister!' Soraya grinned, then she whisked off to catch up with her friends on the endless gantries and ladders.

'Any time you've gotta problem!' she called over her shoulder, tapping on her name badge.

The Earth was making another great circle of the sun, as it had 4 billion times before. This orbit was no more significant than any other, except in the lives of its inhabitants. Even then, it was merely the last year in office of the 48th President of the United States.

His frequent calls to Ford had an increasing sense of urgency, born out of the likely success of his political antithesis; the no-nonsense Peggy Tyler. She was waltzing ahead in the polls and had made it her aim to rid the state of all unnecessary spending. Luther's cherished mission was in her sights. They even dubbed her Peggy 'Crosshairs' Tyler on account of her political targeting and unruly mop of red frizz.

'We can't drop the ball now, Ford. When our train's left the station it don't turn around.'

Ford asked the president if he'd read his last progress report.

There was a 'humph' on the line. 'Listen, I'm too old to read reports – my desk is creaking with them. Tell me straight.'

'OK, sir...'

'Call me Luther!'

'OK, Luther, the Saturn V is complete in Florida and awaiting the crew quarters and capsule. The French have delivered and assembled the boosters in Guiana and the landing module is being shipped from China as we speak.'

'What's the delay on the crew quarters and capsule?' the president demanded.

'The capsules are ready except for the final fitting-out. We had problems with the weight of the quarters, but we've resolved it.' Ford had spent a day preparing his report and here it was, pared down to a few sentences.

'What are we waiting for then?'

Ford took a deep breath. 'Testing, fuelling, testing, fitting-out, testing and choice of the crew.'

Luther continued the grilling. 'OK, who's going to be the crew?'

There was a pause. 'Mmm, we are still evaluating. It's a tough call.'

'You still limited to 200kg, whatdayacallit, "human payload"?'

Ford scratched his hair. 'Sure, a bit less, if you count any samples.'

Luther was in a decisive mood. 'Choose the best team and do the science on the planet. Forget about the rocks, they can test them there.'

Ford was scratching madly now. 'That's the trouble. They are all hanging in there, sir, er, Luther. By the way, we're having a party for them if you want to give them your regards?'

If a smile could come through the phone, it did. 'My pleasure! Hook me up on video. I'll give 'em a bit of inspiration.'


Jane enjoyed parties. Her blood coursed with excitement as she manically prepared for the evening. Ford's stomach was a leaden weight as he tried to help, moving furniture, poaching the salmon and working on the playlists. His only inspirational input was the theme for the party: 'Retro space adventure', echoing the TV dreaming of his youth.

'Shall we give them all a Cinzano cocktail on arrival, honey?' he ventured.

'Don't be ridiculous, cariad! Juices for the kids and dry Martinis for the rest. Have you stuffed the olives yet?' she asked, in her officious voice.

'Isn't life too short to stuff an olive?'

It promised to be a balmy night, so Ford busied himself setting out a dozen faded deck chairs around the pool. The garden and pool were down a level from the cantilevered balconies. The bleached concrete paving framed the deep blue rectilinear pool and led to a pine-lined games room.

He paused as an evening breeze rustled the heads of the clustered palms. Little had changed in the house since its heyday and, returning to the den, he was intrigued to find a hidden shelf behind where the chairs had been stored. On it he discovered the sleek, rounded shape of an old projector and a library of still boxed celluloid films.

Excitedly his finger tracked across the handwritten labels, and alighted on two classics. *The Wizard of Oz* and several episodes of *Lost in Space*. 'Well, that will sort the kids out,' he assured himself. He set up the kit and aimed the beam at the empty white wall opposite the worn leather sofas.

'You've been ages – there's still the avocados to mash!' Jane scolded when he eventually returned to the steam of the kitchen. The sycamore worktop was strewn with salad.

'Mmm, that smells nice, almost good enough to eat,' Ford whispered as he gently kissed the back of her neck.

'It's the Chanel No5 you gave me, my sweetheart.'

Ford distractedly bit into cocktail carrot. 'No, it's the quiches. By the way I've set up some cool entertainment for the kids.'

He excitedly told her about the old projector. She was not as impressed.

'*Lost in Space*? Just how encouraging d'you think that is? What about *Apollo 13* or *Alien*? Let's get them really excited!'

Ford scratched his head. 'OK, it's *The Wizard of Oz* then!' Butterflies fluttered in his stomach as he organised the drinks and glasses. This was the last big get-together before the end of the training. The president was going to join them, albeit on a video link. 'Keep calm,' he told himself. 'After all, what could possibly go wrong?'

The guests arrived in waves, and soon the old house was brimming with chatter and people again. The party was exclusive to the mission team, the would-be astronauts, their mentors and trusted partners. To Ford's great pleasure, the head of NASA, Mike Hermes, made a surprise appearance. Ford, now dressed in a black-collared mustard shirt with old suit trousers tucked into his flying boots, escorted him around the premises, introducing him to old colleagues and new faces alike.

Alim, in dressing gown and towel, particularly hit it off with him, with a mutual interest in hiking the Canadian Rockies and the best curry houses in LA. 'It is the most unassuming place, you know, but the food... fantastic.'

Hermes nodded. 'That's down in Inglewood... wonderful. By the way, why are you here? You're not one of the usual faces?' Alim checked Ford's furrowed features for permission.

'Well, I'm under strict confidentiality, you know... but as the top "bod" you must have clearance. I'm a hanger-on! My son's a candidate and I support the little chap in his science. There's a few of us: Elisabetta's here for Enza, and Zulu for Bheki.'

Mike took a sip of his very dry Martini. 'Ahh! "The Other Things." You're their avatars, or it is the other way round?'

Alim laughed raucously. 'Well, I'm not tall or blue but I have a big nose!'

Ford escorted Mike towards the pool, down the concrete steps beside the lush fronds of crimson bougainvillea. He was hoping to introduce Kirsten, but she appeared to have vanished. As his eyes searched the scattered conversing couples, the lights seemed to dim, like a dark cloud passing over the sun. A chill wind blew over the house as the unmistakable drawl of a black-clad Stephen Dyer broke the silence.

'At least you've got rid of those kids!' Stephen had missed the children in the games room, where *The Wizard of Oz* was weaving its magic. He insinuated himself between Ford and Mike.

'Stephen Dyer, the only sane man on the team!' He proffered a hand to the head of NASA as he fixed him squarely in the eye.

'Ah, you're Stephen. I've heard you have been doing wonders with our allies in the Far East.' Stephen took this compliment as his opportunity to skilfully usher Mike away from Ford, engaging him in his deep misgivings about the project and its management.

Ford suppressed his irritation and decided to leave them to it. He checked out the temporary cinema to see six beaming faces lit in the colourful flicker of a strange world somewhere over the rainbow. He softly closed the door and made his way to the upper level where he hoped to catch up with Jane. People were tucking into food – especially Su-lin, who was demolishing the neatly stuffed olives. Eugene and Felix, in their light-blue uniforms with brightly coloured sashes, were mixing cocktails and raucously encouraged Ford to down their new invention, a 'Venus and Mars'. They were preparing for years of sobriety by making up for it now.

Ford politely nodded to Edward Crumb standing alone in the kitchen, before having a quick word with Sharon and Elisabetta, who reported seeing Jane retreating upstairs with an emotional Kirsten.

The open mahogany treads creaked slightly as he made his way to the first floor, and he stopped on the landing for fear of disturbing a delicate moment.

Kirsten hadn't slept soundly for days. An anxiety had gripped her guts and twisted her mind into paroxysms of doubt. The intermittent sobs were being soothed by Jane's soft tones, as she opened her heart.

'I can't abandon her again, not for two years! I've spent enough time away already!'

Jane quizzed, 'But what if she's chosen? What's the difference?'

Kirsten sniffed. 'It's a big difference, I'm her mother! I can still support her on the mission and children must all fly the nest at some time – it would be her big adventure, not just an absentee parent putting herself first again!'

'Are you sure? You've worked on this for so long.'

'I'm not sure, I'm confused. I don't want to let everyone down.'

Ford stood stock still, listening transfixed but not wanting to interrupt. He then heard Jane's decisive tones.

'Let everyone down? Don't be ridiculous. No one can force you to go. Do what you think is right.'

Kirsten wiped away the tears. 'I'm sorry, I thought I was the tough one!'

Jane then spoke more wise words. 'Listen, my love. You are tough to admit it, it's natural. Even the guys are nervous, that why they're getting hammered down there. Just do what you think is right.'

Feeling betwixt and between, Ford decided to retreat while he considered the prospect of one of the team options evaporating before him.

The strains of 'Born Slippy' wafted up the steps as he descended. The beat had drawn a few guests onto the floor in the living room. Eugene and Felix had abandoned their makeshift bar and held the centre of the parquet. Felix was dancing like an uncle at a wedding, while Eugene grinningly encouraged Yasmin and Soraya to join them.

Glancing at his watch, Ford realised the time. 'Argghh! The president's going to make his call in 15 minutes – must get the crew together.' He shot down to the basement where, in the movie, Dorothy was finally coming home.

'Hey, kids! Upstairs in the lounge in 10 minutes.' He hurriedly made a circuit of the pool to tell an intense Stephen and an exhausted-looking Mike Hermes the same message.

Sharon and her partner followed Ford up the steps, back into an unfolding mayhem. The dance floor was a scene of carnage. Eugene had fallen over a glass-topped Burmese coffee table, while executing his best Travolta move. Soraya, in her white singlet and olive jumpsuit, looked as happy as a snowball in a barbecue.

'Get your hand off my butt, fella!'

Felix stood stock still, hands in the air as 'Thinking Out Loud' reached its inevitable climax. All eyes turned to the pair. Soraya, hands on hips, looked Felix square in the eyes.

'Did I give you permission, man? Did I send you any "Put your hand on my butt signals"? NO... way!'

Felix stood hands outstretched, protesting his innocence like a footballer on a second yellow card. Luckily the glass of Blue Nun Soraya poured over his head was not a great vintage.

The TV screen suddenly broke into life, freezing the scene.

The president's calm face beamed out as Ford hurriedly helped Eugene up from the pool of broken glass.

Jane stood in the background with a red-eyed Kirsten, while the kids trooped in looking bewildered. Luther's oversized visage frowned quizzically as he took everything in.

Ford was brushing the glass off Eugene's back. Felix's hair was dripping with wine and Soraya was glowering. Kirsten turned away to hide her tears and gripped Jane's shoulder.

At which point Stephen, oblivious of Luther's video presence, waded angrily through the crowd. Towering over the innocent kids, he bellowed to the four walls. 'Why the hell are you still here?!'

He was abruptly silenced when the disembodied voice of Luther came over the cherry-wood speakers. 'Good evening. Hum! Quite a party you're having...' His wide eyes scanned the room. 'Hi, young'uns! At least you know how to behave.' The tension was broken by six high-pitched voices.

'Good evening, Mr President!'

Luther's broad smile broke back across the screen. 'Hello, Bheki. How's it going?'

Bheki read his lips intently and replied, 'Watching an awesome movie, sir, about a dog called Toto.'

'Ah, Toto, now that's one of my favourites... So tell me, what would you seek over the rainbow?'

Bheki smiled. 'A home and a dog, like Dorothy.'

The large brown eyes fixed on Stephen. 'And you, Stephen, what do you seek?'

Stephen squinted towards Ford. 'Organisation and order, sir!'

'A rather scarce commodity tonight!'

The president continued to work around the transfixed figures.

'... And you, Ford?'

Ford closed his eyes and replied, 'More time, Luther!'

The president's eyes alighted on Kirsten's back. 'Is that Kirsten?' She turned.

'What would you seek?'

Kirsten pulled herself together. 'Nothing... A little peace of mind, maybe.'

'Well, Bheki. Home is empty without the people you share it with.'

Bheki looked along the line of his new friends and felt maybe he did belong somewhere.

'But you won't find a dog on Mars. Maybe a rover! Stephen, you'll never find what you want without seeking harmony. Ford, there's never enough time, it's all relative.' Then he returned to Kirsten. 'Kirsten, my advice? We all worry too much. Do what you think is right!' Then he laughed, 'And, Felix, I think you're in need of a towel.'

The president addressed each of the other would-be crew members before signing off as the screen returned to a blaze of dancing static.

This house had never seen a greater party, although the stuffed olives left a lot to be desired.

# Chapter 27

## The Equipment Is Coming Together

As the northern hemisphere approached its annual maximum tilt away from our sun, the voters' inclinations had also swung in the definite direction of Peggy Tyler. The razzmatazz of the campaigning over, the voters punched or dropped their ballot papers like the falling autumn leaves.

No scrutinising of hanging chads would affect this result. Peggy, backed by the massive media empire of the Pure Corporation, was going to have a landslide victory.

Her homespun messages of austerity and cost-cutting had hit a chord. As Luther predicted, there was no way the mission would survive if it hadn't left the planet by 20 January, the date of her inauguration.

The launch was thus set for 17 January, giving three days to assemble the parts of rocket in orbit before blasting off past the dark side of the moon and onwards for the greatest adventure in the history of humanity. Luther knew that once it was outward bound, it would be almost impossible to recall.

The two rockets now stood proud and erect, ready to be trundled out to their respective launch pads. Who would sit on top of them was still open, but the smart money would be on 'The Elves' – the women's team. They had performed solidly and professionally in all the tasks and Kirsten's expertise provided a sound scientific base.

The trouble was, she was still fighting against that inner voice which nagged away at her resolve. The training amplified the seed of doubt, which grew and blossomed as the departure date grew ever closer. She bore it until it felt like all the burdens of the world were heaped on her shoulders. Gritting her teeth, she carried on.

From the very start Ford had felt an affinity with Kirsten and wanted to do anything to support her. He asked Jane to work with her, hoping she could offer some support and solidarity.

In Jane, Kirsten found a kindred spirit who slowly patched up her psyche. Jane was also mentoring Buzz and working on the landing site exploration, which enabled them to work together on the planet's geology. They both spent hours scrutinising 3D images of Martian landscapes and volcanic features, looking for an oasis that could still shelter some spark of life.

Oblivious to Kirsten's doubts, Elin was in turn the recipient of her mother's coaching. Kirsten had never spent so much concentrated time with her daughter, transferring her knowledge of science and survival skills. Soon Elin's mind was full of red rocks and planetary geology, all as vivid to the young girl as a first compelling novel.

To a child, adults appear larger than life. Not just physically bigger, but akin to a sensory experience: the whiff of perfume or tobacco, the touch of rough skin, the boom of deeper voices and an air of being in a far away, complex world, where they have all the answers.

Elin would feel immensely comforted by the simple fall of her mother's hair from behind her ear, the sudden tensing of her tattoos as they scrutinised a laptop screen, or the catch of Kirsten's eye or a little pinch to her ribs if she mentally wandered off.

These small intimacies were repeated for all the children as they worked with their closest familiars. Their mentors had also formed a tight group. Kirsten, Jane, Elisabetta, Alim, Su-lin and, of course, Zulu, who were not only mentoring the would-be 'space cadets' but themselves learning the art of being virtual astronauts in case the kids were chosen.

Who *would* be chosen? To objectively resolve the issue, the mission planners, Henrietta, Yasmin and Edward, had devised a complex computer program with more parameters than a neural network. For the whole duration of the selection they assiduously uploaded the data as the results and evaluations came in.

They were a strange trio, each quite different in their outlooks and disciplines. Edward, socially stunted, was shy and introspective and would have died rather than reveal his inner feelings. Instead he tried to impress with his exactitude and thoroughness in the task. He was convinced his role in Safety and Departmental Assurance Manager – SaDAss – gave him a greater authority than the others.

Edward 'The Passion Killer' Stalk had stymied more projects with his statistical analysis than a nun running a hen party.

Stephen was sure that Edward was the trump card against 'The Other Things' ever being chosen.


Ford felt a great sense of achievement as he took in ESA's massive assembly building. Situated on the wooded coastal plain of French

Guiana, it wasn't a bad place to be in December. The summer breezes of the southern tropics shimmered the palms, with their heady hint of warm spice, as he marvelled at the extraordinary contraption before him.

Pierre, his guide, was beside him as they worked their way up the gantries to study the intricate network of spiral latticed ribs which formed the central cradle that held the rockets. Pierre tapped his nose. 'I love – 'ow you say – the contrast. The "high tech" and the ancient.'

**Kourou**, French Guiana
5.1N 52.4W
Altitude: 50ft
Geology: Coastal plain – alluvial deposits

Milt's six refurbished solid rocket boosters, strapped around the lattice, had the countenance of veteran military equipment. Three were fixed at the bottom and three towards the top. They were still being repainted as the pair admired them.

'They look like they mean business, *mon ami*! The blue ones get us off Earth and the *rouge* to Mars.'

'Blue for Earth and red for Mars?'

'*Exactement!*'

'What's that bottom unit?'

Nestled within the bottom section was a short silver rocket.

'That's for the final push into orbit. Your rockets are like brutes! They keep on burning like a firework. We need a small, controllable rocket to get things exact, like the shuttle's engine.'

The lower solid rockets would be jettisoned as the vehicle left the atmosphere and the upper rockets would then propel it into the depths of the solar system.

Compared with those old workhorses, the lattice cage was a perfect jewel of modern engineering: precise, shiny and pared to the bone. Ford pointed to the silver stage.

'So, we remove that in space to make room for the crew's quarters and return rocket?'

Pierre jokingly punched Ford in the arm. 'If they fit! Remember, we work in metres, not feet, you know.'

'Don't you worry, our trusty Saturn V will deliver them safe and sound and they will be as snug as a bug!'

Pierre was glowing with pride. He raised his arm and pointed to the far end of the contraption. '*Celui est formidable! Regardez*, we received the lander from China. It's up there, you know.'

They both gazed intently at the pristine delicacy of the landing vehicle which crowned the edifice. It was like something from another world. It was both the lightest and most intricate object they had ever seen. Three sections of its cylindrical skin had unfurled to reveal the revolutionary solar panels.

Ford stared up beyond the galvanised grillage to see a bevy of technicians testing them.

'They don't look big enough.'

'These are – 'ow you say – *extraordinaire*! It's amazing the power you can get out of these babies.'

'They're tiny, how they do it?'

'Pure accident! We tried a film of graphene to reduce the glare off the glass. *Bang!* It blew all the fuses.'

Ford scratched his head. 'Doesn't that just block the light more?'

Pierre made a small gesture with his hand, indicating something very, very small. 'Ah no, my friend, the thin carbon layer forms a diffraction grating and the light acts as a wave, not a particle! It all literally condenses on the receptor. It doubles the power, *naturellement*!'

Ford thought of all the inventions attributed to the space race. 'Even more useful than Velcro?'

The French man intuitively checked the immaculate cut of his trousers. 'Who has the need of the Velcro, *mon ami*?'

What a long journey it had been: from the old observatory where 'Wilson' had illuminated the night sky to assembling these amazing machines. The only question now was, who was going to sit in the small conical capsule at the top of the edifice?

# Chapter 28

## The Crew Are Chosen

*On the Gantry*

Soraya couldn't believe it. From an idle moment when she filled out a form for an impossible dream, to the point where she was actually going into space.

In stunned amazement she'd heard her named called out with Sulin and Eugene. Without a moment to lose, they were immediately whisked off by private jet to Cape Canaveral where the fully restored Saturn V waited in cryogenic splendour. Soraya was so nervous that her knee jiggled manically all the way, drumming out an adrenaline beat on the hollow floor of the aircraft. Her stomach churned and her mind raced in a cacophony of thoughts. She ran though her duties and training, peppering them with fears of explosions, decompressions and asphyxiation.

**Cape Canaveral**
Florida, USA
28.3N 80.3W
Altitude: 10ft
Geology: Coastal
peninsular –
sedimental deposits

Like a trooper before battle, the excitement of action and the fear of extermination pervaded her body. As the plane took a left bank to align itself with the landing strip, she saw the needle-sharp colossus of the waiting rocket shimmering in the warm haze of the afternoon.

They arrived into a maelstrom of activity. On the various platforms the rocket was crawling with engineers. Their special seats were being fitted and final fuel and stores were being loaded. The astronauts changed quietly, and Soraya was given a stylishly short cropped haircut before they sat down for a last supper of steak and eggs and a final briefing.

Not much was said between them, just cursory comments and nervous pleasantries. When Kirsten had pulled out late the night before, Soraya thought that was an end to it. Now she was here with Eugene and Su-lin, reading their briefing notes. Boy, they were going to be busy. She made just one call to say goodbye.

'Hey, Sis, I hope you're watching the news. Hey! Look out for me on the gantry, but keep shtum! It's still secret, girl!... No, listen, don't worry, I'll be back... Yes, it's all cool... OK, see ya, must fly. Literally, must fly!'

Her stiff orange suit swished as she walked to the silver bus. From anywhere with a line of sight, a hundred photographic lenses strained to catch the astronauts and speculate who they might be.

The bus trundled down the long, hot concrete road towards the looming behemoth. Soraya had spent her life dodging round and about the feet of skyscrapers, but the rocket's splendid isolation made it look extraordinarily tall.

This singular object just went on and on to the sky. Soon it would go beyond. At the base, Soraya could make out the five massive bell-shaped engines that would lift it off the Earth. Through a swirl of frozen fog, formed by the brittle, cold liquid gases being pumped into the tanks at each level, her eyes worked their way up to the top of the rocket.

The skeletal elevator was waiting as Soraya attached her handheld life support unit to the suit. Holding her helmet in the other hand she entered with her fellow astronauts, the steel concertina gates clanging like a prison sentence behind them. The car rose slowly and in the distance, through the flickering bars, they could see the massive assembly building and the ocean beyond.

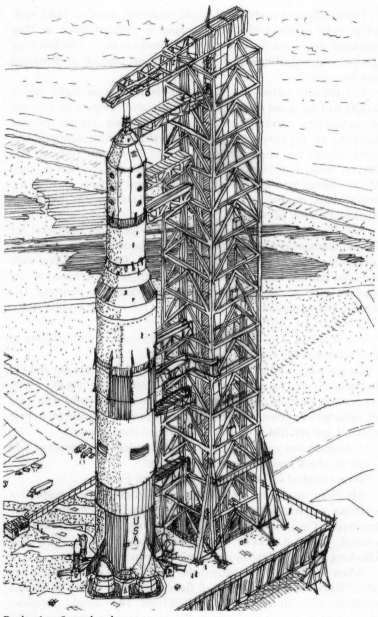

*Rocket 1 on Launchpad*

Turning, Soraya could see the cold, steaming, massive, black-and-white girth of the rocket, diminishing in circumference as they ascended each stage. Su-lin gave her a reassuring smile. She had done this twice already. Eugene, an old veteran, just kept his own counsel and decorum.

The elevator jarred to a halt, their bodies momentarily losing weight and the doors opened to a green-painted bridge with a gaggle of technicians awaiting them. Taking their last breaths of free planetary air, the astronauts helped each other on with their goldfish-bowl helmets and checked the airways of the comms systems. The 20-foot walk was like a marathon. Soraya's legs jellied as they trudged along the metal flooring. She stopped halfway and felt the urge to wave, more to the good Earth that had nurtured her than to any particular human being.

Ahead she saw the conical capsule. The open door beckoned her like an automaton's Wendy house. Many hands helped her into the diminutive dark space, where straps, wires, leads and tubes soon threaded into her outer skin. The bright sunlight was eclipsed by the massive form of Eugene – last in and blocking the doorway. His waving elbow smashed her visor as he half fell into the middle seat.

'Thanks a lot – oaf!' she protested.

'No problem. Any day, lady!' he replied, turning and grinning at the face lost in the visors' golden reflection.

Soraya was given a pat on the shoulder and a thumbs-up and the heavy hatch door swung over them and closed off the outside world. As her darting eyes grew accustomed to the dark interior, a myriad of lights and switches came into focus. A curious mixture of archaic controls and stitched-in modernity presented themselves.

A disembodied voice crackled over the headphones. 'Houston here – can we check your telemetry and systems?'

Soraya studied the scene. 'Sure thing, man! Fire away!'

All three astronauts sat checking and flicking their respective switches and controls, each encouraged by a flight engineer sitting hundreds of miles away in the serried ranks of monitors at mission control, Houston, Texas. Many others around them were also checking the state of the systems up and down the rocket.

When the technicians vacated the gantries and sped away in the silver NASA bus, the three small figures sat alone on top of enough explosive material to devastate a small town. Their checks complete, they could only wait patiently as the countdown ran its course like fine sand falling through an hourglass.

Every couple of minutes the voice would crackle over again, commenting on her heart rate and blood pressure, which, given the circumstances, were holding up pretty well. Her mind was racing. Visions of the Challenger disaster preyed on her imagination. Her small frame ached with the pressure of the straps. She thought of her childhood, her sister, her long-dead parents and what they might have thought. For once she was glad there were no children to worry about or weep for her. Then she heard the number 20. It jolted her back to the present, and the numbers flashed across her eyes, through the teens and down to the 10, 9, 8, 7, 6 – something moved within the rocket way below them; all the valves had opened up to release the fuel – 5, 4… 3… 2…

She heard the word 'ignition', then nothing else except her head cracking back onto the cushioned headrest and a grinding and straining of the massive structure. An extraordinary pressure pushed through her back, arms and legs. Everything was pinned back in the seat and the force was mounting with the acceleration. It was as if she no longer existed but was a crushed flower, preserved forever in a book. She fought against the power of the rocket and screamed to herself, 'Survive, survive, survive!'

A record crowd stood on the beach, watching the rocket receding into the haze. In a small seaside hotel, through binoculars, Dick Gordon Jr wistfully dreamed. He watched the moment when the first stage, having completed its function, detached

**Dick Gordon Jr –** Astronaut due to command the cancelled Apollo 18 moon mission

itself and fell away, with an immediate splay of jets emanating from the second stage as it kicked into action.

For Soraya there was a temporary halt to the ordeal, her body lifted for a moment as she felt the essence of the rocket change, then – *bang!* She snapped back against the seat, the chair pushing through her spine. She concentrated on the rhomboid window, watching the sky change from a dazzling blue to a deep black.

Onwards and upwards they travelled. There were no explosions, no faulty engines, and the rocket did its stuff, behaving beautifully. Milton's work had not been in vain. True to Ford's word, each stage lightly descended on fine silk parachutes, to be recovered and preserved as an exhibit that had an even greater place in history.

The ride was getting smoother. The infernal juddering died down to a point where the astronauts' shaken eyes could begin to examine their screens and each other, and they could start to breathe without straining.

Through the windows, the black starry sky told them they had left the bonds of the Earth. A lightness of mind and body overwhelmed them and informed them that they were 'in space' and weightless.

'Phoenix here, Houston. Looking very good!' Eugene signed in.

There was a massive and relieved cheer as mission control released its pent-up anxieties and reflected on the success of one of the most peculiar chapters in NASA's history.

Soraya released her straps and twisted in her seat to stare through the window at the curve of the Earth beneath them. She cracked her head against Eugene's helmet. 'Sorry, fella! Own back time!'

'You can take that off now, lady,' Eugene suggested, and in no time the three of them were childishly bouncing their helmets around in the weightless environment.

Soraya pressed her nose right up to the thick glass. The rocket was performing a graceful roll. As it turned, the world with its thin skin of atmosphere, swirling clouds and endless seas and oceans, wheeled below them, followed by the inky blackness of the void and the white-hot outpouring of the sun. Earth appeared subtle and benign; the universe beyond, stark and forbidding.

As she thought of all the people down on Earth, a quiver rippled through her. The remoteness and the extremity of it all almost overpowered her, before imperceptibly giving way to the beauty and the awe of the spectacle laid before her.

It was not for long, as Houston's voice burst through with serious things that needed to be accomplished. First were the checks. All three in unison needed to work through the systems again. Then Eugene and Su-lin would ease the remains of their rocket into the correct orbit. It was still a behemoth and a delicate touch was required to gently nudge it into a precise altitude. Their capsule was on top of the crew's quarters, containing most of the supplies and the return rocket.

The alignment was crucial because in six hours they would be docking with the second spaceship, now being prepared for take-off.

Eventually, they slid gracefully into their designated position. There was no time to lose. A lot of preparation was needed outside the capsule before they would be ready to receive. The pumps purred, sucking their precious air out before they could reopen the hatch and venture out. Eugene's training injury had left him restricted and with their helmets back on Soraya gave him a little kick as he struggled to pull himself out of the tight confines.

Soraya's heart pumped and a thrill of excitement flushed through her as she deftly followed him out. There she was, frozen for a moment with the rolling planet spread out below her. A visceral apprehension charged her system, an instinctive fear of falling gripping her. Then an inner voice reminded her that though she was actually falling, it was in a grand circular orbit.

Focusing on the job at hand she watched Eugene with fascination as he made his way down the rocket. This man had spent more time working in space than any other, and there were whole sections of the ISS that owed their existence to his space engineering skills.

With the flick of Su-lin's finger, ranks of external lights suddenly flashed on as they prepared for the 'night' they would be subjected to when they swung around the far side of the Earth. The stark white light of the day began to mellow into hues of yellow, then diminished to orange then red as the great arc of the Earth appeared to rise into the path of the sun.

In an instant they were in a pitch-black void. The natural tones of the daytime Earth were replaced by a cascade of spangles as the major conurbations and highways traced out their presence in artificial light.

Soraya looked in rapt wonder as she contemplated the weight of humanity now evident across the globe. Tearing her eyes away, her vision was gripped by the spectacular starscape emblazoning the heavens above. 'Get a grip, sister!' she muttered as she refocused. Always keeping three points of attachment, she hurried after Eugene, who was now unfurling the great rolls of rubber with which they were to festoon the main body of the crew's quarters.

Once in place, the rubber would be filled with the precious water supplies for the voyage, freeing up valuable internal volume and creating a shield for the crew against the intense radiation of interplanetary space. It was taxing work, and sweat was collecting in small bubbles floating around Soraya's visor by the time 'dawn' broke in a beautiful reversal of the sunset forty-five minutes before.

As the light returned she made out the tongue of Florida, from whence they had escaped the grip of Earth. From this distance the USA looked deceptively peaceful compared with the mayhem that had unfolded shortly after their selection.

It now seemed like a lifetime ago, but it had been only a few hours since they had been sitting in the auditorium, nervously waiting for the outcome of their final selection. Elin caught Mo's eye. 'Nervous, are you?'

Mo's detachment was broken as he fiddled with an elastic band. If it were possible to be smug and disappointed at the same time, he was feeling it.

'Don't be stupid, we're not going, innit!' he hissed.

He had a guilty secret, undivulged even to his friends or father. Unlike those around him, he thought he already knew the results.

Mo hadn't been chosen for his exceptional computer skills for nothing. His sharp eyes had picked up all the secret passwords and programs, as the likes of Sharon and Edward had uploaded the selection data.

Surreptitiously hacking and wending his way through the NASA database, he had discovered their team was lagging behind 'The Elves'.

'Negative, don't be! How do you know?'

'Trust me, I know. There's no way we're going to Mars. Your mum's team are way ahead and we ain't putting the rockets together.'

Elin gave him a conspiratorial look and in hushed tones mouthed, 'My mummia not going! Pulled out she has!'

The rubber band twanged across the room. 'What?! But they were going to be...' He tailed off, realising he could let the cat out of the bag.

Everyone knew there'd be two crews, one for Mars and the other to help assemble the craft in space. Now the cat wasn't even in the bag, but out among the pigeons.

The fine-cut timing meant that the results of the medical samples and tissue testing on ISS had only just been uploaded into the database. Each would-be astronaut's painfully extracted samples had been undergoing a series of tests in space.

The two great health risks to a long-term space traveller are bone loss, due to weightlessness, and the presence of constant radiation.

Two remarkable results were confirmed. Firstly, the growth plate cells of the children's bones were undiminished and actually increased their growth to compensate. In contrast, adults in space suffer from irreversible osteoporosis.

Secondly, the youthful cells of the kids were confirmed to be incredibly resilient to the pervasive radiation of space. Their vigorous cells repaired or replaced themselves at a rate that significantly minimised their risks.

In stark comparison, the adults would suffer an increased threat of cancer or other cell damage. This had only been mitigated by choosing middle-aged adults, who simply had less time to live to develop these illnesses.

Once the late scores were uploaded into the matrix, the results brought the children almost level with the women. Then the bombshell. Kirsten had dropped out.

The senior mission members sat grim-faced around a conference phone. Luther had joined them, remotely 'sitting in' on their deliberations. He'd missed the initial row and was surprised at the stony silence when he asked innocently. 'OK, who's going?'

Sharon took a sip of her americano. 'We're at loggerheads, sir. The results backed "The Elves", but Kirsten has pulled out. So the logical decision is either to cobble together a mixed team or send "The Other Things".'

'OK, give me more detail: who, what and when?'

'Sure. For a mixed team, we could only send Felix with Soraya and Su-lin. He's the lightest of the men and he's been studying the science. However, he's on a warning for groping Soraya at the party and she refuses to be alone in the same room as him, let alone a capsule for two years.'

'What's his science like now?' Luther had seen him working away at it on his visit.

'High school B grade, at best, I'm afraid.'

'OK, what about the alternative?'

Then there was uproar as Stephen broke in. 'The alternative is postponing the mission!' He pointed at Edward. 'And if that idiot was doing his job, he'd back me up!'

'Exactly which idiot are you referring to?' Luther was on voice only.

'I'm not an idiot, I'm a logician,' Edward blurted out. 'He thinks I should veto the children on health-and-safety grounds.'

'Too goddamn right. You won't let me tie up my shoe laces without training!'

'But, Stephen, your previous job was killing people with drones! A completely different health-and-safety environment...'

'Ford, help me out! You're leading this mission!' The president needed a firm hand.

'Well, Edward's right. The logical thing is to send the kids. They will suffer fewer health problems, they naturally love sitting around all day doing nothing and have proved they can do the job, but... We're also worried about the politics and public reaction.'

'How many damned times do I have to tell you? I am the politician – you get on and choose the astronauts on merit. I'll go with Edward's call on this! Choose "The Other Things".'

Ford stuttered, 'Do you actually mean we should send the kids?'

The last thing Luther heard after he answered 'yes' was the slamming of a heavy door as Stephen stormed out.


As Mo and the others waited with bated breath in the small auditorium, they became increasingly aware of raised voices in the room adjacent. Each felt the embarrassment of listening to an almighty row which they ought not to be witnessing, like when your apparently nice neighbours have a major domestic. The voices ebbed and flowed until a distant door slam, then all was quiet.

The children waited, glancing at each other, unable to comment, apart from Enza and Elin, who were snorting with suppressed giggles.

Mo hated rows. At home they were one-sided and usually ended with his auntie in tears. He had cringed as it ebbed and flowed, and welcomed the long silence that followed.

The children looked anxiously at the clock above the empty stage. They knew that today was the day and the project was already behind. Someone should have been chosen by now – what the hell was going on?

Suddenly a flustered group emerged from the connecting room and assembled on the stage. The twelve would-be astronauts faced them on the front-row seats, their families and mentors sitting behind.

Checking his watch, Ford addressed them, glancing sideways to his colleagues on either side but with one notable absence: Stephen Dyer.

'Hi!' Ford shuffled his papers. 'After a lengthy debate...' Several of the group on the stage cleared their throats. '... the crews are selected! No time to lose... we're behind on our programme and need to get to the launch pads straightaway. Crew one – Soraya, Eugene and Su-lin – step forward and follow Sharon.'

The three looked at each other with surprise and hugged; then turning to the others high-fived them one by one, before leaving by the exit to the right of the stage.

Mo watched as they were guided through the forbidding door and assumed they must the Mars crew and looked over at Felix and Virgil as the natural guys who would help them assemble the rockets in orbit. His automatic assumption was tempered with a nagging doubt.

'Why's Eugene going, if he's still not fit, innit? Who gonna to take Elin's mum's role?'

'Crew two.'

To Mo's utter astonishment, he suddenly heard his own name called, followed by Elin, Buzz, Xing and Enza. His mind was swamped with a flood of emotion and confusion. He stumbled forward with his friends, he didn't even register that his father and the other mentors were being called as well. A group of ten filed out of the room, all looking at each other in disbelief.

The door closed and in the desolation of the room, four lonely figures were left seated. The small auditorium felt vast and cold around them.

Bheki stared at the spaces his friends had vacated. Having waited in vain for his name to be mouthed or signed, he felt tears welling in his eyes.

It wasn't that he would have been shocked or upset if none of them had been called, but to be left alone again! Seeing his friends chosen and whisked away was more than crushing, it reopened the void that had haunted him most of his life. His shoulders started to heave, until two familiar arms enveloped him from behind to restrain and soothe him. 'I'm still here, little brother,' said Zulu.

Edward joined them, nominated to tactfully explain why he'd not been picked. He sat down next to Bheki. Disliking social interaction at the best of times, he struggled with the sensitivity required to gently let down this young heart. Avoiding eye contact he shuffled, straining to find the right words. Bheki was sitting head down with his brother's arm resting protectively round his shoulders.

Edward blurted out. 'You can't go because... you're deaf!'

Bheki did not move, totally oblivious to the unseen words. Edward waited a moment before turning to Zulu. 'Does he understand?'

Now Bheki could see his lips. 'Understand what?' he sniffed, adding, 'I have to see you talk – I'm deaf, you know!'

Edward stood up relieved. 'Exactly, young man. I'm glad you understand.'

Beyond the door, a whirl of excitement gripped the children who ran dizzily around, then Enza stopped and thought, '*Dove si trove*, Bheki?'

Before the children could work it out, Yasmin asked them to sit down and started the briefing. But the children were distracted and in rebellious mood on hearing that Bheki had been excluded on health-

and-safety grounds. They all stood up and Enza shouted, '*No e guisto!* You should've decided that ages ago.'

Buzz was enraged. 'We've all learned to sign. He's our friend and we need him!'

Mo chipped in. 'I'm not going, if he's not!' Elin and Xing both sat down with arms crossed and lips pursed.

Ford emerged through the connecting door, scratching his head in a spasm of anxiety. 'Come on, what's keeping you? We need to get going! Pierre is already waiting at the airport to take them to the launchpad at French Guiana and all the papers need signing.'

There was a pile of papers on the table that each of the guardians had to sign on behalf of the children. The guardians stood stony-faced behind the children. It was obvious they were going nowhere.

'OK. I'm really sorry about Bheki. If it were my choice, he'd be with you but Edward was adamant. He can't read your lips with your helmets on.'

'But he has taught us to sign!' protested Mo.

There was a long, pregnant silence, until Buzz piped up. He had to back his granddad.

'Bheki's my best friend and I don't want to leave him, but he'd be more upset if we didn't go because of him.'

One by one the children uncrossed their arms. With heavy hearts, they agreed to go without Bheki. There was a flurried signing of papers before they were whisked onto the waiting coach.

Los Angeles was enveloped in a heavy haze, the watery sun unable to burn off the moisture in the air. The freeway signs flew by as the city gave way to suburbs, and finally the open ground of the airport unfolded before them. The coach took the first exit and pulled into a vast parking lot.

There were no security or customs for them. They just had to give the authorisation papers to Pierre. On the tarmac was an ESA airbus, bearing the logo 'Zero-G' on its airframe.

'*Bonjour, mes amis!* Are you all ready? We have no time to lose!'

Pierre had just been informed that 'The Other Things' had been chosen to go to Mars, but surveying the group counted only ten: five children and their five mentors.

'There should be twelve, *non*? Who's missing? Have we, as you say in NASA, a problem?'

'Bheki's been excluded on health-and-safety grounds!'

'In Europe we are very hot on these topics. What grounds exactly?'

'Because of his disability – he's deaf,' explained Yasmin.

Pierre looked shocked. He had worked with all the potential astronauts and had been particularly impressed with how seamlessly Bheki communicated, despite his lack of hearing.

'We are even hotter on the discrimination! I will have to make a call. This is definitely a problem.'

He stood a little away from the crowd to consult with Toulouse.

After Ford had made his fond farewells, he needed to tie up loose ends before setting off on his journey to mission control.

His composure was ruffled: first Stephen storming out of the briefing and then Edward's insensitivity with Bheki. He was furious with Edward's obstinate stance to exclude Bheki.

Ford couldn't understand how the man could stick his neck out by supporting the kids to go, then to be so punctilious about leaving Bheki behind. Little did Ford know the working of a singularly linear mind.

A call came through on his cell phone as he packed his computer into his travel bag.

'Hi, Yasmin, what's up?'

'Oh, Ford, I don't know what to do! Pierre's gone all technical on us – he says we can't get on the plane!'

'What do you mean, technical?'

'Well, he's talking, like, European legislation and discrimination things. He got kind of animated!'

'Animated?'

'Yup, he's waving his arms around and shouting in French. How we'd, like, discriminated against Bheki. He says they're taking off on French territory and American health-and-safety legislation don't count. Apparently you just can't discriminate against anyone in Europe!'

'So, what's happening?'

'He won't let us on the plane!'

Looking at his watch, Ford's guts suddenly loosened with the gravity of the situation. The timings were tight enough without further delays.

Clutching his bag, he rushed through the centre just in time to catch Zulu and Bheki leaving the foyer for an uncertain future. He slid to a halt across the polished terrazzo floor and shouted, 'Quick, Bheki, I've made an executive decision. You're going!' Then looking towards Zulu said, 'Can you drive? A cab won't take you onto the runway and I've still got critical things to do.'

'Of course, Mr Ford. I've just passed my test!'

'OK, here's my keys – get that boy to the airport!'

Ford pointed to a pale-green VW camper parked 50 yards way.

'I'll set the route on your phone, but be quick!'

The boys whooped with delight as they made it to the veteran vehicle.

'Hey, bro, what's this?'

'It's a gear stick, you idiot! Just like Mr Herman's Land Rover,' answered an incredulous Bheki.

'OK, OK, I learned on an automatic, man.'

There was a grinding of gears. Bheki pointed to the floor. 'There's a clutch, you warthog!'

Zulu depressed the pedal and bunny-hopped along the bays until they turned out screeching into the unsuspecting city roads.

Ford was on the phone. 'It's OK, Pierre. Bheki's on his way. Can you let the team on the plane – it's touch and go!'

'So, there's no discrimination?' quizzed Pierre.

Ford explained he'd taken an executive decision to override the safety concerns and respect ESA's constraints.

'*Merci*, Monsieur Harris. They'd better not be late or we'll have to leave without them!'

Ford was confused. 'I thought you couldn't leave without Bheki.'

'Only if he's been discriminated against!' replied the Frenchman. 'If he's late, he's late. *C'est la vie!*'

'Vive la goddamn difference,' muttered Ford.


Zulu was getting used to the VW's peculiar ways, even second gear. There was a large verdant park to be circumnavigated before meeting the freeway. Zulu glanced down at the threatening clock in the middle of the dashboard. He looked over at Bheki. 'Shall we go African style?' he mouthed at the boy, who gave a thumbs-up, and with a broad smile gave permission for a minor safari across the well-watered sage. Softballers and dog walkers yielded and scattered in all directions to the roar of the mighty flat four as they headed full tilt across the lawns.

Once on the freeway the drive seemed plain sailing, apart from the distraction of the flashing red lights in the distance.

The poor old crate couldn't do much over 60mph, but that was as much as the traffic allowed, and by the time Zulu and Bheki dropped down the slipway, they felt confident of reaching the airport in time. Like most who have just passed their test, Zulu made extravagant use of his mirror. Unfortunately, the red lights were getting closer and the wail of a siren now filled the air.

'Hey, bro, we've got company. Maybe they didn't like our shortcut?'

Bheki scrutinised the map and thrust his arm across Zulu's vision. 'Turn left, then left again,' he gestured. The van wobbled as it cut the corner and nearly rolled on the second turn around a scrubland under the viaduct.

'Behind that hedge!' shouted the navigator, as Zulu glided to a halt in the lee of a screen of tangled bushes.

Amid the scent of honeysuckle and dust they waited while two ardent patrol cars shot off like hounds that have missed their quarry.


Pierre had settled the party on the plane and completed the inevitable paperwork with the ground staff. He glanced nervously at his watch, then his phone blared, with Ford's creased face glowing from the screen.

'Are they there yet? They should be!' quizzed Ford.

'*Non, mon ami.* They are… notable by their absence. We have to go!'

Ford knew airport procedure back to front, and more importantly, how to make up time.

'Taxi the plane up to the runway and wait. It will save at least 10 minutes queueing and it's closer to the access road.'

Ford hurriedly dialled Zulu's number.

The map on Zulu's phone was suddenly interrupted by Ford's face. 'Where are you?'

Bheki turned the phone around and Ford immediately recognised the long perimeter fence and the avenue of palms fringing the sidewalk.

'Great! Go through Gate 7 – it's where I park my plane. Tell Zulu to put on my hat and they'll waive you through. Ignore the signs, go straight onto the tarmac, and look for a big plane with "Zero-G" on its body.'

Pierre's watch ticked insistently to its deadline, but there was still no sign of the boys.

'Que sera, sera,' he thought to himself, as he began to close the doors.

Turning round to look beyond the stark whiteness of the empty interior, he could see the children buckled in the stern, staring intently through the porthole windows. He hadn't told them about Bheki.

'Look, look, it's Ford!' shouted Buzz, instantly recognising the outline of his grandfather's grey-green van hurtling across the hot tarmac – with a posse of flashing yellow lights following at a distance. Pierre glanced through the window and, with a shrug, darted across the starchy white mats to the rear door. He flung it open just as the camper screeched to a halt below.

Immediately, he could see the hole in Ford's great plan. With no ladder or passenger steps, the two boys were way below with no hope of reaching the door. Even if they stood on the van's roof they would still be 4 feet short. The fleet of airport security cars were almost upon them. 'So near, yet so far,' thought Pierre as he saw Zulu disappear back into the van.

Suddenly, with a hydraulic whoosh, the candy-coloured stripes of the pop-top roof raised itself towards the heavens. The two boys deftly clambered up into the grip of Pierre's long, toned, outstretched arms and tumbled into the plane. An astonished gasp and then cheers filled the cabin as the children slipped their belts and clambered along the aisle to hug their friends.

'Attendez!' shouted Pierre. 'Belt up, we have to go. Vite! Allons-y!'

Zulu turned to interrupt the hasty closure of the door. Poking his head out he tossed the camper keys into the path of the running figures closing in from the now parked security vehicles. 'Please give these to Mr Ford!' he called, before Pierre pulled him in.

The great jet juddered into taxiing speed. Quickly they left behind the van and the huddle of uniformed guards, buffeted by the engine blasts and looking lost and forlorn in their wake.

# Chapter 29

## Lift-Off

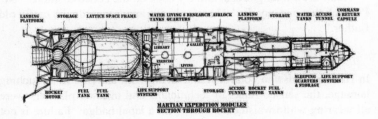

*Section through Rocket*

The world had watched in awe as the three intrepid astronauts blasted off from Cape Canaveral. It held its collective breath for each successive stage to ignite and push them further up and away into the gods. A silent immense sigh of relief echoed round the planet when they attained their orbit. The architect of this grand enterprise stood like a proud father on the distant viewing platform, waving majestically as the great thrusting flame disappeared into the heavens. Then, in his own engaging way, Luther earnestly addressed the world – explaining how this was just the start of humanity's greatest mission. He lauded the intrepid three for their bravery, skill and fortitude.

Although he touched the hearts and minds of most, there were dissenters. High in a Chicago penthouse, a brooding Victor Relish sank further into his white leather sofa and stirred his tea, while watching the show unfold on the Pure News channel. Unable to contain himself during Luther's speech he bellowed to his wife Delilah in the kitchen, 'Come watch this, doll. Look at the man! He's up to something, the sly old fox. It's not what he says but what he doesn't say.'

Delilah came through in her coral silk dressing gown and settled by his side. 'It's probably another hoax like the moon landings, darling.'

Victor grinned conspiratorially and clinked his cup to his wife's Martini. 'He'll be gone in a few days and the gloves will be off. Madame President has invited me over next week to help sort things out! The end of eight years of nonsense.'

With a nonchalant click of a button he changed the channel to the Pure racing channel. 'Huh! Definitely something fishy,' Victor muttered to himself.

Delilah scrutinised the paper. 'Sorry, darling, Something Fishy is not on the card. You'll have to choose another horse.'

Victor drew a long breath and lay back on the cerise cushions. 'No, I'd back that one any day! There's always another card with crafty old Luther.'


In Houston, mission control was heaving with activity. In a touching homage, the serried ranks of technicians and mission planners were all wearing white waistcoats, each with a lapel badge: 'Failure is not an option'. After the euphoria and relief of getting the first crew up, the tricky task of co-ordinating the second flight and its rendezvous was taxing every one of them.

After his own breakneck journey, Ford was buzzing around in the background when the call came through from Luther. The great man was uncharacteristically on edge and he nervously asked about 'The Other Things'. Ford did his best to assure him and after recounting the debacle around Bheki, he joked, 'You're going to have to get me a presidential pardon, if I'm ever going to get my van back!'

'We'll all need one when we're done with this!' the president replied with a hollow laugh. 'Look, we're going to keep "The Other Things" under wraps until the world is ready.' Then, with a more genuine chuckle, 'Hey, trust me! I know about the best time to release information. The world is very happy with our intrepid three astronauts in orbit at the moment.'

The second rocket's capsule had been like a Formula One pit bay, as the technicians feverishly fixed the diminutive seats in place and stuffed the last stores into its cramped confines. The last-minute discovery that Stephen had thrown away the children's specially moulded seats for the Mars lander had sparked a panic, until the training set were purloined and flown in from the simulators. It had been a long, long flight and in the sultry heat of the South American night, the children and their mentors sat fanning themselves in the newly equipped changing rooms.

It was only when their diminutive space suits appeared that the first real frisson of excitement erupted. They would not only be the first children in space, but the very first astronauts to blast off from these sprawling ESA facilities.

'*Allora!* Look at this!' Enza was the first to be squeezed into her suit. She pirouetted to show off her name and the red, white and green tricolour proudly embroidered on her sleeve. Soon, one by one, they were all strutting the catwalk in front of their nearest and dearest. Pierre burst in, accompanied by a hot blast of air from the outside.

'Sorry to break up the party. Time for your fond *adieus, mes amis*.'

The whole room froze. There was a heavy silence, then the surreal nature of their situation condensed into a rock-hard reality. Yes, this was it. It was not a dream and they would be unexpectedly saying goodbye for almost two years, or, with a shudder, maybe forever. The enormity of the enterprise was lost on no one. The time had come and the children stood solemnly with their mentors, each of whom had a small gift.

Alim took Mo's hands between his and surveyed his son's face with a love that comes with a lifetime guarantee. For once this eloquent man was choking, lost for words. He bowed as he silently passed him a small round wrapped gift for the journey.

For Zulu, a brother, there was no parental angst, only the excitement of it all. He swept Bheki up and held him aloft before resting his forehead gently against the young boy's. With a flourish he gave Bheki his farewell package. 'It was Father's,' he explained.

Enza and Elisabetta, mother and daughter, were lost in their mixed emotions: they hugged, laughed, cried and made enough noise for all of them. Tears flowed copiously among the laughter as the mother slipped Enza a long, thin parcel.

Jane, the step-grandmother, first ruffled Buzz's hair with more than a tear in her eye, then gripped him close to her chest, profusely apologising for the absence of his mum or Ford. Buzz was stiff, showing little emotion until his face suddenly brightened. 'Perhaps my dad will notice me?' Jane gave a smile and kissed him on both cheeks, then handed him a brown paper parcel that looked remarkably like a teddy bear.

Elin and Kirsten, Viking-bred, stood staring at each other before they started a slow, slow hand clap high above their heads, increasing and intensifying into a deafening climax, then they hugged, while Kirsten lifted and whirled her petite daughter dizzily around the room. 'It was either you or me, *litla min*, and you're the future.' She patted her own flushed cheeks, then very carefully placed in Elin's hands something weighty yet totally invisible to the rest of the group.

*Rocket 2 on Launchpad*

On the end of the long bench poor Xing sat stoically alone. There was no one there for her, her mother was already in space. Enza, ever aware, suddenly sensed the lonesome void and vigorously beckoned the others to envelop the little girl in a major group embrace.

Then, like toddlers trailing nappies, the children shuffled out into the sultry, starblazing night. The adults stood pensively aside on the still steaming concrete, watching them as they took their protein pills and put their helmets on. Dodging the odd tropical storm puddle, they boarded their transit vehicles. The two groups were like opposite poles, the adults subdued, quiet and apprehensive, guilty even, and the children animated, waving frantically in their excitement from the back of two open jeeps, which picked up speed and scooted down the long drive towards the strangest-looking rocket ever constructed, crouching almost a mile away at the business end of the ballistic range.

Xing's childhood had been one of joy, sadness and fear. Even in the dusty backyards of her home town, the child found joy in the smallest things. A singular infant, she detached herself from close friends, depending instead on the strength of her vivid imagination that could conjure animated personalities and extraordinary adventures from a single thought or whim. She had witnessed her beloved father dying in front of her, struck down by a premature heart attack. She sat with the still warm body for the best part of a day, coaxing and imploring its life force to rekindle and surface, until her mother returned to join her in the unexpected pit of grief.

She had somehow survived, mostly through the energy and diehard optimism of her mother. That was until Su-lin's meteoric rise through the echelons of the Chinese space agency brought yet another existential threat to her life: the fear of losing her surviving parent and her life's anchor. Xing had learned to shut off her worries and visceral fears and gradually gained confidence and boldness with each of her mother's safe returns from the void.

Although heavy with sadness, she held on to these strengths now. On the steaming launchpad, adrenaline and terror coursed through her veins, forcing her to dig deep into her defences. Strapped in, trussed up like a chicken waiting to be roasted, there wasn't much Xing could do or say. She closed her eyes and closed her mind. Then she heard a soft voice over the intercom. '*Commençant compte à rebours... Cinque, quatre, trois...*' The body of the rocket shook, and the voice continued. '*Verifiez l'allumage et que l'amour de Dieu soit avec vous... deux, un, décollage!*'

Xing squeezed her eyelids even tighter, shutting off the outside world, only to feel gloved hands reaching for hers as the children felt the thrust of lift-off pushing against their seats.

In Mission Control Toulouse, the atmosphere intensified as the telemetric sensors streamed back disturbing data from the base. A wave of anxiety struck the flight engineers as it became evident that one of the boosters had not fired. The computers were kicking in to rectify the situation, but they were acutely aware that the rocket would not reach orbit without it. *Click, click, click* – the ignition mechanism re-fired and failed like a broken gas ring.

The crew were only aware of this due to the buzzing of orange warning lights, the slow rate of climb and added tilt of the lifting rocket. Suddenly, to applause and the relief of mission control, the third booster coaxed itself out of its slumber. With explosive force it fired up and the children flinched with the sudden kick it added to the massive boost already pressing on their backs.

The momentary relief was tempered by the fact that the additional untimely power of the rocket appeared to set up a grinding oscillation within the ungainly frame. 'The Other Things' felt a low, swaying rhythm and a rasping vibration creep through their seats and suits. It seemed to invade the very flesh and bone of the six recumbent bodies. Even Xing could not shut it out of her mind and flashed open her eyes to watch the monitors respond to an unfolding crisis. The on-board computers had already started to compensate for the missing booster by directing a stream of pulsed ejections from the ring of boosters fixed onto the main lander's body. But they could not cope with added impetus of the third rocket when it kicked in, and over-compensated like an inexperienced canal boat skipper might weave a boat from bank to bank in a desperate effort to maintain a straight course.

Unlike the lift-off spectacle in Florida, there were no crowds to witness this scene, except a few locals and space agency staff who stood, eyes lifted, watching the rising fire and clouded trail. They witnessed the weaving, spinning corkscrew that painted itself on the darkening sky that night. The nervous technicians back in France had no idea of the consequences of this increasingly violent flexing on the airframe, save that most had seen the appalling vision of the devil's cloud that had blown the Challenger crew out of the pristine blue sky of Florida many years ago.

On that day, a weakness in the 'O' ring seals connecting each segment of the solid rocket burners had allowed an intense flaming tongue to disastrously ignite the main fuel tank of the shuttle. Despite the technicians' re-design, no one really knew how much stress the burners could withstand before again falling apart at the seams. To the horror of all, with each unforgiving minute, the negative feedback appeared to increase exponentially. The computers struggled to fight the problem.

The diminutive bodies of the astronauts were now being jolted violently from side to side, with warning lights buzzing on all panels.

A small high-pitched voice came over the intercom. 'Toulouse, we have a problem!'

Moments later, *'Bolleaux!'* screamed Eric. Inexplicably he had just witnessed the automatic systems suddenly switch off and the flight was now out of his or the computer's control. A gaggle of bodies hurried around his shoulders, shouting fierce orders and invectives at the hapless man and his screen. Eric feverishly hacked at the keys, vainly attempting to impose some semblance of command.

Pierre's blood ran cold as he too realised that the craft appeared to be up Merde Creek without a proverbial *'pas d'elle'*.

'Spam in a can' was a complaint voiced by the early space pioneers about their status, if they were given no human override or ability to fly their missions. Since the 1960s the crew were always able to take the helm.

Xing knew this and so did Buzz. She had not wasted hour upon tedious hour, day upon mind-warping day, sitting in a pretend capsule in a desert for nothing. Their computers were linked to the NASA flight simulators and Xing, the quiet one, had worked on every problem that might be thrown at them. She would ask Buzz and Mo to set the simulator with one disaster or another. Sometimes, they would tease her by setting a boring regular flight or just being spectacularly blown up on the launch pad, much to their gales of laughter. She would then give them the sort of look her mother would be proud of. Often they would all virtually die, or the mission would be aborted. Relentlessly, she would 'work the problem' until she conquered it. Afterwards she would delight in running the autopilot to see what mess or magic it could conjure. For the really difficult scenarios, she would also insist on Buzz having a go himself and competitively kept their scores.

In the midst of this crisis she had opened her eyes and took in the ominous vibes. Immediately she was reminded of one of the most innocuous sounding but taxing situations Mo had set. 'What if one of the rockets kicks in late, innit?!' was the slightly longwinded name for their current predicament. Xing had watched time after time the simulators struggle with the wild oscillations, until an inevitable breakup. She vainly fought it herself until remembering Soraya's sage advice on docking a boat in a tight spot. 'Relax, gain equilibrium, then control. Think ahead!'

Buzz also saw they were entering a bad place and recognised the conundrum. Looking Xing in the eye, or at least the juddering visor, he raised his hand with a prominent thumb. He knew she had always beaten him on this one. A small gloved hand clicked a switch, not once but twice, as was protocol in such matters, and suddenly a self-destructing 200-tonne spaceship's fate was in the hands of an 11-year-old girl.

Eric sat and watched as the correcting retros were switched off, no longer fighting against the strain. Then the rocket started following its own trajectory, a graceful arc, but not one to take it into orbit.

In the cabin, the effect was immediate, the violent vibrations quelled and the screeching and grinding stopped. There was still an immense amount of noise and clatter but at normal levels. Buzz's furious pointing indicated to Xing that she should use the 'Game box' control, rather than the stiff manual ones.

Now that the steaming rocket had stabilised, Xing started to slowly coax it into an ever steeper curve using the large gimballed rocket motor at its base. Finally, she re-introduced the fine controls of the side retrorockets to trim it into what she guessed would be the right alignment. Her eyes darted between the myriad of screens and Mo and Buzz, who were staring intently through the triangular windows, tracking the starscape that revealed itself as they progressed into the stratosphere.

Eric gestured excitedly to his colleagues, his dread changing to a rising elation to see the craft steady itself and rejoin its correct route to infinity and beyond. Xing concentrated on keeping the ship on course and it was a great relief when mission control ordered her to put the craft back into autopilot. She looked for reassurance from Buzz, who gave a shrug then gestured for her to flick the switch.

Xing nervously reached up and hit the toggle.

*Bang! Bang! Bang!*

Immediately three staccato explosions shook the craft. Shocked, she let out a blood-chilling scream, along with her five terrified companions, as they watched in dismay as the main rockets suddenly dropped away and fell back to a diminishing Earth. 'What have I done?' was her frantic thought. 'Forgive me!' she whispered.

The whole of Toulouse mission control erupted into a deafening roar. The spaceship was now right on track and the explosive bolts holding the solid booster rockets had separated exactly on cue. They would return to Earth on parachuted wings, like spinning dandelion seeds. The last rocket engine, which Xing had so skilfully manipulated, was now boosting the rocket into the final stage of their flight into orbit.

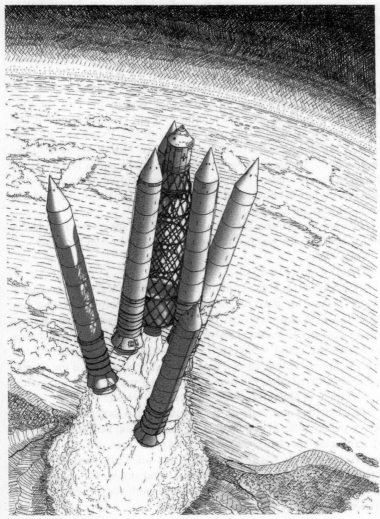

*Rocket 2 Lift-off*

At her moment of despair, Xing, shamed and frightened, had clamped her eyes shut again and waited for what she thought were to be their final moments. It was several minutes before she dared reopen them. She puzzled at the peaceful serenity of the scene, asking in bewilderment, 'Are we in heaven?'

'I'd like to think so!' responded Mo, as he strained his eyes through the reinforced glass, surveying the rolling sphere of the Earth below them and the blackness of space above. In the far distance there was what appeared to be a bright moving star.

Speeding through the sodium-stained freeway, Stephen eased the Pontiac onto the slipway and entered the grid of the city suburbs. Then he was home at last. The nightmare of the last two years felt like a heavy cloak cast off in the tiled hallway of life. Exhausted after the long drive, he collapsed onto the hard black leather of the chrome-framed sofa. Surrounded by a lifetime of books and a lost youth of vinyl, he dropped into a restless sleep. Dreams of tall corn and orchid skies haunted his inner mind until the brightening light beyond the undrawn curtains filtered through his eyelids.

Fortified by a strong black coffee, Stephen tapped feverous tracts on his laptop to the two people he knew might take him seriously.

'Dear Peggy...'

'Dear Victor...'

The message was the same to both. He had served the president out of a sense of duty on the Mars mission. Despite it being run by a bunch of dreamers and incompetents, he had carried on, but the choice of the children and the secrecy still surrounding it was more than he could stand. He had resigned in protest and wanted them to know and put an end to the foolishness. He fired the emails off and received almost immediate replies, noting their automatic reassurances of attention within the next few weeks.

He spent the next half an hour dusting and ordering the room, before pursuing the matter on the telephone. Again he met a stonewall of answering machines and secretaries who took his number and details and politely but firmly fobbed him off. Exhausted, he finally retired to the kitchen to fix some proper breakfast. He checked the news and was privately disappointed that both rockets had made it into orbit and the rendezvous was looming.

Soraya and Eugene had fastidiously completed the preparations for the craft; its rubber suit was now in place ready for the water to be pumped out once it had been united with the lander and three remaining boosters. They were making the final attachments of the umbilical command cables which would run from the base of the vehicle to the re-entry capsule. Soraya's feelings of excitement were giving way to sweat and exhaustion as she helped haul it along the length of the ship.

Working in space takes some getting used to. Despite the training, Soraya struggled with the lack of inertia and resistance. When the cable momentarily snagged, she followed Newton's laws of opposite reactions as she tugged at it. In the background, a green ring of aurora had burst on the southern pole. Struck by its ethereal beauty, she bashed into Eugene instead. Seeing it over his shoulder she could at least point it out to him.

Eugene, an old hand, was less impressed but felt a genuine thrill when he spotted a bright, moving star-like object growing in intensity by the second. Without a doubt it was 'The Other Things' approaching their rendezvous. Hurriedly, Eugene and Soraya snapped home the cable into the socket on the side of the capsule and opened the triangular hatch, squeezing back into their sanctuary.

Su-lin was thrilled to hear the news of the sighting. Checking the systems as the spacewalk progressed, she had been going through her own private hell of waiting. After Eugene and Soraya cross-checked the hatch, the pressure hissed as the air rushed in. They felt emancipated and took their helmets off in sweaty relief. But there would be no respite – they would have to work closely together for at least the next few hours. The re-entry capsule would be disengaged from its main body and Soraya's job was to fly it. Soraya would use the newly fixed data cord to remotely manoeuvre the bulk of the rocket into its coupling with the other craft.

The bright star below them had now become a distinctive shape above them. The pilot rolled and yawed the capsule to get the best vantage point. The Earth was a bright blue and white heaven filling their fields of vision. Eugene had his binoculars trained, straining to make out the detail. Bright puffs of ejecta lifted and glided the rocket into their orbit, and now just a little in front of them.

Butterflies waltzed in Buzz's stomach as he nosed them upwards. This was real – there was no virtual game that could get close to the sheer thrill of flying this craft. Every little touch on his controls shot out a small blast from the tiny rockets surrounding them. The response was immediate, and the swaying of his companions and their giggles simply amplified the thrill. Each of them had pinned their noses to the portholes, and one by one pointed and felt a warm pride as they made out their homelands far below. The sweeping line of dawn had just broken over Iceland as Elin spotted it glistening at the very top of the globe. Soon Mo was thrilled to see a cloud-dappled London, his second home. Simultaneously, Enza spotted the old boot of Italy in the centre as Bheki pointed out the greens and ochres of landlocked Zimbabwe to the south. Xing caught the outline of Beijing just as the shadow of night overtook it.

Their worlds, so distant on Earth, now seemed within a hair's breadth from this vantage point. Their command capsule was never going to be spacious, and as each of them hastily unclasped the straps, they squirmed around each other like a herring ball. Desperately trying to experience their new weightless state, their helmets bashed like so many bobbing apples among the bits of loose kit that had been freed by the crazy vibrations of the eventful take-off.

'Let me see, let me see!' ordered Buzz as he pushed away the bodies to track the path of the main rocket above them. He needed to ease them into the same orbit but just ahead. The capsule glided past the long rolling tube of the final stage, the black-striped crew quarters and then the detached capsule – which filled and vanished from their window view as he eased them in front. Their orbits were now the same, but a delay was necessary before any further manoeuvres. The red glow of the evening light was creeping over them, giving way to the black shadow of Earth.


Back at mission control, Ford's satisfaction with the success of events, was tempered by the need to lift the secrecy on the mission. The press were now baying at the gates and the television stations were abuzz with speculation. The likes of the famous science pundit Professor Ryan Prix had already spotted the two re-entry vehicles, and the convenient assumption that the first crew were the chosen ones was wearing thin.

Ford saw himself as a straight-talking guy, and this evasiveness was for the realms of the politician. He was jittery with anticipation when his phone rang again, this time with an image of the White House on the screen.

'Cease your worrying, Mr Harris. I shall make a statement on the matter tomorrow morning. It shall be my last press conference and it will be nice to go out with a surprise… besides I can bury it in a lot of other stuff and ruminations. Ha! Ha!' Luther lowered his tone. 'How are the preparations going? I'd like to get the technical crew away from the scene beforehand.'

Ford ran his fingers through his hair. 'Pretty darn tense on the way up, sir… er, Luther, but all A-OK now – just need to couple the vehicles up and finish the preparations and then off they go!'

'Good, I want to give that woman a "fait accompli". She's one of the few people who make me nervous.'

Ford laughed nervously. 'She reminds me of my ma.'

'Exactly,' growled the president.

Lake Kariba

Mr Herman put down his sundowner and took in the peace and quiet. He was enjoying a break from the orphanage. Bheki's extraordinary journey had brought great benefits. Even small donations made a great difference and NASA had given an appreciable amount. It was Mr Herman who had to sign the consent forms and keep the secret. His reward was this small holiday. The dusty drive from the granite landscape of the Matopos Hills to Lake Kariba had been long but uneventful, except for the inevitable police checks.

The crimson sun was setting rapidly into the grey-blue haze. The silhouettes of elephants and half submerged trees shimmered in the pink ripples around them as the sun slowly disappeared and night fell around them. He pondered on the order of the universe and the spinning planet that provided this beauty, as the bitter hints of gin lubricated his thoughts.

**Lake Kariba**
Zimbabwe – Zambia
16.6S 28.0E
Altitude: 1,591ft
Depth: 318ft
Geology:
Hydroelectric
reservoir – Zambezi
River

As the tender wound its way back to the houseboat he checked his watch. Looking up, he picked out the twin stars floating across the heavens in tight formation. He did his best to find a future for all the children and here was one who had not only reached for the stars, but had joined them.

One hundred miles above him, the two rockets were preparing to dock.

All had been running smoothly far above. After jettisoning the final stage, Soraya guided the return rocket onto the lattice cage. She and Eugene checked the camera with its crosshairs and made the final alignment with one small thrust. It bounced off. 'Damn it!' she whispered, and lined up and tried again. The kids could feel the bump and vibrations as the rockets attempted to engage. Three times it happened, rocking them forward each time. They all found it amusing, except Xing. She had recovered from the stress of take-off, only to be overcome by the sadness of missing a final goodbye with her mother. The frustration of it all, each floating around in their tin cans far above the world, but not able to communicate other than via the *bleep-bleep* of the intercoms.

'Work the problem,' extolled Eugene as he gestured to Su-lin to manoeuvre the capsule further down the length of the cage to view the connection at close hand. These couplings were tried and tested, and had never failed before. Worryingly, if they couldn't dock, the mission could go no further. As they drew alongside, Eugene took a deep breath and inspected the connections through his raised binoculars. The plastic bubble wrap glistened in the sunshine.

'Goddamn protective packing's still there. I'm gonna have to sort this one out.' He reached for his helmet, indicating the others to do the same and prepare for decompression.

'No, Eugene, if you don't mind, I'd like to.' Su-lin tugged his sleeve.

'No problem, we've already had our fun out there.'

Their suits expanded in response to the drop in pressure and Eugene took control as Su-lin and Soraya eased open the door, and Su-lin cast herself into the void. She grasped the outside of the solid rocket booster and worked her way round to the lattice cage. Squeezing through the gap towards the base of the landers, she could now see the problematic packaging.

*Assembly in Orbit*

Space gloves are not made for dexterity, and it was with some difficulty and a great deal of patience that she managed to prise the compressed and mangled material from the titanium rings of the docking mechanism. Casting it untidily aside, she finally brushed off the surface with her glove. She took a small object from her patch pocket on the suit and attached it on the inner hatch with some of the excess tape she'd just removed.

All finished, she slowly removed herself from the cage and gestured to Eugene that she was going to work herself up the edifice.

Xing was quiet. She was lost in her own thoughts when Mo tugged her shirt. 'Look out of the window, innit!'

They shifted to make room and there was the golden sheen of a space helmet and a gloved hand pointing to the red flag of the People's Republic of China on the suit. Xing's pulse leaped as she realised that her mother had come to say goodbye. They spent a precious minute or two gesturing their love across a vacuum.

Finally, Su-lin stretched her right hand against the outside glass of the window and Xing placed her left in return as if touching a mirror. A small tear worked its track down her cheek. Then, with a wave, Su-lin was gone. Time was pressing, and all that was left was the imprint of a small palm on the condensation which slowly trickled down the glass.

Suddenly, there was a satisfyingly audible click and tremble which shook the whole craft. The children knew then that they had docked. Soraya had eventually done her stuff and all was set. The adult crew could now re-pressurise their capsule and prepare for their fiery descent into the rolling brine of the Pacific Ocean.


'Listen to him, droning on about his so-called successes. Bunkum!'

Peggy 'soon-to-be-President' Tyler was packing her clothes with one ear on the television and shouting comments to 'soon-to-be-first husband' Ryan, who was glued to the Pure News channel. She frowned while choosing the perfect blouse to match the bright-green suit she had carefully chosen for the inauguration. Moving house was always exciting, but moving into the White House was thrilling.

'The first thing I'm going to do is redecorate the Oval Office. It's far too masculine!' she called through to the slouching Ryan.

He didn't answer, fixed to the television, unable to believe his ears. 'What! That's reee...diculous. Sheee... it, that's the stupidest thing ever. Hey, Pegs, you won't believe what that lunatic's done...'

'Ryan, what *are* you going on about? What could he have done that's worse than before?'

'He's sent a bunch of kids into space!' Ryan hastily stood up and to his horror spilled his coffee on the immaculate beige sofa. He hurriedly rearranged the cushions to cover his mishap.

Peggy rushed through to see Luther proudly name each of the kids and their nationalities. Judging by the gasps and general murmuring, the press were as shocked as Ryan.

'Well! Ryan, I think the decoration will now be the second thing! I'm going to put paid to all this nonsense.'

Peggy bustled out of the room to get her phone.

Ryan regarded the room and the packing boxes. 'Maybe we might keep the sofas here after all.'

# Chapter 30

## In Orbit

As Elin slowly opened the hatch, a waft of compressed air streamed through her weightless hair in a cascade of gold, temporarily blinding a bemused Buzz, who was straining to look over her shoulder. The short tube gave way to a hi-tech cave, which held all the necessaries to survive on the Martian surface and was lined with six small vertical beds. These bright-white quarters would also serve as their dormitory during their long journey to the planet and back. One after another they floated through the tube and jockeyed to claim the best beds, only to find them pre-allocated with their names and flags embroidered, like their overalls, on the fabric.

Rushing to their next task, like the frantic opening of Christmas presents, they released the gauges to pressurise the main working and living quarters.

To enter they had to slip through an even longer connecting tube. The hexagonal plan of the lander allowed for nine fuel cylinders: three for oxygen and six for hydrogen, with just enough space in the middle to accommodate the connecting tube. With a whoosh of air, the last hatch was released.

There, in the torchlight was a small package still taped to the hatch. To Xing's absolute delight it contained her beloved kimekomi doll.

They all flooded through, tumbling into the dark compartment in a scrum of bodies and limbs. Bheki was the first to reach the controls. He knew this layout like the back of his hand. As he flicked through the switches, banks of lights and buzzers sprang to life. The chattering children spread out like the fingers on an unfurling hand, excitedly rolling and spinning as they enjoyed the spacious living quarters – at least compared with the cramped command capsule.

Slowly settling down, Xing and Buzz joined Bheki, packing away the collapsed water containers and checking everything under the watchful presence of an attentive mission control. They were carefully preparing everything for the grand tour ahead. The unplanned delay in docking had upset all the schedules, and Houston prudently decided to rest the crews before they engaged in the demanding blast out of Earth's orbit into interplanetary space. After all the extraordinary events of the last day, fatigue enveloped 'The Other Things'. They snuggled down in their state of excited exhaustion. Even the adult astronauts were allowed a cat nap before preparing for their own descent back to Earth.

Very soon to be ex-President Luther Garvey sat for the last time at his desk of state. Before him were the national newspapers and they all bore similar headlines: 'What Off Earth Is He Playing At?', 'Get the Kids Down' and 'Astronomical Mistake' were just a sample of the negative headlines. The creases on Luther's brow deepened as he frowned and stroked his chin. The delay in orbit had meant that the mission was yet to cross 'the line of no return'. The bevy of phones sitting menacingly before him had been buzzing manically and the penultimate call he took that day was from an iridescently irate Peggy 'due-to-become-president-tomorrow' Tyler. No word or reasoning from Luther, however short, could be squeezed in edgeways, except a reluctant 'OK' when she demanded him back in this very room to face the music in the new president's first meeting after her inauguration. Luther then called Ford to give him the lowdown, pressing him to expedite matters on the mission as soon as possible. To Luther's dismay, Ford revealed that he too had been given a royal scolding and told to be present tomorrow.

'Sounds like "book down the trousers time", sir,' Ford joked thinly.

Luther ruefully smiled as he remembered own his father's discipline. He wished he still had the ragged copy of *The Boy's Book of Wonders*, which been so useful in more circumstances than he cared to remember. With a sigh, he surveyed the interior of the Oval Office, the focus of his daily existence for the last eight years. He realised it looked as shabby as he felt at present.

An idle thought came to him. Much as he disliked 'That Darn Woman', he grudgingly recognised her as a person of conviction and maybe, just maybe, it was time for change, but hopefully not tomorrow. He shuffled around the carpet, slowly packing each of his portable personal items into his worn leather briefcase. Turning round, he took his last look at the room and the portraits of many great men who had held the privilege of this office. He chuckled out loud when he remembered the joke about Nixon, who had asked the portrait of Abraham Lincoln for advice about what to do in his own darkest hour. It is said that from the bowels of the past came an unearthly voice: 'Go to the theatre, Dick. Go to the theatre.'

Slowly and carefully he closed the door behind him.

Ford's stomach churned. All the blood, sweat and tears of the last two years could be wasted. Anxiety surged through him. He had to get moving. Tomorrow was a new dawn and the dark clouds were massing.

'Wake all the astronauts up,' ordered Ford. 'We gotta move our butts! Get the Mars crew ready for the first burn. Then as soon as all's well, get the maintenance crew down.'

A whirl of activity broke out in the ranks of the technical staff and programmers. This was a crucial stage and they all felt the pressure. Everything had to work perfectly, not just now but for the next two years. Even with a following wind it would take a full day.

The young astronauts had to rehearse their drills. They knew that from now on, communications would get more and more challenging as they headed away from Earth. Their parents and mentors had to take advantage of this opportunity to finesse their partnerships with their little 'avatars'.

These tyros were still organising and checking the stores when Luther and Ford found themselves waiting in the anteroom outside the Oval Office.

They were as nervous and pensive as defendants before a court hearing, whispering to each other between the long silences. With a slight creak the doors opened and Belle walked in with a slightly sheepish smile to her old boss. 'President Garvey and Mr Harris, please come through. President Tyler is ready to receive you.'

Ford scanned the room. The new president sat behind the very desk that Luther had greeted him from all those months ago. It felt so different. The place appeared to have shrunk, in all probability because it was so full of grim-faced advisers. There were two chairs, onto which they were ushered. Ford sat down. Luther excused himself and remained standing.

The new president stood up in her immaculate green suit and orange blouse. After minimal pleasantries, she fixed him with a gimlet eye. 'Mr Harris, pardon me if I cut to the chase. Was all this – sending vulnerable children to their certain death on an inhospitable planet – your idea?'

Ford stood up, cleared his throat and looked around the room with an innocent countenance. 'It's quite logical really, ma'am. It's a scientific choice – the safest and most viable option.'

President Peggy Tyler surveyed the faces in the room with an air of incredulity. 'Don't give me science, Mr Harris. I believe in faith and opinion, so please answer my question: was this your idea?'

Ford's confidence to carry the argument was melting into slush. 'Er, it was a joint decision...' he stuttered.

Peggy took a long, deep breath and tapped the leather-topped desk in a slow beat with her right purple-nailed index finger.

'Whose idea?' she slowly repeated.

Ford scratched his head and glanced sideways to a stony-faced Luther.

'Well, I suppose... er... yes, it was one of my initial options! But everyone's right behind it.'

Peggy sat down in her chair and made an infinitely small gesture towards the back of the room. The phalanx of advisers parted like the Red Sea waters and through the gap emerged a familiar face.

'Not everyone, Mr Harris. I believe you know Mr Dyer? He resigned over it. Stephen's been very kind and filled me in on all the details of this debacle.'

She cleared her throat. 'This not a time for "blue sky thinking". I'm afraid I need someone with more conventional ideas. Mr Dyer is taking over your role forthwith.'

There was a heavily pregnant pause while Ford's bewildered eyes flickered around for inspiration or help. Peggy tapped again on the leather. 'Must I make it plain to you? Mr Harris... you're fired! Please use the servant's door yonder.'

The stunned silence seemed to echo around the curved walls. A sly smile broke on Stephen Dyer's thin lips. A dumbfounded Ford slowly realised he had been ordered to leave the proceedings and his only comfort was that this time he knew where the door was. There was a murmuring of whispers as he left dewy-eyed in a daze of thoughts and emotions. As he closed the secret door, he paused on the threshold for just long enough to hear Peggy inform Luther, with haughty disdain, that she was cancelling 'his impossible dream', as she put it.

It had all been so perfunctory. Ford's naive hope that he could reason and argue the case had been dashed and replaced by such a dire hollowness that he now operated solely on instinct. He had no plan B or thoughts other than to fly from this place and get back to Houston and tell the team the bad news. He implored the stern-faced driver to rush him to the airport, where his old plane was waiting. He simply had to get there before Stephen Dyer could wreak his mayhem.

There was an agonising wait for a take-off slot while the big jets trundled their course to the main strip and lumbered heavily into the evening's honeyed skies. The city's haze of smog and persistent headwinds would not help. Finally airborne as the night took over,

| Houston |
| Texas, USA |
| 29.5N 95.2W |
| Altitude: 80ft |
| Geology: Gulf |
| coastal plain |

Ford followed the freeway lights from one twinkling city spiderweb to another.

By the time he got to Houston, he was exhausted and overcome with the immeasurable sadness of seeing his good works about to be dismantled and cast aside by fools and philistines.

Stephen Dyer, on the other hand, was brimming with unexpected triumph as he boarded the white-and-silver Boeing. What a couple of days it had been! His frustration in having his phone calls and emails ignored had been overturned by unexpected missives from Victor Relish and then the White House. Victor's news organs had been vicious in their condemnation of the sending of 'The Other Things' and here on a plate was his opportunity to terminate the mission. Stephen was the obvious executioner.

Victor had already been relishing the prospect of meeting Peggy and receiving accolades for his vigorous support of her campaign and discussing future media relationships with the administration. So he was intrigued to be invited to join her in a pre-meeting before the showdown with Luther and Ford. It was Victor's suggestion that Stephen Dyer also join them. Basking in his moment of vindication, Stephen had laid out the failings of the mission and its proponents. Victor joined in with his zealous pitch for the commercialisation of space exploration. Peggy felt she was among kindred spirits and made her first presidential decision.

'There's nothing in this mission for me. If it's a success, Luther'll get the glory and if it's a disaster, I'll have to pick up the pieces.'

The mauve lipstick cracked a little and she gave Stephen an encouraging smile. 'OK, Mr Dyer. I'm going to put you in charge of aborting this tomfoolery.' In a reversal of Luther's peace initiatives, she added, 'Then you can have your old job back!'

Stephen's flight was not delayed, and his sleek airliner cut through the stratosphere at such a pace that although he had two hours of briefing with his new masters following Ford's departure, his aeroplane landed in the slot just behind Ford's vintage crate.

The yellow taxi that took Ford to the space centre was rusting and beaten up, but it sped through the night with a comforting wallow around each corner or dip in the road.

On arriving, Ford hurriedly pressed his card against the barrier but crashed his legs into the glass when it didn't open. He tried again but to no avail.

Pedro Santo was engrossed on his cellphone when he saw Ford's predicament. Leaving the security kiosk, he rushed out to help. 'Meester Harris, let me help.' He held Ford's card against the sensor with the same result. 'Let me check.'

He returned from his kiosk with an apologetic shake of the head. 'Eets been cancelled, my friend.'

'Can you let me through, Pedro?' appealed an anxious Ford. Pedro Santo had been in security and gatekeeping as long as he cared to remember and was well versed in the cardinal law: 'Rules are rules.' However familiar the individual or urgent the reason for their passage, if the card didn't work or the dress code was not conformed to, then 'they shall not pass!'

All argument was futile and after ten minutes of increasingly tetchy discussion, Ford had to simply give up. One hundred yards away was a twenty-four-hour burger joint where he could refresh his body and mind and call Jane. As he trod the cracked sidewalk a smart new yellow cab flashed past, spreading its dust far and wide.

Stephen Dyer paid the driver and boldly strode into the centre flashing his card at the sensor. *Bump!* Just like with Ford, the glass barrier remained obstinate. This was going to be a busy night for Pedro. He bustled out, checked Stephen's card and returned to his office. Stephen stood there impatiently drumming his fingers on the top of the stainless-steel gate housing until Pedro returned. 'I am very sorry, Mr Dyer, but this is your old card. I print you a new one.'

Stephen bristled. 'This is ridiculous. Do you know who I am?'

He looked at the card and checked Stephen's features. 'You are Stephen Dyer.'

'Yes, of course, that's darn obvious. I'm the new boss! So let me through!'

There is nothing more enlivening to a door man than a stroppy customer. Like a noose that tightens the more you struggle, the angrier

Stephen got, the more adamant Pedro became. 'Eets more than the very value of my job. I don't care if you have the authority of the president. You can't pass without a card.'

'But I *do* have the authority of the president, you fool!' Stephen delved in his case and brought out his treasured letter of appointment.

'Did she give you a card?' Pedro quizzed impassively.

'No, of course not.' Stephen hammered his fist against the housing.

'Well, you will have to wait until I print you a new one. Have you a photograph?'

Stephen's face went a shade of red yet to be named. He sped off to the photo booth. When he returned, Pedro had company. Edward Stalk, the health-and-safety co-ordinator, had joined them. Stephen had arrived at the centre with precious little time to organise the return of all the astronauts. This would involve the maintenance crew docking with 'The Other Things' capsule and the transfer of one of the children to swap with Eugene who would then disengage their descent capsule and pilot the young crew on their journey back to Earth. The clock was ticking and Stephen was growing more and more impatient to get on with it.

'OK, here's the photo – now get on with it.' Pedro left for his office and Edward awkwardly shook Stephen by the hand.

'Hello, Mr Dyer, I'm going to take you through the safety training.'

'Don't be goddamn stupid, Stalk! I have done that already!'

'Mr Dyer, you know the regime. Safety first on everything. All new employees have to do this. Usually, I do this in the working day and am already making an exception for you. Would you prefer to wait?'

Pedro returned with the precious card and Edward took charge of it until the training had been completed.

Enza's mind was adjusting to the lack of gravity, difficult for such a 'down to earth' girl. Struggling with her first proper job in space, she was not used to ingredients wandering off randomly as she prepared their first meal. Bheki loved it, free from the bonds of Earth. Like a sprite, he tumbled as he fetched and carried sachets and bottles of hot water while Enza prepared the fresh elements.

The pasta and tomato sauce was pre-made, but the salad was to be fresh. As she worked, her frown of frustration turned into a smile of amusement, watching each newly cut slice of cucumber bounce off the surface in a line of floating green discs. Tearing at the green leaves, she delighted in the novelty of them rebounding off each other as she cast them into the bowl. Toying with the idea of just trendily calling it a 'deconstructed salad', she finally discovered that when she added the olive-oil-based vinaigrette, the leaves clumped together into a recognisable entity. She christened it her 'gravity dressing'.

She and Bheki revelled in setting the table, or lack of it! They very carefully positioned bowls and cutlery floating on an imaginary plane in the centre of the quarters. Except for the salad bowl, which they positioned upside down hovering above the rest. Elin was so impressed she glided in to take a closer look, just clipping the first bowl, which cannoned off the next. The chain reaction sent their meals spinning to the circular walls and bouncing back to the middle, before bouncing out again.

Eugene, Soraya and Su-lin did not relish their last meal in space, sucking on tubes of nourishing pastes before they set their own course for home.

In Ford's absence at mission control, Sharon was in command. Ford had managed to call her from the burger joint. Her blood was boiling at his news of the tumultuous events in Washington. She had had no official orders and was steadfast and determined that until Stephen's arrival, she had no brief to change any plans whatsoever and took on a stoic 'business as usual' approach to the threatening circumstances.

Edward sat Stephen down on the demonstration chair. 'No, no, no. Lower yourself gently, using your arms.'

Stephen stood up, pushing it angrily away. 'I know how to sit on a goddamn chair. Get on with it!'

Edward took a deep, patient breath. 'Do you recognise these?' He placed before Stephen two yellow self-standing signs, one with 'Trip Hazard!' and another with 'Caution – Slippery Surfaces!'

'What the f— This is stupid… One warns you of a trip hazard and one of slippery surfaces.'

'Very good, Mr Dyer, full marks for that. And where might you find them?'

'In the maintenance cupboard!'

Edward thought for a while. 'Not the conventional answer, but accurate. OK.'

'Can I go now?' pressed Stephen, trying to snatch the security card.

With a wag of his finger Edward placed the vital card in his back pocket. 'Oh no, there are many more risks to be taken account of. We'll skip the mouse and keyboard posture training. That's optional, but the paper training, of course, is compulsory.'

'Paper training?' An incredulous Stephen almost shouted.

'Oh yes, you won't believe how many paper cuts we have to deal with.' Edward took out a packaged ream of printer paper and fastidiously showed Stephen how to unwrap it and fan the paper to prepare it for an imaginary machine.

'Are we going to do toilet training? Tying shoe laces? Crossing the road?' Stephen asked facetiously.

Edward looked at his list. 'No, that's reserved for the legal department.'

Sharon's mind was racing as she studied the screens and serried ranks before her. 'Almost there,' she thought.

She gave the command, 'Eugene, start descent procedure – check!'

At that moment Stephen Dyer, card in hand, burst into the room.

'Retrorockets fire! Check,' came Eugene's dry voice over the speakers.

'Re-entry procedures commenced – check,' answered the mission planner.

'Yaw 180 – check.'

'Yaw completed and stable – check.'

'Roll 30 – check,' came another order.

'Roll completed – check.'

Stephen barged a startled Sharon from her position. 'I'm taking charge!'

Sharon turned, hands on hips and fixed him with a vexed stare. 'Taking over what, Mr Dyer?'

Stephen cocked his head and rolled on his heels. 'Ford's post. What's the status?'

Sharon remained in place. 'Where are your credentials?'

Stephen thrust the president's letter at her. She read it carefully.

'For God's sake!' hissed Stephen. 'What's the status?'

With an air of weary resignation, she turned and slowly wandered over to one of the mission planners and, after a long discussion, returned.

'The Mars crew are ready to embark and the re-entry is underway for the maintenance capsule, Mr Dyer.'

'Sheeeit!' Stephen whispered to himself.

Stephen picked up Sharon's water glass from the desk top, and chinking it with his stainless-steel pen, he gained the attention of the room. 'I'm your new commander. Mr Harris has been retired. I'm here to bring the crews back. The mission is being aborted.'

The was a discontented hubbub within the ranks and a few catcalls.

'Silence! Let me reiterate: THE MISSION IS OVER! Order Eugene to take the capsule back up to the main rocket and dock.'

'But, sir...' protested Rocky, the chief engineer.

Stephen whirled around. 'Just do it, man, or you can go home too!'


What an adventure it had been for Soraya. From the girl steering a motorboat in Zanzibar to piloting a spacecraft. Her mind raced as she tried to relax in her straps. There was nothing to do now but cross her fingers and experience the second most exhilarating and frightening ride of her life. Through the ice-crystal fringes of the toughened glass, she watched the main rocket slowly spin, glide away from them and diminish as they descended towards the upper fringes of the atmosphere.

Soon would come the natural braking, followed by the increased juddering and buffeting of the building air pressure and streams of hot ionised gas of the searing bow wave. Bracing herself, she became aware of Eugene's raised voice over the intercom.

'Negative! Houston, can't do! Check.' She tuned into the conversation.

Stephen's flat voice responded. 'Commander, return to the main ship, that's an order! Check.'

She saw Eugene turn to Su-lin and put his gloved finger to his head with the universal 'crazy' gesture. 'This is a capsule, not a rocket. We are in the descent phase with no means of return – check.'


Stephen's black polo-necked form paced the floor in frustration. He wheeled around to Edward Stalk, who had followed him into the room. 'This is your fault, Stalk. Get out, you're fired!'

This unprecedented sacking of the mission-safety planner caused confusion among the mission planners and technicians, and there was much whispering and scratching of heads.

His initial plan thwarted, Stephen finally calmed down and set his mind to work out what to do next. He appealed in more conciliatory tones to Chief Engineer Rocky for advice on plan B.

Unaware of events, with excited smiles and a few farewell tears, the children waved from the portholes at the diminishing maintenance capsule as it disappeared into the glare of the Earth and the impossibly thin veneer of glowing atmosphere which sustains all terrestrial life. As they one by one withdrew their straining eyes, it began to dawn on them they were finally all alone and would be for the best part of the next two years. That spell was broken when the sheer excitement of their adventure overtook them. Gaily chatting and joking, they were suddenly brought to book by the detached voice of mission control.

'Would the crew make their way to the capsule and buckle up?'

This was it!

Nervously they filed into the tubular link through to the sleeping quarters, where they donned their suits, before following Buzz into the command capsule itself. The tail-end Charlie would be Bheki, charged with locking the hatches. Buzz, like a whippet, shot ahead into the capsule and settled in his seat with eager anticipation. Despite this there was something bothering Buzz. He had not heard the comforting voice of Granf for two days and he desperately needed to say his farewells before the 'big burn'.

'Houston, can I speak to my Granf, please? Check,' he requested as soon as he had plugged in his intercom.

'Who the hell's Granf?' demanded Stephen.

'His granddad, you know... Ford,' whispered Rocky.

'Tell him Ford's ill!' replied Stephen.

Rocky leaned back and took a long hard look at Stephen. 'Tell him yourself, you're the boss! Anyway, I need a comfort break.'

Rocky got up defiantly, exiting the room and leaving Stephen to deal with it. Stephen reluctantly decided to tell the truth.

'Mr Harris... has been let go. I'm boss now. I'll send your regards – check.'

The strange euphemism of 'letting someone go' had never entered Buzz's vocabulary. Had he been tied up? Put in prison? What the flip could have happened? He was confused.

'What? Why? Check.'

There was no avoiding the issue and Stephen decided it was time to show his authority. 'He's been dismissed, and I've taken over. The mission's off, on the orders of the new president herself! Unfortunately, the maintenance crew have left so we're going to bring you home remotely. You're going to stay in your capsule and we'll detach it from the rest of the spaceship and you'll re-enter, as you've been trained. So, get everyone strapped in – check.'

It was like cancelling a trip to Disney World. Buzz was stunned but defiant. He unstrapped his buckles and shot like a diving seal down the connecting tube to his friends. Wide-eyed with indignation he told them the terrible news.

The voice came again. 'Enough chatting! Back to the capsule!'

The children gathered, floating in a rough circle. A loquacious babble erupted in several different languages, but they all said more or less the same thing: 'It's not fair!'

They ignored the increasingly stern tannoy giving out repeated orders. In a slight dip in the hubbub, Bheki could be seen shaking his head.

'Jeez! Eich!' he cursed with earnest sentiments. Catching his friends' attention Bheki looked at them with a flickering light in his eye and a conspiratorial grin. 'Let's make a plan,' he signed.

Bheki had taught 'The Other Things' this visual language during the many 'otherwise bored out of your brain' hours in selection and training. He lifted his finger to his lips and signed, 'Here's my plan. Do what they ask but don't buckle up.'

Obediently they followed the orders to take up their seats in the capsule. A light was winking in the gloom of the cabin. 'Seat belts undone!' The same light flashed on the monitors in Houston. 'Seat belts undone!'

'Oh, for heaven's sake,' complained the new controller. 'Do what you're told, you cretins! I order you to buckle up! Check.'

Yasmin was looking mortified. She sidled up to Stephen and dropped a word in his ear. 'This is going out live!'

Buying time, Buzz retorted, 'We're working the problem, Houston – check.' He then signed to Bheki, 'What's the plan?'

'Cheeky little...!' Stephen cursed under his breath. With a dismissive wave, he turned to Rocky who had returned to his station.

'Get control of the craft and bring it down! If they don't buckle up they can take the consequences.'

With one eye to the watching millions, Stephen decided to address the mini-astronauts in kinder tones. 'Now, children, be good little space cadets and do what you're told – check.'

Bheki signed to the other five, 'No, no, no, no, no!'

Bheki signed to Xing, 'OK, take control, we'll go for the big burn.'

Xing flicked the switches and for a moment she had control but they were immediately overridden by the technicians below. Mo immediately understood what he had to do and gave them all a sign.

'Stop messing about – check,' commanded Stephen.

Elin took over. 'We are very sorry, Mr Stephen, we didn't mean to be difficult, it's just really disappointing. We're buckling up now! Check.'

As she did this she leaned over and had a word in Mo's ear, appearing to spell something out.

Finally satisfied with their compliance, Stephen puffed out his chest and strutted around, before hustling Rocky with an open-palmed pushing gesture of his right hand. 'OK... now, just get on with it!'

Mo was typing madly on his keyboard as Rocky surveyed his checklist. 'Oh, darn! They've left the last hatch open. Get someone to close it!'

Stephen gave the order. 'Astronaut Bheki, close the hatch, then return to your seat! Check.' There was silence.

'Astronaut Bheki, are you deaf or something? Close the hatch! Check.'

Once again Yasmin sidled up to Stephen and had a word in his ear.

'Sorry, sorry, I forgot. Astronaut Enza, will you please close the hatch?'

'Which hatch, Houston? Check,' Enza replied, looking around the cabin with sugar-coated innocence. Bheki winked at her. He could sometimes choose not to hear.

Stephen, who would never have made a hardened teacher, was fuming. He stood with hands on his hips in a double 'teapot' as the screen focused on Enza.

'That darned hatch, the one you just came through! Check.'

The farcical nature of the proceedings was now spreading like wildfire in the alternative universe of social media. The 'Alumni' pages were brimming with videos of Stephen as he lost his cool and berated the children. Out there on the World Wide Web a worm was starting to turn.

Enza, like a gymnast in slow motion, pirouetted down the tube and then inch by inch secured the hatch. She beamed at the camera as she carefully and slowly re-did her strappings. Mo with a flourish on the keyboard completed the reprogramming of the mission's computer software. He flashed the universal thumbs-up and Xing surreptitiously reached up and toggled the override switches yet again.

Rocky was unaware of her actions. He shrugged his shoulders ruefully as he reflected on the last two years going down a long fiery drain. 'Ready, sir,' he announced in weary resignation, and then on Stephen's behest pressed the command buttons that would jettison the descent module from the rest of the spacecraft. Nothing happened. Rocky pressed again. Nothing. He then noticed the override had been triggered.

'Pesky kids,' he snorted and tried to take control. The computer asked him for a password. 'They've blocked me out! Little SOBs!'

Mo had successfully delved into the software and inserted Elin's favourite password, 'Eyjafjallajökull'. Mo signed to Buzz and Xing, 'Yes!' they fervently signed back.

It was now a race against time. The 'big burn', as they called it, was what would blast them out of Earth's orbit on their journey to Mars. It would accelerate them from their already brisk 15,000 miles per hour to 35,000 in a few minutes. That's fast – faster than any humans have ever travelled. To initiate the 'big burn', the engines needed priming and the systems shut down in the quarters. Mo, Buzz and Xing would have to work together in record time and without the help of any ground technicians. They knew what to do – they'd practised it enough times – but this was the real thing and under pressure.

On the ground the technicians were crazily trying the obvious passwords. They tried a program that would crunch them, but to no avail. Rocky forced himself into Mo's position. 'What password would I use under pressure?'

It was obvious – a familiar one, he delved in the database and found Mo's records. His cellphone password was deceptively easy: 'Innit'. 'Try "Innit"!' Rocky called over. They entered the text and the words 'password incorrect' sprang up. Stephen was looking over the shoulders of the guys. 'I saw that little ice maiden whisper to him! Find hers!'

Back in the capsule the feverish toil had abated. They couldn't believe it; they were ready to go! With great care and comradeship, they checked each other's straps and dimmed the lights. All Buzz needed to do was press the middle button on his trusty hand control.

Back on the ground, Elin's files had been searched and the illusive phone code was discovered. 'Eyjafjallajökull – found it!' shouted Rocky.

'OK, what is it?' was the impatient reply from the flight controller. Unfortunately, no one could pronounce it. Letter by letter he shouted it out: 'E y j a f j...'

Buzz was suddenly consumed by nerves and doubt. The words 'on the orders of the new president herself!' were drumming in his ears. He had been defiant before, but only with his ma. This was the President of the United States! No standing in the corner or being grounded in his room – this was serious! His finger hovered over the switch, willing himself to push it, but his body was frozen with fear.

Houston was almost there; the last letters were being entered to override the children's control. '... l a j... Christ, where's the key for the ö?' Rocky fiddled around with the keyboard settings.

'The Other Things' watched in alarm as Buzz dithered. 'I can't do it! I wanna, I wanna... I wanna go home!' he sobbed.

The small hand of the little African boy stretched over. 'I'm not going home, my friend!' he said, and struck the button.

The ignitions sparked and arced and 48,000 kilonewtons of thrust hit them like a crashing truck. Pinned to their seats, eyes bulging and skin stretching, immobilised by the crushing acceleration, there was only one thought on the minds of the six children.

'Here we, here we, here we goooooooo!'

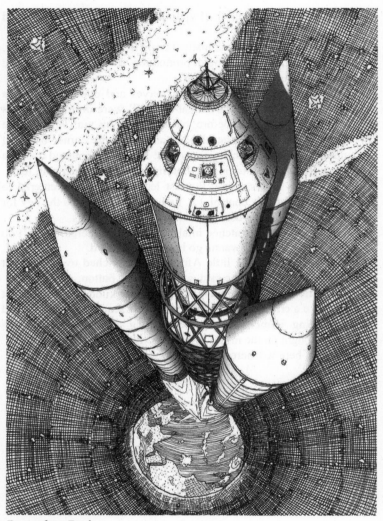

*Escape from Earth*

# Acknowledgements

This book started on a long drive to Cornwall. Despite the roar of the VW camper engine, I listened intently to a report about two planned missions to Mars. One was to send an elderly couple to loop around the planet and return and the other was to send a group of volunteers on a one-way mission to establish a colony.

The first mission included an older couple because they would be less affected by the prolonged radiation exposure of deep space, but did not include landing on the planet because of the difficulty of returning. The second mission sidestepped that issue by leaving a larger crew there forever. Neither of these options seemed great!

As a natural problem solver, my mind worked on how one might plan a successful return mission. Obviously the payload or weight posed real issues in getting back off the surface, so why not choose the lightest crew possible? An average American man or woman weighs more or less the equivalent of three nine-year-old children. Why not send kids? In addition young kids have a vigorous immune system and their growth plates are still functioning, so they may be better suited than most to weather the journey. I thought it would make a great film!

I met script writer Kirsty McNeil at a party. She thought the idea had potential and encouraged me to develop it. Not used to writing, I used storyboard techniques to develop the plot and when it was finished Kirsty suggested we next develop the characters. She also proposed to write it as a novel rather than a film script. Without her inspiration or assistance, this novel would never have been written.

I continued with the storyboard method to help with the writing and sketched out many of the scenes. I'm an architect and visual person and am more comfortable with drawing on a blank sheet of paper than writing on it! This is how it became an illustrated novel.

My partner Kathryn McAdam Freud has encouraged me from the start and, as willing victim, listened to the whole novel – read in its rawest state! Our kids (we have three each and have adopted three) have given us a constant youthful presence for the last twenty-nine years, and more than an insight into children's behaviour. They are Samuel, Adam (scientific advisor), Owen (early reader), Nathan, Eva,

Kayd (Unbound video maker) and Samantha (cameo actor), Luke and Emerald (star of video and reader), and have been a wonderful source of enthusiasm and encouragement for the project.

Many friends have helped on the way to publication and I'd particularly like to thank Dom Welby, Rima Boz, Ruky South and Nigel Draube for their initial readings and suggestions; Botts for the idea of 'The Museum of Practical Jokes' and generous sponsorship; Dr Jim Rice for his technical input and interest; and especially Bernadette Sheehan and Janet Chequers for their reading, criticisms and initial editing.

Through Kwaku's stewardship, my friends and family and even the odd stranger have been amazing in their sponsorship of the publication process and enabled Unbound's designers and editors to work with me to bring you the finished novel. I'd like to thank Josephine, Xander, Annabel, Kate, Petra, Julia, Sara and Mark at Unbound.

# Patrons

Gillian Abela
Marji Abela
Nesher Asner
Garry Atkins
Naomi Beer
Henry Bird
Louise Bishop
Lewis Blomfield
Charles Boot
Stephen Brough
Leanne Brown
Angela Browne
James Butcher
Pip Carr
Anthony Carrick
Jan Clark
Lin Clarke
Monica Creek
LD
Louise Davies
Bo and Malcolm Davies and Vaughn
Suzanne Davis
Becca Day-Preston
Joel Dela Cruz
Julie Devine
Nancy Dolores
Nigel Draude
Bruno and Lou Etienne
Emese Fulop
Sara Gappa / Greening
Luke Gregg
Samantha Gregg
Tim Gowler
Lizzie Haigh
Benny and Mel Hazlehurst
Pat Hicks
Jen & Glenn at Hop Burns & Black
William Hulse
Neil Isaacson

Richard Kalmar
Sebastian Kalmar
Pat Kent
Maryja, Lee & Ebony Kimberley
Annette Kobak
William Lawrence
Stefan Lipinski
Nat Low
Dhiraj Madan
Deirdre Malone
G Mazzarini
Eva McAdam Freud
Nathan McAdam Freud
Ana Mafalda Menéres Tello
Eve Moralee
Carlo Navato
Nicky Neate
Angela Nescerry
John Newing
Chris Nicolson
Katharine Norbury
Mark Pearson
Jim Reynolds
Gary Rice
Paul Ruffles
Elad Schwarz
Chiara Sensi
Bernardo Siv
Alan Smith
Ruky South
Allison Stamatis
Annie Stone
Parma Sulh
Will Templer
Sylvie Toutain
Mark Vent
Andrew Wadsworth
John Wallace
Jeffery Woodward